Susanna Gregory was a police officer in Leeds before taking up an academic career. She has served as an environmental consultant during seventeen field seasons in the polar regions and has taught comparative anatom

She is the creator of the M mysteries set in medieval Camb adventures in Restoration Lo with her husband, who is also

Praise for Susanna Gregory

'A lively and intelligent tale set vividly in turbulent medieval England'   *Publishers Weekly* on *An Unholy Alliance*

'A good, serious and satisfying read'
                            Irish Times on *A Masterly Murder*

'Excellent . . . the historical research is first rate. All in all, great entertainment for cold winter days'
                            Eurocrime on *To Kill or Cure*

'Once again Susanna Gregory has combined historical accuracy, amusing characterisation and a corking good plot to present a section of British history that is often overlooked: the emergence from the Dark Ages to Renaissance in the field of education and medicine'
                            Historical Novel Society on *A Poisonous Plot*

'Carefully researched, imaginative and evocative . . . this is a gritty but humorous period mystery'
                            Good Book Guide on *The Cheapside Corpse*

'Gregory never fails to impress with her immaculate research, creating an exciting and vivid historical, social and political backdrop and embellishing her stories with authentic detail and thrilling atmosphere'
                            Lancashire Evening Post on *The Chelsea Strangler*

Also by Susanna Gregory

The Matthew Bartholomew series

A Plague on Both Your Houses
An Unholy Alliance
A Bone of Contention
A Deadly Brew
A Wicked Deed
A Masterly Murder
An Order for Death
A Summer of Discontent
A Killer in Winter
The Hand of Justice
The Mark of a Murderer
The Tarnished Chalice
To Kill or Cure
The Devil's Disciples
A Vein of Deceit
The Killer of Pilgrims
Mystery in the Minster
Murder by the Book
The Lost Abbot
Death of a Scholar
A Poisonous Plot
A Grave Concern
The Habit of Murder

The Thomas Chaloner series

A Conspiracy of Violence
Blood on the Strand
The Butcher of Smithfield
The Westminster Poisoner
A Murder on London Bridge
The Body in the Thames
The Piccadilly Plot
Death in St James's Park
Murder on High Holborn
The Cheapside Corpse
The Chelsea Strangler
The Executioner of St Paul's

SUSANNA GREGORY

THE MARK OF A MURDERER

THE ELEVENTH CHRONICLE OF
MATTHEW BARTHOLOMEW

SPHERE

First published in Great Britain in 2005 by Time Warner Books
First published in paperback in 2006 by Time Warner Books
This edition reissued in 2018 by Sphere

3 5 7 9 10 8 6 4 2

A CIP catalogue record for this book
is available from the British Library.

ISBN 978-0-7515-6951-3

Typeset in Baskerville by Palimpsest Book Production Limited,
Falkirk, Stirlingshire
Printed and bound in Great Britain by Clays Ltd, Elcograf S.p.A.

Papers used by Sphere are from well-managed forests
and other responsible sources.

Sphere
An imprint of
Little, Brown Book Group
Carmelite House
50 Victoria Embankment
London EC4Y 0DZ

An Hachette UK Company
www.hachette.co.uk

www.littlebrown.co.uk

For Uncle Ed
With love and with enduring appreciation
for his support, encouragement and enthusiasm.

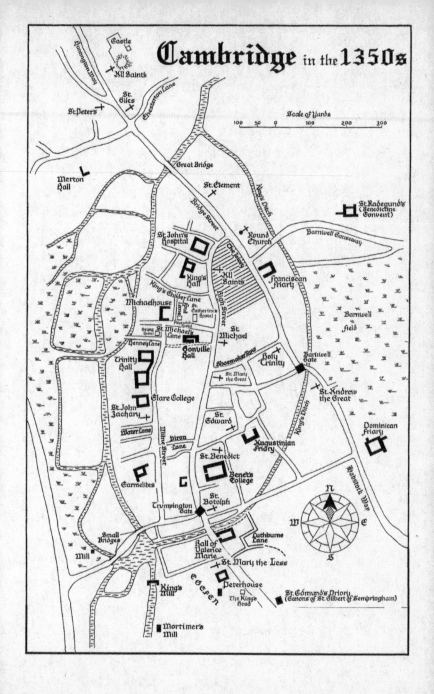

Cambridge in the **1350s**

Castle
+ All Saints
St. Giles +
St. Peters +

Huntingdon Way
Chesterton Lane

Scale of Yards
100 50 0 100 200 300

Great Bridge

Merton Hall

St. Element +

Bridge Street

St. Radegund's
(Benedictine
Convent)

King's Ditch

Barnwell Causeway

St. John's Hospital
King's Hall

+ Round Church
All Saints

Franciscan Friary

King's Childer Lane
Michaelhouse
Foul Lane
Pilgrim Hostel
St. Catherine's Hostel
Ovyng Hostel
St. Michael's Lane
Gonville Hall

St. Michael +

Barnwell Field

Henney Lane

Trinity Hall

Shoemaker Row

Clare College

+ St. Mary the Great

Holy Trinity +

Barnwell Gate

St. John Zachary +

St. Edward +

St. Andrew the Great +

King's Ditch

Water Lane
Mill Street
Piron Lane

Dominican Friary

Augustinian Friary

St. Benedict +

Carmelites

Benet's College

Trumpington Gate

St. Botolph +

Luthburne Lane

Babraham Way

N
W   E
S

Small Bridges
Mill

Hall of Valence Marie

+ St. Mary the Less

King's Mill

Peterhouse

The King's Head

Mortimer's Mill

St. Edmund's Priory
(Canons of St. Gilbert of Sempringham)

PROLOGUE

The Swindlestock Tavern had been painted a delicate pale gold the previous summer, so it stood handsome and resplendent among its more shabby neighbours. The inn was noted for the quality of its brewing, its fine spit roasts and the genial hospitality of its landlord Master Croidon, a squat, cheery-faced man who possessed the kind of belly that indicated he had no small liking for ale himself. His kind brown eyes invited confidences, and this made him popular among those for whom drinking also required a ready listener.

The tavern was peaceful when the scholars entered, but the low murmur of amiable conversation and the busy clatter of pots from the kitchen were not to last. Walter Spryngheuse and his friends walked to a table near the fire, and set about divesting themselves of their ice-clotted cloaks and hats. The wind rattled the window shutters and sent a frigid blast down the chimney, scattering ashes and sparks across the flagstone floor as Croidon came to tend the new arrivals, wiping his hands on his apron and exchanging pleasantries with other patrons as he went.

'What can I fetch you, sirs?' he asked, smiling an affable welcome. Drinking in the town's hostelries was forbidden to members of the University, and the ones who flouted the rules nearly always caused trouble. But Croidon knew Spryngheuse and his colleagues to be sober, decent men, who often used his inn as a venue for their lively discussions

1

on philosophy and natural science, and he did not fear bad behaviour from them. He glanced around as pellets of snow pattered against the window shutters, and did not blame the scholars for choosing his cosy tavern over the cold, draughty halls they called home.

'Ale,' replied Spryngheuse, edging closer to the fire. 'Warmed, if you please. And what are you cooking today?'

'Mutton,' replied Croidon. 'The poor animal froze to death inside her byre two nights ago. It has been a long and bitter winter, and I shall be glad to see it end.'

The clerks nodded heartfelt agreement. It had been one of the worst winters anyone could remember, with roads choked by snow since Christmas, and the river frozen hard, like stone. Life in many University foundations could be dismal even in good weather, and the atrocious weather had rendered some unbearable. Spryngheuse longed to abandon his studies and escape to the relative comfort of his family's manor in the diocese of Hereford, but the roads west were all but impassable, and only a fool undertook long journeys while violent storms raged.

The scholars finished ordering their meal, then huddled around the table to discuss the latest theories emanating from Merton College on speed and motion. Spryngheuse was a Merton man himself, and used his association with the foundation's great philosophers to impress the others. His good friend Roger de Chesterfelde was a member of Balliol, which also had its share of clever thinkers, and they began a bantering, light-hearted argument, while the others listened and laughed at the quick-witted insults that were tossed this way and that.

One did not smile, however. He was a slight, serious-faced man who wore the dark habit of a Benedictine. Croidon had not seen him before, and was under the impression that he had attached himself to Spryngheuse's party without an invitation – the taverner doubted the monk's tense, dour demeanour would have encouraged the others to befriend him. As soon as Croidon had gone to fetch the ale, the Benedictine made his first move.

'Heytesbury of Merton is an ass,' he declared, so harshly and unexpectedly that even the Balliol scholars were taken aback by his vehemence. 'His theories about uniformly accelerated motion are flawed and illogical.'

Spryngheuse stared at him in astonishment. 'You are mistaken, Brother: Heytesbury is widely acclaimed as the best natural philosopher Oxford has ever known.'

'Nonsense,' retorted the monk aggressively. 'That honour belongs to Wyclif of Balliol. Is that not true, Chesterfelde?'

'Of course,' agreed Chesterfelde, although the tone of his voice was uneasy: it was one thing to assert supremacy with good-natured raillery, but another altogether to be downright rude about it. He jabbed the bemused Spryngheuse in the ribs in an attempt to revert to their former levity. 'Wyclif is still young, but he is already the superior of your bumbling Mertonians. Just imagine what he will be like when he is the same age as Heytesbury!'

'Here is your ale, gentlemen,' boomed Croidon jovially, bearing a tray loaded with jugs. 'Warmed against the chill of winter.'

'But you have not heated it as much as you would a townsman's,' said the monk, sipping it with distaste. 'And I asked for wine, anyway.'

'You did not!' declared Croidon indignantly. 'You all ordered ale, and if it is not as hot as you would like, then you can blame the weather. I assure you, I treat all my patrons the same.'

'Bring me wine,' ordered the monk, thrusting the ale back at the landlord, so hard that some spilled on the man's apron. 'I cannot drink this vile brew.'

Croidon knew better than to argue with bellicose

customers. Wordlessly, he took the jug and went to fetch a different drink. The monk's companions regarded him uncomfortably.

'That was unmannerly, Brother,' said Chesterfelde. His face, usually bright with laughter, was flushed, and Spryngheuse was reminded that his friend had an unfortunate tendency to lose his temper rather more quickly than most men. 'Croidon is right: how can he warm his ales when the weather is so bitter? He is only mortal, and cannot magic hot ale from cold casks.'

'We are breaking University rules by coming here, but Croidon turns a blind eye as long as we are well behaved,' said Spryngheuse, resting a hand on Chesterfelde's arm to calm him. 'So keep a civil tongue in your head, if you please, Brother. I do not want to be reduced to drinking my ale at Balliol, for God's sake!'

The others laughed, easing the tension that had arisen at the prospect of an unpleasant altercation between Chesterfelde and the Benedictine. Chesterfelde smiled, too, his flare of temper subsiding. He was always ready to enjoy a joke, and was about to retort with a teasing insult aimed at Merton, when Croidon arrived.

'Here is your wine,' the landlord said, placing a goblet in front of his awkward patron, along with several coins that were the change from Spryngheuse's groat. 'It is the best we have, and I warmed it myself with the poker from the fire.'

'It is filth,' declared the Benedictine, spitting it on the floor. Croidon gaped in disbelief as the monk turned to his companions. 'Will you allow this scoundrel to sell poor quality brews to scholars, while he saves the best for the secular scum who infest the city?'

'Hey!' shouted a listening mason indignantly. 'Watch your mouth! It is scholars who are scum around here, with their uncouth manners and slovenly ways.'

'Well?' demanded the monk, ignoring the mason and fixing Chesterfelde with a challenging glare. 'Will you sit there and let this vagabond insult your University?'

'No harm has been done,' said Spryngheuse hastily, aware that Chesterfelde was beginning to rise to the bait. 'I think—'

'And we have been *cheated*, too!' interrupted the monk, pointing at the money Croidon had left on the table. 'Look how much we have been charged. He has one price for students and another for the rest of his patrons.'

'I must have made a mistake,' said Croidon, bewildered. He was certain the number of coins had been correct.

'That is not good enough,' snapped the monk. 'Frozen ale, filthy wine and now you try to swindle us.' He appealed to his companions. 'Will you let this thief treat us like ignorant peasants?'

'Not I!' declared Chesterfelde, incensed by the very notion. He snatched up the monk's goblet and brought it down hard on Croidon's head. The landlord dropped to his knees with a howl of pain, and blood dribbled between the fingers he lifted to his scalp.

Men were rising to their feet all over the tavern. The mason's friends began to advance menacingly, while a group of hitherto silent, unobtrusive Franciscans from Exeter College set their sights on an apprentice who had recently jibed them about their celibacy.

'He tried to deceive us!' shouted the Benedictine, jabbing an accusing finger at the bleeding landlord. 'And in so doing he insults Balliol – and Exeter and Merton, too! Will you allow this to happen? Or are you soldiers of God, ready to fight for what is right?'

'Balliol!' yelled Chesterfelde, bloated with fury as he struck the hapless landlord a second time.

The mason leapt at him, and they rolled to the floor in an undignified mêlée of arms and legs. The craftsman's companions surged forward to join in, while the apprentice threw a punch at one of the Franciscans, whose head jerked back and struck the wall with a soggy crunch. Skirmishes broke out all across the room.

'Come outside!' the monk urged Spryngheuse, grabbing his arm. 'I have bows and arrows. You must protect yourself against these murderous townsmen, or they will kill you.'

He dragged the reluctant Spryngheuse through the door and out into the street. Their friends followed, leaving Chesterfelde and the mason embroiled in a scuffle that was becoming deadly: the mason had drawn his dagger, and there was blood on Chesterfelde's arm.

'Murder!' Chesterfelde screeched, his outraged wail audible in the street as he tried to wriggle away from his furious opponent. 'He has stabbed me!'

'The town has slain a scholar!' bawled the Benedictine to several passers-by, as he thrust bows and arrows into his bemused companions' hands. They were too startled by the sudden escalation in violence to ask why he had thought to store such objects so conveniently close to hand. The situation was spiralling out of control, and there was no time to stop and think logically.

Chesterfelde staggered out of the inn, shrieking from the agony in his wounded arm. The mason followed, and the expression on his face as he wielded his dagger made it plain that he was intending to finish what he had started. Spryngheuse shot him dead.

Then the bells in St Mary's Church started to ring in an urgent, discordant clamour, warning scholars that their University was under attack. Within moments, the streets were full of students. Word spread that several of their own had been brutally slain in the Swindlestock Tavern, and it was not long before they had armed themselves with staves, clubs and swords, inflamed by the jangle of bells and the calls for vengeance. They flocked to the inn like wasps to honey, and within moments several neighbouring houses were ablaze.

Children and women screamed, horses whinnied in terror, and scholars and townsmen alike howled in savage delight at the prospect of a serious brawl. The University's Chancellor hurried from his sumptuous lodgings and tried to appeal for calm, but a gang of apprentices recognised his gorgeous robes and began to pelt him with mud. Some struck his face. The mob surged towards him, and would have torn him apart, had his clerks not dragged him back inside and barred the door.

Meanwhile, the Mayor, seeing what happened to the Chancellor, decided the only way to resolve the situation was to make sure the town won the fracas, so he exhorted his people to rise up against the scholars. A group of unarmed friars from University Hall went down amid a flailing fury of sticks and spades; all six were killed within moments. News of the slaughter spread like wildfire, and more scholars ran on to the streets with weapons. Croidon watched the unfolding massacre with open-mouthed horror, while the monk who had started it all hid in a doorway, a smile of satisfaction stamped across his dour features. Then he slipped away to complete his own business while chaos reigned.

Cambridge, May 1355

Only the merest sliver of moon was visible on the eve of the festival to celebrate Ascension Day. John Clippesby, the Dominican Master of Music and Astronomy at the College of Michaelhouse, liked this soft, velvety darkness, because it meant he was less likely to be seen, and he could sit quietly and listen to the sounds of the night without being disturbed.

7

He was glad to be away from the College, to escape from fat Brother Michael and his tediously fussy preparations for the following day. Clippesby would not have minded if some of the arrangements had focused on the religious ceremonies, but the gluttonous monk made no bones about the fact that his chief interest lay in the feast that was to follow the mass. Clippesby was tired of hearing about the vast quantities of meat and wine that were to be consumed, and the number of Lombard slices that had already been baked.

The Dominican often left his College at night. He disliked being obliged to spend too much time with his quarrelsome, earthly minded colleagues, and preferred the more peaceful, honest company of animals. Like Clippesby himself, they were soft-footed and silent, and together they witnessed all manner of happenings when people did not know the shadows held observant eyes. Clippesby had already watched Father William sneak into the cellars to raid Michael's wine, and he had seen a pair of Doctor Bartholomew's medical students climb over the College walls to enjoy an illicit assignation with some of the town's prostitutes.

He walked along the High Street, stopping briefly to greet the University stationer's mule, and then spent some time near King's Hall, admiring the bats. When his neck became stiff from craning to see their intricate aerial ballet, he made his way towards All-Saints-in-the-Jewry. A cat regularly prowled in the church's graveyard, and Clippesby enjoyed talking to her. Sometimes, she talked back, and told him what she had seen as she hunted mice and rats. Clippesby knew his colleagues thought he was insane because he conversed with animals, but he did not care – his furred and feathered friends invariably made a lot more sense to him than the diatribes of his human companions.

He passed a row of houses that had been rebuilt after

their collapse the previous winter. The largest was occupied by a yellow dog called Edwardus Rex, named for the King; he graciously shared his home with Yolande de Blaston, her husband Robert and their ten children. The Blastons were so desperate for money to feed their ever-growing brood that Robert was only too pleased his wife was able to provide extra by selling her body to other men, and saw nothing odd in her using the family home for such purposes. Clippesby did not hire her: he was a friar, and he took his vows of chastity seriously. He edged behind the trees opposite the house, thinking it had been some time since he had seen Edwardus and that he should enquire after his health. Edwardus barked, and Clippesby smiled.

But it was not Clippesby that Edwardus was acknowledging: it was someone else. Intrigued as always by the steady procession of men who made their way to Yolande's door during the secret hours of darkness, Clippesby waited to see who had an appointment with her that night. He grimaced when he recognised a scholar he did not like, who regularly visited Yolande and who was a hypocrite, because he condemned others for sins he committed himself. However, he knew there was no point in exposing the man: Clippesby's penchant for animals meant that most people considered him a lunatic, and few believed anything he said.

The scholar carried a package under his arm, which Clippesby knew from past observations contained marchpanes for Yolande's children; he supposed the gift eased the man's conscience about cavorting with their mother while they and their father slept upstairs. When Yolande opened the door to her suitor's soft taps, Edwardus eased past her and began sniffing the parcel. The scholar tried to kick him, but Edwardus had been hurt by the man before, and was ready to dodge out of the way. Then the dog stiffened and started to growl.

9

Clippesby raced forward as fast as he could. He heard Edwardus's furious yaps and the scholar's exclamation of annoyance that he should be disturbed as he was about to enjoy himself. Then Yolande screamed, and blood spurted from a gaping wound in the scholar's shoulder.

'The wolf!' Clippesby yelled. 'It is the wolf!'

CHAPTER 1

Cambridge, Pentecost 1355

Dawn was not far off. The half-dark of an early-June night was already fading to the silver greys of morning, and the Fen-edge town was beginning to wake. Low voices could be heard along some of the streets as scholars and friars left their hostels to attend prime, and an eager cockerel crowed its warning of impending day. Matthew Bartholomew, Master of Medicine and Fellow of Michaelhouse, knew he had lingered too long in Matilde's house and that he needed to be careful if he did not want to be seen. He opened her door and looked cautiously in both directions, before slipping out and closing it softly behind him. Then he strode briskly, aiming to put as much distance between him and his friend as possible. He knew exactly what people would say if they saw him leaving the home of an unmarried woman – some would say a courtesan – at such an unseemly time.

He slowed when he emerged from the jumble of narrow alleys known as the Jewry and turned into the High Street. The elegant premises of the University's stationer stood opposite, and Bartholomew detected a flicker of movement behind a window. He grimaced. If John Weasenham or his wife Alyce had spotted him, he was unlikely to keep his business private for long. Both were unrepentant gossips, and the reputation of more than one scholar – innocent and otherwise – had been irrevocably tarnished by their malicious tongues.

11

Once away from Weasenham's shop, he began to relax. The High Street was one of the town's main thorough-fares, and Bartholomew was a busy physician with plenty of patients. Anyone who saw him now would assume he had been visiting one, and would never imagine that he had spent the night with the leader of and spokeswoman for the town's unofficial guild of prostitutes. The University forbade contact between scholars and women, partly because it followed monastic rules and its Colleges and halls were the exclusive domain of men, but also because prevention was better than cure: the Chancellor knew what would happen if his scholars seduced town wives, daugh-ters and sisters, so declaring the entire female population off limits was a sensible way to suppress trouble before it began. However, rules could be broken, and even the prospect of heavy fines and imprisonment did not deter some scholars from chancing their hands.

It was not far to Michaelhouse, where Bartholomew lived and worked, and the journey took no time at all when the streets were quiet. When he reached St Michael's Lane, he continued past his College's front gates and aimed for a little-used door farther along the alley. He had left it ajar the previous evening, intending to slip inside without being obliged to explain to the night porter where he had been. He was startled and not very amused to find it locked. Puzzled, he gave it a good rattle in the hope that it was only stuck, but he could see through the gaps in its wooden panels that a stout bar had been placed across the other side.

He retraced his steps, wondering which of the students – or Fellows, for that matter – had crept out of the college the night before and secured the door when he had returned. Or had someone simply noticed it unbarred during a nocturnal stroll in the gardens and done the responsible thing? It was a nuisance: Bartholomew had been using it for ten days now, and did not want to go to the trouble of devising another way to steal inside the College undetected. He walked past the main gates a second time, and headed for nearby St Michael's Church. All Michaelhouse men were obliged to attend daily religious offices, and no one would question a scholar who began his devotions early – particularly at Pentecost, which was a major festival. He wrestled with the temperamental latch on the porch door, then entered.

Although summer was in the air, it was cold inside St Michael's. Its stone walls and floors oozed a damp chill that carried echoes of winter, and Bartholomew shivered. He walked to the chancel and dropped to his knees, knowing he would not have long to wait before his colleagues appeared. Smothering a yawn, he wondered how much longer he could survive such sleepless nights, when his days were full of teaching and patients. He had fallen asleep at breakfast the previous morning, a mishap that had not gone unnoticed by the Master. He was not entirely sure Ralph de Langelee had believed him when he claimed he had been with a sick patient all night.

The sudden clank of the latch was loud in the otherwise silent church, and Bartholomew felt himself jerk awake. He scrubbed hard at his eyes and took a deep breath as he stood, hoping he would not drop off during the service. The soft slap of leather soles on flagstones heralded the arrival of his fellow scholars; they were led by Master Langelee, followed closely by the Fellows. The students were behind them, while the commoners – men too old or infirm to teach, or visitors from other academic institutions – brought up the rear. They arranged themselves into rows, and Bartholomew took his usual place between Brother Michael and Father William.

'Where have you been?' demanded William in a low hiss. William was a Franciscan who taught theology, a large, dirty man who had fanatical opinions about virtually everything. 'You left shortly after dusk and have been gone ever since.'

His voice was indignant, as if Bartholomew's absence was a personal affront, and the physician wondered whether it was he who had barred the door. William was narrow minded and intolerant when it came to University rules, despite the fact that he did not always heed them scrupulously himself.

'Fever,' he replied shortly. William had no right to question him: that was the Master's prerogative – and Langelee was mercifully accommodating when it came to the activities of a physician with a long list of needy customers. He encouraged Bartholomew to treat the town's poor, in the hope that this might induce some of them to spare Michaelhouse during the town's frequent and often highly destructive riots.

'What kind of fever?' asked William uneasily.

'A serious one,' replied Bartholomew pointedly, wishing the Franciscan would begin his prayers. He did not want to elaborate on his story – and he certainly could not tell the truth.

'Fatal?' asked William, covering his nose and mouth with his sleeve. His voice went from accusing to alarmed. 'Is it the Death? There are rumours that it is coming a second time. Not enough folk mended their wicked ways, and God is still angry with them.'

Bartholomew smiled despite his irritation, amused by the way that William did not consider himself one of those with 'wicked ways'. 'It is not the plague.'

'Then who has this fever? Anyone I know?'

'A labourer – one of the men hired to clean the town for the Archbishop of Canterbury's Visitation next week.' This was true: he had indeed been summoned to tend one of the hollow-eyed peasants who worked all day for the

14

price of a meal. He had physicked the fellow before visiting Matilde.

'I do not mingle with such folk,' said William loftily – and wholly untruthfully, since meeting the poor was unavoidable in a small town like Cambridge, and William was not a callous man, despite his pretensions of grandeur. 'They are beneath the dignity of the Keeper of the University Chest and Cambridge's best theologian.' Smugly proud of himself, he turned his attention to his devotions.

'That is not how *I* would describe him,' muttered Brother Michael, who had been listening. 'Well, he *is* the Keeper of the University Chest, but he is no more a theologian than is Matilde.'

Bartholomew glanced sharply at him, and could tell from the sly gleam in the monk's eyes that more was known about his nocturnal forays than he would have liked. The obese Benedictine held the post of the University's Senior Proctor, and was responsible for maintaining law and order among the scholars and a good deal more besides. He had a legion of beadles who patrolled the streets, hunting out students who broke the University's strict rules – and any academic caught in a tavern or fraternising with women could expect a hefty fine. Bartholomew supposed that one of the beadles had spotted him visiting Matilde, and had reported the transgression to Michael.

Bartholomew was not only Michael's closest friend, but also his Corpse Examiner, which meant he was paid a fee to investigate any sudden or unexpected deaths among members of the University or on University property. These occurred with distressing frequency, because life in Cambridge – as in any town across the country – was fraught with danger. People were killed in brawls; they had accidents with carts, horses and unstable buildings; they died from diseases, injuries and vagaries of the weather; and sometimes they took their own lives. Bartholomew and

Michael explored them all, which meant that although any beadle would think twice about arresting Bartholomew for visiting a woman, he would certainly not hesitate to tell the Senior Proctor about the event.

'You should be careful, Matt,' whispered Michael. 'Cambridge is a small town and very little happens that someone does not notice – even when you are being cautious.'

'I know,' said Bartholomew, closing his eyes prayerfully to indicate the conversation was over.

Michael was not so easily silenced. 'I needed you earlier, and you were nowhere to be found. Then I discovered the orchard door unbarred – for the tenth night in a row.'

Bartholomew opened his eyes and regarded the fat monk accusingly. 'Did *you* close it?'

Michael pursed his lips, offended. 'Knowing you planned to use it later? Of course not! What sort of friend do you think I am?'

'I am sorry,' muttered Bartholomew. He rubbed his eyes again, and wished he felt more alert; Michael was the last man to lock him out, no matter what rules he was breaking. He changed the subject. 'Why did you need me? Were you ill?'

'There was a murder.'

'How do you know it was murder?'

'I am told there is a dagger embedded in the corpse's back,' replied Michael tartly. 'And even a lowly proctor knows a man cannot do that to himself.'

Despite the fact that there was a body awaiting Michael's inspection, and that he and his Corpse Examiner had been summoned before dawn – almost two hours earlier – the monk refused to attend his duties until he had had his breakfast. Personally, Bartholomew felt the fat monk could do with missing the occasional repast, and encouraged him to forgo the egg-mess, pickled herrings and rich meat pottage provided as part of the Pentecost celebrations, but his advice fell on stony ground. Michael intended to make the most of all the meals on offer that day, and no cadaver was going to lie in his way. When he had first been appointed proctor, Michael had chased recalcitrant students all over the town with considerable vigour, but he had since trained his beadles to do that sort of thing, and the only exercise now required was the short walk between College and his office in St Mary the Great. Over the past year, Bartholomew had noticed that the monk now waddled rather than walked, and that even a short burst of activity left him red-faced and breathless.

Langelee led his scholars back to Michaelhouse, where a bell rang to announce that breakfast was ready. Since it was Sunday, and the religious observations were always longer and later in starting, the scholars were peckish, so there was a concerted dash for the stairs that led to the handsome hall on the upper floor. The chamber's window shutters had been thrown open, filling the room with light, and a gentle breeze wafted through the glassless openings, bringing with it the scent of summer. Benches and trestle tables had been set up, and loaves of bread, hacked into lumps, awaited the scholars' consumption.

Michael charged to the high table, where the Fellows ate, and shuffled in agitated impatience while Langelee waited for the others to take their places, so he could say grace. Some masters used grace as an opportunity to hold forth to a helplessly captive audience, but Langelee was a practical man with plenty to do – little of which included studying – and his prayers were invariably short and to the point. He spoke one or two insincere words in a loud, confident voice, and was sitting down with his knife in his hand before most scholars even realised he had started. In view of the special occasion, he decreed that conversation was

17

permitted that day, and dismissed the Bible Scholar, who usually read aloud during meals.

As soon as he had finished speaking, servants began to bring the food, which was served in 'messes' – large ones to be shared by four in the body of the hall, and smaller ones for two at the high table. Bartholomew was grateful he was not obliged to share with Michael, knowing it would be an unequal contest and that he would almost certainly go hungry. The monk reached for the largest piece of bread, then leaned back so that pottage, heavily laced with diced meat, could be ladled into the dish in front of him, demanding more when the servant stopped before it was fully loaded.

'I see one of us does not miss Clippesby,' said a morose Carmelite friar called Suttone, as he watched Michael's gluttony with rank disapproval. 'He is your mess-mate, and the fact that he is ill means you do not have to give him half.' He glanced at Langelee, who shared his own dishes, and added pointedly, 'Clippesby is considerate, and *always* divides the best parts evenly.'

Langelee responded by eating more quickly, and Bartholomew thought Suttone would be better fed if he did not waste time on futile recriminations: Langelee rarely spoke until he had finished feeding, and Suttone needed to do the same if he wanted an equal division of spoils. Bartholomew's own mess-mate was William, who also ate more than his own allocation, but at least he usually asked whether the physician minded.

Michael was unashamedly gleeful that he could enjoy his food without competition. 'I dislike teaching his music classes, but I do not miss him at meals.' He released a sudden exclamation of horror and recoiled from his dish as though it had bitten him. 'There is cabbage in this!'

'Only a little,' said Bartholomew. It was such a minute shred that he could barely see it. 'It will not kill you.'

'It might,' countered Michael vehemently. 'I do not eat food that is popular with caterpillars. I am always afraid that one of them might still be on it.'

'Then it will be meat,' replied Bartholomew. 'And you have no objection to that.'

'But caterpillars are green, and nothing green shall pass *my* lips,' said Michael firmly, picking out the offending sliver and flinging it away with considerable force. It landed on William, who did not notice. Then the monk took an enormous horn spoon from his pouch, and began shovelling pottage into his mouth as if it might be the last food he would ever enjoy.

'Slowly, Brother,' said Bartholomew, aware that they went through this particular routine almost every day. 'It is not a race – especially now Clippesby is not here.'

'Yes and no,' said Michael, glancing at Langelee. The Master was a rapid eater, and it was not unknown for him to gobble his own food, then leap to his feet, say the final grace and dismiss the servants before some scholars had even been served.

'When can we expect Clippesby back?' asked William. He rubbed his dirty hands on the front of his filthy habit, before breaking a piece of bread and passing half to Bartholomew. 'Personally, I think he should stay where he is for ever. The man is not only a lunatic, but a Dominican.' As a Franciscan, William detested Dominicans generally, and Clippesby in particular.

'Having Clippesby incarcerated at Stourbridge hospital is highly inconvenient,' said Suttone critically. 'Not only does it mean we are missing a master – and his classes still need to be taught – but it does not look good to have our Fellows declared insane.'

Everyone except William glared at Bartholomew, who spread his hands helplessly. His colleagues were not the only ones who had been landed with additional duties;

19

Bartholomew himself had been given the responsibility of looking after Clippesby's astronomers, and fitting them into his already crowded schedule was far from easy. 'I am sorry but, as his physician, I am under an obligation to do what is best for him. He is ill, and he needs to be somewhere he can recover.'

'We are better off without him,' declared William airily. He alone of the Michaelhouse Fellows had escaped the burden of extra teaching, because his fanatical hatred of Black Friars was certain to cause offence to Clippesby's Dominican students. 'And we should throw away the key to his cell. The man is mad, and he is where he belongs.'

'I suppose we are lucky Brother Paul agreed to take him in,' said Langelee, finishing his meal and wiping his lips on the back of his hand. Michael ate faster, seeing the final grace was not far off and there was still plenty to be devoured. 'Most hospitals refuse to accept madmen, because they can be disruptive, and we can hardly treat him here.'

'No,' agreed William. 'The man truly believes he can commune with the beasts, you know.'

'He communes with them a good deal better than he does with his students,' said Michael, cheeks bulging. 'His musicians have not read half the texts they should have learned this term, while Matt says his astronomers are sadly deficient in even the most basic methods of calculation.'

'That is irrelevant,' said Langelee, not a man to be fussy about the academic standards of others when his own were so sadly lacking. 'I just want him back. It is not just the teaching – he is also wine steward and manages our loan chests. I have enough to do, without adding his work to my burden. When can we expect him home, Bartholomew?'

'When he is well again.' Bartholomew thought, but did not say, that Clippesby might never recover.

'He is not the only one enjoying a life of leisure while the rest of us toil,' said Suttone, sanctimoniously disapproving. 'Two King's Hall masters left Cambridge in the last few days, too – right in the middle of term, and when us teachers are at our most busy.'

'Richard de Hamecotes and Robert de Wolf,' said Michael immediately, to show that the Senior Proctor knew all about unofficial leaves of absence. 'Hamecotes left a note to say he was going away on King's Hall business, but Wolf simply vanished. They will both face heavy fines when they reappear.'

'That is what comes of accepting Fellows who are deficient in Latin,' said William, blithely unaware that most of his colleagues considered his own grasp of the language somewhat below par, too. 'Hamecotes and Wolf are men with heavy purses, who think a few months at our University will advance their careers at Court. The Warden of King's Hall takes anyone who can pay these days, and cares nothing that his scholars do not understand a word of the lectures they are obliged to attend.'

'They are not alone in wandering off without the requisite permission,' Suttone went on. 'Doctor Rougham – that surly physician from Gonville Hall – has gone home to Norfolk, and sent a letter informing his colleagues that he would return "when he could". All I can say is that I am glad such presumptuous behaviour is not permitted here, at Michaelhouse.'

'Rougham is a terrible *medicus*,' announced Langelee in the dogmatic tone of voice that suggested disagreement was pointless. 'I would not want him anywhere near me, should Bartholomew be unavailable. I would sooner die.'

'You probably *would* die, if Rougham touched you,' said Suttone cattily.

'Clippesby's sin must be very great,' said William, reverting to a topic that held more interest for him.

21

'Madness is caused by an imbalance of the humours and, in Clippesby's case, this imbalance is a direct result of an unnatural enthralment with all seven of the deadly sins. It is the only explanation.'

'Is it indeed?' said Bartholomew, wishing William would keep his bigoted ideas to himself. The students were listening, and he did not want them to think badly of a man who was simply ill.

'Reason is the thing that ties us to God,' William went on. 'And all lunatics have wilfully alienated themselves from Him by purposely destroying their powers of reason with wickedness. A soul weakened by sin is easy prey for the Devil. *Ergo*, Clippesby is the Devil's agent.'

'He is not,' said Bartholomew firmly, unwilling to allow such a statement to pass unchallenged, even though he knew from experience that there was no changing William's mind once it was set: it was as inflexible and unyielding as baked clay. 'His humours are in temporary disorder, but they are being restored by diet and rest. He is *not* the Devil's agent. On the contrary, he is a kinder, better man than many I know.' He was tempted to add that these included William.

'We all croon to the College cat when it comes to sit in our laps,' said Langelee unhappily. 'But Clippesby claims it talks back, and *that* is what makes him so different from the rest of us. However, insanity is a small price to pay for the work he does, and I am prepared to overlook it. I want him back, Bartholomew, preferably before the Visitation next week.'

'I am looking forward to Archbishop Islip's visit,' said William keenly. 'He will want to come to Michaelhouse – the best of all the Cambridge colleges – and he will certainly insist on meeting *me*.'

'God forbid!' muttered Langelee, standing to say the final grace. 'If he thinks all Michaelhouse men are like

22

you, then we will *never* persuade him to become one of our benefactors.'

Summer had definitely arrived, Bartholomew realised, as he walked along the High Street with Michael. He had been so preoccupied over the past ten days – not only with Matilde, but with the additional teaching made necessary by Clippesby's illness – that he had not noticed the trees were fully clothed in thick, green leaves, that flowers provided vibrant bursts of colour in unexpected places, and that the sun shone benignly in a clear blue sky. It was warm, too, and many of the casual labourers, who had been hired to make the town beautiful for the Visitation, had dispensed with tunics and presented pale, winter-white skin for the sun to touch as they enjoyed their day of rest.

As they passed the Jewry, Bartholomew stole a furtive glance along Matilde's lane. Her door was closed, and he hoped she was managing to catch up on some of the sleep she had missed the previous night. He smothered a yawn, and wished he could do the same. Neither the glance nor the yawn escaped the attention of the observant Michael.

'It will not be long before the whole town knows. I thought you liked life at Michaelhouse, but if you are caught defying the University's prohibition against women you will lose your Fellowship *and* your students. You will be reduced to practising medicine in the town and nothing else.'

'That would not be so bad,' replied Bartholomew, thinking about the mountain of academic work that loomed ahead of him until term ended. His third-year students had not finished Galen's *De criticis diebus*, while he was still dissatisfied with the lectures his postgraduates intended to deliver on Hippocrates' *Liber aphorismorum* for their inceptions. The Regent Master who would examine them was his arch-rival Doctor Rougham, who would not grant them their degrees unless they were perfect.

'You would starve,' said Michael brutally. 'Your Fellowship provides you with a roof over your head, regular meals and funds to squander at the apothecary's shop. Most of your patients are too poor to pay for their own medicines, and without Michaelhouse you would not be able to help them. So, think of *them* as you brazenly stride away each night to frolic with Matilde.'

Bartholomew thought of the care he had taken on his nocturnal forays. 'I am not brazen . . .'

Michael gave a snort of laughter. 'Your students know what you do and they are beginning to follow your example. I caught Deynman and Falmeresham with a whore two nights ago. I have told you before: enjoy Matilde if you must, but do it with at least a modicum of discretion.'

'I have never—'

'Do not argue, Matt: you know I am right. And if you do not care about yourself or your patients, then think of me. I am the Senior Proctor. Imagine how it looks for me to have a Corpse Examiner who flouts the rules night after night, and I do nothing about it.'

Bartholomew rubbed his forehead tiredly. 'But what can I do? She needs me.'

'I am sure she does,' replied Michael primly. 'But that is beside the point. I am giving you some friendly advice, and you would do well to listen. Practise discretion.'

'I will bear it in mind,' replied Bartholomew, thinking that if sneaking out quietly when no one was awake, always waiting for total darkness, and making sure no one watched when he entered the Jewry was not discreet, then he was defeated. He had been as careful as he could, and was horrified that so many people seemed to know what he had been about.

'We are going to Merton Hall,' said Michael, changing the subject. He saw Bartholomew's blank expression, and added in exasperation, 'To see this corpse we have been asked to inspect, man!'

'Oh,' said Bartholomew without much interest. 'That.'

'My beadles say the victim is a visiting scholar from Oxford.' Michael glanced at his friend when he received no response. 'Matilde must be wearing you out, because you have not asked a single question about the body and the circumstances of the man's death, and you are normally full of them.'

'Merton Hall,' mused Bartholomew, trying to make an effort. 'That is the house over the river, which is owned by the College I once attended in Oxford.'

'I forgot you have connections to the Other Place,' said Michael, not entirely approvingly. England had two universities – in Cambridge and Oxford – which were rivals for students and benefactors. Cambridge was newer and smaller, and its scholars invariably regarded its larger, more influential sister with rank distrust. 'Merton is one of its biggest and richest Colleges, I understand?'

Bartholomew nodded. 'Its founder, Walter de Merton, was afraid his scholars might eventually be driven out of Oxford by rioting townsfolk, so he purchased a house and several parcels of land in Cambridge for them – a refuge should they ever be obliged to flee.'

'Well, they *have* flown,' said Michael. He saw Bartholomew's puzzled expression, and elaborated. 'Surely you remember the news? On St Scholastica's Day – four months ago now – there were violent disturbances in their city that ended in the murder of sixty scholars. Several Oxford men have arrived here recently, although one evidently learned last night that we are not the safe haven he anticipated.'

'A Merton man is dead?' asked Bartholomew, feigning an interest he did not feel. His years as an undergraduate in Oxford seemed a long time ago, especially that morning, after his tenth night of interrupted sleep.

'Not Merton. Balliol. Perhaps you knew him: his name is Roger de Chesterfelde.'

Bartholomew shook his head. 'I studied there two decades ago, and my contemporaries will have moved on to other things by now.'

'Then what about Henry Okehamptone?' asked Michael. 'Is that name familiar?'

Bartholomew shook his head again. 'Why?'

'Because Chesterfelde is not the first Oxford man to have died in Cambridge recently. That honour went to Okehamptone, who passed away ten days ago – on Ascension Day – the morning after this large party from Oxford arrived. His friends said he had been unwell the previous night, probably from drinking bad water along the way, and he perished in his sleep. These things happen, and catching a contagion is just one of the many dangers associated with gratuitous travel.'

Bartholomew smiled. Michael disliked lengthy journeys, and always believed he took his life in his hands when he embarked on one. However, he had a point about the perils of drinking in strange places: it was not unknown for travellers to arrive and immediately fall prey to some ailment they had contracted *en route*. As a physician, Bartholomew encountered such cases regularly.

'Was Okehamptone old?' he asked. 'Frail and more susceptible than his companions?'

'He was a young man. I saw his corpse myself.'

'Did you?' asked Bartholomew, surprised he had not been summoned, too.

Michael shot him a nasty look. 'I wanted *you* to do it, but you were nowhere to be found. You have become very elusive over the last two weeks.'

Bartholomew ignored the comment. 'Why were you called? Merton Hall is not *our* University's property, and Oxford scholars do not come under your jurisdiction.'

'I beg to differ – they can hardly be investigated by the secular authority invested in the Sheriff, so of course they fall to me. However, there was nothing to suggest Okehamptone's companions were lying about his fever.' Michael cast Bartholomew another resentful glance. 'My Corpse Examiner should have confirmed their diagnosis, but he was mysteriously unavailable.'

'Ascension Day,' mused Bartholomew, refusing to acknowledge the barrage of recriminations. The festival was a favourite of Michael's and, after a solemn mass, the monk had furnished plenty of food and wine so that Michaelhouse could celebrate in style. Bartholomew recalled the occasion clearly, unlike some of his less abstemious colleagues. 'I was obliged to tend Master Weasenham that morning. For a toothache.'

'Then it is no wonder I could not find you,' remarked Michael testily. 'I did not think to look for you at Weasenham's house, because he is not your patient: he is Doctor Rougham's. You should take care, Matt. The University stationer is a rich man, and Rougham will not approve of you poaching one of his best sources of income.'

'Rougham was unavailable, and Weasenham said he could not wait,' replied Bartholomew, thinking it was ironic that he had treated the stationer out of compassion, and yet it was probably Weasenham who had been spreading the rumours about him and Matilde.

'I did not need you anyway,' Michael went on airily. 'I met Paxtone of King's Hall on the way, and he agreed to do the examination in your stead. He confirmed what Okehamptone's friends said about a fever.'

Bartholomew frowned. 'And now there is a second death at Merton Hall. Are you sure you cannot pass this to the Sheriff, on the grounds that these scholars are aliens in our town? If Chesterfelde has been murdered, then any investigation is likely to be time consuming.' He was uneasy

27

with the notion that helping Michael solve an unlawful killing might impinge on his understanding with Matilde.

'Dick Tulyet is busy at the moment, supervising arrangements for the prelatical Visitation.'

'You are busy, too,' Bartholomew pointed out.

Michael was one of the most powerful men in the University, and holding on to such authority entailed a good deal of work; it was generally known that the monk made the most important decisions and that Chancellor Tynkell just did what he was told. Michael also had students to teach and, like Bartholomew, had been obliged to undertake extra classes because of Clippesby's indisposition. In addition, he was heavily involved with preparations for the Archbishop's Visitation – it fell to him to ensure that England's highest-ranking churchman would be impressed by what he saw of Cambridge's *studium generale.* Since there were rumours claiming that Islip intended to found a new College at one of the two universities, impressing him was particularly important.

Michael grinned in a predatory manner. 'This will provide a challenging diversion from my usual routines – Tynkell is so malleable that he is no fun to manipulate any longer, while my students virtually teach themselves – and it will be interesting to probe the affairs of our sister University.'

'What about the challenge associated with teaching Clippesby's musicians?'

Michael did not dignify the question with an answer. He was resentful that he had been saddled with the class; although he was proud of his achievements with the Michaelhouse choir, being able to sing was a long way from understanding the discipline's theoretical framework, and he was hopelessly out of his depth. Clippesby's astronomers had been inflicted on Bartholomew, because physicians were obliged to maintain a working knowledge of the celestial bodies in order to treat their patients, but at least the field was not a complete mystery to him, as academic music was to Michael.

The two scholars turned on to Bridge Street. The sun shed a golden glow across the fields behind St John's Hospital, catching in the thin mist that rose from the river. The air was balmy and smelled of new crops, with only a slight odour from the marshes that lay to the north, and the sky was light blue with a delicate membrane of high-scattered clouds. Birds sang loud and shrill and, in the distance, sheep bleated in water meadows that were carpeted with buttercups.

Bridge Street was busy, as people made their way to and from their Sunday devotions. There were orderly processions of scholars led by the masters of the Colleges and halls, there were friars in black, white or grey habits and cloaks, and there were townsfolk in their best clothes. Bells rang in a jubilant jangle, with the bass of St Mary the Great providing a rumbling accompaniment to the clanking trebles of Holy Trinity and All-Saints-in-the-Jewry.

Bartholomew and Michael reached the Great Bridge and started to cross it. Bartholomew gripped the handrail uneasily; the bridge was notoriously unstable, and comprised a gravity-defying mess of teetering stone arches, rotting wooden spars and a good deal of scaffolding. Funds were desperately needed for its repair – or, better still, for its complete replacement – but moneys raised by the burgesses always seemed to be diverted to some more pressing cause at the last moment. Bartholomew supposed the situation was set to continue until the whole thing toppled into the river; he only hoped no one would be on it when it did.

When he was halfway across, he glanced up to see someone standing near a section that was particularly afflicted with broken planking and crumbling masonry.

The river was deep and fast at that point, and anyone jumping into it might well drown if he were not a strong swimmer. The man looked like a scholar; he wore dark, sober clothes and a cloak with a fringe of grey fur, but Bartholomew did not recognise him. He supposed he was a member of one of the many hostels that were scattered around the town. The fellow's face was pale and shiny, as though he had been crying, and the physician watched in horror as he took a deep breath, then stepped hard on to one of the most precarious parts of the bridge.

Bartholomew darted forward as the plank bowed under the man's weight. The fellow stumbled to his hands and knees, but the wood held just long enough for Bartholomew to reach out and drag him away by his hood. The man put up a feeble struggle, as several lumps of rotten timber splashed into the river below, but his heart was not in a serious escape. After a few moments, he went limp in Bartholomew's restraining arms, and stared at the water rushing past below.

'This is too public a place for self-murder,' said Michael gently. One or two people stared, but there were better things to do than watching three scholars murmur in voices too low to be heard, and they soon moved on. 'What brought you to this? Your studies? Love of a woman?'

'It was an accident,' mumbled the man, looking away. 'I was not going to kill myself.'

'No?' asked Michael. 'Surely you can see this side of the bridge is not safe.'

'I am a stranger,' said the man miserably. 'I do not know your town and its buildings.'

'You do not need to be local to tell which bits of *this* structure to avoid,' retorted Michael. 'What is your name? Which hostel are you from?'

'I would rather not say,' replied the man in a whisper.

'You will report me for trying to break the Church's laws against suicide, and I was not . . .'

'I will do no such thing,' said Michael firmly. 'And if you say it was a mistake, then I shall believe you, although I will not allow you to linger here. Do you have friends who—?'

The man suddenly pulled free of Bartholomew and raced away, heading for the centre of the town. The monk raised his eyebrows in surprise, then shook his head helplessly.

'He is probably pining over a woman. It is a pity he dashed off without giving us his name – I could have warned his principal to watch over him. But there is nothing I can do if he will not confide in me. Come on, Matt. If we do not visit Merton Hall soon, they will think we are never coming.'

'And whose fault is that?' asked Bartholomew archly, brushing splinters from his clothes. 'We should not have eaten breakfast first.'

They reached the crossroads near St Giles's Church, and turned along the road known as Merton Lane. Merton Hall was to the left, set amid its own neat strip-fields. Bartholomew had been inside it only rarely, usually when it was rented to the University as a venue for debates or public lectures. Most of the time it was a private dwelling, owned by a distant landlord and leased to a tenant who farmed the land. He and Michael followed a narrow path that wound pleasantly through an orchard, and approached the house.

It was a massive affair, built entirely of yellow-grey stone. It was old, but looked as though it would stand for many centuries to come, because its walls were thick and strengthened by sturdy buttresses placed at regular intervals along all four sides. Its lower floor comprised vaulted chambers used as offices, cellars and pantries; the upper

31

floor contained a hall, with a solar at right angles to it, so the building was L-shaped. Bartholomew supposed it had been raised during a time of civil unrest, as everything about it suggested defence. He was not surprised that Merton's founder had considered it a suitable refuge for scholars driven out of Oxford by force.

Besides the house were stables, barns and a small granary. In the distance was an enclosure for pigs and a large, square structure that Bartholomew knew was a cistern for storing water. A flock of pigeons clustered and cooed around a dovecote, and the fields bristled with vigorous shocks of barley and rye. The manor exuded an air of prosperity, and he was sure Merton College was grateful for the handsome profits it would almost certainly yield.

Michael knocked on the door, which was opened by a small man with hair so fair it was almost white. The fellow looked Michael up and down with rank distrust.

'What do you want?' he demanded.

'I was summoned to inspect the body of Roger de Chesterfelde. Who are you?'

'John de Boltone,' replied the man. 'Bailiff of this estate. That means I oversee everything that happens here, and I present the accounts to Merton College – usually every twelve months, although I did not go this year, winter being so severe.'

'I know what a bailiff does,' said Michael, impatient with the man's self-important rambling. 'However, I am surprised to find one here. I thought Merton *rented* the manor to a tenant, rendering a bailiff unnecessary.'

'The tenant is Eudo of Helpryngham,' replied Boltone. 'He pays an agreed sum each year and, in return, takes a share of the manor's profits from crop-growing and the like. That is why I am employed: to make sure he does not keep more of the income than he should.'

'I see,' said Michael. 'So, was it you who sent me the message about the dead man? I was under the impression the summons came from scholars.'

'They arrived almost two weeks ago,' said Boltone, in a way that suggested he wished they had not. 'There were riots in Oxford, so these brave souls decided it was time to inspect "some of the more distant outposts", as they describe this fine manor. The reality is that they were too frightened to stay in their own city.'

'What can you tell me about Chesterfelde?' asked Michael, since the garrulous bailiff seemed to be in the mood for chatter. 'Do you have any idea who slipped a knife into his back last night?'

'Not specifically,' said Boltone, standing aside to allow them inside. The door opened into a stone-vaulted entrance chamber packed with storage barrels and an eclectic assortment of agricultural implements. Merton Hall evidently placed a greater emphasis on accommodating its farming needs than on appearances, since the chaotic jumble could hardly be said to provide an attractive welcome to visitors. A spiral staircase in one corner led to the hall and solar above. 'He was a happy sort of man – although he had a temper – and he has been here before. I think he liked Cambridge.'

'Anything else?'

Boltone shrugged. 'He was more cheerful than that miserable lot upstairs, so perhaps his gaiety led them to dispatch him. Not everyone likes a smiling face in the mornings.'

Michael raised his eyebrows. 'You think he was killed because he was a morning person? That does not sound like much of a motive.'

'Do not be so sure,' said Boltone sagely. 'I imagine it would be very annoying, day after day. As I said, the others are a morose rabble who seldom laugh about anything.

But you took so long to answer their summons that some grew tired of waiting and have wandered off.'

'I was delayed because I am busy,' said Michael stiffly, not liking the censure in the bailiff's tone. 'I cannot drop important business the moment anyone snaps his fingers.'

Boltone shot him an unpleasant glance, offended by the implication that events at Merton Hall were insignificant. He sniffed, then his eyes took on a spiteful gleam. 'The scholars refused to eat their breakfast with a body in the room, and insisted on moving it to the solar – I told them they should leave it where it was until you arrived, but they ignored me. Still, it is obvious what killed Chesterfelde. All you need do is work out which of his so-called friends did it.'

Michael and Bartholomew were about to follow Boltone upstairs to the hall, when the door clanked and someone else entered the vestibule. While Michael introduced himself, Bartholomew, feeling sluggish again, wondered whether he could manage to snatch an hour of sleep that afternoon or whether he would have to spend the time preparing lessons for Clippesby's astronomers.

'My God!' breathed the newcomer. The shocked tone of his voice dragged the physician out of his reverie. 'Matthew Bartholomew! I heard you had settled in Cambridge, but I did not believe it. I thought even *you* had more taste than to come here.'

Boltone was affronted. 'Hey! This is a nice place, not like Oxford, which has riots every week.'

It took a few moments for Bartholomew to identify the face that was gazing imperiously at him, not because it had been forgotten, but because it was not one he had ever expected to see again.

'William de Polmorva,' he said, startled. It was not a pleasant surprise. He and Polmorva had not been on good terms when they had been undergraduates together at

Oxford, and had come to blows on several occasions. 'What are you doing here?'

'You two know each other?' asked Michael, looking from one to the other.

'Obviously,' drawled Polmorva, employing the aggravating sarcasm Bartholomew recalled so vividly.

'Why are *you* here?' asked Bartholomew, before Michael could formulate a suitably cutting retort. He had barely given Polmorva a thought in the twenty years since he had left Oxford, but memories started to crowd unbidden into his mind now, most of them centred around the fellow's arrogance and condescension.

Polmorva shrugged. 'Oxford is dangerous at the moment, and a man like me cannot be too careful.'

'A man like you?' echoed Michael, arching his eyebrows. The tone of his voice indicated that the comment could be taken in one of several ways and that he was busily sorting through them for the worst. Bartholomew had known Michael long enough to see he had taken a dislike to Polmorva.

'Wealthy and erudite,' elaborated Polmorva with a wolfish grin. 'However, this squalid little village is every bit as dangerous as Oxford, and a good deal less charming. I arrived here eleven days ago, and two of my party have died already – one of them murdered.'

'It will be three dead if he insults Cambridge again,' hissed Boltone, addressing Michael. 'I will not stand here and see my lovely town maligned by the likes of *him*.'

'Go about your business,' ordered Polmorva icily. 'You should not be here, listening to your betters. Be off with you!'

'You see?' said Boltone to Michael. 'Rude and miserable. That is what these Oxford scholars are – and one of them killed Chesterfelde.' He turned on his heel and stalked out, slamming the door behind him.

'You will not find Chesterfelde's killer among Oxford's scholars,' said Polmorva in the ensuing silence. 'But townsmen like *him* should be worth a long, hard look. And now, let me look at you.'

He walked around Bartholomew as if he was inspecting a prize bull. The physician forced himself not to show his irritation, knowing perfectly well that his old nemesis would be delighted if he succeeded in irking him. The physician saw time had not mellowed the man, and that he was just as spiteful and rebarbative as he had been in his youth.

Polmorva had always taken pride in immaculate grooming and he was perfectly attired now. His hair was fashionably cut, his gipon – a padded, above-the-knee tunic – fitted snugly around his waist, and he wore a sword-belt that aped the recent fashion among knights. The cloth of his cloak was expensive, while his soft-leather shoes were modelled into impractical points in the style popular among those who were not obliged to walk very far. In his patched and faded garments, still rumpled from his time with Matilde, Bartholomew felt grubby and impoverished. But for all his finery, Polmorva was unable to disguise the fact that his hair was thinning and there were puffy pouches under his eyes. By contrast, Bartholomew's complexion was unblemished, resulting from plenty of exercise and the fact that his College rarely provided him with enough wine to allow debauchery. His hair was still mostly black, and he lacked the paunch that Polmorva's expensive clothes could not disguise. He stood a little taller under the scrutiny, feeling that the years had been kinder to him than they had to his rival, and that he cut a finer figure, despite the disparity in the quality of their costumes.

'Well,' drawled Polmorva, reverting to spoken insults. 'I see you have not used your education to earn your fortune. How have you managed to fall on such hard times?' He reached for the pouch that hung at his belt, and his voice dripped with contempt. 'Perhaps I can oblige with a loan? At least you could buy a decent tabard.'

'Who is this cockerel?' demanded Michael of Bartholomew, affronted on his friend's behalf.

Polmorva gave one of his infuriating smiles. 'I see you are a forgetful man, Brother. We were introduced last week, when you examined Okehamptone's corpse.'

'I do not recall you,' said Michael with calculated insouciance. 'As Senior Proctor, I meet many important men, and tend to dismiss lesser mortals from my mind.'

Polmorva gave another of his nasty sneers. 'I am William de Polmorva, formerly Chancellor of the University of Oxford, and now Fellow of Queen's College.'

Bartholomew could not stop himself from gaping. 'They elected *you* Chancellor?'

Polmorva preened himself. 'A two-year appointment.'

'Queen's College?' asked Bartholomew. 'You were a Fellow of University College when I knew you – after you had been expelled from Exeter.'

'I was not expelled,' objected Polmorva stiffly, and Bartholomew saw he had annoyed him. 'I resigned, because University College offered me a better room.'

Bartholomew turned to Michael. 'There were rumours that he was dismissed for embezzling.'

'The rumours were false,' said Polmorva coolly, while Michael gazed at Bartholomew in astonishment. It was unlike his mild-mannered friend to be so brazenly uncivil.

'What are you doing here?' asked Bartholomew again. 'In a house owned by Merton?'

'I was invited,' replied Polmorva silkily. 'I expressed a desire to be away from Oxford's unsettled atmosphere, and Warden Duraunt asked if I would like to accompany him here. When I did not see you at the public debates last week, I made the assumption – wrongly, it would seem

– that you had moved away. I confess I am surprised to see you today: if you have no time to attend compulsory disputations, then surely you have no time to satisfy a ghoulish interest in cadavers.'

'He has been busy,' said Michael, 'with no time for old acquaintances – not even ones of your evident charm.'

'Warden Duraunt is here?' asked Bartholomew with eager pleasure. Some of his happiest Oxford memories were associated with Duraunt, a mentor who had been acutely intelligent, but also patient and gentle. 'He is Warden of Merton now?'

Polmorva inclined his head in a nod, and returned to his own quest for information. 'Are you some sort of lackey to this monk, Bartholomew? Or do you make use of your medical skills to lay out corpses? We employ pauper women for that sort of thing in Oxford.'

Michael eyed him with distaste. 'I must remember to thank the good Lord that Cambridge has William Tynkell as its figurehead, and not a chancellor like you. I would not give much for its chances during a riot if it had to rely on your tact and diplomacy to soothe an enraged mob. Is that why Oxford was aflame in February?'

Polmorva gave a short bark of laughter. 'Master Brouweon was in office then, not I – if *I* had been Chancellor, the rabble that attacked us would have been put down with proper force. But do not allow me to detain your from your important duties. Come upstairs and see about removing this body. It is a damned nuisance, lying in the way.'

'Tell me about Chesterfelde,' said Michael, indicating that Polmorva was to precede them up the stairs. He tried to sound detached, but did not succeed: Polmorva's manners had irritated him far too deeply, and his next question came out like an accusation. 'Who killed him?'

'I thought that was why *you* were here. If we knew the

identity of the killer, we would have dealt with the matter ourselves, not invited outsiders to meddle.'

'That is not how things work in this town,' said Michael coolly. 'I investigate all suspicious deaths and the perpetrators are *always* brought to justice.' He looked hard at Polmorva, and the unmistakable message was that he hoped the ex-Chancellor would prove to be the culprit.

Merton Hall's main chamber was a large room with narrow lancet windows set into thick walls, which made it a dark and somewhat cheerless space. There was a hearth in the middle, and a door at the far end led to the adjoining solar. The floor was of wood, and was badly in need of cleaning, while ancient cobwebs hung thickly from the rafters. Bowls containing herbs had been placed on the windowsills, but they had long since finished emitting their sweet scent; they were dry, dusty and mixed with dead flies, and should have been changed. In all, the hall looked in desperate need of someone who would care for it.

'Matthew!' exclaimed an elderly man who sat by the fire. 'I assumed you had moved away from Cambridge.'

Smiling with genuine affection, Bartholomew went to greet the man who had taught him the Trivium – grammar, logic and rhetoric – so long ago. Duraunt had aged since Bartholomew had left Merton to complete his studies in Paris. His hair was white, and there were deep lines in his kindly face. He had taken major orders with the Austin Canons, too, and wore a friar's habit, rather than the traditional Merton tabard Bartholomew recalled. When he clasped his teacher's hand it felt thin and light-boned, although the grip was still firm and warm. His grin was warm, too, and his face lit with joy as Bartholomew sat next to him.

'You did not write as often as you promised,' Duraunt

said, gently chiding. 'Nor did you accept my offer of a Fellowship at Merton. What does Cambridge have that we could not provide?'

'My sister,' replied Bartholomew. 'She wanted me near her. Besides, I like the Fens. They produce a poisonous miasma that is the cause of several interesting agues.'

Duraunt smothered a fond smile. 'Well, that is a virtue with which Oxford cannot compete.' He glanced at Polmorva. 'I hope you two will behave respectfully towards each other, and do not continue that silly feud you began as students. It was a long time ago, and I doubt you even recall what started it.'

'I do,' said Polmorva coldly. 'It is not something I am likely to forget – or to forgive.'

'You could have asked me about Matt when I came to inspect Okehamptone,' said Michael, after a short and tense silence; out of respect for Duraunt, Bartholomew refrained from responding in kind. 'You did not mention then that you knew him, and I was with you for some time.'

Duraunt shrugged. 'You are a Benedictine and Matthew detests that particular Order. I did not imagine there was any possibility that you and he would be acquainted.'

'Is that so?' asked Michael, startled. 'And what, pray, is his problem with Black Monks?'

'He is very vocal about their venality,' explained Duraunt, oblivious to his former student's discomfort. 'And then there was that business with them and the set of artificial teeth provided at feasts for those who had lost their own. He made no secret of what he thought of *that*.'

'I can imagine,' said Michael, intrigued by a hitherto unknown episode in his friend's past. 'But perhaps you would elaborate?'

'Another time,' said Duraunt, finally noting the mortified expression on Bartholomew's face.

'You have still not explained why you have come to deal with a corpse,' said Polmorva, addressing Bartholomew. 'Have I underestimated you, and you have reached the dizzy heights of *Junior* Proctor?' He smirked disdainfully.

'He is the University's Senior Corpse Examiner,' replied Michael, making the post sound a good deal grander than it was, 'and one of our most valued officers. So, lead us to Chesterfelde's body, and we can set about bringing his killer to the hangman's noose.'

'Polmorva said it was not decent to leave him on the floor while we ate breakfast, so we put him in the solar,' said Duraunt. 'However, he was killed here, in the hall, during the night – we know, because he was found at dawn today, and he was alive when we retired to bed.'

'Where did the rest of you sleep?' asked Michael. 'In the solar?'

Duraunt shook his head. 'The solar is used by Eudo, who rents this manor, and Bailiff Boltone. It is the best room in the house, and it would not be right to oust the man who pays to live here.'

'I disagree,' said Polmorva, and from the weary expression on Duraunt's face, Bartholomew saw this was not the first time this particular issue had been aired. 'Merton owns this building, and its bailiffs and tenants should evacuate the "best room" when College members visit.'

'I do not want our people claiming we treat them shabbily,' said Duraunt tiredly. 'We are the visitors, so we shall sleep in the hall and leave them the solar.'

Michael brought the discussion back to the murder. 'But you said Chesterfelde died in the hall. How could that happen, if you were here?'

Duraunt's expression was sombre. 'That is precisely why we were all so shocked. I sleep lightly, and wake at the slightest sound, but I heard nothing last night, and neither did anyone else. I suppose I was exhausted – I was in church

41

most of yesterday, preparing myself for Pentecost.'

Michael was bemused. 'Are you telling me Chesterfelde was killed while he was in the same room as you both?'

Duraunt nodded unhappily. 'I am afraid so, Brother.'

Michael raised his eyebrows and gazed dispassionately at Polmorva. 'I see. Were the three of you alone, or were there others present, too?'

Duraunt rubbed his eyes. 'There was Spryngheuse, who is a Merton man, like me. Chesterfelde was from Balliol, but he and Spryngheuse were friends regardless. And there were three Oxford burgesses called Abergavenny, Eu and Wormynghalle.'

'Chesterfelde was murdered in the presence of *six* other people?' asked Michael, making no attempt to hide his incredulity. 'And none of you heard or saw anything?'

'That is what we said,' replied Polmorva insolently. 'Would you like me to repeat it, so it can take root in your ponderous mind?'

Bartholomew blocked Michael's way, as the monk took an angry step towards him. He knew from experience that Polmorva could goad people to do or say things they later regretted, and he did not want Michael to strike him and face some trumped-up charge of assault that would divert attention from Chesterfelde's death. Then it occurred to him that Polmorva might have antagonised Chesterfelde, and the resulting fracas had ended in a death. It would not be the first time such a thing had happened and, as far as Bartholomew was concerned, Polmorva was at the top of his list of murder suspects.

'Where are Spryngheuse and the three merchants now?' he asked.

'Out,' replied Polmorva shortly. 'They grew tired of waiting for you to come, so they left.'

Michael was now in control of himself. He smiled pleasantly as he took a seat opposite Duraunt. 'Then we shall have to make do with you two. What can *you* tell me about Chesterfelde? Why did he come here? Because he was friends with Spryngheuse?'

Polmorva sighed. 'We answered these questions when you came to poke into Okehamptone's death. Do you have nothing better to do? Cambridge scholars are a wild and undisciplined rabble. Surely your time would be better spent in taming them?'

'I hardly think we need that kind of advice from you,' retorted Michael tartly. 'You have been obliged to run away from your University because it is so unsettled. At least here we can walk the streets without resentful townsmen coming after us with pitchforks and spades.'

This was not strictly true, and the relationship between University and town was uneasy, to say the least. But there had been no serious disturbances for several months, and Cambridge was as calm as could be expected. Bartholomew hoped it would stay that way until the Archbishop had been and gone.

'We all came for different reasons,' replied Duraunt, striving to keep the peace. 'As I told you before, Brother, I am here to do an inventory of Merton property in Cambridge. There is evidence that Bailiff Boltone and Eudo are keeping some of the profits that should come to us . . .' He trailed off unhappily, clearly uncomfortable with his role in investigating others' dishonesty.

'The man who let us in?' asked Bartholomew. 'He did not seem worried about you being here.' He did not add that the bailiff seemed more concerned with the scholars' maudlin spirits than bothered by what they might learn about his accounting practices.

'Probably because he thinks he has covered his tracks,' said Polmorva. 'But why do you think I told him to be about his work, and not to stand gossiping with you? It is because I want to impeach the fellow, as he deserves, so

43

we can move to another of Merton's manors and leave this nasty town.'

'So, Polmorva is here because Oxford is too dangerous for him,' said Bartholomew, addressing his summary to Duraunt. 'And you came to investigate a dishonest tenant. What about the others? Why are three Oxford burgesses staying here, and what about the dead men: Okehamptone and now Chesterfelde? Why did they come?'

'I am not the only one who believes it is prudent to let Oxford settle before we return to our studies,' replied Polmorva. 'Chesterfelde and Spryngheuse also left because they feared for their safety. As Duraunt said, they were friends – Spryngheuse decided to flee, so he invited Chesterfelde to run with him.'

'And the three merchants are here to look for a killer,' explained Duraunt. 'They believe a scholar used the St Scholastica's Day riot as an excuse to kill one of their colleagues, and they have evidence that suggests the villain came to Cambridge afterwards. Okehamptone was their scribe.'

Michael pursed his lips. 'You did not mention this when I was here last time. You said then that these merchants were here for business. This is poor form, gentlemen. The proper procedure for such matters is to inform the appropriate authority – me, in this case – immediately upon arrival. It is not polite to investigate crimes in other people's towns without asking.'

'They are with your Chancellor as we speak – obtaining official permission for something they have been doing anyway,' said Polmorva smugly.

'That is not true,' said Duraunt sharply. Bartholomew recalled Polmorva's unpleasant habit of rumour-mongering, and was disgusted the man had not grown out of it. 'These are merchants – men always looking for opportunities to expand their trade. They have been visiting

44

other burgesses in the area – not just in Cambridge, but in the surrounding villages – and have been so busy that they have had no chance to investigate the death of their colleague.'

'Then Chesterfelde was murdered, and they realised Cambridge is just as dangerous as Oxford,' finished Polmorva. 'They decided they had better find their killer and go home before anyone else dies.' He sighed, and glanced meaningfully at the sun. 'Do you want to see Chesterfelde's corpse or not?'

He led the way to the solar, where a body rested on the floor, covered with a sheet. A bulge near its shoulders indicated that although it had been moved to a more convenient location, nothing else had been done: Chesterfelde was lying on his front with the dagger still protruding from his back. Bartholomew pulled the cover away and began his examination, childishly gratified when he heard Polmorva's soft exclamation of disgust, followed by a walk to the window for fresh air.

Bartholomew was thorough. He did not like the idea of a man being murdered in the same room as six other people, and no one noticing. He also felt there was more to the case than either Duraunt or Polmorva had led them to believe. Seeing Polmorva again reminded him of how much he had detested the man, and he admitted to himself that at least some of his attention to detail was in the hope that he would discover something that would incriminate him.

'Whoever stabbed Chesterfelde did so after he was dead,' he said eventually, sitting back on his heels and looking up at Michael. 'No dagger killed this man.'

Astonishment flashed in Michael's eyes, but was quickly suppressed; he did not want to appear at a loss in front of men from Oxford. 'Matt is good at this kind of thing,' he said, rather boastfully. 'It is why we always – *always* – solve any crimes that are committed here. If a man has been killed in Cambridge, then you can trust us to bring his murderer to justice.'

'I am glad he is useful,' said Duraunt, although distaste was clear in his voice. 'But what do you mean, Matthew? Of course he died from being stabbed. Look at the knife buried in his back!'

'But there is very little blood. His clothes would have been drenched in it had the dagger killed him, and you can see they are not. This wound was inflicted after he died.'

'Someone stabbed a corpse?' asked Polmorva in a tone that suggested he thought the physician was wrong. 'Why would anyone do that?'

'I have no idea,' said Bartholomew. He pointed to a ragged gash in Chesterfelde's wrist. 'But this is the injury that caused him to bleed to death.'

CHAPTER 2

When Bartholomew had finished his examination of the dead scholar, he and Michael left Merton Hall. Duraunt was troubled, and urged Michael to solve the murder as quickly as possible. Polmorva informed the monk that there was nothing to solve, and that Chesterfelde had been killed by Bailiff Boltone or the tenant Eudo, claiming they must have mistaken him for Duraunt in the dark – Duraunt had come to expose their dishonesty, and it was obvious they had reacted to the threat he posed. Unfortunately for Chesterfelde, in the unlit room and with so many men sleeping, an error was made.

'Duraunt seems decent, but Polmorva is an ass,' declared Michael, as he and Bartholomew walked down Bridge Street. The monk was alarmed by the notion that three merchants planned to conduct their own murder enquiry in his town, and hoped to interrupt their meeting with the Chancellor before he granted them the requisite permission. The last thing he needed with the Archbishop's Visitation looming was burgesses asking scholars if they had committed a savage crime. It would bring about a fight between town and University for certain.

'Duraunt *is* a good man,' agreed Bartholomew. 'However, Boltone and Eudo have little to fear from an investigation into these alleged accounting irregularities: if Boltone says they made an honest mistake, Duraunt will believe him. Boltone no doubt knows this, which is why he seems unconcerned. However, if Duraunt recruits Polmorva, then Boltone will be in trouble: Polmorva will see him dismissed – or worse – on the most tenuous of evidence. Duraunt may be keen to see the good in people, but Polmorva always looks for the worst.'

'I do not understand why Duraunt should invite Polmorva to travel with him in the first place. Gentle men do not choose that sort of company without a compelling reason.'

Bartholomew shrugged. 'I imagine Polmorva heard that Duraunt planned to leave Oxford, and seized an opportunity to escape the turmoil for a few weeks.'

'I would love to discover that Polmorva killed Chesterfelde. I do not like his sneering smile or his condescending manners. But tell me about this feud of yours. You clearly detest each other, and since it is unlike you to harbour such feelings over two decades, it must have been a serious quarrel you had.'

'It was a long time ago,' said Bartholomew tiredly. 'It hardly matters now.'

Michael gave a derisive snort. 'That was not how it appeared to me! If Duraunt had not been there, you would have been at each other like fighting cocks.'

'It sounds ridiculous now,' said Bartholomew, smiling ruefully. 'But it started with those teeth Duraunt mentioned. Polmorva designed them, and hired them out to edentulous monks so they could eat the same amount of meat as their fully fanged colleagues. Obviously, metal teeth are not as good as real ones, and several monks became ill – partly because they were swallowing food that was not properly chewed, and partly because the wretched things were used communally.'

Michael started to laugh. 'They *shared* them – passed them around like a jug of wine?'

Bartholomew nodded. 'And they did not clean them, so contagions passed from one to another. I was young and insensitive, and informed the monks that they owed their

48

resulting sicknesses to greed, because they ate fine foods after God and Nature had decided it was time for them to stop.'

Michael regarded him with round eyes. 'You said that? Do you not think it was a little sanctimonious? It is not for some student to tell an old man what he can or cannot eat.'

Bartholomew winced. 'As I said, I was young.'

'And this is why you and Polmorva are at loggerheads?' asked Michael, thinking it ludicrously petty. 'He invented some teeth and you denounced them?'

'Eventually, a monk died. I accused Polmorva of bringing about the fatality and he objected. Once the gauntlet was down all manner of quarrels and fights followed. But then I left Oxford and that was the end of it.'

'Until now,' mused Michael. 'Is that why you went to Paris, instead of continuing your studies at Oxford? You wanted to escape from Polmorva?'

'He was one factor,' admitted Bartholomew. 'But the chief reason was that I wanted to study with an Arab physician – their medicine is so much more advanced than our own. Paris had such a master, Oxford did not.'

Michael thought about what he had been told. 'You are right; your feud *is* ridiculous – although, having met the man I can see why you fell out. But he will be gone soon, and you can forget about him again.'

'Not if we find him guilty of Chesterfelde's murder.'

'There are other suspects – Boltone and Eudo for a start, although it would be galling to admit that Polmorva is right. So, what can *you* tell me about Chesterfelde? Are you sure that small wound on his wrist was the fatal one, and not the huge hole in his back? I did not want to question you in front of Polmorva, but I confess I am unconvinced.'

'Chesterfelde's sleeve was bloodstained, and the fact that the injury bled so profusely means he was alive when it

49

was inflicted. However, the comparative lack of blood seeping from his back indicates he was dead when that happened. There is only one conclusion: his wrist was slashed, bringing about death by exsanguination, and the wound in his back was added later – to his corpse.'

'You also said there were no other marks on his body – no bruises and no indication that he struggled. Why would he allow his wrist to be sliced, and then do nothing while he bled to death?'

'Perhaps he was drunk. I doubt it was something that happened in his sleep, because it would have hurt enough to wake him up – unless he was fed some sort of soporific, I suppose.'

'A soporific would explain why Duraunt slept through the incident, too,' mused Michael. 'He said he is usually a light sleeper.'

'That means the entire party from Oxford – all four scholars and the three merchants – was dosed. They all claim to have slept through whatever happened last night.'

Michael nodded slowly. 'We shall have to ask Boltone or Eudo whether they provided their guests with something more than wine.'

Bartholomew was silent for a moment, while he organised his thoughts. 'I do not think Chesterfelde died in the hall. There would have been a lot of blood, and Duraunt and the others would definitely have woken up had someone started to scrub the floor in the middle of the night – sedated or otherwise. I think he must have been killed elsewhere.'

'We shall have a good look around Merton Hall and its grounds later,' promised Michael. 'If as much blood was spilled as you say, then it will not be hard to find out where this foul deed took place. We can also search for stained clothing – his killer should be drenched in the stuff.'

'Not necessarily. He may have slashed Chesterfelde's

wrist, then stood back. But it is worth looking, I suppose.' Bartholomew gave a sudden, uncharacteristically malicious grin. 'It will definitely be worthwhile if we discover something incriminating among Polmorva's belongings.'

The town was busy by the time Bartholomew and Michael reached the High Street and started to walk to St Mary the Great, where Chancellor Tynkell had his office. People were out, enjoying the Feast of Pentecost before work began again the following morning. Merchants rode in carts drawn by sleek ponies or strutted in their Sunday finery, displaying to their colleagues that they were men of influence, who could afford the finest boots, the best cloth for their cloaks, and the richest jewellery for their wives and daughters. Apprentices gathered in gangs, yelling insults to passing students in the hope of goading them into a fight, while Michael's beadles patrolled the streets, alert for any scholar who might be tempted to respond.

Even the poor were out in force, spending carefully hoarded pennies on jugs of strong church ale or the aromatic pies sold illegally – Sunday trading was an offence punishable with a heavy fine – by Constantine Mortimer the baker. Entertainers had flooded into the town, too, ready to take advantage of the holiday spirit among the townsfolk. Troops of jugglers vied for attention with singers and fire-eaters in the Market Square, although only the very best could compete with the threadbare bear that danced an ungainly jig in the graveyard of St Mary the Great. It revealed broken yellow fangs as it scanned the fascinated spectators with its tiny, malevolent eyes, and gave the impression that it would dearly love to maul someone.

The atmosphere was generally amiable, although Bartholomew did not like the way the townsmen congregated in sizeable gaggles to savour their ale, or the fact that students from various Colleges and hostels tended to form distinct bands. He knew from experience that it took very little to spark off a riot – as Oxford had learned that February – and large gatherings of men with access to strong drink was often more than enough.

He considered the pending Visitation, and hoped the town would be peaceful when the Archbishop arrived. Simon Islip was deeply concerned about the number of clerics who had died during the plague, and had made it known that he intended to establish a new College for the training of replacements. He had studied in Oxford himself, and most people thought he would build it there, but every Cambridge scholar was united in the hope that he might be persuaded to change his mind. It was therefore imperative that he should find a town that was strife-free, clean and peaceful, filled with industrious, law-abiding scholars – and with townsmen who would welcome another academic foundation. Bartholomew thought uneasily of Chesterfelde's death, and three merchants intent on investigating a murder, and prayed they would not spoil Cambridge's chances of winning Islip's patronage.

Then his mind drifted to the St Scholastica's Day riot in Oxford, and he wondered whether the wanton destruction and indiscriminate killing would encourage Islip to look more favourably on Cambridge. Both towns and their universities were notoriously unstable, and fights were commonplace, despite Cambridge's current attempts to pretend they were not. It occurred to him that Oxford's disturbances must have been particularly serious, if they had encouraged ambitious and scheming men like Polmorva to abandon their homes. He said as much to Michael.

'It was the most devastating incident Oxford has ever known,' replied Michael gravely. 'Did you not pay attention when I told you about it? We had the news four months ago, and I remember very clearly regaling you with details.

I thought you seemed distant at the time, and now I see why: you were not listening.'

'I am sure I was,' said Bartholomew. He vaguely recalled the conversation, but it had been about the time when Clippesby had taken a turn for the worse and, as his physician, Bartholomew had been more concerned with him than with Michael's gossip about a fracas in a distant city.

'Well, I am sure you were not,' retorted Michael. 'Or we would not be having this discussion now. The riot started when scholars began an argument over wine in a tavern called Swindlestock.'

'I know it,' said Bartholomew with a smile. 'I have done battle in it myself – against Polmorva, in fact, when he referred to Merton as a "house of fools". The landlord threw us into the street, and told us to take our quarrels to University property, and leave his alone.'

'Well, he was not so fortunate this time. He was hit over the head with a jug. His patrons came to his defence, and the scholars were obliged to take up arms to protect themselves. And then everything flew out of control. The townsfolk also grabbed weapons, and the Mayor urged them to slaughter every student they could find, so Oxford would be rid of the curse of academia once and for all.'

'I doubt he did any such thing! There are thousands of clerks in Oxford and he could not possibly hope to dispatch them all. Your version of events came from a scholar with a grudge against the town, Brother.'

'My "version of events" came from Chancellor Brouweon himself, in his official report to Tynkell,' argued Michael. 'The fighting continued into the next day, and only stopped when every scholar had been killed, wounded or driven from the city. Eventually, the Sheriff managed to impose calm and the King was informed. Four days later, all privileges and charters were suspended and the whole city was placed under interdict.'

'The *whole* city?' Bartholomew was astounded: these were Draconian measures. 'When was this interdict revoked?'

Michael nodded in satisfaction. 'You see? You did not listen back in February, or you would not be asking me this. You would have remembered that the University was pardoned and encouraged to resume its studies almost immediately, but that the town remains under interdict to this day.'

'Still?' asked Bartholomew in horror. 'But that means the functions of the Church are suspended: no masses can be said, no townsman can have a Christian burial, his children cannot be baptised—'

'I know what an interdict is. And Oxford's looks set to remain in force for some time yet.'

'I suppose this is good for us, though,' said Bartholomew thoughtfully. 'I cannot see Islip founding a College in a city under interdict.'

'No,' agreed Michael. 'However, he will not build one in a town rife with unsolved murders, either – which is possibly what someone is hoping. So, I intend to have Chesterfelde's killer in my prison before Islip arrives.'

'You think Chesterfelde was killed to harm Cambridge's chances with the Archbishop?' Bartholomew was unconvinced. 'It seems a drastic step, and not one that will necessarily work – especially if you discover that Polmorva is the culprit. Exposing an Oxford scholar as a murderer will only serve to make our case stronger, and theirs weaker.'

Michael's expression was wry. 'I suspect it is not as simple as that – not when men like Polmorva and Duraunt are involved.' He overrode Bartholomew's objection that his teacher would have nothing to do with such a plot. 'I do not like the fact that as soon as Islip announces his intention to come here we have an invasion of Oxford men. Eight of them is a significant number.'

'But two are dead,' Bartholomew pointed out.

'And the survivors include three merchants intending to solve a murder; Polmorva and Spryngheuse claiming they came for their safety; and Duraunt investigating his bailiff, despite the fact that you tell me he is the kind of man to believe good of Satan himself.'

'Duraunt did *not* come for sinister purposes,' reiterated Bartholomew firmly.

Michael shrugged. 'Perhaps, but he is the Warden of a powerful Oxford College, and he is here. That is all *I* need to know at the moment. But leave him for now, and consider the others. Polmorva is the kind of fellow who enjoys feuds, while Chesterfelde made himself an enemy so bitter that he ended up dead. These Oxford men are clearly not peace-loving citizens.'

'And the merchants?' asked Bartholomew. 'Oxford's burgesses hate scholars just as much as do the ones in Cambridge. Surely it would be in the interests of these three merchants to see Islip found a new College *here*, rather than in their own city?'

Michael's green eyes gleamed, pleased by the prospect of a challenge that would require his wits. 'I have been restless lately. Tynkell does everything I say, and the University is operating exactly as I want it. Michaelhouse thrives under Langelee's surprisingly enlightened rule, and there is little for me to do there. We solved that crime involving the Mortimers and Gonville Hall recently, and since then I have been bored. Now things are looking up.'

'Looking up?' echoed Bartholomew, startled by his choice of words. 'A man has been murdered.'

'Quite,' agreed Michael gleefully. 'And we have clever scholars from Oxford and three cunning merchants involved. This promises to be interesting, Matt. And it will need a man like me to solve it!'

'Then you had better do it quickly, Brother. Before Islip arrives.'

'I shall!' vowed Michael confidently. 'Believe me, Matt, I shall.'

St Mary the Great was the University Church. Since it was the largest building under the academics' control, and could accommodate huge numbers of scholars, it was used for public disputations, for when the Fellows were required to vote on issues pertaining to the running of their University, and for when they needed to resolve some of the frequent and bitter disputes that raged between its Colleges, hostels, friaries and convents. The church boasted a stalwart tower that housed their various deeds, documents and stockpiles of coins, and the Chancellor and his clerks had offices located off its aisles.

'This really is a beautiful place,' said Bartholomew, pausing to admire the way the sunlight poured through the windows to form delicate patterns on the newly laid chancel floor. 'The coloured light virtually dances across the flagstones.'

Michael regarded him stonily. 'You need a night away from your exertions with Matilde. It is not normal, talking about buildings as though they were women.'

He moved away, leaving Bartholomew too bemused to point out that the association between the church and a lady was entirely one of the monk's own devising. He opened the door to the Chancellor's office, and Bartholomew could not help but notice that he did not bother to knock. Tynkell was so much under Michael's spell after his third year in office that when the monk marched into the room as if he owned it, Bartholomew half expected him to leap from his seat and offer it up.

Tynkell had not been lawfully elected to his exalted office, although few people other than Michael knew it. There had been violent objections when Tynkell had first been declared the victor, but these had gradually died away, and now people were reasonably satisfied with the way Michael ran matters. Indeed, Michael's power was so absolute that Bartholomew had once asked why the monk did not simply declare an election and have himself voted in properly. He replied that he did not have the patience to endure the many dull civic functions that chancellors were obliged to attend – and there was the fact that while he could take the credit when things were going well, he could always stand back when they were not, and let Tynkell weather the consequences.

Tynkell was a thin man with an aversion to water that led to a problem with his personal hygiene. He doused himself liberally with scents in an attempt to disguise the fact that not so much as a drop of water ever touched his skin, with the result that his office reminded Bartholomew of a rank public latrine sited near a lavender field. Tynkell suffered from digestive ailments, which the physician insisted would ease if the man were to rinse his hands before eating. Tynkell declined to follow the advice, and that morning sat clutching his stomach with one hand while the other played nervously with a pen. He was visibly relieved when Michael entered his domain, and Bartholomew supposed the three men who were with him had been pressing him for the unthinkable: a decision.

'This is my Senior Proctor,' said Tynkell, ushering Michael inside. 'And my Corpse Examiner.'

'Corpse Examiner?' asked one of the men. 'What sort of post is that?'

'One that is useful,' replied Michael enigmatically. 'He has examined a corpse of your own, as a matter of fact.'

'Chesterfelde's,' said the man. 'His death was a pity. He was a cheerful fellow, although he did have a habit of quoting the Bible at you in Latin. At least, that is what he said he was doing. He could have been damning us all to Hell for all I know.'

'Why would he do that?' asked Michael. 'Did you harm him in some way?'

'Of course not,' replied the man impatiently. 'I am trying to illustrate my point. I am a spicer, and have no time for foolery like Latin. French and English were good enough for my father, God rest his soul, and they are good enough for me.'

'We can hardly read the Bible in French!' exclaimed Tynkell, shocked. 'We are at war with France, and it would be an odd thing to do, anyway. Latin is the only tongue for sacred texts – and for proper academic discourse.'

'Allow us to introduce ourselves again, Brother,' said another of the trio, interrupting the spicer's tirade. He spoke with the soft lilt of a man from Wales. 'I am William of Abergavenny, burgess of Oxford and Master of the Guild of Saints.' He indicated the spicer, who sat on his left. 'This is Philip Eu, also a burgess and a past Mayor. And finally, this is Thomas Wormynghalle.'

The absence of any reference to title or claim to fame did not escape Wormynghalle's notice, just as it did not the scholars', and Bartholomew immediately sensed there was tension between the three merchants.

'I will be Mayor next year,' snapped Wormynghalle, shooting Abergavenny an unpleasant glance, 'and I was elected a burgess in January. It is about time Oxford had a tanner as Mayor. It is just as respectable a trade as spicery or wine-selling.'

As he gazed challengingly at his companions, Bartholomew took the opportunity to study them. Abergavenny was black-haired and fair-faced, like many Celts, and his eyes held a humorous glint, as if he found much of what he saw amusing. His cloak was embroidered with a tiny vine motif, and Bartholomew surmised that he was a vintner. Eu was tall and thin, and spoke English with a thick French accent. The inflexion was inconsistent, and

Bartholomew suspected English was his mother tongue, but that he liked to emphasise the fact that he hailed from old Norman stock. There was a carving of a nutmeg on his ring, which was exquisitely made and a symbol of tastefully understated wealth.

Wormynghalle was Eu's exact opposite: short, heavily built and pugilistic. He did not wear his fine clothes as comfortably as his companions, and the rings on his fingers and his heavy gold neck-chain were ostentatious examples of his riches. The chain carried a heavy pendant in the shape of a sheep's head, to represent his trade as a curer of skins; the workmanship was poor, despite the high quality of the medium, and the carving possessed a set of very un-ovine teeth. When inspecting him, Bartholomew was unfavourably reminded of the overweight peacock that lived at Michaelhouse, and was not surprised the man's companions did not seem to like him. His trade as a tanner would not endear him to men who dabbled in the rarefied worlds of exotic spices and wines, either. Tanning was a foul, stinking business involving bloody, flayed skins and vats of urine.

'We have come to investigate a murder,' stated Wormynghalle, when no one replied. 'The culprit fled to Cambridge, and we intend to hunt him out and take him home with us.'

'It happened during the St Scholastica's Day riot,' elaborated Abergavenny, 'while the town was in flames and there was murder and mayhem everywhere. It was then that this evil fellow chose to strike down an innocent man.'

'With a sword,' added Wormynghalle.

'That unrest was months ago,' said Michael, startled. 'Why search for this culprit now? And how do you know he is in Cambridge anyway?'

'His victim was left mortally wounded, but not dead,' explained Eu. 'The poor man – Gonerby was his name –

59

gasped with his dying breath that he overheard his assailant telling a friend that he intended to hide in Cambridge until the hue and cry had died away. I was there: I heard Gonerby's words with my own ears. Then he charged us to catch the killer and make him answer for his crime. I am from an ancient family, who believes in the sanctity of oaths and sacred vows—'

'So do I,' interrupted Wormynghalle, not to be outdone on the chivalry front.

'—so I gave my word to Gonerby, as he died, that I would find his murderer,' finished Eu, looking Wormynghalle up and down in disdain, to deny that he and the tanner shared common ideals.

'Tell me this killer's name,' said Michael. 'If he is guilty, then he is yours to take to Oxford.'

'Gonerby did not know it,' replied Abergavenny. 'That is why we came ourselves, and did not entrust servants to find him.'

'Tracking a killer is not easy, and will need men of intelligence and cunning,' said Wormynghalle, oblivious to the long-suffering glances his colleagues exchanged behind his back. 'That means us. Besides, Gonerby was popular, and if I catch his killer, everyone will vote for me as Mayor.'

'Many people died during that riot,' said Michael. 'What makes Gonerby's death worthy of investigation, when others are not?'

'He was wealthy, popular and influential – a parchment-maker,' replied Eu, twisting his nutmeg ring around on his finger. 'We cannot afford to have men like *him* murdered and their killers going free. What message would that send to the general populace?'

'We do not want scholars thinking they can slaughter us as they please, and nothing bad will ever happen to them,' elaborated Wormynghalle, who did not seem averse to stating the obvious. 'It might encourage others to try their luck.'

'This is an odd tale,' said Michael, frowning. 'You know more about Gonerby's death – and about his killer – than you are telling, since you cannot possibly hope to snag the culprit with the information you have shared with us. It is simply not enough to allow you to start.'

'We know the killer is a scholar,' offered Abergavenny. 'Gonerby said he wore a student's dark garb *and* he heard him say Oxford was too dangerous, so he would study in Cambridge instead.'

'That does suggest you should look to a University member for your culprit,' admitted Tynkell. 'But it does not tell us whether he was an Oxford student who saw Cambridge as a safe haven, or whether he was a Cambridge student who happened to be visiting Oxford at the time of the riot.'

Abergavenny nodded. 'So, we intend to look at both possibilities. Gonerby's widow told us we cannot go home unless we bring her a killer. She made us promise to fulfil her husband's last wish, even if we die in the attempt.'

'She is a forceful lady,' said Eu, not entirely admiringly. 'Just because we three happened to stumble on the dying Gonerby, she decided *we* should be the ones to hunt down his murderer. I did not want to oblige, but we had made that promise to Gonerby, so it became a point of honour.'

'*I* was only speaking to comfort the man in his final agonies,' said Abergavenny ruefully. 'But Wormynghalle here made the promise public and Mistress Gonerby held us to it.' He cast an admonishing, resentful glance at the tanner.

'I did what was right,' declared Wormynghalle defensively. 'How was I to know you were only humouring Gonerby when you swore to avenge him? I was under the impression that you held the same principles as me, and

61

I was astonished to learn you were ready to renege.'

'You are deliberately misrepresenting us,' snapped Eu, seeming to forget he was in the Chancellor's office and the argument was being witnessed by strangers. 'Of course I believe in honour and the sanctity of oaths, but this was different. I was trying to calm him, not agree to sacrifice weeks of my life searching for a fellow whose name and description we do not know.'

'It has cost you little so far,' said Wormynghalle nastily. 'You arrived here eleven days ago, and you have spent virtually all that time establishing new business contacts.'

'We did not promise to hunt this killer to the exclusion of all else,' said Abergavenny reasonably. 'And the opportunities that have arisen in and around Cambridge have been irresistible.'

'For spicers and vintners maybe,' snapped Wormynghalle. 'But not for tanners. Mine is not a trade that benefits from distant agreements – it is cheaper to buy and sell *my* materials locally.'

Abergavenny smiled to acknowledge his point, then turned to Michael. 'But we have drawn our personal affairs to a close, and now we are ready to begin our hunt.'

'But this *still* does not explain why you did not visit Cambridge sooner,' said Michael. 'If this quest is so important, then why the delay? Gonerby has been dead almost four months.'

'We could not just up and leave,' declared Eu. 'We had arrangements to make, and there were important matters that required our attention. We came as soon as we could.'

'We came when it became obvious we had no choice,' corrected Abergavenny ruefully. 'We thought the task an impossible one from the start, and were reluctant to begin something we could not finish. But Widow Gonerby is a forceful woman, and she was backed by the guilds. Gonerby was well liked, and everyone insisted that his last wish should be carried out.'

'Because the city is under interdict, Gonerby was buried without the appropriate rites and his wife was furious,' added Eu. He shuddered. 'I would not like to see *her* lose her temper again – and she will, if we return without a culprit.'

'An interdict is a terrible thing,' agreed Tynkell. 'Corpses rot in the streets, because their kin refuse to allow them to be buried without a requiem mass. The stench offends my delicate senses.'

For a moment, no one spoke, and all three merchants, Bartholomew and Michael regarded him in wary disbelief. Then Eu pointedly lifted a heavy pomander to his nose and mouth, while Abergavenny was clearly struggling not to snigger.

Michael dragged his thoughts away from the Chancellor and back to the merchants. 'Your task would be difficult if the killer had remained in Oxford, but how will you find him here, in a town where you have no friends and where no one has any reason to help you?'

'And even if you do discover a scholar who was in Oxford the day Gonerby died, it will be impossible to prove he is the culprit,' added Bartholomew. 'Unless he confesses.'

'There were many vicious murders that dreadful day,' added Tynkell softly. 'Sixty scholars were slaughtered as they tried to go about their lawful business. Sixty!'

'And how many townsmen?' demanded Eu. 'Probably twice that number!'

'More,' said Wormynghalle, tugging aggressively on his sheep-head pendant.

'But the scholars were unarmed,' insisted Tynkell. 'Chancellor Brouweon wrote to us, and described dreadful acts of savagery.'

'If the scholars were unarmed, then why did so many

townsmen die?' asked Abergavenny quietly. 'The killing – with weapons – was carried out by both sides.'

'You clearly dislike scholars,' said Bartholomew to Eu. 'Yet you travelled to Cambridge in their company. Why?'

'It made sense,' explained Abergavenny, resting his hand on Eu's arm when the spicer looked as if he was about to make a curt response about his travelling arrangements being his own affair. 'Duraunt was due to inspect Merton's Cambridge holdings, and three of his colleagues were itching to leave the city, because they fear reprisals. Thus there were four academics, and we were four – if you count Okehamptone the scribe among our number. It seemed safer to make the journey as a single party, given that the highways are so dangerous these days.'

'I appreciate your predicament,' said Michael, regarding the three merchants soberly. 'You have been charged to find a killer and you are determined to carry out your duty. But I must refuse you permission to do it here. The Archbishop of Canterbury is due in a few days, and I cannot have merchants asking inflammatory questions of scholars. You may cause a disturbance here, too.'

'But you must!' cried Eu, coming to his feet. 'Widow Gonerby will be furious if we return empty-handed, and will denigrate us to our fellow burgesses.'

Abergavenny also stood. 'Worse, she may come after this scholar herself, and then you will have a riot for certain. She is not a woman to be denied.'

'I do not care,' said Michael. 'If she comes, she will be told what I am telling you: to go home.'

'Then we shall see the Sheriff,' declared Wormynghalle, making for the door. 'He will not condone universities protecting scholars who slay innocent merchants.'

Wormynghalle's tirade faltered when he found his way blocked by a small man with pale hair and a wispy beard.

Despite his diminutive size, the man exuded an aura of confidence and authority, and even though Wormynghalle was at least a head taller, he stopped dead in his tracks when the fellow raised a hand to indicate he was to return to his seat. Sheriff Tulyet had approached so silently that no one was sure how much of the discussion he had heard. Bartholomew liked Tulyet, who was able, intelligent and more than a match for the criminals who tried their luck in his town. He introduced himself, and Bartholomew was gratified to see Wormynghalle at a loss for words.

'Well?' asked Abergavenny when he had repeated their request. 'Will *you* see justice done?'

Tulyet walked to a window and stared across the grassy churchyard, hands clasped behind his back. 'I know what happened on St Scholastica's Day, and I do not want hundreds dead here because you interrogate our scholars. Brother Michael is right to forbid you from conducting your enquiries.'

'But what shall we do?' demanded Wormynghalle. 'We cannot go home without a culprit, and I shall not stay here for ever.'

'And we do not want you here,' said Tynkell with a deplorable lack of tact. 'But it is not our fault you agreed to this ridiculous quest. You must devise a solution to your predicament yourselves.'

'You cannot let a killer go unpunished, any more than we can,' reasoned Abergavenny. 'He will be so delighted to get away with one murder that he may commit another.'

'Perhaps he has already struck,' said Eu uneasily. 'Chesterfelde was stabbed last night: perhaps *he* knew the killer's identity, and was murdered before he could tell.' He appealed to his colleagues. 'The Sheriff is right: we cannot do anything here, and we should leave while we are still able.'

'I suppose we could go home,' said Abergavenny cautiously. 'But . . .'

'We could not,' stated Wormynghalle firmly. 'We are not Chesterfelde – a grinning fool who spouted Latin at every turn – and *we* will not slink away like beaten curs.' He gazed defiantly first at Michael, and then at Tulyet.

'Tell me a little about Chesterfelde, since you are here,' said Michael opportunistically. 'I heard you were in the hall when he was killed.'

'We were,' said Eu with a shudder. 'It was not pleasant to wake up and find a corpse in our midst, I can tell you! We were all tired and slept heavily – even old Duraunt, who usually only naps. We doused the lamps at dusk – about nine o'clock on these light evenings – and none of us knew any more until Bailiff Boltone woke us shortly before dawn.'

'It was a vile shock,' agreed Abergavenny quietly. 'Knowing you slept through a murdered man's final agonies. There are similarities between the deaths of Chesterfelde and Gonerby, Brother, and you would be rash to ignore them.'

'And those similarities are?' asked Michael, surprised.

Abergavenny raised his hands in a way that suggested he thought the answer obvious. 'Both were killed with blades, and both were killed in such a way as to leave no witnesses.'

'Gonerby was killed with a sword, and Chesterfelde with a knife,' mused Bartholomew. 'Chesterfelde died during the night, and Gonerby during a daytime riot. Gonerby was a parchment-maker and Chesterfelde a scholar. They do not sound similar to me.'

'However,' said Michael, 'if these two deaths are related, then we shall have confirmation of it when I find Chesterfelde's killer – which I will do, gentlemen.' He looked at each one in turn, and Bartholomew thought that if any of the three merchants are the culprit, then he should be experiencing some serious unease. 'I intend to have Chesterfelde's killer in my prison before the Archbishop arrives, and if the fellow also did away with Gonerby, then your problem will be solved.'

'How do we know we can trust you?' asked Wormynghalle suspiciously.

Michael did not dignify the question with a reply. 'You will return to Merton Hall and throw yourself on Duraunt's hospitality while I make some enquiries. Then, when I have my culprit, you can question him about Gonerby.'

The three merchants looked at each other. Bartholomew could see Eu was ready to accept, because it was the easiest and safest option – and it would leave time free for business. Wormynghalle was against it, because he did not trust the monk to apprehend the right man. Abergavenny wavered, torn between wanting to be amenable to the authorities and preferring to conduct his own investigation.

'Very well,' said the Welshman eventually. 'We shall do as you ask.'

'We will bide by your decision until the Archbishop arrives – next Monday,' said Wormynghalle, clearly irritated by the decision. 'It is Sunday now, so you have seven full days. But then I am going home, and I *will* take a culprit with me. Either you will hand him to me, or I shall find one myself. I will not return to Oxford empty-handed.'

The warmth of the day, combined with the relaxed atmosphere of a Sunday and several nights of interrupted sleep, made Bartholomew drowsy. He knew he would be unable to concentrate on reading that afternoon, so did not mind when Michael suggested they return to Merton Hall to search for stained clothing and the place where Chesterfelde had died. Tulyet walked with them, heading for his house on Bridge Street, where he lived with his wife and their hellion son, Dickon.

'I am not sure it was a good idea to volunteer to find their killer,' said Bartholomew, watching a group of children play with a discarded cartwheel. Their shrill, excited voices drew disapproving glances from a group of Carmelite friars, who were chanting a psalm as they walked to their friary.

'I had no choice,' said Michael, turning a flabby white face to the sky, relishing the sun's caressing rays. 'What a trio! They would have Cambridge in flames within a day.'

'I agree,' said Tulyet. 'They care nothing for our town, and want only to give this vengeful widow someone to hang. Eu, who is the most dangerous of the three, is not a reasonable man.'

'You think Eu was the worst?' asked Michael in surprise. 'I had the Welshman marked as the villain. He pretends to be amiable, but he manipulates the others like puppets.'

'The tanner was the one I did not like,' said Bartholomew. 'He is desperate to be accepted by ancient and respected families, and I think he will do anything to prove himself worthy. He is also determined to have himself elected Mayor. It would not surprise me to learn that *he* had engineered this whole business of avenging Gonerby, just to show voters his mettle.'

'He is not clever enough,' argued Tulyet. 'But Eu is cunning. I am from an old Norman family myself, and I recognise his kind. You mark my words: if Michael does not hand him a culprit in a week, it will be Eu who selects a victim.'

'We shall have to agree to differ,' said Michael, 'because you are both wrong. But it is a strange business that brings them here. Hundreds of folk died in the St Scholastica's Day riots, and I find it difficult to believe that these men travelled all this way to investigate one death. Perhaps they instigated the disorder themselves, for reasons we have yet to fathom.'

'Actually, scholars were responsible for that,' said Tulyet. 'I had a letter from the Mayor, and he said it was *all* the fault of the students – a fight started over wine in a tavern.'

'A Mayor would say that,' declared Michael disparagingly. 'I heard the whole thing began with a quarrel over claret, too, but it was *townsmen* who took it to its bloody conclusion.'

'There was a sinister set of coincidences in the chain of events that led to the trouble,' mused Bartholomew, thinking about what Michael had told him. 'First, weapons were readily available – for scholars and townsfolk alike. And second, alarm bells sounded very quickly after the initial squabble in the Swindlestock Tavern. It was almost as if someone was fanning the spark of an insignificant incident, to ensure it caught and ignited the rest of the city.'

'Do you think it had something to do with the death of Gonerby?' asked Tulyet. 'It would explain why these merchants are so determined to have his killer. The fellow also left their town in ashes.'

'If that is true, then you are putting yourself in considerable danger,' said Bartholomew to Michael. 'Eu capitulated very quickly when you refused him permission to investigate: he was glad to see someone else take the risks.'

Michael waved a dismissive hand. 'I am more than a match for anyone from Oxford. However, the real reason Eu gave way so readily was that he and his cronies have no intention of obeying my orders. They plan to make their enquiries, regardless. I read it in the Welshman's eyes.'

Tulyet agreed. 'I will set a sergeant to follow them, and ensure they do not cause trouble. I would just as soon lock them up until the Archbishop has gone, but I do not think we can get away with it – not with prosperous merchants. Our own burgesses would claim I had overstepped my authority, and they would be right. But we may be worrying over nothing: there are hundreds of scholars in Cambridge, and any one of them could be this killer. Our merchants will never identify their man.'

'Not so,' argued Bartholomew. 'Most of our students were here on the tenth day of February, keeping University term. There will not be many who were away.'

'That is easy to find out,' said Michael. 'Any scholar wanting to leave during term must apply in writing for permission, so his request will be documented. Of course, the murderer may be an Oxford man who is visiting us for a few weeks – but we have lists of those, too. So if Gonerby's killer really is an academic who was in Oxford in February, and who then came here, he will not be difficult to identify.'

Tulyet began to tell Michael about the arrangements the town was making to entertain the Archbishop, and Bartholomew listened with half his attention; the rest was engaged in a sluggish contemplation of the lurid pink wash that adorned the home of the town's surgeon. The guilds had united to organise a splendid feast, Tulyet was saying, while public buildings and the Market Square were being cleaned. The Sheriff pointed out the parallel drains that ran along the High Street, and declared proudly that they had never been so empty. Bartholomew knew this perfectly well: he had been summoned to tend several people who had been taken unawares by the sudden appearance of deep trenches in Cambridge's main thoroughfares, and had fallen down them. Tulyet had also raised funds to pay for additional dung collections, and the High Street was oddly bereft of the odorous piles that usually graced it. People with horses had been ordered to remove what their animals left behind, and the public latrine pits had been emptied. Bartholomew thought it a pity the improvements would last only as long as the Visitation was under way. As soon as Islip departed, business would be back to normal, and Cambridge would revert to its usual vile, stinking state.

'And I do not want any lepers hanging around,' Tulyet said sternly to Bartholomew, as if the physician was in a position to oblige. 'They are invited to a special service in St Clement's Church, where they will receive Islip's blessing, but then they will make themselves scarce.'

'Right,' said Bartholomew, tiredness making him uncharacteristically caustic. 'We do not want sloughed fingers and noses littering our clean streets, do we?'

'No, we do not,' agreed Tulyet, equally tart. He turned to Michael. 'And *you* can make sure *he* has a good night's sleep. I do not want him snapping at Islip, because he is overly weary.'

'He will not listen to me,' said Michael. 'Nor am I bold enough to prise my way between a man and his paramour.'

'Now, just a moment,' began Bartholomew indignantly. 'I do not—'

Tulyet cut across him. 'Rougham is away in Norfolk, so you must be ready should the Archbishop require a physician. I know you are busy, with Clippesby indisposed, but it cannot be helped. You are better than Lynton of Peterhouse and Paxtone of King's Hall, and I want you to tend Islip, should the occasion arise. It is our duty to ensure he has the absolute best we can offer – of everything.'

'I am surprised Rougham has chosen now to leave for a family reunion,' said Michael conversationally. 'He is an ambitious man, and I would have thought he would be here, showing off to important people. Still, he has a nasty habit of polishing his teeth on his sleeve after formal dinners – presumably to improve the quality of his smile – so perhaps it is just as well he is gone.'

'Teeth polishing will not bother Islip,' said Tulyet disapprovingly. 'He does it himself. How is Clippesby, by the way? Still ailing?'

'I plan to visit him today,' replied Bartholomew, 'and hope to find him a little recovered.'

'You had better find him more than "a little recovered",' said Michael testily. 'I cannot imagine why you have so suddenly decided he is unfit to teach. He has always been insane, and it has never bothered you before. I do not know how much longer I can teach his classes – I know nothing of musical theory and I am not interested in learning. So, either declare him well and reinstate him, or declare him irrecoverably mad, so we can hire someone in his place.'

'Soon,' promised Bartholomew. 'Give him time. He has been gone only a few days.'

'Since Ascension Day,' said Michael, aggrieved. '*Ten* days. I know, because that was when Langelee so blithely ordered me to teach a subject I have never studied. Does he think we are King's Hall, with no standards?'

'King's Hall?' asked Tulyet. 'You criticise their teaching practices? I thought most of its scholars were men destined for high ranks within the Church or the King's Court.'

'Quite,' muttered Michael venomously. 'I met one Fellow last week who knew no Latin. None at all! I was obliged to speak to him in French, for God's sake! And there are others who do not know the most rudimentary aspects of the Trivium. It must be like teaching children!'

Tulyet bade them farewell when he reached his house. Even from the street, Bartholomew could hear the excited screeches of his son Dickon as he played some boisterous – and probably violent – game with the Sheriff's long-suffering servants, and did not miss Tulyet's grimace of anticipation as he knocked on the door to be allowed in. It could not be left open for people to come and go as they pleased, because Dickon would be out in a trice, and his parents were afraid he would come to harm. From what

Bartholomew had seen of Dickon's developing personality over the past few months, he was not entirely sure it would be a tragedy. Michael grinned as they walked on alone.

'Poor Dick! That is the only child he will ever sire – within his marriage, at least – and the boy is a monster. How did it happen, do you think? William believes the Devil slipped into his bedchamber and fathered the brat. Dickon is so unlike his parents that I cannot help but think he may be right.'

An ear-shattering scream of delight followed them as Dickon greeted his father. Several people jumped in alarm, while those who knew Dickon shook their heads in mute disgust. Bartholomew walked a little more quickly, in case the boy spotted him through a window and demanded a visit, setting a pace that had Michael gasping for breath. They crossed the Great Bridge, where there was no sign of anyone thinking of self-murder, and turned along Merton Lane. For the second time that day, Michael hammered on the door. As before, it was answered by the pale-headed bailiff.

'Now what? The body has been taken to the church, and everyone else is out.'

'Good,' said Michael, pushing his way inside. 'That will make our task here all the easier. And I want a word with you anyway. Where were you when Chesterfelde died?'

'Why?' asked Boltone, looking shifty. 'What does that have to do with you?'

'Just answer the question,' snapped Michael.

'I was asleep,' replied Boltone. 'It is common knowledge that Chesterfelde died between after the curfew bell at eight and before dawn. I was asleep all that time, and so was Eudo.'

'Eudo?' asked Bartholomew. He sensed he should know the name, but his tired mind refused to yield the information.

'Eudo of Helpryngham,' said Boltone impatiently. 'He rents the manor from Merton College – I told you about him earlier. He and I sleep in the solar, while the scholars have the hall.'

'Were the scholars alone last night?' asked Michael. 'Or did they entertain guests?'

'They might have done,' replied Boltone unhelpfully. 'I went to bed immediately after the curfew, so I have no idea what they did. I am a heavy sleeper. I snore, too, and Eudo always wraps a cloth around his ears to block my noise, so neither of us heard what that miserable rabble were doing.'

'What happened after you retired at eight?'

'I heard nothing until the cockerel crowed before dawn. When I went to wake the Oxford men for their breakfast, there was Chesterfelde with a knife in his back. It was my yell of horror that roused the others from their slumbers.'

'They were all there?' asked Bartholomew. 'Three surviving scholars and three merchants?'

'Yes,' replied Boltone. 'But I cannot say whether they were all there the whole night. Sometimes they debate and argue, and keep me awake, but I was exhausted yesterday, and I heard nothing.'

'Argue?' pounced Michael. 'You mean they antagonise each other?'

Boltone shrugged. 'Sometimes. Polmorva called Spryngheuse a sludge-brained pedant last week, and Chesterfelde responded by referring to him as a slippery-tongued viper. But I am busy today: Duraunt accused me of being dishonest in my accounting, so I have to prove him wrong. Do you want anything else, or can I go?'

'Go,' said Michael. 'We only want to inspect the hall again.'

'All right,' said Boltone. 'But do not touch any of the scholars' belongings, or they will accuse me of doing it.'

Michael and Bartholomew climbed the stairs to the hall.

The room was much as it had been the last time they were there. Straw mattresses were stored on one side, ready to be used again that night, and blankets were rolled on top of them. The trestle tables employed for meals had been stacked away, and only the benches left out, so there would be somewhere to sit when the visitors returned. The window shutters had been thrown open to allow the hall to air, and the fire Duraunt had enjoyed earlier had burned out – the day was warm and heating unnecessary, even for chilly old men.

'Right,' said Michael, rubbing his hands. 'Do you want to go through these saddlebags for stained clothes, or keep watch to make sure no one catches us?'

'You just told Boltone you would not touch anything.'

'I lied,' said Michael carelessly. 'It comes from dealing with the likes of Abergavenny and Polmorva. Well? Hurry up and decide, or they will be back before we have started.'

'You do it,' said Bartholomew distastefully. 'I will make sure no one comes.'

While Michael rummaged through the visitors' bags, Bartholomew sat on a windowsill and struggled to stay alert. The sun was warm on his face, and he felt pleasantly relaxed. When Michael spoke, he started awake. For a moment, he did not know where he was, and gazed around him, blinking stupidly.

'I see my integrity is safe under your vigilant care,' remarked Michael caustically. 'You really do need a good night's sleep, Matt. Now I cannot even trust you to keep watch while I ransack people's belongings. What would we have said if they had caught us?'

'That they are all suspects until you have Chesterfelde's killer under lock and key,' replied Bartholomew, rubbing his eyes as he stood. 'Duraunt will not object, but Polmorva will, which would be satisfying. Well? Did you find his clothes drenched in gore?'

'No,' said Michael in disgust. 'Not so much as a spot. There are a few drips on the floor where we found the body, but that is not surprising. I found this in Duraunt's bag, but it cannot have any relevance, given that no one has been poisoned.' He handed Bartholomew a tiny phial.

The physician took it carefully, knowing that small pots often contained fairly powerful substances. This one was no exception, and it released the pungent odour of concentrated poppy juice when he lifted it to his nose. He recoiled. 'There is enough soporific here to put half the University to sleep!'

Michael regarded it thoughtfully. 'And it is partly empty, which means some of it has been used. Is there enough missing to make half a dozen merchants and scholars doze through a murder?'

Bartholomew inspected the vial. 'Yes, but Duraunt is not your culprit. He was appalled by the murder, and he is a kind, gentle man.'

'So you said earlier,' said Michael. 'But people change, and you have not seen him for years. Who knows what he might have become in the interim?'

Bartholomew had a better explanation. 'Polmorva is not beyond hiding something incriminating among another man's possessions. He did it to me once, and almost had me convicted of theft. I only just managed to hurl them out of the window, before my chest was searched.'

'Them?'

'Those teeth – the ones he made for the Benedictines. He claimed they had been stolen and accused me of taking them. When I went to my room, there they were, hidden under a book.'

'How do you know it was he who put them there?'

'The servants saw him. But this is getting us nowhere. Put the phial back where you found it, Brother. We can ask Polmorva and Duraunt about it later.'

76

'No,' said Michael, slipping the bottle into his scrip. 'I do not want a potentially toxic substance in the hands of my suspects. I shall keep it, and we will know to whom it belongs when its disappearance is reported.'

'That is dangerous,' warned Bartholomew uncomfortably. 'Boltone knows you have been here. It will not look good for the Senior Proctor to be on the wrong end of a charge of theft.'

'I shall deny it,' said Michael. He walked towards the solar. 'Since we are here, we may as well be thorough. We should see whether Boltone and Eudo own stained clothes, too.'

The solar was far less tidy than the hall, and was strewn with bedding and discarded clothes. Filthy shirts sat in a pile in one corner, where they were evidently picked through to be worn again on subsequent occasions, while boots and shoes lay where they had been cast off. Two smelly dogs lounged in a shaft of sunlight from the open window, and watched with uninterest as Michael began to sift through the mess. Bartholomew remained by the door, standing so he would not fall asleep again.

'There is nothing here, either,' said Michael. He wiped his hands on his habit in distaste. 'Eudo and Boltone live like pigs! I am not surprised Duraunt declined to wrest the solar away from them.'

'Someone is coming!' said Bartholomew urgently, hearing footsteps on the stairs. 'Come into the hall and pretend to inspect the blood where the body was found.'

Michael had only just reached the place and leaned down to look where Bartholomew was pointing before the door was flung open. The man who stood there was tall, and Bartholomew supposed he was handsome, although there was something in his arrogant demeanour that was highly unattractive. His dark brown hair was long and wavy, and his blue eyes were surrounded by dark lashes, giving

77

him the appearance of a foreigner, although his clothes were solidly English, with none of the cosmopolitan fripperies flaunted by many men of substance.

'Who are you?' he demanded, hands on hips as he regarded the scholars imperiously. 'And what are you doing here?'

Michael straightened, irked by the man's manner. 'Senior Proctor, investigating the murder of Roger de Chesterfelde.'

'He smiled a lot,' said the man, making it sound sinister. 'And he cited a good deal of Latin – not that those stupid merchants could understand him. Unlike me. I attended the King's School when I was a boy, and *I* can read.' He drew himself up to his full height and looked as if he expected them to be impressed.

'I imagine reading will be helpful to the man who rents this manor,' said Michael evenly. He had surmised that the man was Merton's tenant, Eudo of Helpryngham.

'Actually, no,' replied Eudo. 'If there is any reading to be done, Boltone does it. I prefer to be outside, with the sun on my face and fresh air in my lungs.'

'I am not surprised,' said Michael, casting a significant glance at the squalor of the solar. 'What do you know about Chesterfelde's death?'

'Nothing,' replied Eudo. 'I was at the King's Head last night, and then I came here. I was drunk and heard nothing at all – not even Boltone's infernal snoring. I probably downed seven or eight jugs of ale.' He looked as if he was fishing for compliments, in the same way that Bartholomew's younger undergraduates bragged about the amounts of wine they could consume without being sick. But Eudo was in his thirties, and should have grown out of such foolishness.

'You have hurt yourself,' said Bartholomew, pointing to a crude bandage that adorned Eudo's left arm. 'What happened?'

'I probably fell over when I was staggering home last night. You are a physician, are you not? Tend it for me. It is very sore.'

Without waiting for Bartholomew's consent, Eudo unravelled the dressing to reveal an injury on the inside of his forearm that was no more than a scratch. It was slight enough to have been caused by brambles or even a cat, and the reams of material enveloping it were far in excess of what was needed. Despite its superficial nature, Eudo grimaced and sucked in his breath when Bartholomew examined it.

'You do not need to keep it wrapped,' said Bartholomew. 'I will smear it with salve, but the best thing would be to leave it open to the air. It will heal more quickly.'

'It is a serious injury,' declared Eudo, watching Bartholomew apply a balm of woundwort and hog's grease. 'Besides, I told Boltone I was too sick to work, and he will think I am malingering if he sees me without a bandage. Put it on again.'

'No,' said Bartholomew, replacing the salve in his bag. 'It will not heal if you keep it covered. Besides, you *are* malingering if you claim it is stopping you from working.'

Eudo's handsome face creased into a scowl as he bound the afflicted limb himself. 'You are no good. Doctor Rougham would have ordered me to spend a week in bed and buy half an apothecary's shop in poultices and purges, but he is away at the moment, more is the pity. Still, it has saved me money, because I am not paying you for bad advice and a smear of pig oil.'

'So, you can tell us nothing about Chesterfelde's murder?' asked Michael, seeing Bartholomew about to take issue. 'You saw and heard nothing?'

'No,' said Eudo proudly. 'Not with nine jugs of ale inside me.'

'You said seven or eight.' Bartholomew pounced.

79

'Did I?' asked Eudo carelessly. 'It was a lot. Probably nearer ten.'

'I wish it had been twenty,' muttered Bartholomew in an undertone. 'That would have wiped the smile off your face this morning.'

Bartholomew and Michael left Merton Hall and began to walk towards their College. On the way they met Duraunt and Polmorva, who said they had been visiting Duraunt's fellow Austin Canons at nearby Barnwell Priory. Polmorva's expression hardened when Michael told him that he and his Corpse Examiner had re-inspected the place where Chesterfelde had died, and Bartholomew thought he detected an uneasy flicker in his eye; he wondered whether he guessed they had searched his possessions and was afraid of what might have been found. Duraunt contented himself with reciting a short prayer for Chesterfelde, then started to discuss the next University Debate. Michael fretted impatiently as the old man gabbled on about his favourite topics for such occasions, while Bartholomew listened with interest, recalling disputes on similar issues they had attended together in Oxford – an erudite, careful teacher and his eager but inexpert student.

When they eventually parted, Michael went to search the University's records for any scholars who had been granted leave of absence to study in Oxford, and to peruse applications from Oxford students who wanted to visit Cambridge, while Bartholomew walked to the hamlet of Stourbridge, outside the town. He wanted to see Clippesby, and assess whether there was any improvement in his condition. As it was such a fine day, he strolled slowly, enjoying the sweet scent of ripening crops and the damp earthiness of fertile soil. The sun lay golden and warm across the fields, occasionally cooled when fluffy white clouds drifted across its bright face.

The hospital was a sprawling complex of buildings enclosed within a fence of woven hazel. It had originally been founded for lepers, so their disease would not contaminate others, but now it accepted patients with a variety of ailments. It comprised the Chapel of St Mary Magdalene, an ancient two-celled church with thick walls and tiny windows, and a number of huts with thatched roofs, where the inmates lived. The community had its own well, fish-ponds, fields, orchards and livestock, and its residents were seldom obliged to deal with the outside world.

The warden who cared for the eclectic collection of people who had been banished from 'normal' society was an amiable Austin Canon called Paul. He tended his thirty or so patients with the help of a small staff of lay-brothers, and Bartholomew considered the man little short of a saint. He was tall and sturdy, which was a useful attribute when dealing with the obstreperousness of madness and the heavy lifting required for the bedridden, and his brown hair lay thickly around his untidy tonsure. He was nearly always smiling, and it was not unusual for the compound to ring with his laughter.

There was no humour that day, however, because he was troubled. Michaelhouse's Master of Music and Astronomy was afforded a fair degree of freedom in the hospital, and had been helping to care for some of the sicker inmates. But Clippesby had a habit of wandering away without telling anyone where he was going, and Bartholomew was disturbed to learn that he had vanished several times since he had been enrolled at Stourbridge. Most worrying was the fact that he had been gone for part of the previous night, when Chesterfelde had died.

'I was with the ducks near the river, Matt,' said Clippesby dreamily, when the physician asked him about it. He laughed merrily. 'They will provide me with an alibi, should you require one.'

Bartholomew studied him intently, trying to ascertain whether the man was genuinely trying to be helpful, or was playing him for a fool. He rubbed his hand through his hair when several moments of staring into Clippesby's clear grey eyes told him nothing at all.

'You promised you would stay here,' said Paul reproachfully. 'Why did you break your word?'

'I was needed elsewhere, Brother,' said Clippesby with a serene smile. 'You have duties towards your charges, so you will understand these obligations. Besides, I do not like being shut up all night. There are too many interesting things happening elsewhere.'

'What sort of things?' asked Bartholomew uneasily.

'Things *you* would not understand. Why do you want to know?'

'A man was killed in Merton Hall last night. You should not wander around the town, Clippesby. People know you are unwell, and we do not want them to accuse you of a crime because they cannot find the real culprit and need a scapegoat. I brought you here for your own safety.'

'So you say,' replied Clippesby acidly. He did not like Stourbridge. 'But that is the second death at Merton Hall. A fellow called Okehamptone perished there a week or two ago. I was visiting some geese at the time, and they were very unhappy that he died so suddenly after arriving in their town.'

'Were they,' said Bartholomew. The Dominican's nocturnal wanderings meant he was often a witness to criminal activities, and he had provided Michael with valuable clues in the past. The difficulty, however, lay in deciding what was true and what was fancy.

'They were,' asserted Clippesby. 'Tell Michael not to forget Okehamptone. It will please the geese to know they have a Senior Proctor who takes all deaths seriously. Can you see that lark, Matt? High in the clouds? I have just

82

heard her say she saw you leaving Matilde's house at dawn again this morning. You *must* be more discreet when you visit her, my friend, or you will tarnish her good name.'

'Matilde the courtesan?' asked Paul, regarding Bartholomew askance. 'You visit her during the night? This lark is right, man! You should show some discretion. Leave while it is still dark, not once the sun has started to rise.'

'I will bear it in mind,' said Bartholomew shortly. 'Although the lark should mind her own damned business, and keep her gossip to herself.'

He spent the rest of the day with his ailing colleague, but even after several hours still had no idea whether the Dominican was improving. It was frustrating, and he walked home helpless and angry, wishing there were not so many ailments that his medical training could not cure. He was light-headed from tiredness, but when he flopped on to his bed at Michaelhouse, intending to doze until it was time to meet Matilde, sleep would not come. Images of Clippesby, Polmorva and Duraunt rattled around his mind, along with Chesterfelde and the knife embedded in his back. He sensed he was about to embark on an investigation where nothing would be what it seemed, and that would take all his wits to solve. The unsettling part was that he did not think his wits were up to the task.

CHAPTER 3

The following morning heralded another glorious day, clear and blue. Michael told Bartholomew that he had been reviewing the evidence surrounding Chesterfelde's death and had eliminated none of the suspects from his enquiries. He had visited the King's Head tavern and ascertained that Eudo had indeed consumed copious quantities of ale on the night in question, but pointed out that being drunk did not preclude anyone from committing murder. He also distrusted Boltone, and thought Polmorva might well be right to accuse him of the crime on the basis of mistaken identity in the dark. But he distrusted Polmorva more, and considered him exactly the kind of man to kill and confuse the evidence by thrusting knives into dead men's backs. The result was a wealth of suspects.

'But not Duraunt,' said Bartholomew as they walked up the High Street, Michael to ask yet more questions of his potential culprits, and Bartholomew to answer a summons from Sheriff Tulyet. Tulyet's son had stabbed himself with one of his toy arrows, and his anxious parents wanted to ensure the injury was not serious. Bartholomew regarded the prospect of a session with Dickon without enthusiasm, sensing the nagging ache behind his eyes that had been plaguing him all night was likely to become worse once Dickon's enraged screeches had soared around it.

'Duraunt seems kindly,' acknowledged Michael. 'But do not forget that phial we found in his bag – and the fact that we suspect everyone was fed a soporific before Chesterfelde was killed.'

'It probably belongs to Polmorva,' insisted Bartholomew doggedly. 'Besides, the merchants or the scholar we have not yet met – Spryngheuse – might have killed Chesterfelde.'

'That is why I want to question Duraunt about the poppy juice and why I want to meet Spryngheuse – so I can at least try to eliminate some of them from my investigation. I will keep you company while you tend Dickon, and then you can help me. I would like you to watch Polmorva and assess his reaction when we produce that vial.' He gave Bartholomew a sidelong glance. 'And I assure you that you have the better half of the bargain: a few moments with Dickon is far more dangerous than an entire week with murderers from Oxford.'

'What about our teaching?' asked Bartholomew with arched eyebrows. 'It is Monday, and we have lectures all day. I paid Falmeresham to read *De criticis diebus* aloud for an hour while I tend Dickon, but he cannot do it all morning.'

'He can,' said Michael. Bartholomew saw a crafty look in the monk's eye. 'I anticipated we might be assisting each other, so I slipped him a little extra. Galen's *De criticis diebus* is a lengthy work, and Falmeresham has promised to keep your students enthralled with it until noon – or at least, occupied so they do not wander around the hall and make a nuisance of themselves. I cannot imagine anyone being interested in a medical view of diet. Food is not for the cold analysis of science.'

'What about Clippesby's astronomers? Galen's thoughts on vegetables are not relevant to *their* studies, and they are my responsibility now he is indisposed.'

'You have only yourself to blame for that,' said Michael haughtily. 'You went to see him yesterday; you should have pronounced him fit and brought him home. But, as it happens, you can set your mind at rest over the astronomers, too. Young Rob Deynman has agreed to supervise them while they calculate every movable feast in the ecclesiastical year for the next decade.'

'Deynman?' spluttered Bartholomew in appalled disbelief. '*Deynman*? He can barely calculate the time of day when he hears the dinner bell ring! He is not capable of helping other students.'

'He is not going to teach them,' said Michael, unmoved by his objections. 'He will just make sure they do not make too much noise or escape early. And at least he can read, which is more than can be said for the scholars of *some* Colleges.'

He glanced meaningfully to the other side of the street, where Thomas Paxtone, the Master of Medicine from King's Hall, was passing the time of day with Bartholomew's sister. Paxtone was a rosy-cheeked, smiling man from a village near Huntingdon and, unlike the other two physicians in the town – Lynton of Peterhouse and Rougham of Gonville Hall – he was willing to tend the poor, as well as those who could afford to pay for his services. His charity meant that some of the burden was lifted from Bartholomew, who was grateful.

'Mistress Edith is telling me that she and her husband are about to embark on a journey,' said Paxtone, nodding a friendly greeting as Bartholomew and Michael approached. 'The weather is fine, so they will leave for London today.'

Edith kissed her brother, her face flushed with excitement at the prospect of an adventure. 'Oswald is packing the last of our belongings and the horses are saddled. It is a week earlier than we anticipated, but our son will not mind.'

'He might,' warned Bartholomew, suspecting his nephew would be appalled by the unannounced arrival of his parents. Richard was a lawyer, and youth and a high income had combined to render him wild. Bartholomew trusted he would outgrow his dissolute lifestyle in time, but the lad had not shown any indication of encroaching sobriety so far. He hoped Edith would not find her beloved son entwined in the arms of a prostitute, or drunk and insensible – or both – because it would hurt her.

Edith waved away his concerns with the happy optimism he had always envied, then became serious and pulled him to one side, so Michael and Paxtone could not hear. The two scholars immediately began a rather strained discussion about whether the Archbishop should spend more time at King's Hall, which was one of the University's richest foundations, or Michaelhouse, which had a reputation for academic excellence. The decision would depend on whether the University wanted Islip impressed by Cambridge's scholarship or its capacity for lavish entertainment.

'You know I am fond of Matilde,' Edith whispered to her brother, 'and I think she would make you a good wife. But your nightly visits are damaging her reputation and yours.'

'You know about them, too?' asked Bartholomew, mortified.

'She nodded soberly. 'But I do not want my parting words to be nagging ones, so I shall say no more. Just this: be careful and trust no one – especially sweet old men from your past.'

Bartholomew stared at her. 'You mean Master Duraunt? Why? What has he done to make you wary of him?'

Edith lowered her voice further still. 'I was in the apothecary's shop when he bought a good deal of poppy juice. Now, there is nothing wrong with that, but when the apothecary questioned the high potency of the dosage, Duraunt said *you* had recommended that strength to him the previous evening. I happen to know you did not, because you were with Matilde all that night. He lied, Matt.'

Bartholomew's thoughts whirled. 'I have never recommended a sedative to him – weak or strong.'

Edith grimaced. 'So, beware of him. But I must go, or Oswald will wonder where I am.'

She kissed Bartholomew again, and darted off down the High Street, more like a girl than a mature woman ten years Bartholomew's senior. He watched her go fondly, trusting she would have a safe journey along the King's highways, and that she would not be too distressed by what he was sure she would find when she invaded her debauched son's domain.

'I bought a new set of urine flasks recently,' Paxtone said conversationally when she had gone. 'Would you like to see them, Matt?'

'He is going to visit Dickon Tulyet,' said Michael, before his friend could accept the enticing offer. 'He should not dally.'

'He should,' argued Paxtone fervently. 'Because then the brat might have expired by the time he arrives – with luck.'

'Thomas!' exclaimed Bartholomew, shocked. 'Dickon is a child.'

'So his parents claim,' said Paxtone grimly. 'But I think otherwise. The boy is a monster, with his hot temper and unruly behaviour. You *should* dally, Matt. It will allow him to use up his strength by tormenting his helpless parents, so he will be more docile with you. I would not tend him if Tulyet made me a gift of Cambridge Castle!'

Without further ado, he took Bartholomew's arm and guided him towards the impressive edifice that comprised King's Hall. Not averse to Dickon expending some of his violent energy before their visit, and accepting the sense in Paxtone's logic, Michael followed.

Founded almost forty years earlier, King's Hall was a

training ground for men who wanted to enter the King's service or for those destined for exalted posts in the Church. Because it was a royal foundation, it was never short of funds, and no expense had been spared in providing its scholars with a supremely comfortable home. It comprised buildings gathered around a neat, clean yard, and well-tended grounds of orchards, fields and vegetable gardens that extended to the river. As a senior Fellow, Paxtone had been allocated two stately rooms for his personal use – an unthinkable luxury in a University where space was at a premium – both of which were elegantly furnished.

As they strolled across the scrubby grass in front of Paxtone's window, someone hailed them. It was the Warden, a quiet Welshman with long front teeth and a shock of lank grey hair. Thomas Powys had been in office for several years and was a popular master, being kindly, tolerant and ready to grant his Fellows considerable freedom on the understanding that they did not break College or University rules. He was more strict with his students, though, which Bartholomew thought was a good thing: there were more of them in King's Hall than in any other Cambridge institution, and the possibility of serious trouble with such a large body of closely knit young men was very real.

'Brother Michael,' said Powys, baring his impressive incisors in a smile. 'I have been meaning to report to you that we are down two Fellows this term. You need to know for your attendance records.'

'Robert de Wolf and Richard de Hamecotes,' elaborated Paxtone. 'It is highly inconvenient to be without them, actually – as you will know yourself, Brother. I understand Michaelhouse is missing poor Clippesby at the moment. Insanity again, is it?'

'Are they absent with your permission or without it, Warden?' asked Michael, ignoring the impertinent query and not revealing that he already knew about the King's Hall truancies from his University spies.

Powys looked uncomfortable. 'Hamecotes wrote to us saying he has gone to Oxford to purchase books for our library. We are short of legal texts, so his journey will be of great benefit to the College.'

'If he wrote telling you what he planned to do, then it means he asked for permission after he had gone,' Michael surmised. 'You did not grant him leave: he just went.' He eyed the Warden questioningly.

'I do not want trouble,' said Powys softly. 'Hamecotes had no business abandoning us during term, but he has never done anything like this before. I confess I am surprised by his conduct, but if he returns loaded with books, then I am prepared to overlook the lapse.'

'What about the other Fellow?' asked Michael. 'Wolf. Did he just decide to slip away, too?'

Powys nodded unhappily. 'He is in debt – expenses unpaid from last year – but we had agreed to postpone the matter for a few weeks, because he was expecting an inheritance. I am astonished he decided to take unauthorised leave, too, and we miss him sorely. He is an excellent teacher and a popular master.'

'Debt?' asked Michael. 'How much does he owe?'

'Quite a bit,' admitted Powys. 'I know scholars with serious financial troubles sometimes abscond, so they will not have to pay their dues, but I do not think Wolf is one of them.'

'Hamecotes's room-mate was as surprised as the rest of us when *he* left, but Wolf's was not,' said Paxtone, rather imprudently, given that he was talking to the Senior Proctor – the man who might later penalise his colleagues for breaking the University's rules. 'Wolf likes women, and I suspect he is enjoying himself with one and has lost track of time.'

'For eleven days?' asked Powys archly. 'She must be quite a lady!' He turned to Michael. 'Come to my office, Brother, so I can write down their details for your records.'

'You are very honest,' said Michael, as he started to follow. 'Most Colleges would have tried to conceal the matter, because Wolf and Hamecotes will certainly be fined when they return.'

'I considered keeping quiet,' admitted Powys. 'But we have too many students, and we cannot trust them all not to chatter. Besides, it is always best to tell the truth.'

'I wish everyone believed that,' said Michael wistfully.

Bartholomew left Michael to deal with the absent Fellows, and went with Paxtone to his chambers. These overlooked the herb gardens at the back of the College, and when the window shutters were thrown open, the rooms were filled with their rich scent, fragrant in the warmth of early summer.

'You look tired,' said Paxtone sympathetically, as Bartholomew flopped into a large oak chair that was filled with cushions. 'Did a patient keep you up again last night?'

'Yes,' replied Bartholomew shortly, wondering whether this was his colleague's discreet way of mentioning that he, too, knew about Matilde. Since even his sister was aware of it, he supposed it was not out of the question that the Fellows of King's Hall were, too.

'You must learn to refuse,' advised Paxtone, peering into Bartholomew's face, concerned. 'You will make yourself ill if you persist in burning the candle at both ends. A man needs his rest just as much as he needs his daily bread.'

'There are just not enough hours in a day to do everything,' said Bartholomew wearily. He rubbed his eyes and sat up straight, knowing he would fall asleep in Paxtone's peaceful chamber if he allowed himself to settle too deeply into the chair.

'I know you are overburdened,' said Paxtone kindly. 'So, to help you, I visited one of your patients in the hovels at All-Saints-next-the-Castle last night – a morbid obstruction of the liver. He sent for you, but your porter said you were out, so his woman came to me instead, although she had no money to pay for my services.'

'That couple barely have enough for bread, and only ask me to visit because I forget to charge them.'

'I "forgot", too,' said Paxtone, removing the first of his urine flasks from a chest for Bartholomew to admire. 'But that is not all I have done for you recently. Michael asked me to inspect a corpse for him a couple of weeks ago. I agreed, because you are my friend and I wanted to be of use, but I shall not do *that* again! I am a physician, not a Corpse Examiner, and I deal with the living, not the dead.'

'I used to think that, too,' said Bartholomew, taking the flask and thinking nostalgically of the days when his time had been filled solely with healing and teaching. 'But the additional income from examining bodies is very useful – it is how I provide medicines for patients like the one you saw last night. Besides, I have learned a great deal from corpses that can be applied to the quick.'

'Anatomy,' said Paxtone with distaste, taking the flask from Bartholomew and presenting him with another. 'I hear they are teaching that at the Italian universities these days, but I shall have nothing to do with it. Christian men do not prod about inside the dead. That is for pagans and heretics.'

'What I do is hardly anatomy,' protested Bartholomew, who had never dissected a corpse in his life, although he would not have objected to doing so. He had been an observer at several dismemberments at the University in Padua, and believed much could be gained from the practice. He turned the flask over in his hands as he spoke. It really was a fine thing, made from thin glass that would allow the urine to be seen clearly through it from any angle. 'I only assess the—'

'I do not care,' interrupted Paxtone firmly. 'I did not like looking at the dead man from Oxford, and I shall not oblige you again. I told Michael as much.'

'What did you learn from Okehamptone's cadaver?' Bartholomew asked absently, wondering whether there had been a wound on the body's wrist, like the one on Chesterfelde's.

'Learn?' echoed Paxtone in distaste. 'Nothing. His companions said he had died from a fever.'

'But you examined the body, to make sure they were telling the truth. So, what did you—?'

'I most certainly did not,' replied Paxtone fervently. 'Michael left me alone with the thing, and told me to "get on with it", to quote his eloquent phrasing. But I saw no reason to disbelieve an honest man like Warden Duraunt, so I knelt next to Okehamptone and prayed for his soul. I considered that far more valuable than poking around his person. Besides, we all know corpses harbour diseases. I do not know how you have lived so long, given your penchant for them.' He presented another flask with a flourish. It was beautifully engraved; clearly he had saved the best for last.

'So, the only reason you know Okehamptone died from a fever is because his companions told you so?' asked Bartholomew, taking the object without seeing it.

'No,' said Paxtone shortly. 'I knew because there was a thick blanket around his body and one of those liripipes – a combined hood and scarf – enveloping his head and neck. In short, the corpse was dressed just like any man who had been laid low with an ague in his last hours. I possess some common sense, you know.'

'You did not strip the body, to see if there was a dent in his head or a wound under these clothes?'

93

'Is that what you do?' Paxtone was clearly repelled and did not wait for a reply. 'Well, such a distasteful task was not necessary in this case, because Okehamptone looked *exactly* like a man who had died of a fever: bloodless around the lips and chalk-faced. Besides, there were seven people at Merton Hall, and they all told the same story: Okehamptone contracted some virulent contagion on the way to Cambridge and died the night they arrived. They have no reason to lie.'

Bartholomew was not so sure, given what had subsequently happened to Chesterfelde, but Paxtone reminded him that Okehamptone had been in his grave almost two weeks, and they could scarcely dig him up to confirm the diagnosis. There was nothing he could do to rectify Paxtone's ineptitude, and it was none of his affair anyway. He put the matter from his mind and concentrated on the flasks. After each bottle had been re-examined and admired, Paxtone offered to show him his new clyster pipes, too, stored in a shed in the garden. He led Bartholomew into the yard, where Michael was waiting.

'I smell smoked pork,' said Michael as they approached.

'We always dine well on Mondays,' said Paxtone, a little smugly, aware that Michaelhouse fare was mediocre on a good day and downright execrable on a bad one.

Michael watched a student trot across the courtyard and begin to pull on a bell rope. Tinny clangs echoed around the College. 'Is it not a little late for breakfast?' he asked, rubbing his stomach in a way that declared to even the most obtuse of observers that he was peckish.

'The bell is for our mid-morning collation – it tides the more ravenous over until noon.' Paxtone smiled engagingly. 'We are going to see my clyster pipes. Would you like to come?'

'*I* am ravenous,' declared Michael, opting for brazen, now that subtle had failed. 'And not for the sight of clyster pipes, either. I am sure there is room at your high table for a slender man like me.'

Bartholomew stifled a laugh. Michael was the last man who could be called slender, and the physician was worried that his overly ample girth meant he could no longer move at speed. It was not just friendly concern, either: he was aware that if he chased wrongdoers on Michael's behalf, then he would be fighting them alone until the fat monk managed to waddle to his aid.

'There is always room for friends,' said Paxtone. 'Would you like to eat before or after you see the clyster pipes.'

'Before,' said Michael, before Bartholomew could respond. The physician grimaced, knowing he would be unlikely to see Paxtone's enema equipment that day, because once Michael had been fed, they would have to visit Dickon.

The King's Hall refectory was a sumptuous affair, with wall hangings giving the large room a cosy but affluent feel. Since monarchs and nobles often graced it with their presence, the Warden and his Fellows were in constant readiness to receive them, with the result that they lived like kings and barons themselves most of the time. Their hall was furnished with splendid oak tables and benches, a far cry from the rough elm, which splintered easily and was a menace to fingers and clothes, that Bartholomew was used to in Michaelhouse. There was no need to scatter the floor with rushes, for the polished wood was a beauty to behold. Bowls of fresh herbs and lavender stood along the windowsills, while servants burned pine cones in the hearth; the scent of them along with the smell of bread and smoked meat was almost intoxicating.

Paxtone led his guests to a raised dais near the hearth, and gestured that they were to sit on either side of him. Several men were already there, and nodded amiably to the newcomers. Bartholomew noticed that they did not seem surprised or discomfited by their unexpected guests; at Michaelhouse it would have meant a shortage of food.

Bartholomew found himself sitting next to a man called John de Norton, who was something of a scandal, for he had been admitted to a College despite the fact that he could barely read and knew virtually no Latin. He could, however, pay handsomely for the privilege of a University education, and made no secret of the fact that he intended to use his sojourn in Cambridge to further his career at Court. He spent a good deal of time cultivating friendships with men he thought would later become similarly successful, ready for the time when they would be in a position to trade favours.

Michael's neighbour was a man named Geoffrey Dodenho, infamous for his unbridled bragging. Short, squat Dodenho was no more scholarly than Norton, although he considered himself a veritable genius and seldom hesitated to regale folk with his various theories, most of which were either untenable or poached from more able minds.

'I gave an excellent lecture last week,' he announced to the table at large. Several of his colleagues struggled to stifle sighs of irritation. 'It was on the notion that the world was created by the self-diffusion of a point of light into a spherical form. It is complex, of course, but *I* have the kind of mind that can assay these matters.'

'You concur with Grosseteste, then?' asked Bartholomew, surprised that Dodenho should lay claim to this particular theory. He was aware of smirks around the table, although it did not occur to him that his comment to Dodenho was the cause of them. 'He first explained the Creation in terms of a diffusion of light into a specific form.'

'Grosseteste did not pre-empt *me*,' said Dodenho indignantly. Michael sniggered, while Paxtone looked uncom-

96

fortable, and Norton's blank expression showed he had no idea what they were talking about – that Grosseteste might be a kind of cabbage for all he knew. 'He proposed something entirely different. Where is Powys? I am hungry, and we cannot eat until he says grace.'

The Warden was walking slowly towards the dais. He was in earnest conversation with a young, fresh-faced man who sported half a faint moustache and whose boyishly wispy beard sprouted from odd and inconvenient places, bristles springing from under his chin rather than on it. Bartholomew supposed that, like many adolescents, he was so pleased to have grown any facial hair at all that he was loath to shave a single strand. The vague aura of femininity was enhanced by his long-lashed eyes and well-manicured fingernails.

'Grosseteste talked about his particular notion in *De luce*,' said Bartholomew, turning his attention back to Dodenho. He smiled encouragingly, waiting for Dodenho to take up the challenge in time-honoured academic fashion, but when he saw a reasoned answer was not to be forthcoming, he added, 'We have a copy at Michaelhouse, if you would like to read it.'

'I do not need to read it,' cried Dodenho, offended. 'The man's logic will be inferior to mine in every way, and if it is the same, then he has copied from *me*.'

'I doubt it,' said Michael dryly. 'He has been dead for a hundred years.'

'Well, he still cannot be compared to me,' declared Dodenho uncompromisingly. '*I* am a scholar of great renown, and will be remembered longer than a mere century. My writings are—'

'Good morning, Warden,' interrupted Paxtone, as Powys and his companion approached. 'Brother Michael and Doctor Bartholomew have agreed to join us for our humble refection this morning.'

This was not how Bartholomew thought the invitation had been inveigled, but was grateful to Paxtone for his gracious manners.

'They are welcome. The good brother is looking particularly undernourished this morning, so we shall have to see what we can do to put some colour into his cheeks.' Bartholomew gazed at Powys, trying to assess whether he was making a joke, while Michael inclined his head with quiet dignity. Then Powys indicated the young scholar at his side. 'Have you met John Wormynghalle? He has been with us since the beginning of term, and we are glad to have him. He is an excellent philosopher and is also helping with the music curriculum.'

'Yes,' agreed Paxtone warmly. 'Wormynghalle has already proved himself to be a valuable asset.' He glanced at Dodenho and Norton, as though he would not have said the same about them.

'Wormynghalle?' asked Bartholomew. The name was familiar, but his sluggish mind refused to tell him why. Then it snapped into place. 'There is another Wormynghalle in Cambridge at the moment.'

Wormynghalle nodded with a smile that revealed even but sadly stained teeth. 'A tanner. I sought him out when I first heard about him, but we own no common ancestor, despite our shared name. He is from Oxford, while I hail from Buckinghamshire.'

'You are fortunate,' said Norton in distaste. 'It would be dreadful for a decent man to learn he has relatives in the tannery business. Tanneries reek and so, invariably, do tanners.'

'This one does not,' replied Wormynghalle pleasantly. 'But he said he is a burgess, so I imagine he no longer soils his own hands with skins. However, although I studied briefly in Oxford, I never came across him or his kin. He must be a relatively new member of the city's government.'

'I do not know him, either,' said Dodenho, not liking a conversation that did not have him as its focus. 'I spent last term at Merton College, but I never encountered any Wormynghalles. They must be inferior businessmen, or they would have been introduced to me.'

'I may have run into him, now I think about it,' said Norton, scratching his chin thoughtfully. 'I stayed at Oxford Castle once, and I vaguely recall a common trader named Wormyngton or Wormeley or some such thing. But I was more interested in the hounds than in meeting local dignitaries.'

'Why does that not surprise me?' said Dodenho caustically. He turned to Michael and murmured, 'Norton should never have been admitted to King's Hall, given that he has not even attended a grammar school, but the King wanted him to "study" here – and no one refuses the King. Still, it does little for my reputation to belong to a College that appoints Fellows who can barely read.'

'I doubt it makes much difference to a man like you,' Michael whispered back, leaving Dodenho to ponder exactly what he meant.

'My first love is philosophy,' said Wormynghalle, his eyes shining at the mere mention of the subject. 'But in my spare time I study music. When I was at Oxford I had the pleasure of visiting Balliol, where there are manuscripts ascribed to the theorist William Gray.'

'I know all about Gray,' said Michael resentfully. 'I have been obliged to read him of late, in order to pass his wisdom to Clippesby's students. His notions about plainsong and metrics are complex.'

'But they are also logical when you think about them,' said Wormynghalle. He flushed furiously when he realised he might have insulted Michael's intelligence, and hastened to make amends. 'Perhaps you might permit me to invite your lads to the lecture I intend to give on Gray next week?'

'You most certainly may,' said Michael, transparently relieved to share some of his responsibilities. 'I shall attend, too, and perhaps then I will understand what the wretched fellow was getting at with his discant styles and reference pitches. But meanwhile . . .' He rubbed his hands and gazed at the servants who were waiting to serve the meal.

'Wormynghalle is doing well with our College choir,' said Dodenho, before Powys could open his mouth to say grace. Michael grimaced. 'Of course, he is not achieving as much as *I* did, when I was choral master, but that would be too much to ask.'

'He has made vast improvements,' said Powys, smiling encouragingly at Wormynghalle. 'I know a good teacher when I see one. I spotted him when I was in Oxford, and I am afraid I resorted to poaching: I offered him a Fellowship. I am glad I did, especially now Hamecotes and Wolf are away.'

'Richard de Hamecotes is my room-mate,' said Wormynghalle to Michael. 'We rent a large chamber, and I rattle around like a pea in a barrel without him. I hope he comes back soon.'

'Speaking of peas,' began Michael. 'I—'

'Count yourself lucky,' said Dodenho. 'Hamecotes is clean and tidy, but I share with Wolf, and he is a slut – clothes strewn across the floor, ink spots on the desks, parchment in untidy piles . . .'

'A man with debts,' said Norton disapprovingly. 'You can never trust them not to run away without making good on what they owe.'

'Wolf will pay,' said Wormynghalle charitably. 'His family were tardy in forwarding an inheritance, so he has doubtless gone to collect it in person. He lives in Suffolk, no great distance. I am sure he will return laden with gold soon, and prove his doubters wrong.'

'You should have taught him to sing,' said Dodenho, a little spitefully. 'Then he could have earned pennies by warbling in the Market Square.'

'I will sing, if it means the food is served,' offered Michael pointedly.

'Wormynghalle might know his music, but he knows nothing of horses,' said Norton. He grinned approvingly at the young man. 'Still, he is a crack shot with a bow.'

'My brother taught me,' said Wormynghalle, to explain what was an odd skill for an academic. 'He said a scholar, travelling between far-flung universities, should know how to protect himself.'

'This learning game is all very well,' Norton went on, whetting an inappropriately large knife on a stone he had removed from the pouch at his side: the blade was already sharper than most of Bartholomew's surgical implements. 'But it means nothing if you do not also know how to hunt and ride. If a man cannot mount a horse and canter off to shoot himself a decent supper, then all the books in the world will not prevent him from starving.'

'"Learning game"?' echoed Powys. 'Is that any way for a Fellow to describe academia?' He turned to Wormynghalle, and Bartholomew saw that the Welshman regarded the youth as his best scholar, and one who would be equally affronted by Norton's description of their profession.

'You have a long way to go with our tenors,' said Dodenho. The golden newcomer was stealing attention usually afforded to him, and he did not like it. 'They are too shrill in their upper reaches.'

'They are supposed to be shrill up there,' said Michael. 'Now, the meat is getting cold, and—'

'I am a tenor, and *I* am not shrill,' interrupted Dodenho. 'But enough of my singing. We were discussing my theories about light being the origin of the universe.'

'Your theory sounds heretical to me, Dodenho,' said

101

Powys. He grinned wickedly. 'Father William of Michael-house has a deep interest in heresy, and considers himself an expert on the subject. Perhaps you should take your ideas to him, and have them assessed.'

'God forbid!' declared Dodenho. 'The man is a lunatic. Of course, Michaelhouse is famous for that sort of thing.'

'Famous for what sort of thing?' demanded Michael coldly.

'For lunatics,' replied Dodenho. 'Everyone knows it. You have Father William, who is so rabidly against anything he considers anathema that he is wholly beyond reason. And then there is Clippesby, and we all know about *him*.'

'What do we all know about him?' asked Michael quietly.

'I am *very* hungry,' stated Paxtone, rising quickly to his feet when he saw the dangerous expression on the monk's face. 'Perhaps you could say grace, Warden.'

Powys obliged, waiting until all the scholars were standing with their heads bowed before saying the familiar Latin with a heavy Welsh inflexion that meant not all of it was readily comprehensible. Bartholomew struggled to follow him, while Norton nodded knowledgeably and muttered 'amen' in inappropriate places.

'Lord!' muttered Michael, when Powys finished and they took their seats again. 'I am not sure your idea of eating here was a good one, Matt. It is a bizarre experience, to say the least.'

'I hear a man was killed at Merton Hall on Saturday night,' said Norton, as servants brought baskets of boiled eggs and dried fruit. Pats of butter were placed at regular intervals along the table, along with substantial slabs of an oily yellow cheese; the smoked pork was sliced and placed on platters, one to be shared by two Fellows.

'News travels fast,' said Michael, rubbing his hands in gluttonous anticipation. 'Matt inspected the corpse, and says Chesterfelde was murdered with a knife.'

Norton nodded eagerly. 'I heard a dagger had been planted so hard in his back, that it pinned him to the floor.'

'Please!' said Paxtone sharply. 'Not at the table!'

'You are a physician,' said Norton, startled. 'Surely you are used to a bit of blood and gore?'

'Not while I am dining,' replied Paxtone firmly. 'We can talk about the Archbishop's Visitation instead. He is going to sleep in King's Hall, you know. Wormynghalle has been persuaded to give up his room, since it is huge and Hamecotes has taken himself off to Oxford.'

'I hope Hamecotes brings back some books on philosophy,' said Wormynghalle wistfully. 'The last time he went, he concentrated on theology and law.'

'He has been on book-buying missions before?' asked Michael, reaching for the meat.

'Twice,' said Powys. 'He is rather good at it, actually, because he has contacts in some of the richer Colleges – Balliol, Exeter and Queen's.'

'I only hope he remembers the discussion we had about spurs,' said Norton, giving the impression that he thought a journey solely for books was a waste of time. 'There is a smith in Oxford who makes excellent spurs. I wish he had told me his plans to travel in advance, rather than slinking off in the middle of the night. Then I could have reminded him.'

'What happened to this corpse in Merton Hall?' asked Dodenho, overriding Paxtone's distaste for the subject and determined to have some gossip.

'He died from a wound in his wrist,' replied Michael obligingly. 'The blood vessels had been severed, and you know how quickly a man can die from such wounds, if the bleeding is not stanched.'

'Then the rumours that he was stabbed are wrong?'

asked Norton. 'That will teach me to listen to scholars. They are a worthless rabble for garnering accurate information.' He gnawed on a piece of cheese, and seemed oblivious of his colleagues' astonished – and offended – expressions.

'Chesterfelde *was* stabbed in the back,' acknowledged Michael. 'But the fatal injury was to his arm. It was odd, because he died elsewhere, and his body must have been dumped among his companions as they slept.'

'Chesterfelde,' mused Norton, pondering the victim's name. He turned to Dodenho. 'You know a Chesterfelde, do you not? I recall you entertaining him in your room last term. You got drunk together, and he was sick on the communal stairs.'

'It was probably a different Chesterfelde,' said Dodenho shiftily.

Michael narrowed his eyes. 'Bailiff Boltone told me the murdered Chesterfelde had visited Cambridge on several previous occasions.'

'Names mean nothing,' said Wormynghalle lightly, seeing Dodenho's face grow dark with resentment. 'Look at me, with the same name as a tanner. There may be more than one Chesterfelde from Oxford who regularly travels to Cambridge.'

'This fellow was burly, with dark hair,' offered Norton obligingly. 'In his early twenties.'

'That is him,' said Michael, looking hard at Dodenho.

'Well, perhaps I did meet him,' admitted Dodenho reluctantly. 'But I do not *know* him.'

'Nonsense,' said Norton. 'You sniggered and whispered in your room like a pair of virgins.'

Dodenho saw he was cornered, and that continued denials would be futile. He sighed. 'He was a sociable sort of fellow who liked to drink – it was the wine that made him giggle – but he was not a friend. Simply an acquaintance.'

'Then why did you deny knowing him?' demanded Michael.

'Because I wanted to avoid being interrogated,' snapped Dodenho, finally giving vent to his anger. 'I know how you work – quizzing people who have even the most remote associations with the deceased – and I did not want you adding *me* to your list of suspects.'

'Do you know who killed this poor man?' asked Powys of Michael, breaking into the uncomfortable silence that followed. Paxtone pointedly set down the little silver knife he used for cutting his food, and declined to eat as long as the discussion was about corpses and murder.

'Not yet,' replied Michael.

'Were these Merton men deep sleepers?' asked Wormynghalle curiously. 'You say they dozed through the dumping of a body in their chamber.'

'We suspect a soporific was used on them,' said Bartholomew.

'That would make sense,' said Paxtone, intrigued, despite his antipathy to the subject. 'I read about a similar incident that took place in Padua: a murder carried out in the presence of insensible "witnesses". I recall that poppy juice was used.'

'These men *are* from Oxford,' said Michael, taking an egg with one hand and more meat with the other, 'so they may well have access to sinister texts from foreign places, telling them how to render men senseless while they murder their colleagues. What a feast! And what makes it so especially fine is that there is not a vegetable to be seen. Only meat will help me solve the mystery surrounding this particular victim's death, because it is complex and nothing is what it seems.'

'I have a theory,' said Dodenho, who had recovered from his embarrassment at being caught out in a lie, and was back to his confident self.

'You do?' asked Michael, cheeks bulging with pork. 'Let us hear it, then.'

'Well, it is a *reductio ad absurdum*, really.' Dodenho cleared his throat and adopted an expression he imagined was scholarly. 'Consider this proposition: what I am now saying is false.'

'The "liar paradox",' said Bartholomew, wondering what the man was getting at. 'Expounded by Bradwardine in his *Insolubilia*. What does it have to do with Chesterfelde?'

'Nothing,' replied Dodenho impatiently. 'I never said it did – I just said I have a theory. It relates to the paradox I have just mentioned, and it is *my* idea, not this Bradwardine's. I could grow to dislike you, Bartholomew, always telling a man his ideas belong to someone else.'

'I thought you meant you had an idea relating to Chesterfelde, too,' said Norton accusingly. 'But all you did was change the subject to something that revolves around you.'

Dodenho shrugged. 'I can think of worse things to discuss.'

Eventually, Powys stood and said the final grace, dismissing the Fellows to their teaching. Paxtone walked with Bartholomew to the gate, with Michael trailing behind, his large face glistening with grease. Reluctantly, Bartholomew declined Paxtone's offer of a visit to the clyster pipes, knowing duty called him to the Tulyet household and Dickon.

'Good luck with the Devil's brat,' said Paxtone. 'And with your murder. I hope you solve it quickly, so it does not plunge us into a series of riots, like those at Oxford.'

'So do I,' agreed Michael. 'Especially with the Archbishop's Visitation looming.'

As it transpired, Paxtone's recommendation to dally before visiting Dickon was a good one, and, by the time

Bartholomew and Michael arrived, the boy had recovered from his initial shock and was back to normal. The injury comprised a small bruise surrounding a minute perforation, and needed no more than a dab of salve. The operation was over in a moment, and Bartholomew and Dickon were relieved to discover it was painless for both of them. This was not always the case, because Dickon employed fists, teeth, feet and nails to fight off the physician's ministrations, often resulting in Bartholomew being just as badly mauled as his small patient.

Tulyet then invited Bartholomew and Michael to his office and, wanting to hear more about the town's preparations for the Visitation, Michael accepted. The Sheriff led the scholars into the ground-floor chamber he used for working, and barred the door so Dickon could not follow. He was amused when a tousled head appeared at the window a few moments later: Dickon had discovered an alternative entrance. While Tulyet crowed his delight at the child's resourcefulness, Bartholomew and Michael braced themselves for an invasion. They were not to be disappointed.

'Bang!' yelled Dickon, leaning through the window with a small bow in his chubby hands. There was an arrow nocked into it, and the missile was pointed at Michael.

Although Dickon hated Bartholomew tending the results of his various mishaps – and anything went when treatment was in progress – he did not mind the physician at other times, and was perfectly happy to sit on his knee and insert grubby fingers into his medical bag in search of something dangerous. But Michael was a different matter. Dickon did not like Michael, and the feeling was wholly reciprocated. Michael was not averse to doling out the occasional slap while Dickon's doting parents were not looking, and was unmoved by the boy's shrieks of outrage when he did not get his own way. In essence, Dickon knew that in Michael he had met his match, although that did not prevent him from trying to score points over the monk whenever he could. That morning it looked as if he might do it with a potentially lethal weapon.

'God's blood, Dick!' exclaimed Bartholomew, leaping up to interpose himself between boy and target. 'I thought you said you would not let him have that again after he shot himself in the foot.'

'That was a freak accident,' objected Tulyet. 'The drawstring was too tight, and made the arrows fly with too much power. But we have loosened it again, and now it is quite safe.'

'I do not feel safe,' snapped Michael, cowering behind Bartholomew. 'Tell him to put it down.'

'Dickon!' said Tulyet sharply. 'Do you remember what I said? You can only have the bow if you do not point it at anyone. If you aim it at Brother Michael, I will take it away and burn it.'

Dickon's small face lost its expression of savage delight and became sombre as he considered his options. He studied his father hard, as if assessing how seriously to take the threat, then moved to one side so he could see the tempting target that quailed behind the physician. Then he looked back at Tulyet. His fingers tightened on the weapon and Bartholomew saw that the little arrow had a nasty point on it, and while Dickon was probably too small to shoot it with sufficient power to kill, he could certainly cause some painful damage. He moved again to block Dickon's line of vision, and wondered what the Sheriff was thinking of, to give the lad such a dangerous plaything.

'Come and watch me,' ordered Dickon imperiously, lowering the bow when he saw he would not have a clear shot at Michael anyway. 'By the river.'

'We are busy,' replied Michael shortly. 'Go away.'

'Come!' insisted Dickon firmly. 'Now.'

'Go and see your mother, Dickon,' suggested Tulyet, wheedling. 'She may have a cake.'

'Now,' repeated Dickon, and the bow came up again. 'I shoot.'

'We shall have no peace unless we oblige,' said Tulyet resignedly. 'He only wants us to watch him in the butts at the bottom of the garden for a moment.'

'You should not give in to him, Dick,' grumbled Michael heaving himself out of his seat and preparing to hike to the end of the Tulyets' long toft. 'It will make him worse than he already is.'

'What do you mean?' asked Tulyet indignantly. 'He is a little more boisterous than some lads his age, but only because he is unusually intelligent. Besides, what do you know about being a parent? You are a monk.'

'I know more than you can possibly imagine,' replied Michael, aloofly enigmatic and leaving Bartholomew and Tulyet wondering exactly what he meant.

'But a bow, Dick,' said Bartholomew. 'It is not wise. He may harm himself again or, worse, decide to shoot a person or an animal. He could do real harm.'

'He must to learn how to handle weapons,' insisted Tulyet. 'It will be part of his knightly training, and the younger he is, the faster he will become accomplished in their use. He will be Sheriff one day, and I want him properly prepared, or the first armed outlaw he meets will make an end of him.'

'I must have myself promoted to Chancellor before you relinquish your post,' muttered Michael, as they followed the boy to the end of the vegetable plots, where a sturdy wall had been erected to keep the child away from the river. 'Dickon will not work as smoothly with me as you do.'

Tulyet draped an arm around his shoulders. 'Give the lad a chance, Brother. He will be a splendid man in time

109

– taller than his father and with the sweet temperament of his mother.'

'He will be tall,' agreed Michael.

'Watch,' commanded Dickon, aiming his arrow at a circular target made of straw. Bartholomew was perturbed when the boy sent the missile thudding neatly into its centre, and even more so when he saw how hard Dickon had to pull to extricate it. His father may have loosened the bowstring, but it was still taut enough to drive the arrow home with considerable force. Tulyet grinned in proud delight.

'You can see Merton Hall from here,' said Michael, peering over the top of the wall and refusing to admire anything Dickon did.

'Our properties are divided only by the Bin Brook,' said Tulyet, applauding as Dickon repeated the exercise, which indicated that the first shot had been skill, not chance. 'We are neighbours, although my house fronts on to Bridge Street and Merton Hall is accessed from Merton Lane.'

'I do not suppose *you* saw anything odd the night Chesterfelde was murdered, did you?' asked Michael hopefully.

Tulyet shook his head. 'Eudo is a noisy fellow, and his loud voice occasionally disturbs us while we sit in our orchard of an evening, but we *usually* hear nothing from the others who are currently staying there – those scholars and the merchants.'

Bartholomew and Michael exchanged a bemused glance that Tulyet should dare to complain about Eudo when he had sired such a raucous brat. 'Usually?' asked Michael. 'There are exceptions?'

Tulyet nodded. 'They were quite noisy on Saturday night, as a matter of fact. They were not arguing or fighting, just speaking loudly and laughing a lot.'

'Laughing?' asked Michael. 'Laughing about what?'

'Chesterfelde was guffawing, and encouraging the others to enjoy themselves,' elaborated Tulyet. 'I met him once or twice on his previous visits to our town, and he was always smiling.'

'Bailiff Boltone said the same,' said Bartholomew. 'So did Norton. He seems to have been a cheerful sort of man.'

Michael rubbed his chin. 'I wonder whether Dodenho's initial denial that he knew Chesterfelde is significant. His excuse for the lie may be valid – that he does not want a passing friendship to implicate him in a murder enquiry – but now I find myself wary of what he told us. Still, Chesterfelde sounds as though he was a likeable sort of fellow.'

'Yes,' agreed Tulyet. 'Generally speaking.'

'What do you mean?' asked Michael.

Tulyet folded his arms, watching his son shoot off the head of a flower. 'He had a hot temper, and I recall Dodenho telling me that it took very little to set it off. But, like many quick-to-anger men, his fury faded fast, and I do not think it was a serious flaw in his character. I am glad this is not my investigation, Brother. It takes a partic-ular kind of skill to explore scholars and their cunning ways, and it is not one I shall ever possess. I am just grateful that my boy will never attend a University.'

'Yes,' said Michael wholeheartedly. 'So am I.'

It was noon by the time Bartholomew and Michael reached Merton Hall. Michael rapped sharply on the door and it was answered, as previously, by Boltone. There was ink on the bailiff's fingers, and his eyes were red and raw, as if he had been straining them. Bartholomew supposed he had been working on his accounts so that Duraunt could assess whether he had been cheating.

'Tell me, Master Bailiff,' said Michael, smiling in a friendly fashion, 'when did you last visit Oxford?'

'I am obliged to present yearly accounts,' said Boltone, looking furtive, 'but I go there as rarely as possible. It smells, and all the streets look the same. Why?'

'Were you there in February?' asked Bartholomew. He could think of no reason why a Cambridge steward should kill an Oxford merchant, but that did not mean it had not happened.

'No,' said Boltone, a little too quickly. 'I have not been since last October, and February was too cold for long journeys. The roads were closed by snow then, anyway.'

'They were,' acknowledged Michael. 'But not for the whole month.'

Boltone stood aside to allow them to enter. 'Have you decided which of these Oxford men killed Chesterfelde? Was it a scholar or a merchant? I do not know who I would prefer you to hang: I dislike that condescending Eu, but I hate the sly Polmorva.'

'What makes you think it was one of those two?' asked Michael.

'Who else could it be?' asked Boltone, his eyes wide with surprise that there should be other culprits. 'Chesterfelde was murdered in *their* room while *they* were present – sleeping or otherwise. You do not need one of your University degrees to assess that sort of evidence. And Polmorva and Eu are the nastiest of the group, so they are the best suspects for this vile murder. It is obvious.'

Michael regarded him thoughtfully. 'You think Abergavenny, Wormynghalle, Spryngheuse and Duraunt are innocent, do you?'

Boltone returned the appraising stare, then seemed to reconsider, apparently afraid the monk might be laying some sort of trap that would see him in trouble. 'Well, I suppose the killer *could* be one of them,' he said after a long pause. 'Except Duraunt, of course. He would never harm anyone.'

112

'Is that so?' asked Michael flatly. 'Of course, Polmorva has *you* marked down as the assassin. He thinks you killed Chesterfelde by mistake, because you are desperate to do away with Duraunt and prevent him from exposing your dishonesty.'

'Polmorva is a fool,' snapped Boltone. 'If I did kill Duraunt, then what do you think would happen? That Merton will forget these accusations and leave me alone? Of course not! They will send another man to look at my records, and then what would I do? Kill him, too? And another, and another? Polmorva is deranged if he believes I would see murder as a way to clear my name. Besides, I have nothing to hide – no reason to stab anyone.'

'I see,' said Michael. 'Well, I would like to speak to Duraunt myself today. Do not bother to escort me; I can find my own way. Go back to your accounting.'

Bartholomew followed Michael up the stairs into the hall. The three merchants sat there, talking in low voices that still contrived to sound hostile. Wormynghalle presented a grotesque sight that day, in a fashionably close-fitting gipon made from gold cloth that gave him the appearance of a shiny grub. His sheep's head pendant and the rings on his fingers glinted in the sunlight, and he looked exactly what he was: a man of humble origins who found himself rich, and who did not have the taste to accommodate it decently. He played restlessly with a silver disc, and when Bartholomew looked more closely he saw it was an astrolabe, although he could tell from the way the tanner handled the instrument that he did not know how to use it. To him it was just a pretty object made of precious metal.

Eu, meanwhile, wore a gipon of dark green, with a discreet clasp on his cloak that carried his nutmeg motif. He carried himself with a natural dignity, and Bartholomew wondered how the two merchants, diametrically opposed

113

in all respects, managed to stomach each other's company. He supposed it was because Abergavenny was there, to keep the peace and remind them that they had a common purpose. The Welshman seemed relieved to have company, and Bartholomew suspected he was finding his role as arbitrator hard work.

'Where are the scholars?' asked Michael.

'In the solar,' replied Wormynghalle with an unpleasant sneer. 'They claim they are afraid of boring us with their debates, but the truth is that they prefer their own company.'

'What they prefer is conversation that does not revolve around tanning,' said Eu acidly. 'And who can blame them? I do not want to be regaled with the difference between dog and horse urine while I am at table, either.'

'Better than one bristling with cleverly disguised aspersions,' retorted Wormynghalle. '*You* were the one who offended them on Saturday with your sly tongue and ambiguous "compliments".'

'We should all moderate our conversation, and—' began Abergavenny.

'I am surprised you remember,' snarled Eu to the tanner. 'You drank so much wine that you were asleep most of the evening.'

'You were drunk when Chesterfelde died?' pounced Michael. 'And the night ended in insults?'

'No,' said Abergavenny hastily. 'Wormynghalle provided a casket of claret for us all to share, but no one was insensible and no discourtesies were exchanged – just one or two harmless jests . . .'

'Then why do you occupy separate rooms now?' asked Bartholomew, knowing what happened when wine and poppy juice were combined, and thinking that he and Michael now had the answer to at least one part of the mystery. If the men at Merton Hall had swallowed such a mixture, they would probably not have stirred from their slumbers if the King of France had mounted an armed invasion; a body placed carefully among them would almost certainly have passed unnoticed.

'Because we are *trying* to be good guests,' said Abergavenny with a strained smile. 'The scholars enjoy long, pedantic debates and I do not see why these should be curtailed by our presence. It was my suggestion that they adjourn to the solar during the day for their erudite discussions. Duraunt was kind enough to allow us to stay here, so the least we can do is stay out of his way.'

'Why did he invite you?' asked Michael. 'You seem odd bedfellows.'

'Because we are rich,' replied Wormynghalle smugly. 'We are all in a position to make handsome benefactions to his College when we return to Oxford, and wealthy merchants are always being courted by scholars – like whores after men with full purses.'

Abergavenny winced at Wormynghalle's coarse analogy, while Eu shook his head. Bartholomew watched them closely, and thought about what Michael and Tulyet had said. The Sheriff distrusted the laconic, noble-born Eu, because he had met his kind before, while alarm bells had jangled in Bartholomew's own mind over Wormynghalle, because he was aggressive, overconfident and brutal. But it had been the diplomatic, reasonable Abergavenny that Michael had elected as the villain, on the grounds that the Welshman's congeniality was good cover for evil intent.

'It suits us to stay at Merton Hall,' said Abergavenny, again calming troubled waters. 'The best taverns are inside your town gates – where we have no desire to be.'

'Why not?' asked Michael.

Eu sighed impatiently. 'Why do you think? We have just left a city ravaged by scholars, and we do not want to be trapped inside another. We are safer here on the outskirts.'

'That is why I bought claret on Saturday,' explained Wormynghalle. He glared at Eu, implying that the spicer's failure to do likewise indicated he was cheap. '*I* wanted to thank Duraunt for his hospitality. He declined to accept coins, no doubt hoping for a larger donation when we return, but he is fond of wine, and I felt I should do something pleasant for him while we are here.'

'Never mind this,' said Eu. Bartholomew saw the tanner's barb had hit its mark. 'Have you come to give us Gonerby's killer, so we can go home?'

'It is him!' said Wormynghalle, pointing at Bartholomew. 'He is our culprit.'

'How in God's name have you deduced that?' asked Michael, startled.

'It is obvious. He knows Oxford, because he was an Oxford scholar himself. Polmorva told me. He must have visited our city in February, perhaps to meet old acquaintances, killed Gonerby and fled home again.'

'Why would I do that?' asked Bartholomew, not bothering to hide his contempt for the man. 'I have never met Gonerby.'

'So you say,' countered Wormynghalle. 'But, for all we know, you may have been enemies for years. Polmorva said you were a Merton man two decades ago, and Gonerby was living in the city then. Perhaps you ordered some parchment from him, and were dissatisfied with the result. There could be all manner of reasons why you did not like each other.'

'Did Gonerby supply parchment that was of inferior quality, then?' asked Michael.

Abergavenny intervened, as usual. 'Of course not. His parchment was excellent, and few scholars had cause for complaint. But I do not think this physician is our man, Wormynghalle.'

'He is a suitable suspect, though,' said Eu. He looked

Bartholomew up and down appraisingly. 'He looks poor, so no one will miss him. We will take him with us when we leave.'

'You will not,' said Michael, 'because he is not your culprit. He gave the University Lecture on St Scholastica's Day, and more than five hundred people – scholars *and* townsmen – will vouch he was here, in Cambridge, not off stabbing merchants in Oxford.'

'Am I to understand from this discussion that you have learned nothing about Gonerby's killer?' asked Wormynghalle, sounding disgusted.

'Give me time,' said Michael coldly. 'I have other matters to attend, besides looking into the murders of men I do not know in cities I have never visited. But I have spoken to a number of Cambridge students who were in Oxford during February, and some Oxford scholars who are here now. I have several promising lines of enquiry.'

Bartholomew knew for a fact he did not, but said nothing to contradict him. He did not like the merchants and their assumption that money made them important, and he resented Wormynghalle's accusations. He did not know whether he would prefer Chesterfelde's killer to be Polmorva or the tanner, and began to hope they were in cahoots, and had done it together. Then he realised he was allowing his dislike to interfere with his reason, and tried to control his growing antipathy.

Michael turned to Wormynghalle. 'We met a relative of yours this morning.'

Wormynghalle was aghast. 'It was not my wife, was it? She is heavy with child, so I hope you are mistaken. I would not like to think of her travelling so far when she is about to provide me with a son.'

'A scholar named John Wormynghalle,' said Michael. 'Of King's Hall.'

'Oh, him,' said Wormynghalle uninterestedly. He gave

the astrolabe a vigorous shake. Something rattled, and Bartholomew saw that his fiddling had broken it. 'He is no kin of mine. He came sniffing around as soon as I arrived, doubtless hoping we were related, so I would be obliged to donate money for his education. We talked for an hour, but could find no common kin, and he left disappointed. Did he tell you we were from the same stock? Cheeky beggar!'

'I came to speak to Duraunt,' said Michael, suddenly heading for the door that led to the solar. His abrupt departure had the effect he intended: the merchants were puzzled and uneasy, suspecting he knew more than he had told them about Gonerby's murder and the repercussions it might have on the men who had decided to avenge it. 'I will keep you informed of my progress.'

Bartholomew caught Michael's arm before he reached the solar door and spoke in a low voice as the merchants began a carping argument among themselves, debating what the monk might have learned that he declined to share with them. 'Why did you ask Wormynghalle the tanner about Wormynghalle the scholar? He told us this low fellow is not his kin, and we have no reason to disbelieve him. There was no reason to check his story.'

'His, no,' agreed Michael. 'But I did not like the way the tanner accused you of murder, just because he has been listening to Polmorva. I wanted to see if I could catch him out in a lie – to see whether he would deny meeting young Wormynghalle on the grounds that he will not want to be associated with anyone at Cambridge. But he was more honest than I imagined he would be.'

Bartholomew considered. There was definitely something unsavoury about the tanner, and it went further than his coarse manners and penchant for wild accusations. 'I told you the first time we spoke to him that I had a bad feeling about the fellow.'

'*You* have not met him before, have you?' asked Michael, pausing to look hard at Bartholomew. 'In Oxford, when you were a student?'

'No. I would have told you.'

'Would you? You keep a lot from me these days, and I do not know what to think.'

'What do you mean?'

'You slip out every night to meet Matilde, but you refuse to tell me why your relationship has taken this sudden and unexpected step. You do not usually hide secrets from me.'

'Just because I decline to share details about Matilde does not make me a liar,' said Bartholomew, faintly irritated. 'You should know me better than that.'

Michael did not reply. He knocked on the solar door, but did not wait for an answer before pushing inside. Duraunt sat near the hearth, a book on his knees, while Polmorva diced with a man who wore a distinctive grey-fringed cloak. The man's jaw dropped in horror when he recognised the visitors, while Michael regarded him thoughtfully and Bartholomew's mind whirled with questions.

'So,' said the monk amiably to the man who had been contemplating suicide on the Great Bridge the previous morning. 'We meet again, sir.'

'You know each other?' asked Duraunt, surprised.

'No,' replied the man quickly. His eyes held a mute appeal for Michael's silence. 'Not really.'

Duraunt closed his book and indicated that the visitors were to sit with him on the stools that were clustered around the hearth. Bartholomew obliged, but Michael remained standing.

'Who are you?' the monk asked of the stranger.

'Walter Spryngheuse.' The man began to gabble, and Bartholomew sensed he would say anything to prevent Michael from telling Polmorva and Duraunt about the

119

incident on the bridge. 'And you are here to look into Chesterfelde's murder. I cannot believe someone killed him. He was good company and everyone liked him.'

'Someone did not,' Michael pointed out.

Spryngheuse's eyes became watery. 'I miss him. He was a Balliol man and I am from Merton, but we were friends nonetheless. I wish he had not died.'

'We all do,' said Duraunt comfortingly. 'But he has gone to better things.'

Spryngheuse pulled himself together. 'Duraunt has been telling me about you, Bartholomew.'

'Not very accurately,' said Polmorva nastily. 'He has been far too kind in his reminiscences.'

'And you have been too harsh,' said Spryngheuse immediately.

'Your tongue *is* overly sharp, Polmorva,' agreed Duraunt, leading Bartholomew to wonder what the man had been saying.

'Meanwhile, I have learned that *you* like to drink and argue,' said Michael to Duraunt, preventing the physician from responding with some reminiscences of his own. 'You were making so much noise on the night Chesterfelde died, that you disturbed your neighbours.'

Duraunt was astounded. 'Really? It was quite unintentional, I assure you, and I shall apologise to them at once. We were discussing Bradwardine's mean speed theorem, and it was so exciting that we may have been a tad raucous.'

'Chesterfelde had interesting opinions,' explained Spryngheuse shyly. 'He was an amusing debater, so we laughed a lot. We did not mean to annoy anyone, though.'

'It was the merchants' fault,' said Polmorva testily. 'They were the ones guffawing at Chesterfelde's inanities. Debates are not meant to be funny – they are serious expressions of philosophical ideals, and I disapproved very strongly when you all made that one into a joke.'

'Do not be so ready to frown,' admonished Duraunt mildly. 'There is nothing wrong with laughter. Indeed, I am glad we were merry that night, since it was Chesterfelde's last. At least he died after a lovely evening in pleasant company.'

'Mostly pleasant,' said Bartholomew, suspecting Polmorva had been a terrible misery.

'You drank plenty of wine,' fished Michael. 'It made you sleep more deeply than usual.'

'We did not imbibe that much,' objected Duraunt. 'And I seldom sleep well these days. It is one of the curses of old age.'

'Is that why you take poppy juice?' asked Bartholomew.

Duraunt stared at him. 'I do not dose myself with poppy juice or any other kind of soporific. When I am restless, I pray, and eventually sleep overtakes me.'

'Then what about the tincture you bought from the apothecary?' asked Michael. 'You claimed Matt had recommended that you swallow a strong dosage, but he has done no such thing.'

'He did,' said Duraunt firmly. 'Twenty years ago, when I had stomach pains, he recommended poppy juice at a specific strength that cured them instantly. I have used his remedy ever since on rare occasions, particularly when I undertake long journeys. My digestion is adequate at home, where I am used to the food, but it occasionally misfires when I travel and am obliged to eat unfamiliar fare.'

'You have been taking concentrated poppy juice for two decades?' asked Bartholomew in horror.

A note of genuine irritation crept into Duraunt's voice when he replied. 'You are not listening, Matthew. I said I take it *on rare occasions when I travel.* But Okehamptone's death upset me, and I felt the need for a dose. I thought I had brought some with me, but I could not find it, so I purchased more from the apothecary. And now you know everything about my stomach and its sporadic irregularities. Does that satisfy your morbid and unwarranted curiosity?'

'I am sorry,' said Bartholomew, startled and hurt by the reprimand. He was aware of Polmorva's smirk. 'But it *is* odd that you all slept through Chesterfelde's murder, and that a dose of strong medicine was added to your wine is not an unreasonable conclusion to draw.'

'Especially since we found some in your bag,' added Michael.

But it was Bartholomew who bore the brunt of Duraunt's outrage. 'You *searched* my possessions? Without my permission?' He shook his head and there was a hard, unforgiving look in his eye that cut the physician to the quick. 'I expected better of you, Matthew. I do not know what you have become here in Cambridge, but I do not like it.'

'I did not like what he was before,' said Polmorva. 'I am not surprised to learn he is the kind of man to go through our belongings. It would also not surprise me to learn that *he* killed Chesterfelde, since he seems to have developed a talent for skulking and prying.'

'I would not go that far,' said Duraunt, his faded blue eyes still fixed unblinkingly on the physician. 'But the next time you want to know something, Matthew, you can ask. You will *not* rifle through my bags. Is that clear?'

Bartholomew nodded, feeling like an errant schoolboy, and fumed at the gloating expression on Polmorva's face.

'Good,' said Duraunt, leaning back in his chair. 'Then we shall say no more about the matter. Why are you here? Was it just to ask about the poppy juice, or do you have another purpose?'

'We came to inform you that we have been busy with Chesterfelde's case,' said Michael. 'And that progress has been made. We would also like to ask Spryngheuse some questions, since he is the only one we have not yet interviewed.' He turned to the man. 'Why did you come to Cambridge?'

'I told you that yesterday,' said Polmorva. 'Did you not listen?'

Michael rounded on him. 'I am not talking to you, so keep your answers to yourself until you are asked for them. Spryngheuse?'

'I fled because I was afraid for my life,' replied Spryngheuse. He hung his head. 'It is disconcerting to arrive at another university, only to have your closest friend murdered within days.'

Michael included Duraunt and Polmorva in his next question. 'You did not come because you know the Archbishop is due to visit, and you hope to ensure he founds his new College in Oxford?'

Duraunt was appalled by the accusation. 'Of course not! What a terrible thing to say! No wonder Matthew has turned bad, if he listens to men like you.'

'Now, just a moment,' said Michael indignantly. 'Oxford is in a state of turmoil – and under an interdict. It is not so far-fetched to imagine someone might take steps to make Cambridge appear similarly uneasy, to ensure we do not gain Islip's patronage at your expense.'

'It *is* far-fetched,' insisted Duraunt angrily. 'None of us are so low-minded.'

'Really,' said Michael, giving Polmorva a stare to indicate he thought otherwise. 'But let us return to Chesterfelde, and who might have wanted him dead. Spryngheuse, do you have any ideas?'

Spryngheuse was thoughtful. 'Chesterfelde visited Cambridge several times, but he was not here long enough to make enemies. He only had friends – not like in Oxford, where he and I are shunned and hated.'

'That is the price of instigating a riot that left hundreds dead,' said Polmorva unpleasantly.

Bartholomew stared at Spryngheuse. '*Chesterfelde* was one of the scholars who began the argument in the Swindlestock Tavern?'

'He was,' said Polmorva, before Spryngheuse could speak. 'And Spryngheuse was another.'

'Let me explain,' said Spryngheuse tiredly. 'We were in the alehouse, happy and good humoured, when this Benedictine attached himself to our party. We had never seen him before, but were too polite to send him away. I wish to God we had. He seemed to know Chesterfelde had a quick temper, and needled him with inflammatory state-ments until he reacted with violence – against Croidon the landlord. It was the monk who started the fight, not me and not Chesterfelde, although we are the ones being blamed.'

'But it was Chesterfelde who smashed the pot over Croidon's head,' said Polmorva. 'And it was *you* who shot the mason. No one – except you – recalls this elusive Benedictine.'

'Our friends did,' objected Spryngheuse. 'The two others who were with us.'

'But they were killed,' said Polmorva. 'Of the original party, only you and Chesterfelde survived – other than this monk, of course.' He turned to Michael. 'I am sure many Benedictines enjoy a good riot, but they are innocent of inciting this one. I made enquiries among the Oxford brethren myself, and this mysterious monastic does not exist.'

'Is this true?' asked Michael of Duraunt, his voice cold and angry. 'Why did you not mention it before? If Chesterfelde was responsible for bringing about these riots, then there is probably an entire city full of people who would like to see him dead.'

124

'I did not tell you for two reasons,' said Duraunt calmly. 'First, because Spryngheuse and Chesterfelde have always maintained their innocence.' Here Spryngheuse nodded and Polmorva made a sceptical moue. 'And second, if they do have enemies, then they are in Oxford, not here.'

'Not necessarily,' said Michael. 'How do you know one of your three merchant friends did not exact revenge? After all, it was the riot Chesterfelde started that saw their friend Gonerby murdered.'

Duraunt shook his head. 'If that were true, then the killer would have struck during the journey to Cambridge, when there were better opportunities.'

Michael was unconvinced. 'Perhaps that is what we are supposed to think. Personally, I shall reserve judgement until I have more evidence.'

'So, what *have* you learned so far?' asked Polmorva, in the kind of voice that indicated it would be nothing of significance.

'I never compromise my investigations by indulging in idle chatter with suspects,' said Michael haughtily. 'But I have finished with you for now. Tomorrow I shall have another word with Boltone and Eudo, and see what they can tell me about rowdy debates that kept half the town awake.'

'My bailiff,' said Duraunt, closing his eyes. 'A landlord cannot be held responsible for the character of his tenant, so I disclaim anything Eudo might have done. But I confess to appointing Boltone. He and Eudo have been stealing from us regularly, as became obvious when I examined their records this morning. I have known for some time that our Cambridge estate was not yielding the income it should, but I was ready to trust Boltone's explanation that times were hard. After all, there was the plague to consider: many properties became unprofitable after the Death, and I saw no reason to suppose this manor was not one of them.'

'So what made you suspicious of him all of a sudden?' asked Bartholomew.

'The losses have grown steadily larger, and a few months ago, Okehamptone – the clerk who died of fever here recently, and who had friends in Cambridge – suggested I should review Bolton's sums. When I followed his advice, I discovered inconsistencies that required clarification.'

'What did Boltone say when you confronted him?' asked Michael. 'When we first met, he did not seem overly concerned by the fact that he was under investigation by the Warden of Merton.'

Duraunt shrugged. 'I think he believed he had covered his tracks well enough to deceive me, and that he had nothing to worry about. But I pointed out one or two problems today, and I think it has finally dawned on him that he may be in trouble.'

'He is now extremely concerned,' agreed Polmorva with satisfaction. 'Had he been my bailiff, I would have dismissed him at once, but Duraunt has given him an opportunity to acquit himself.'

'He says there has been a mistake,' said Duraunt tiredly. 'It is difficult to find reliable men these days, and I have known him for years. I have decided to give him the benefit of the doubt, and allow him to prepare a considered defence.'

'Was he – or Eudo – sufficiently angry about the accusations to kill?' asked Bartholomew. While Boltone claimed that killing Duraunt would not solve his problems, Bartholomew was not sure that Eudo was equally rational, especially after numerous jugs of ale. He thought it entirely possible that Chesterfelde might have been the victim of mistaken identity, as Polmorva claimed, and the real target was the man who was in the process of exposing a collaborative dishonesty.

'No,' said Duraunt immediately. 'That was the first thing

that crossed my mind when we found Chesterfelde. But Eudo or Boltone are not the kind of men to kill.'

'Any man can kill,' said Polmorva, looking at Bartholomew in a way the physician found disturbing. 'All he needs is enough incentive.'

CHAPTER 4

Bartholomew was angry with Michael for putting him in an awkward position with his former teacher and earning him a reprimand that stung. It was, after all, not he who had rifled through Duraunt's belongings. Michael pointed out that by keeping watch Bartholomew had made himself an accessory to the crime, and was just as much to blame. Since they could not agree and Bartholomew was too tired to argue, they returned to Michaelhouse in silence.

The physician turned the facts about Chesterfelde over in his mind. Was the death a case of mistaken identity – something hard to believe, given the strange mode of execution – and Eudo or Boltone responsible? Or had he been murdered as retribution for starting a riot that had left hundreds dead and Oxford ablaze? Answers were not forthcoming, even when he lay on his bed in the comparative peace of his room and gave the matter all his attention.

Later that evening, Michael was summoned by his beadles to quell trouble brewing at the King's Head. The monk was unsettled by the notion that what had happened in Oxford might be repeated in Cambridge, and was inclined to regard any symptom of unrest with more than his customary concern. The fact that the St Scholastica's Day trouble had exploded from a relatively minor incident made him feel as though he should be on his guard at all times. Meanwhile, Bartholomew dozed in his room until every light had been extinguished in the College, then set out to see Matilde.

As he made his way through the dark streets, he tried to

keep to the shadows, lingering in some to assess whether he was being followed or watched. He was too weary to be properly vigilant, and although he saw the occasional movement out of the corner of his eye, he could not determine whether it was just a leaf blowing in the soft breeze, a cat hunting rodents, someone who would gossip about him the next day, or the product of an overwrought imagination.

When he arrived, he told Matilde that their 'secret' was now common knowledge, and that even his sister knew about their assignations. Matilde's expression was wry when she mentioned that Edith had quizzed her ruthlessly until she had extracted a confession, but together the two women had devised a plan that they hoped might ease the situation. Bartholomew flopped on to one of Matilde's comfortable benches and rested his head in his hands, feeling exhaustion wash over him in a great unstoppable tide. Matilde looked fatigued, too; there were dark rings under her eyes and she was less immaculately groomed than usual.

'Well?' he asked, his voice muffled. 'What have you and my sister decided will protect us from wagging tongues?'

'This,' Matilde replied, presenting him with a lurid, gold-coloured liripipe – a fashionable hood-come-scarf that could be donned in a variety of styles.

He regarded it without enthusiasm. 'What am I supposed to do with that?'

Matilde sighed, her own lassitude making her unusually irritable with him. 'You wear it, Matthew.'

'No,' said Bartholomew, pushing it back at her and thinking how bizarre it would look with his sober academic attire. 'This is not the kind of thing I favour. It is yellow, for God's sake.'

She shoved it firmly into his unwilling hands. 'You must try to get some sleep tonight, because you are uncommonly slow witted. The fact that this is *not* something you would

129

normally wear means that people will not associate you with it and it will hide your face if you wrap it properly. Folk will see only an amber-hatted man.' She saw his blank expression and sighed again. 'It is what is generally known as a "disguise".'

Reluctantly, he pulled the thing over his head. It felt ridiculous, and he disliked the scratchy sensation around his neck. 'Will it work, do you think?'

'Edith chose it as being the least likely thing you would ever select for yourself. But do not forget to conceal it during the day. If you leave it out for all to see, then it will have the opposite effect – it will advertise what you are doing.'

When he returned to the College, well before dawn this time, Bartholomew was annoyed, but not surprised, to discover that someone had barred the orchard door again. This time, however, he had a contingency plan – one that did not involve arriving early at the church and pretending to be at his devotions. He walked to the bottom of the lane, where a tall wall separated Michaelhouse's grounds from the towpath that ran along the river. A heap of discarded barrels and other riverine clutter lay at the foot of the wall, and he clambered up it. There was a long drop over the other side, but he had spent an hour moving compost the previous afternoon, and it provided him with a soft landing. He jumped, rolled easily and made his way back to his room. He even managed to sleep for a while before the College bell and an answering shriek from the night porter's peacock announced that it was time for the scholars to rise for the morning service.

He prised himself from his bed, and washed and shaved with the water his book-bearer left for him each night, feeling its icy chill revive him. He rummaged in a chest for a clean tunic, and pulled it over his head, acutely aware that the old one was scented with the rosemary Matilde kept in her bedroom. A jerkin followed, and his hose and academic tabard completed his uniform. His boots were near the door and, as he walked across the yard, he saw they were stained with mud from his nocturnal tramp through the gardens. Hoping no one was watching, he stood on one leg to scrub first one and then the other on the backs of his hose, before joining the line that formed as the scholars emerged from their rooms, most complaining about the early-morning chill, the shrillness of the bell, the fact that it was drizzling, and anything else that bothered them before the first sunrays touched the eastern sky.

The Fellows were in a huddle behind Langelee, waiting to follow their Master in their daily procession to church. Michael stood next to Father William, and Bartholomew was repelled to see that the strand of cabbage Michael had flicked away two days before still adorned the friar's shoulder, crusted and dry. The morose Suttone, whose pre-dawn conversation usually revolved around the imminent return of the plague, was with a lawyer named Wynewyk, who was invariably more concerned with predicting Michaelhouse's imminent fiscal collapse. The last Fellow was Kenyngham, an ancient Gilbertine friar who was oblivious to his colleagues' grumbles and proclamations as he stood with his hands clasped in reverent prayer.

'Any news about Clippesby?' Langelee asked Bartholomew, wincing when the wind blew drizzle directly into his face. 'I heard you visited him on Sunday.'

'He is still unwell.'

'Unwell!' snorted William. 'He is insane, man, so say what you mean! However, we must remember that he is a Dominican, and men of that Order are prone to madness. It comes from being obliged to put up with each other's company.'

'Visit him again today,' ordered Langelee, while Suttone pointed out to William that he himself was enough to drive

131

sane men to lunacy with his bigoted opinions. 'God knows, I was relieved to have him gone for a while – his philosophical discourses with bats and pigs were becoming an embarrassment – but we need him back. His students complained about Michael's teaching again last night.'

'Did they indeed?' demanded Michael archly. 'And what is wrong with it, pray?'

'They say you do not know what you are talking about,' replied Langelee baldly. 'And do not look at me with such outrage, Brother. You told me yourself that you are not qualified to take these classes. The astronomy students are disgruntled, too, but *they* say they are being taught subjects that are too advanced. It is a pity you two cannot get together and provide something in the middle.'

'I could teach them theology,' offered William. 'I am busy, of course, but I could manage an hour to tell them something worth knowing – something better than music *or* astronomy.' He almost spat the last words, making no secret of what he thought about any subjects taught by a Dominican.

'No, thank you,' said Langelee, without a moment's hesitation. 'I do not want them to grumble that they are being railed at by a fanatic, either.' He turned to Michael while the Franciscan spluttered with indignation. 'The whole town is talking about that murder at Merton Hall. Should we be concerned? It is rumoured that scholars from Oxford are trying to besmirch our good name, to encourage Islip to found his College there instead of here.'

'Lord!' muttered Michael. 'Who has been spreading these tales?'

'Probably that Doctor Rougham,' said Suttone gloomily. 'He is a nasty fellow, and it is the sins of men like him that will bring the Death down on us again.'

'Rougham is not here,' said William, who listened to a good deal of gossip himself. 'He has gone to see his family in Norfolk, although I do not think he should have been granted permission to leave in the middle of term.'

'He was not,' said Michael. 'He sent his Master a letter after he left, at a point when his "request" could not be refused. Hamecotes of King's Hall did the same. They both knew what they were doing: once they have gone there is nothing we can do about it, and fines mean little to rich men.'

'Hamecotes's colleague Wolf did not send any such letter, though,' said William. 'He just left – probably because he is in debt.'

'Probably,' agreed Michael. 'But I am more concerned with these tales about Oxford than in disobedient scholars. Where did they originate?'

'With Weasenham, the University stationer,' said Langelee. 'You know what *he* is like for chatter.'

'I do indeed,' said Michael grimly. 'But this is more dangerous than idle gossip. It may send our scholars in a vengeful horde to the Oxford men at Merton Hall, and we shall have yet more murders on our hands. And that will certainly not impress Islip.'

'Do you think Chesterfelde was murdered by Cambridge students?' asked Langelee. 'Because they think he came here with the express purpose of harming us? That is what Weasenham was speculating, yesterday.'

'I shall do some speculating with him,' said Michael angrily. 'Does the man *want* us to lose Islip? What is he thinking of, spreading those sorts of tales at a time like this?'

'He has been fabricating rumours about Matt, too,' said Wynewyk, shivering as the drizzle became a more persistent downpour. He pulled his cloak closely around his slight frame. 'He said Matt has serviced Matilde every night for the last twelve days.'

'Damn the man!' exclaimed Langelee angrily. 'Just

because a man emerges from a woman's boudoir does not mean that they have "serviced" each other. Bartholomew and Matilde could have been playing dice for all Weasenham knows.'

Bartholomew was appalled that the rumour should be so explicit, and wondered whether the liripipe ruse would work. He sincerely hoped so, for Matilde's sake as much as his own. He was aware that his colleagues were waiting for him to deny the accusation, but was at a loss for words. He could hardly say he had not visited Matilde night after night, when he had done exactly that.

'It does not look good,' said Suttone, after a lengthy silence. 'You should not be there, Matthew, even if you pass the time reading sacred texts. Not at that time of night.'

Langelee addressed Bartholomew more kindly. 'I know a lusty man needs a little female attention now and again, and I do not condemn you for that – even though it is against College statutes – because I indulge myself on occasion, and I am no hypocrite.'

He glowered at Suttone in a way that indicated the same could not be said for him. Bartholomew was astonished: Suttone was the last man he would have imagined dealing with women.

Suttone looked decidedly furtive. 'I do not—'

Langelee overrode him, still addressing Bartholomew. 'But you must learn discretion, man! You *must* avoid being seen.'

Without further ado, the Master moved to the front of the procession and led his scholars to St Michael's Church. Rob Deynman, the College's least able student, walked in front, bearing the large cross that was only ever brought out for ceremonial occasions. There was nothing special about that particular Tuesday, but Langelee wanted it used during the Visitation, and since Deynman was apt to be clumsy, he needed all the practice he could get. Michael fell into place next to Bartholomew, speaking in a low voice so he would not be overheard.

'You are lucky. Any other Master would have fined you or had your Fellowship revoked. But you should heed his warning – you cannot continue to flout the rules like this, because even he will not be able to protect you much longer, no matter how much he wants to keep you here.'

'He does?' asked Bartholomew, surprised. He was gradually beginning to like – and even to respect – Langelee, despite the man's many faults and his appalling lack of scholarship, but he had been under the impression that medicine was barely tolerated at Michaelhouse, and was regarded as a necessary evil rather than the equal of the venerated disciplines of theology and law.

Michael nodded. 'Your concern for Cambridge's poor and their nasty diseases is good for Michaelhouse, and he would never risk antagonising them by dismissing you. He is also fond of you in his own brutish way and feels a certain kinship – you, he and Wynewyk are seculars among us monks and friars. Wynewyk prefers men, but you and Langelee are alike in your love of women.'

'I love Matilde,' acknowledged Bartholomew, thinking the clerics were no more chaste than he was, if Suttone's reaction had been anything to go by, while he strongly suspected Michael was not always faithful to his vow of celibacy, either. 'I am not lusting after half the women in town, as you imply.'

'Neither is Langelee – at least not any more. He has curbed his appetites, and confines himself to a single paramour. However, *they* do not fling themselves into the bedchamber on a nightly basis without caring who sees them.'

'Who is she?' asked Bartholomew, intrigued. He experienced a sudden pang of alarm when he considered Langelee's patient tolerance of him. 'It is not my sister, is it?'

Michael gave a startled snort of laughter that drew the unwelcome attention of William. He lowered his voice further still. 'Edith is a loyal wife, and you should be ashamed of yourself for thinking such thoughts about a woman who is above reproach. Besides, she has far more taste than to entertain Langelee. However, you will never guess the identity of our Master's lover, because you would not believe he could seduce her without unhappy repercussions.'

'No talking!' snapped William. 'We are about to witness a sacred mass, and you should be inspecting your souls for sin, not gossiping about women. Who *is* Langelee's lover, then?'

Fortunately for Michael, Langelee was listening to Wynewyk's diatribe about the alarming state of the College accounts, and was far too concerned by the predictions of impending bankruptcy to pay heed to the conversations of others.

'Agatha the laundress,' said Michael flippantly, selecting the least likely candidate imaginable. Agatha was the formidable woman who ran Michaelhouse's domestic affairs, and who intimidated every male who lived or worked there. His jest went wide, however, and the Franciscan's jaw fell open in astonishment as he took Michael's comment at face value. Bartholomew grinned as William fell back to consider the implications of such a liaison, and wondered what trouble Michael had just created for the Master.

'Surely not!' exclaimed Deynman, who had also been listening. The cross swung precariously as he shifted his grip, knocking the hat from Wynewyk's head. 'Agatha will be too manly for him.'

'Who is too manly for whom?' asked Langelee, waiting for Wynewyk to retrieve his headwear.

'Yolande the prostitute for Wynewyk,' prevaricated Michael, shooting Deynman a glance to warn him to silence.

Wynewyk was startled to be the subject of such a discussion, but shook his head to indicate Michael was wrong. 'She is not manly enough,' he said meaningfully.

'There are plenty of men in the University who look like women,' mused Deynman, off in a world of his own. 'It is difficult to tell them apart in some cases. For example, Chancellor Tynkell—'

'No,' said Michael briskly, not wanting the student to dwell on that particular topic. Deynman had once attributed the Chancellor's aversion to washing as evidence that he was a hermaphrodite, and had started wicked rumours that still plagued the man.

'Let us take John Wormynghalle of King's Hall instead, then,' said Deynman. He tried to give Michael a meaningful look, catching Wynewyk a painful blow on the shoulder as the cross sagged to one side. 'He is an odd sort of fellow.'

'Watch what you are doing with that thing,' yelped Wynewyk, cowering away from him. 'And there is nothing odd about Wormynghalle, other than the fact that he is able to resist my charms.'

'You tried to seduce him?' asked Bartholomew uneasily, thinking that sort of behaviour might well bring about a fight between the two Colleges as each tried to defend its honour.

'Of course not,' said Wynewyk indignantly. 'But I attempted to steer a conversation around to personal matters – to test the waters, if you take my meaning – and he refused to be diverted. He is interested in natural philosophy, musical theory and nothing else. He is dull, but not strange – except perhaps for the fact that he declines to set foot in taverns and never employs whores. That was why I thought he might be approachable, but it transpires he has no interest in the intimate company of men *or* women. All he wants to do is learn.'

'He is fanatical about his studies,' agreed Deynman. 'He attends *all* the public lectures, and you can tell from his face that he is listening.' The bemusement in his voice indicated that he did not.

'I would not like to sit next to him at a feast – he would be tedious company,' said Michael. 'But you cannot suspect *him* of being a hermaphrodite, just because he enjoys scholarship. He and Tynkell cannot be compared.'

'You admit it, then!' crowed Deynman triumphantly. 'I knew there was something singular about that Chancellor!'

'That is not what I meant,' objected Michael, alarmed by the way his words had been twisted. 'I meant that Wormynghalle and Tynkell are completely different, and . . .'

He trailed off as Deynman, armed with new 'evidence', strode ahead, doubtless working out how to apply the information to the dubious medical theories he had accrued from half listening to lectures.

'That has torn it, Brother,' said Bartholomew, stifling a yawn. 'Now you will never persuade him there is nothing wrong with the Chancellor that a bath would not cure.'

'Damn Tynkell and his peculiar habits,' muttered Michael. He saw the physician smother a second yawn and shook his head in disgust before changing the subject. 'Langelee's lover is Alyce Weasenham, wife of the town's biggest gossip. You have to be impressed, Matt, because very little escapes our stationer's sharp eyes. Still, I suppose Weasenham has more than enough to occupy him at the moment, what with fabricating tales about Merton Hall, about Oxford and its riots, and about you and Matilde.'

138

'Alyce?' asked Bartholomew, startled. 'How do you know?'

'Few things happen here without someone telling me – and that includes reports about you. You think you were careful last night, but tongues are still clacking. I warn you again, Matt: stop this dalliance with Matilde, at least for a while.'

'I cannot,' said Bartholomew tiredly. 'I wish I could explain, because I know you would understand. But I cannot stop seeing her, and I cannot tell you why.'

Michael sighed. 'Then you will lose your Fellowship, and the fine you will be ordered to pay will be so vast that you will spend the rest of your life in debt. Just think about that as you creep along the High Street tonight.'

'Agatha the laundress,' breathed William, still thinking about a relationship between Langelee and the only woman permitted to live inside Michaelhouse's sacred portals. Even the morose Suttone was smirking at the way the Franciscan had so readily accepted Michael's careless remark, and Suttone rarely smiled about anything. 'He is a braver man than I thought.'

'I am concerned about this Merton Hall murder,' said Suttone, leaving the Franciscan to his musings and stepping forward to speak to Michael. 'Another College founded in Cambridge would be greatly beneficial, and it would be a pity to lose Islip's goodwill just because an Oxford man died in our town. Do you have any idea who killed Chesterfelde?'

'None. But I plan to interview Merton Hall's servants this morning.'

'Do not neglect to speak to Eudo and Boltone,' said William, reluctantly dragging his thoughts away from Agatha and Langelee. 'They are an unpleasant pair – you may find they are your killers.'

'What makes you say that?' asked Michael, surprised the

friar should know them at all. They were unlikely to move in similar circles.

'They came to visit that relic I made available for public veneration earlier this year, and I saw then what kind of men they were. They probably killed Chesterfelde to keep their crimes a secret.'

'What crimes?'

'They have been cheating Merton for years,' replied William, a little impatient that the monk should not know. 'It is the talk of the whole town. Why do you think Warden Duraunt is here? It is to confront them. But that is not all: they steal from others, too – scholars and townsfolk alike.'

'Such as whom?' asked Michael, trying to recall whether he had received complaints in the past.

'Geoffrey Dodenho at King's Hall,' replied William. 'And if you want a witness from the town, then ask Matthew's lover: Matilde.'

Michael and Bartholomew did not finish teaching until mid-afternoon. At that point, Michael's sober Benedictines astonished him by showing they were an entire term ahead with Peter Lombard's *Sentences* and were given their leisure for the rest of the day as a reward – they smiled polite thanks and immediately resumed their studies – while Clippesby's musicians were dispatched to King's Hall to hear Wormynghalle's lecture on plainsong. Bartholomew's medical students had been given a passage in Galen's *De simplicibus medicinis* to learn, while the astronomers were to evaluate Ptolemaic epicycles using the mathematical tables constructed by an Arab scholar in the tenth century and translated into Latin by Adelard of Bath. They objected vociferously, and claimed the exercise was too advanced for them, while Bartholomew firmly maintained it was elementary.

'You need the practice,' he said, unmoved by their cries

of dismay at the mountain of work he had set them. 'Your calculations yesterday were entirely wrong.'

'That was not our fault,' said one, sulkily. 'Brother Michael ordered Deynman to supervise the lesson, and he got us confused. We were figuring movable feasts, and his formula had Easter taking place the day after Christmas! We do not want him to "help" us again. He has set me back weeks by forcing us to use his convoluted equations.'

Bartholomew knew Deynman had taken a more active role in the class than he had been allocated. He was older than the astronomers, and eager to display his superior knowledge. Instead of merely making sure they kept at their work, and did not wander away before the session was over, he had stepped in to teach, and the result was seven very confused astronomers and an even more bewildered Deynman. That day it was the considerably more intelligent Falmeresham who had been left in charge, while Deynman was told to sit at the back and keep quiet.

'We should visit Matilde,' said Michael, who had accompanied the physician when he had tended a patient in nearby St John's Hospital. The rain had stopped and the sun was out. 'I want to know what they stole from her.'

'Not now,' said Bartholomew absently, still bemused by the students' indignation at being asked to do some serious thinking. 'I will ask when I see her tonight.'

'I would rather talk to her myself,' said Michael. They were near the Jewry, and he took a couple of steps in that direction.

'No,' said Bartholomew, grabbing the monk's arm and snapping out of his reverie. 'I said I will speak to her later.'

Michael turned to face him. 'Why? Are you ensuring she has her rest, so she will be better able to frolic with you tonight?' He took an involuntary step backwards when he saw the dark expression on his friend's face, then reached out to touch his shoulder. 'I am sorry, Matt. I should not have said that. But Matilde is my friend, too, and you have no right to prevent me from seeing her.'

'I am asking you to leave her alone,' said Bartholomew, fighting to keep the anger from his voice. He rubbed his head, supposing tiredness was making him prone to losing his temper. 'Please.'

Michael shook his head slowly. 'This is an odd state of affairs, Matt. I am not sure Matilde . . .' He faltered when he became aware that someone was close behind him, and turned around fast.

The University stationer was standing there, with his wife Alyce on his arm. He was grinning in triumph, and it was clear he had overheard at least part of the conversation and was anticipating the pleasure of repeating it. It was equally obvious that the snippet would be embellished so that soon it would bear little resemblance to what had actually been said. Bartholomew closed his eyes in despair.

'Weasenham,' said Michael amiably. 'You startled me, approaching so softly from behind.'

'So I imagine,' said Weasenham with a leer. 'I startle many folk with my silent-footed tread. I have surprised Doctor Rougham on occasion, too, as he creeps out to dally with his sweetheart.'

'Not Rougham,' said Michael immediately. 'No woman would take *him* as a lover.'

'Well, he *is* obliged to pay her,' acknowledged Weasenham spitefully. 'He is away from Gonville at the moment. I am told he sent a letter saying he was in Norfolk, but I do not think that is true.'

'Why not?' demanded Bartholomew. He probably disliked Rougham more than anyone, but he still objected to him being the subject of gossip. 'He does have family there.'

'He would never *willingly* leave during term, and especially not with the Archbishop about to visit,' Weasenham

142

pointed out with impeccable logic and a clear under-standing of the man. 'He would want to be here, to be seen and to curry Islip's favour.'

'What do you want?' asked Michael coldly. 'Why are you accosting us when we are busy?'

Weasenham ignored his hostility and gestured behind him. 'My shop is there, gentlemen, and when I saw you chatting, I felt compelled to come out and pay my respects. I am always ready to pass the time of day with Michaelhouse men.'

'So is your wife,' said Michael baldly. Alyce swallowed uneasily, but Weasenham did not seem to grasp the monk's meaning. He glanced at her, then back at Michael, and a frown of puzzlement creased his face.

'Master Langelee does a good deal of business with us,' blurted Alyce.

'He is always in our shop,' agreed Weasenham. He smiled, dismissing his confusion as he considered the prospect of lucrative future contracts. 'He says Michaelhouse is plan-ning to expand its membership, which means that a lot more writing supplies and exemplar texts will be required.'

'Is that so?' asked Michael, while Bartholomew recalled Wynewyk's bleak analysis of the College's finances with its current quota of scholars, and marvelled at the baldness of the lie.

'He says Michaelhouse will soon be the largest College in the University,' Weasenham went on, oblivious to his wife's squirming mortification. 'He is always in our solar, confiding his grand plans to my Alyce. That man has vision.'

'I planned to visit you later,' said Michael, bringing the discussion to a merciful end. Bartholomew was relieved; Alyce's discomfort was too close to his own circumstances to be even remotely amusing. 'The Chancellor is running short of vellum again.'

'I always have vellum for Chancellor Tynkell. He is a

good, decent man who sleeps in his own bed at night.' Weasenham smirked at Bartholomew in a way that made the physician want to punch him.

'But perhaps I will send to Ely Abbey for it instead,' said Michael, rubbing his chin thoughtfully. 'My Benedictine brethren produce remarkably fine vellum.'

The smug grin faded. 'Yes, they do. I buy mine from them – to sell in my shop.'

'I could save the University a good deal of money,' said Michael, appearing to think aloud. 'The monks know me and are sure to give me a good price. Better than anything you can offer.'

'But you would have to pay to have it transported here,' argued Weasenham uneasily. 'And that road is very dangerous – plagued by robbers.'

'It would not be worth the inconvenience to you,' added Alyce, also alarmed. Her voice dropped to an appalled whisper as she glanced at her husband. 'We cannot survive without the patronage of the Chancellor's Office.'

'Is that so?' asked Michael softly. 'Well, I suppose I *could* persuade Tynkell to continue to buy from you. Of course, it would very much depend.'

'Oh?' asked Weasenham nervously. 'On what, exactly?'

Michael's voice was low and menacing. 'The Chancellor's Office will purchase nothing from a man who damages my colleagues' reputations. Furthermore, I shall urge the Colleges and hostels to follow my example. Do I make myself clear?'

'Perfectly,' replied Weasenham. He swallowed hard. 'If I mention what I just overheard between you and Bartholomew, you will drive me out of business.'

'Then can I assume we have reached an understanding?' asked Michael, not bothering to deny the charge of blackmail, or even attempting to couch what he was doing in more pleasant terms.

'Yes,' said Weasenham shortly. His face was dark with resentment as he stalked back to his house, and Bartholomew saw the monk had just made himself a new enemy. Alyce lingered, however.

'If our business fails because Tynkell takes his custom elsewhere, we will have nothing to lose,' she said coldly. 'Extortion works both ways, you know.'

'You are right,' said Michael softly. 'Your husband will have no reason to keep quiet about Matt if he loses all his customers. But *you* will. You do not want me to inform Weasenham that you and Langelee discuss far more intimate matters than Michaelhouse's fictitious expansion, do you?'

She glowered at him. 'But that would damage your College, too. Michaelhouse will not want its Master exposed as a man who possesses a lover.'

'True,' agreed Michael amicably. 'So I suggest we both keep still tongues in our heads. Then no one will be harmed and we will all be happy.'

She thought for a moment, then gave Michael a curt nod before following her husband. Bartholomew watched her open the door and bustle inside the shop, where scholars were waiting to be served with orders of pens, parchment, ink and the cheap copies of selected texts known as *exemplar pecia*. She did not look back, but Bartholomew could tell she was livid. He wondered whether she would inform Langelee about Michael's threats, and plunge the College into a bitter dispute between its Master and its most influential member.

'Thank you,' he said sincerely. 'But you should not have intervened, Brother. I do not want you involved in this mess.'

'In what mess?' The physician's odd choice of words to describe his romance did not escape the astute Michael. He looked searchingly at his friend's face, and spoke kindly. 'What are you not telling me, Matt?'

'Nothing,' mumbled Bartholomew, acutely uncomfortable. 'But thank you for taking care of Weasenham. I will tell Matilde what you did, and will ask her about whatever it is that Eudo and Boltone are supposed to have stolen when I visit this evening.'

'There *is* something amiss,' said Michael, catching his arm and preventing him from walking on. 'You never normally pass up an opportunity to see Matilde.'

Bartholomew searched desperately for a way to change the subject, knowing it would not be long before the monk smoked out his most intimate secrets if the discussion were to run its course. He was simply too tired for convincing prevarication, and Michael was too skilled an interrogator. He was transparently relieved to see John Wormynghalle and Dodenho coming towards them, deep in the throes of a debate. He did not know them well, but they served his purpose.

'Good afternoon!' he called, hailing them with considerable enthusiasm. 'How are you?'

Wormynghalle was startled to be so buoyantly addressed, but Dodenho considered it only natural that someone should be interested in the state of his health.

'I am in need of a physic,' he announced. 'Paxtone says I should take a purge but I detest those. I am sure there is a less dramatic way to remedy this burning in my innards.'

'Yes,' said Bartholomew, feeling on safer ground now he was talking about medicine. 'A chalk solution might help, or perhaps some charcoal mixed with poppy juice and wine.'

'Yes,' agreed Dodenho, nodding keenly. 'The latter remedy sounds acceptable. But omit the charcoal, if you please. Come to King's Hall and write the recipe for this concoction now, so I can send it to the apothecary.'

It was difficult to refuse, having initiated the conversation in the first place, but Michael did not object as

146

Dodenho led them into his College. The chance encounter presented a good opportunity for the monk to ask Dodenho whether Eudo and Boltone had stolen something from him, not to mention probing further into his relationship with the dead Chesterfelde. However, the boastful scholar was not Michael's main concern at that moment: he was more troubled by what he now thought of as Bartholomew's 'predicament' with Matilde, and resolved to add it to his list of problems to solve.

Dodenho led Bartholomew to his chamber, Michael and Wormynghalle trailing behind them, but then realised he had run out of ink. He claimed it was because he used so much for scribing his erudite masterpieces, but Bartholomew looked around the room and knew he was lying. It was arranged in such a way that writing would be difficult: its two desks were shoved in a corner where the light was poor, and the area near the window – where the tables should have been – held a pair of comfortable chairs that were obviously used for dozing in the sun.

The rest of Dodenho's quarters was equally a shrine to easy living. Feathers clinging to the rugs on the floor suggested that he and his room-mate pampered themselves with down mattresses, rather than the more usual straw ones. A table held several jugs of wine, and on a tray stood a large plum cake, some cheese and a bowl of nuts.

'How do you write with the desk so far from the light?' asked Michael guilelessly.

'He does not scribe as much as he would have you believe,' whispered Wormynghalle, amused by the question. 'But he reads by the window – learns theories that he then claims as his own.'

'I work better in the gloom,' pronounced Dodenho with considerable authority. 'Now, where is my ink? Damn that Wolf! He must have made off with it.'

'Wolf left on Ascension Day – almost two weeks ago,' pounced Michael wickedly. 'Does this mean you have only just noticed you have none left?'

'Perhaps it was not Wolf,' blustered Dodenho, caught out. 'I must have used the last of it committing my mean speed theorem to parchment yesterday.'

'You mean the one devised by Bradwardine?' asked Bartholomew, who loved the complex physics entailed in the Mertonian's theories about distance and motion.

'I mean the superior one devised by *me*,' snapped Dodenho, striding to what appeared to be a private garde-robe and inspecting the shelves. Bartholomew thought it an unlikely place to find ink, and, judging from the grins of Michael and Wormynghalle, so did they. Wormynghalle began to whisper again, taking the opportunity to speak while Dodenho was out of earshot.

'His plagiarism may deceive uneducated men like Norton, but I do not appreciate him trying to mislead me, too. I am no knuckle-brained courtier, but a man who takes his studies seriously. I find it extremely irritating, and expected a better quality of scholarship from a Cambridge College.'

'There are plenty of men like Dodenho at Oxford, too,' objected Michael, conveniently forgetting the fact that he had never been there.

Wormynghalle inclined his head apologetically, aware he had trodden on sensitive toes. 'I know; I have met them. They are partly why I came here – to be away from boasters and theory-thieves.'

'You will never escape those,' said Bartholomew, thinking him naïve to suppose he could.

Wormynghalle smiled. 'But I have met many brilliant men since I arrived here. I particularly enjoyed your lecture on Grosseteste's notion that lines, angles and figures of geometry are a useful tool for understanding natural philosophy. Perhaps we could debate that some time?'

'When?' asked Bartholomew eagerly. His fatigue miraculously evaporated. 'Now?'

Wormynghalle indicated Michael with a nod of his head. 'It had better be later if we do not want to make an enemy of the Senior Proctor. I will set our students an exercise that will keep them occupied, and we can use the time for informal disputation. But you will be here all day if you wait for Dodenho to find his non-existent ink. Come upstairs and I will give you some of mine. *I* write all the time, and have a plentiful supply.' He gave Dodenho a disparaging glance and led the way to the floor above.

'It is much nicer here without Wolf and Hamecotes,' declared Dodenho, following. 'I am glad they have gone away on business of their own. I like having a room to myself.'

'Ah, yes,' said Michael. 'Your truant Fellows. Have you heard from them?'

'I had a letter from Hamecotes today,' said Wormynghalle, pulling a crumpled missive from the pouch on his belt. 'He arrived safely in Oxford, and has already bought Gilbertus Angelicus' *Compendium medicinae* and William of Pagula's *Oculus sacerdotis* for our library.'

He seemed delighted, and Bartholomew supposed that, to an earnest scholar like Wormynghalle, securing books was far more important than staying in College to teach.

'*I* have heard nothing from Wolf, however,' offered Dodenho. 'I doubt *he* is buying books, given how much money he owes the College. I do not miss him or his nasty habit of dropping nutshells all over the floor, where they hurt my bare feet. And Hamecotes has a habit of waking me far too early in the day with his damned pacing. He makes the floorboards creak, right above my head.'

'He is thinking,' said Wormynghalle defensively, pausing at the top of the stairs to open a window. The stairwell had the musty, sour odour often associated with places inhabited exclusively by men, even relatively wealthy ones like the scholars of King's Hall, and Wormynghalle wrinkled his nose fastidiously. 'He is especially sharp-witted in the mornings, and we always rise early and pass the time in scholarly discourse – and when he thinks, he walks back and forth. All you and Wolf talk about is the quality of College ale.'

'That is important, too,' argued Dodenho, watching him struggle with the latch before shoving him out of the way and opening it with brute force. He regarded his young colleague with dislike. 'At least we *can* discuss something other than work. You cannot, and it is tedious in the extreme.'

'I heard you were the victim of a crime recently,' said Michael to Dodenho, seeing Wormynghalle's angry look. He did not want to be caught in the middle of a petty row between two men who should have better manners than to bicker in company.

'What crime?' demanded Dodenho. 'Do you mean the time when Hamecotes defamed me, by publicly accusing me of stealing his ideas on the meaning of time?'

'No,' said Michael. 'I mean a theft. Something was stolen from you.'

'Nothing was stolen,' said Dodenho, and his face flushed red. 'I found it again.'

Wormynghalle regarded him in disbelief. 'You *found* it? But you stormed around the College for days, accusing people of making off with your astrolabe, and now you say it was not taken after all? Why did you not say so sooner? We have been thinking there was a thief under our roof all this time.'

'An astrolabe?' asked Bartholomew, recalling that he had seen such an object in the hands of the tanner at Merton Hall. 'It was not silver, was it?'

'Show it to me,' ordered Michael.

'I sold it,' said Dodenho uneasily. 'It *was* silver, and therefore too valuable to keep in a place like this, where impecunious students are in and out of our rooms all the time.'

'A student stole it?' asked Michael, confused. 'And then you got it back and sold it?'

'Yes,' replied Dodenho. 'No.'

Michael raised his eyebrows. 'Well, it must be one or the other. However, I was under the impression that Bailiff Boltone or Eudo might have laid sticky fingers on the thing.'

Dodenho appeared to be bemused. 'What makes you mention them in particular?'

'No reason,' hedged Michael. 'Why? Do you know them?'

Dodenho seemed to consider his options. 'A little,' he replied eventually. 'I met them once or twice through my friend . . . through my *slight acquaintance*, Chesterfelde. But they did not steal my astrolabe. That was students.' His face took on a grim, stubborn look.

'Misleading the Senior Proctor is a serious matter,' said Michael sternly. 'You would not be lying, would you, Dodenho?'

'Of course not,' bleated Dodenho. 'Why would I do such a thing?' He gave one of the falsest smiles Michael had ever seen and changed the subject. 'Now, where is this ink, Wormynghalle?'

He pushed past the younger man and opened the door to an airy chamber where two desks were placed in the windows, to make best use of the light. Bartholomew looked around and saw a neat, functional room, obviously occupied by two people dedicated to academic pursuits. Shelves contained books and scrolls, all carefully stacked, while ink and pens were kept on a windowsill, to avoid accidental spillage that might damage the precious tomes.

It was a clean place; Bartholomew could not see so much as a speck of dust anywhere.

Wormynghalle placed a tray on one of the tables and fetched a scrap of parchment. Bartholomew dipped his pen in the inkwell, and was amused when the first word he wrote came out bright green.

'Sorry,' said Wormynghalle, hurriedly supplying another pot. 'That is Hamecotes's. He has a liking for this particular colour, because he says it does not fade as readily as black.'

'He is a verdant kind of man,' said Dodenho, not entirely pleasantly. 'He wears a green hood on Sundays, and dons emerald hose under his tabard. And he likes vegetables, especially cabbage.'

'And folk think Clippesby is insane,' muttered Michael.

Bartholomew wrote out the prescription, ignoring Dodenho's insistence that wine and poppy juice would work better without the unnecessary addition of charcoal. Michael followed Dodenho when he went to find a servant to carry the recipe to the apothecary, to see if he could shake loose any more details about the mysterious movements of the astrolabe, while Bartholomew remained with Wormynghalle, who showed him a scroll containing quotations from the Arabic scholar al-Razi. The physician was pleasantly surprised when Wormynghalle listened attentively to his explanation about why Western medicine could benefit from the wisdom of the East, and even more pleased when he offered a number of intelligent comments. Wormynghalle was single-minded, perhaps a little fanatical, about learning, but Bartholomew preferred him to the shallow Dodenho.

All too soon, Michael returned, and Wormynghalle reluctantly relinquished his guest. He walked with them to the gate, clasping and unclasping his hands as he expounded a theory he had devised based around Grosseteste's precepts of geometry. While he listened, Bartholomew noticed again Wormynghalle's downy moustache and the few bristles that sprouted from the underside of his chin, and supposed he left them there to make himself appear older. He understood why, recalling the frustration he had experienced himself when mature scholars had dismissed his ideas, simply because he was young.

When they reached the road, Michael found it hard to prise the two men apart. Each time he tried to draw their discussion to a close, one would think of another point he wanted to raise. The monk was about to leave them to it, when his attention was caught by three people walking down the High Street together.

'What are they doing out, when I expressly forbade them to stray from their lodgings?'

Wormynghalle dragged his attention away from Bartholomew's analysis of radiant lines, and followed the line of the monk's pointing finger. 'It is the tanner – the one from Oxford who has the same name as me. But, Bartholomew, have you considered the *pro contra* abstraction, which—'

'Well?' demanded Eu imperiously, directing his question at Michael and cutting across the King's Hall scholar's erudite exposition. 'What have you learned about Gonerby's murder?'

'Gonerby?' asked Wormynghalle the scholar in puzzlement. 'I thought you said the dead man from Merton Hall was called Chesterfelde.'

'Gonerby was an Oxford merchant,' explained Abergavenny politely. 'He died during the St Scholastica's Day riots, and Brother Michael has agreed to look into the matter for us.'

'Only because he is afraid our questions will spark off civil unrest,' said Eu nastily. 'He does not want a war in progress when the Archbishop is here.'

'Of course he does not,' said Wormynghalle the scholar sharply. 'Only a fool would.'

Eu regarded him coldly. 'You must be a fool yourself, for approaching my colleague here in the hope of discovering some common kinship. He is a tanner, for God's sake!'

The scholar's eyebrows rose in surprise at the crude insult, but he clearly did not want to become embroiled in a row between merchants. Before his namesake could frame a suitable response to the jibe, he made a tight bow, turned on his heel and marched back inside King's Hall, giving the impression that he had better things to do than to squabble with burgesses.

'Are you sure you two are not kin?' asked Eu archly. 'You both have poor manners.'

'I will kill any man who suggests I have ties to *that* ruffian!' snarled Wormynghalle. 'He wants to claim an association with me, so he can demand a donation towards his studies. He probably assumed my name for that express purpose, but I will not be taken in by charlatans.'

'He is not poor,' said Bartholomew. Wormynghalle's chamber was an expensive one shared only with one other man, and with a private garderobe. In Michaelhouse such a large room would have been used as a dormitory for at least six.

'Never mind him,' said Eu impatiently. 'I want to know about Gonerby.'

'We have narrowed our list of suspects,' replied Michael. 'So, it is only a matter of time before we have your man.'

'Good,' said Eu, beginning to move away. 'As we agreed, you have until the Visitation. If you do not have our culprit by then we shall follow Wormynghalle's advice and take this physician to Oxford for hanging.'

Michael glowered at their departing backs, although Abergavenny shot the Michaelhouse men an apologetic smile as he left. 'Eu *is* a nasty piece of work. Perhaps Dick was right, and he is the one in that unholy trio we should watch. But I still have a hunch about Abergavenny. Did you see the way he leered at us just now?'

'Not really,' said Bartholomew. 'Were you honest in the reply you gave them? Have you narrowed your list of suspects? Men who were in Oxford in February, and who are now here?'

'Yes,' said Michael. 'That was the absolute truth. However, I have eliminated so many of them with conclusive and incontestable alibis, that I now have a very short list indeed.'

'How many are left on it?'

'None,' replied Michael. He shot his friend a rueful grin. 'I told you it was short.'

Bartholomew was worried that Michael had no suspects for Gonerby's murder, since he thought that Eu might be as good as his word, and try to abduct him if the real culprit was not produced. There was also a nagging anxiety that Langelee might just let it happen, on the grounds that it would rid Michaelhouse of the embarrassing situation involving his relationship with Matilde.

'He will not,' said Michael, when he voiced his concerns. 'As I said before, he is fond of you. Besides, I shall soon have their man and, if worse comes to worst, I intend to fob them off with a tale about their culprit fleeing to London – send them chasing phantoms while Islip is here.'

'And what if they catch someone innocent? They will execute him.'

'Perhaps, but there is no point worrying about that yet, since we have several days to uncover the truth.' Michael was silent for a moment, thinking. 'I have the feeling that Abergavenny was right when he mooted the possibility that the murders of Gonerby and Chesterfelde might be related.'

'What makes you think so?'

'One man is murdered, then a second is killed and his body dumped in the presence of those avenging the death of the first. I dislike such coincidences. However, since I *will* have Chesterfelde's killer before the Visitation, hopefully that means I shall have Gonerby's, too.' Michael scratched his chin. 'I need to know more about Boltone and Eudo and their dishonest dealings. The best solution would be to learn that they *were* in Oxford in February, and once we have proved they murdered Gonerby, we can encourage them to confess to Chesterfelde's killing.'

'The merchants said it was a scholar who made an end of Gonerby. Eudo and Boltone are not members of any university.'

Michael shrugged. 'Gonerby was dying, and dying men do not always make good witnesses – even assuming these merchants have been scrupulous in repeating his alleged last words. Is that Spryngheuse over there, wearing his grey-hemmed cloak, despite the sunshine? He looks dreadful.'

Bartholomew agreed: Spryngheuse's eyes were red-rimmed, there were dark pouches under them, and his face had an unhealthy, waxen appearance. 'What is wrong?' he asked as their paths crossed. 'Are you ill?'

Spryngheuse's voice was hoarse when he replied. 'Remember that Benedictine I told you about – the one Polmorva claims does not exist? I saw him last night, lurking in the garden.'

'Did you speak to him?' asked Michael. 'Did he say what he wanted?'

Spryngheuse shook his head. 'I told the others to come and look, but by the time they reached the window, he had gone. Polmorva told them I imagined it. I detest that man.'

'I understand why,' said Michael. 'He is sly and spiteful. But will you tell me what your friend Chesterfelde thought of Polmorva? Did you ever discuss him together?'

Spryngheuse regarded him unhappily. 'You want to

know whether Polmorva is Chesterfelde's killer. Well, he is certainly bold enough to do such a thing, especially since he knew he could.'

Michael frowned. 'What do you mean?'

Spryngheuse sighed and massaged his temples, eyes tightly closed. 'Ignore me – I meant nothing. I am speaking nonsense, because I am so tired. I do not sleep well these days.'

'I know how that feels,' said Bartholomew wryly. 'But if you know something about Chesterfelde's death, please tell us. We would like to see his killer brought to justice.'

Spryngheuse swallowed, and for a moment looked as though he might weep, but he pulled himself together. 'Very well. Polmorva declined to drink much wine the night Chesterfelde died – unlike the rest of us. He abstained in a discreet way – often raising his goblet, but seldom drinking.'

'Why did you notice that?' asked Bartholomew curiously.

Spryngheuse's expression was grim. 'I have become much more observant since the riots – terror of reprisal does that to a man. Also, you told us Chesterfelde was murdered somewhere other than in the hall, so perhaps he was killed when he went to the latrines. He had imbibed copious amounts of liquid, and would have needed to relieve himself, while Polmorva has an unusually small bladder and is often obliged to get up in the night. It is not impossible that they were out there alone together.'

'So, you were all intoxicated except Polmorva?' asked Bartholomew. 'Does that include Chesterfelde?'

Spryngheuse gave a sad smile. 'He was used to wine, and could drink a lot without his head swimming, but he was merry, too, that evening. It just made him laugh a lot – giggle, rather.'

'Interesting,' said Michael. 'We must have words with Polmorva.'

Spryngheuse paled. 'Please, no! He will know it was I who told you about his deception with the wine, and life is bad enough without having him after me with his sharp tongue.'

'Better that than with his sharp knife,' Michael pointed out. 'But I will ensure he does not know you are our source. Besides, he may even confess once he learns I have him trapped.'

'I doubt it,' said Bartholomew, knowing the monk would need more than speculation to corner the likes of Polmorva. 'But we need to speak to Eudo and Boltone first. Are they at home?'

'In the garden,' replied Spryngheuse. 'There is a cistern, which provides fresh water for the house, and they are repairing its pulley. They have been fiddling with it all day.'

Bartholomew and Michael walked through Merton Hall's neat vegetable plots to where they ended in a small arm of the River Cam known as the Bin Brook. The manor cultivated turnips, cabbages, onions, peas and beans using labour hired by the bailiff, although no one was working there that day. It was a pleasant garden. Walls and trees protected it from the wind, and the paths that wound through it were attractive and peaceful. Bartholomew took a deep breath of air laden with the scent of earth soaked by the morning's shower, and paused to admire the line of red-tiled roofs belonging to the houses on Bridge Street. He recalled that Merton Hall and Tulyet were neighbours, their grounds separated only by the stream and the Sheriff's Dickon-proof wall.

At the very bottom of the toft was the cistern. It comprised a huge, stone-walled chamber that was sunk into the earth, like a deep, square well. Its walls rose above the ground to knee height, and a massive wood and metal lid fitted snugly across them to prevent animals and leaves from dropping inside and contaminating its contents. An intricate system of drains and sluices allowed river water to enter it, and it was invariably at least half full, even in times of drought. Merton Hall thus always had a source of fresh water, albeit at times a murky one.

'This design is clever,' said Bartholomew, impressed as always by skilful feats of engineering. 'Its builders have ensured that, as long as the Bin Brook is flowing, there will always be water. It is deep, too – two or three times the height of a man.'

'Then I would not like to fall in it,' said Michael with a shudder. 'I cannot swim.'

'You would not get out, either,' elaborated Bartholomew, oblivious to the monk's uncomfortable reaction to this news. 'At least, not easily. The walls are too slick, and there are no handholds for climbing. That is why the lid remains in place at all times – a hatch can be opened when anyone wants to draw water, but the lid is always closed. I suppose it is possible to tumble through the hatch, but you would have to be very careless.'

'Fascinating,' said Michael, wishing he would stop. Even the thought of deep, stone vaults filled with water was enough to make his stomach churn, and the notion of being trapped inside one made him feel sick. 'But I am more interested in the men mending it.'

As they came closer, they heard the sound of a hammer, and saw Eudo swinging furiously at the mechanism that allowed buckets to be raised and lowered, looking as if he was more intent on destroying it than fixing it. His handsome face wore a vicious scowl, while Boltone stood to one side with his arms folded, watching dispassionately. To belie Bartholomew's recent statements, the gigantic lid of the cistern had been raised for the occasion, and was flipped back, so that one edge rested in the grass; its opposite side was attached to the wall by massive iron hinges.

'Having trouble?' asked Michael mildly.

Eudo glared at him. 'The pulley has jammed, and I have been playing with the damned thing all day to no avail. Whoever built it is an imbecile.'

'You will not repair it by attacking it like a maniac,' said Boltone, earning himself a foul look. 'I have been telling you for hours that a contraption like this needs coaxing, not brute force.'

Eudo shoved the hammer into his belt. As he did so, Bartholomew noticed the cut on his arm had almost healed, and probably would not even scar.

'You do it, then,' Eudo snapped, sweaty and irritable. 'You have been giving advice and making suggestions all afternoon, but nothing has worked. I am tired, hot and my wrist hurts. *You* do it.'

'Never mind that for now,' said Michael, raising one hand to prevent Boltone from accepting the challenge. 'We have come to ask about this unpleasant business at Merton Hall.'

'*We* did not kill anyone,' said Boltone firmly. 'Duraunt claims I falsified the accounts – which is untrue, as I shall demonstrate when I have devised a way of doing so – but we had nothing to do with Chesterfelde's demise.'

'No?' asked Michael, throwing down the gauntlet in the frail hope of learning something by unnerving them. 'Prove it.'

Eudo gave an insolent shrug. 'We do not need to prove it: we are innocent, and that is that. We are not obliged to explain ourselves to you or to any other man.'

Boltone adopted a less confrontational attitude. 'Neither Eudo nor I has a reason to hurt anyone at Merton Hall – least of all a pleasant man like Chesterfelde.'

'What about that scratch on your arm?' asked Bartholomew, pointing to Eudo's cut. 'Chesterfelde had one rather like it – and it killed him.'

160

Eudo did not seem to find the association a worrying one. He shrugged again. 'Perhaps the killer tried to murder me, but, finding me too manly, decided to slaughter the cackling Chesterfelde instead.'

Michael was unconvinced. He doubted that someone had been so determined to kill by exsanguination that he had moved to a second victim when his first attempt was unsuccessful. 'Where were you when Chesterfelde died?'

'In the King's Head, as I told you the last time you asked,' replied Eudo with a bored sigh. 'However, since you do not know *exactly* when Chesterfelde died, I cannot know *exactly* where I was.' He sneered. 'Is that clear enough logic for you, Proctor?'

'It is very clear,' said Bartholomew, leaning forward to peer into the cistern. Its contents were dark and muddy, and the sides slick with slime. 'So here is some logic for you: Chesterfelde did not die in the hall – he was killed when someone sliced his wrist and allowed him to bleed to death. His corpse was stabbed and dumped later. Do you have any logic to explain how that happened?'

Eudo regarded him coldly, and removed the hammer from his belt. It was a large one with a thick oak handle and a mass of metal for a head. 'That is rubbish,' he said, swinging it like a weapon. 'I saw the knife embedded in his spine myself.'

'I am sure you did,' said Bartholomew, ignoring the threat. 'However, we cannot always believe what we see, particularly when it is intended to mislead us.'

'We shall talk about this another time,' said Michael, taking a step away. He had seen the kind of damage expertly wielded tools could do, and decided he would rather discuss Chesterfelde's murder when he had a posse of beadles at his heels, all armed with knives and swords.

Eudo regarded him with rank disdain. 'And do not come here again with nasty accusations and no way to prove them.'

161

'Very well,' said Michael, edging further away. 'Matt, come with me.'

Boltone shot his companion an uneasy glance. 'Put the hammer down, Eudo, and let us see to this pulley. We have done nothing wrong and have nothing to fear from the Proctor and his lackey.'

'Not so,' said Bartholomew, leaning down to inspect the ground. He poked the turf with his finger, and it came away stained reddish-brown. He held it up for the others to see. 'Chesterfelde was killed here – and his blood in the grass proves it.'

Even before he had finished speaking, Eudo moved. He swung the hammer at Bartholomew's head in a savage, deadly arc. Startled by the speed of the attack, the physician jerked away and lost his footing. Without breaking stride, Eudo lunged at Michael.

'No,' screamed Boltone in horror. 'Eudo! There is no need for violence!'

Michael moved with surprising speed for a man of his girth, and managed to twist out of the way. He staggered backwards, where the low wall of the cistern bumped against his calves, and windmilled his arms furiously in an attempt to regain his balance. Boltone darted forward. Bartholomew could not tell whether the bailiff intended to push or help the monk, but before he could do either Michael disappeared over the edge with a piercing shriek. A splash indicated that he had landed.

'Now you have done it,' growled Eudo to Boltone. 'There is no turning back now.'

Bartholomew rolled in an effort to put as much distance between him and Eudo as possible, then tried to scramble to his feet. Eudo was quicker, and the hammer plunged downward again. Bartholomew squirmed out of the way and heard it connect hard with the pulley, so the whole structure shuddered. While the physician's attention was

162

taken with Eudo, Boltone approached from the other side, evidently deciding attack was the only way to extricate himself from the situation his friend had created. He was unexpectedly strong for so small a man, and when he grabbed one of Bartholomew's wrists and shoved him roughly towards the cistern, he was difficult to fend off. From inside the well, Bartholomew could hear the panicky gurgling of a man who could not swim.

He struggled hard, seeing that the bailiff intended to hold him while Eudo battered him to death. Seizing the medical bag he always carried, he hurled it with all his might at the approaching Eudo, skidding and dropping to one knee as he did so. Boltone fell with him, his small hands still fixed firmly around the physician's left arm. Eudo faltered when the bag struck him, but then advanced again, while Bartholomew raised his free arm to protect his head. Eudo's first blow went wide, and the hammer struck sparks as it smashed into the wall with devastating force. Bartholomew saw he did not have much time, and was acutely aware of the terrified choking sounds emanating from the cistern. He attempted to bring Boltone in front of him, to use as a shield, but the bailiff saw what he was trying to do and resisted. With a grin that verged on the manic, Eudo approached.

CHAPTER 5

Just when Bartholomew thought his life was about to end and that Eudo was going to dash out his brains and kick his body into the cistern, where no one would find it until Merton Hall's residents started to sicken from drinking bad water, Eudo's smile became forced. Then it faded altogether. The tenant put his hand to his chest, and when he pulled it away, there was blood on his fingers.

'Someone is shooting at us,' cried Boltone in alarm. He released Bartholomew, who dropped to the ground, certain that if someone was loosing arrows, then it would be no friend of his. The bailiff darted forward and tugged the quarrel from Eudo's chest, making his friend shriek in pain. 'I *told* you to go back to work and not answer questions, and now look what has happened. You should have known the Proctor would not come here alone. We are doomed!'

'Not yet,' said Eudo, grimacing at the redness staining his palm. 'We will finish the physician, hunt out this archer, and—' Another arrow hissed into the ground at his feet, making him jump like the dancing bear Bartholomew had watched in the Market Square. 'But then again, perhaps not.'

Without further ado, he raced away. Startled by his abrupt flight, Boltone tore after him, howling for him to stop, but Eudo had no intention of waiting to be shot, and within moments both men were lost from sight. Bartholomew crawled towards the spent missile, his thoughts whirling in confusion. It was tiny, although still large enough to have pierced Eudo's skin. He scanned the trees that lay across the Bin Brook, and sure enough, there was Dickon's tawny head poking over the wall. The boy was wearing a grin that almost split his face in half.

'Splat!' shouted Dickon in delight. 'I kill him.'

Bartholomew climbed unsteadily to his feet, edging towards the cistern, half his mind on the fact that Michael had gone ominously quiet, and half on the fact that Dickon might have enjoyed his live target practice so much he would try it again.

'Put the bow down,' he ordered sternly. 'Your father forbade you to shoot at people. He will be angry when he learns what you have done.'

He moved closer to the well and glanced inside it. Michael was not there. Then he saw a scrap of the monk's habit floating in one corner, and his stomach lurched in horror.

'Dickon!' he yelled, all thoughts of his own safety gone. 'Call your father! Hurry! Go now!'

'Pow! I kill him dead!' yelled Dickon, but obligingly disappeared from the wall. Bartholomew only hoped he would not encounter something more interesting before he summoned assistance – and that Tulyet would take the boy seriously and not put his story down to childish imagination.

Meanwhile, Bartholomew himself was faced with an agonising decision. If he jumped inside the cistern, he would not be able to climb out unaided – and if Dickon did not manage to raise the alarm, he would eventually drown. But Michael was already unconscious, and would die for certain if he took the time to fetch help himself. He glanced at the pulley, wondering whether he could use it to haul them both to safety, but Eudo had dismantled it to the point where it was useless. There was only one thing to do if he was to save Michael.

Taking a deep breath, he sat on the wall and launched himself forward. The water was agonisingly cold, and he felt himself descend for some time before he was able to kick his way to the surface. He blinked algae from his eyes and looked for the floating material he had seen in one corner. It was not there: Michael had sunk.

Trying to quell his alarm, Bartholomew dived. The water was cloudy and no sunlight penetrated the pool, which meant it was impossible to see. He flailed around in increasingly desperate circles, searching for anything grabbable. The tips of his fingers encountered something waving near the side of the pit, and he moved towards it, his lungs almost ready to burst. He located an arm and seized it, kicking towards the surface and surprised at how heavy Michael had become.

He dropped his prize in horror: the face that emerged was not the monk's, nor was it anyone he could save. Whoever else was in the well was long past earthly help, and there was a deep, gashing wound in the throat that looked as if someone had hacked it with stunning ferocity. Bartholomew had a fleeting image of a moss-coloured liripipe and a youngish face before he released the corpse and dived again, concentrating on the area where he had seen Michael's habit.

He felt something bulky that moved when he touched it, and struck out for the surface yet again, dragging the body with him and praying it was Michael and not another cadaver, because time was running out. He was relieved when he recognised the thin, brown hair and beefy features, and pressed his ear against his friend's chest. A faint hammering told him the monk was alive. He opened Michael's mouth and breathed hard into it, as he had been taught to do by his Arab master in Paris. Immediately, Michael gagged. His eyes fluttered open and he began to flail, strong arms made even more powerful by panic.

'Keep still,' Bartholomew ordered, ducking to avoid being hit. Michael was weighty, even when buoyed up by water, and his struggles would make keeping him afloat difficult. 'Or you will have us both under.'

'I cannot swim!' shrieked Michael, grabbing him around the throat.

Bartholomew went under, desperately trying to dislodge the monk's vicelike grip. They both started to sink, and one of Michael's knees struck him under the chin. He kicked his way free and surfaced some distance away. This time, he approached the monk from behind and hauled him up backwards, so he would not be able to drag them down a second time. Michael struggled frantically, and Bartholomew was hard-pressed to maintain his hold.

'Stop!' he shouted, when he could speak without water slopping into his mouth. 'You are not going to drown. I have you. But you must trust me. Relax.'

'Relax?' screeched Michael. 'What an inane thing to say to a drowning man!'

'Well, try,' snapped Bartholomew. 'And stop making so much noise or you will have Eudo and Boltone back. We are sitting ducks inside this thing.' He coughed, and the rhythm of his treading water was momentarily broken.

'We are sinking!' howled Michael, at once embarking on a new bout of struggles. 'Water is going up my nose. I cannot breathe!'

'Then stop splashing and making waves,' gasped Bartholomew. 'I will not let you go, I promise.'

Michael went rigid, every muscle in his body straining with the effort of keeping still. His breath came in short, shallow hisses, and he screwed his eyes tightly closed, so he would not be able to see the slick green walls and the rectangle of sky above him. Bartholomew admired his self-control, not sure he could have complied so readily, if the situation had been reversed.

167

'No,' whispered Michael after a few moments. 'This will not work. You are not strong enough to keep us both afloat. Let me go.'

'I cannot,' said Bartholomew caustically. 'As soon as I release you, you will grab me and we will drown together.' He paddled towards one of the walls, hoping to find a handhold that Michael could take, and ease some of the weight. There was nothing.

Michael retched as he scrabbled at the stones, trying in vain to hold himself up. 'My feet are nowhere near the bottom,' he squeaked. 'And the sides are as slippery and as smooth as ice.'

'Help is on its way,' said Bartholomew, to calm him. 'We do not have long to wait.'

Michael twisted around to look at him. 'Who? Not Eudo and Boltone. They want us dead.'

'Dickon. He is fetching his father as we speak.'

Michael was appalled. 'Dickon? But he would love to see me perish. Indeed, I am surprised he is not here to watch. I suppose the garden wall is too high for him to scale.'

Bartholomew said nothing. His legs were already beginning to ache from the effort of swimming, and he dared not ease his hold around the monk's neck, for the instant he did so Michael would panic again.

'Drowned in a latrine pit!' muttered Michael, making a valiant attempt to control his hysteria by talking. 'I can just imagine what my adversaries at the University will make of *that*.'

'This is not a latrine pit,' said Bartholomew, thinking of the other corpse that lurked under the murky surface, but deciding it was not a good time to mention it. In an attempt to ensure it did not slip out inadvertently, he changed the subject, then winced when he ended up saying something equally inappropriate. 'If Dickon neglects to call his father, your enemies will never know what happened to you anyway. You will just fail to return home tonight, and that will be that.'

'A mystery,' said Michael weakly, spitting and fixing one meaty hand around Bartholomew's arm. It was a grip of tremendous strength, and Bartholomew felt his own begin to slacken. He struggled to maintain it. 'I have always hated water. Swim harder, Matt – we are sinking again.'

'You are heavy,' said Bartholomew breathlessly, aware that already his burning muscles were not obeying him as they should. 'Try to float.'

'A man of my girth does not float,' stated Michael, with a trace of his habitual hauteur. He was silent for a moment. 'What if help does not come?'

'It will,' said Bartholomew, trying to sound confident, and deciding not to point out that a three-year-old child could hardly be expected to understand the importance of what he had been asked to do. Dickon's attention span was short and, even if he did go directly to his father and tell him the improbable story that the Senior Proctor and his Corpse Examiner were in his neighbour's cistern, there was a good chance that Tulyet would not believe him.

'Save yourself,' said Michael, after what felt like an age. 'Let me go and climb out. You are fit and strong. You will make it. Then come back for me later, being sure to present my corpse in its best light for mourners. All I ask is that you never tell anyone what really happened.'

'What did happen?' asked Bartholomew. He glanced at the sky, and strained his ears, but could hear or see nothing to indicate rescue was on its way. Michael slipped a little, and gagged as water slapped into his mouth. Bartholomew made a monumental effort to heave him up, and was horrified when he found he was barely able to do it. Without relinquishing his hold, he decided to see if they would fare better by swimming, than treading water. He leaned backwards and began to move. Michael screeched in horror.

'Do not paddle away from the walls! The water is deeper in the middle than at the sides.'

Bartholomew coughed. 'It makes no difference when we cannot touch the bottom at either place. I think I can keep going longer this way than by staying still.'

'But I do not like it!' protested Michael. 'Water is going in my ears.'

'Well, you will just have to put up with it,' said Bartholomew unsympathetically. 'Talk to me. Tell me what happened with Eudo and Boltone.'

'They wanted to kill us. And it was *your* fault. I tried to stop you from interrogating Eudo, because I could see the way it was going to end. He grabbed that hammer as soon as you came close to guessing what had happened to Chesterfelde, and I knew we would be hard pressed to defeat him once he was armed. You should have followed my lead, and . . . Matt, we are going under!'

Bartholomew struggled to lift him. Time was ticking past, and he began to accept that help was not coming after all. The sun started to set, sending orange-red rays across the cistern wall, and he saw it would soon be night. He could not stay afloat much longer, and then he and Michael would be finished. Michael had been right: it was an ignominious way to die, and not one he would have chosen, especially given that he had spent most of his professional life warning people about the dangers of water – the diseases it harboured and the risks associated with swimming. He thought about the body he had found, hoping to distract himself from the agonising ache in his limbs. Had Eudo and Boltone put it there, after they had cut its throat? Or was there another killer?

'You mean in here with us?' asked Michael. 'Who is it?'

With a shock, Bartholomew realised he must have spoken aloud. 'I did not recognise him,' he said, bracing himself for the panicky flailing he was sure was about to begin.

170

'Another of Eudo and Boltone's victims?' Michael showed admirable self-restraint, however, and, although the pincer-like grip on Bartholomew's arm increased, he held himself in check. 'It must have been. They are using this cistern as their personal charnel house.'

Bartholomew barely heard him, although he sensed the monk was talking; the voice was a buzz in the back of his consciousness. Then, just when he thought he was truly doomed and could continue paddling no longer, a silhouette appeared in the rectangle of darkening sky above.

'God's blood!' breathed Tulyet. Dickon stood behind him, still gripping his tiny bow. 'What are you two doing down there?'

Tulyet was a decisive, resourceful man, and it was not long before he had organised the merchants and scholars from Merton Hall to form a rescue team. With the help of a rope, they hauled first Michael, then Bartholomew to safety. Duraunt, too elderly and frail to assist with the physical labour, dropped to his knees and prayed for their well-being, while the three merchants, Spryngheuse and Polmorva managed the heavy work.

By the time Bartholomew and Michael were out of the cistern and on to solid ground again, they were covered in the green ooze that coated the walls. It stank foully, and Polmorva made a point of telling them so, adding as an aside to Bartholomew that only a fool would willingly leap into such a place, no matter how honourable his intentions. He jumped away in alarm when the physician rounded on him with a murderous expression in his eyes.

'There is a bucket,' said Tulyet, thrusting a leather pail at Polmorva with one hand, while he held Bartholomew back with the other. 'Bring water from the river to wash Michael's face. Matt, this is no time for fighting. See to your friend.'

Giving Polmorva one last, furious glower, Bartholomew went to where Michael, exhausted by his ordeal, lay with his eyes closed and an unnatural pallor to his face. The physician was alarmed, seeing the incident had had a more serious effect on him than he had appreciated, and began to consider the unpleasant prospect of a seizure. When Polmorva handed him the bucket, he carefully dribbled water over Michael's cheeks, rubbing away the more stubborn marks with his hand. Wordlessly, he shoved the pail back at Polmorva, indicating he was to fill it a second time. Polmorva obliged, but when he returned, he up-ended the pail over Michael himself. The monk shot upright, spluttering and gagging, while Bartholomew launched himself at Polmorva. This time, Tulyet could not stop him, and he managed to land two solid punches before Polmorva sat down hard on the ground with his legs splayed in front of him. It was a satisfying moment, and Bartholomew was surprised at the depth of feeling that had festered for so many years.

'Enough, Matthew,' said Duraunt, standing between them. Intervention was no longer necessary, though, because Bartholomew's anger had dissipated the moment Polmorva had toppled backwards in an inelegant sprawl. 'He meant no harm.'

'I was trying to help,' said Polmorva resentfully, raising one hand to his split lip. 'And I did. Your friend is sitting up now, having regained his wits. You could have dabbed delicately all night and not had the same effect.'

'I did not want him to leap up like that,' snapped Bartholomew. 'Sudden shocks are bad for the heart after this kind of event, especially in the obese. You might have killed him.'

'Well, I did not,' said Polmorva, gesturing to where Michael was being helped to his feet by the three merchants. They struggled under his immense weight, and at one point he managed to haul all three down on top of him. Tulyet stepped in and offered to show them the method he employed for raising pregnant mares. 'He is perfectly all right.'

'You lied to us, Polmorva,' said Bartholomew, aware that the strain of the last few hours was depriving him of his self-control. 'First, you said you had all slept deeply the night Chesterfelde died, and only later admitted that you had enjoyed some claret. But we have since learned that you were all so intoxicated that the sounds of your merriment could be heard on the far side of the river.'

'*I* was not inebriated,' said Polmorva indignantly.

'Not you, perhaps,' said Bartholomew, deliberately not looking at Spryngheuse. 'But everyone else was. You included.' He rounded on Duraunt.

The elderly Warden was taken aback. 'We had a sip of wine, but we were certainly not drunk!'

Bartholomew did not know whether to believe him. Tulyet was not a man given to exaggeration, but he claimed to have heard the revelry, and Bartholomew knew they were unlikely to have made such a racket had they been sober. So, was Duraunt lying about the amount he had imbibed, and if so, why? To protect his own reputation, or because he did not want Oxford men accused of murder in a rival University town? Meanwhile, Spryngheuse refused to meet his eyes. Was it because he had overstated the extent of their sottishness, or was he was afraid his tale-telling would annoy his colleagues? Or was he simply appalled by the blunt interrogation, since Michael had promised discretion?

'Do not try to pit your meagre wits against killers, Bartholomew,' said Polmorva disdainfully, still fingering his damaged mouth. 'Stay with what you know best – examining urine and lancing boils – and leave the investigation of crime to those who know what they are doing.'

173

'This bitterness between you two must stop,' said Duraunt, stepping forward to take their hands in his own. 'The affair with the Benedictines and the metal teeth is long forgotten, and it is time you ended this ridiculous feud.'

'I have not forgotten it,' said Polmorva frostily. 'He accused me of bringing about a death.'

'But you *did* bring about a death,' argued Bartholomew, equally cold. 'You knew the teeth were making men ill, but you continued to rent them to the greedy and gullible. Had you stopped when I asked, none of those monks would been laid low and the sub-prior would not have died from a surfeit of beef.'

'He ate that of his own free will. Do not blame me for what he did to himself.'

'But you provided him with the means to do it. You knew what was likely to happen, and you should accept some responsibility for the tragedy.'

'The sub-prior was a grown man; he made his own decision.' Polmorva's face was dark and dangerous. 'But there is a question that has been nagging at me for years, and I would like an honest answer: did you steal my fangs after he died? They disappeared, and I was deprived of a valuable source of income. You took them once before – you no doubt recall how I found them on the ground outside your window. Did you make off with them a second time?'

'Of course he did not,' said Duraunt firmly. 'He could not have done.'

'You seem very sure of that,' said Polmorva suspiciously.

'I am – because *I* took them,' said Duraunt. Both men gaped at him. 'Matthew was right: they were a danger to incautious old men. But you were also right: borrowing them conferred great pleasure. So, seeing the conundrum was insoluble, I decided it would be best if they simply ceased to exist. I carried them to the nearest forge, and watched the blacksmith melt them into nothing.'

Polmorva was astounded. 'Why did you not tell me this at the time? I have believed Bartholomew to be a thief for nigh on two decades.'

'Because I was afraid of your temper. But all this happened a long time ago, and it is high time it was set right. Clasp each other's hands, and consign your differences to the past.'

'No,' said Polmorva, dragging his arm away. 'I have endured too many insults, and I am no hypocrite, smiling falsely at men I hate. But tend your fat friend, physician. He is reeling like a drunkard. Perhaps *that* is the reason he toppled inside the cistern, and this claim about bowmen and hammers is the invention of an intoxicated mind.'

Bartholomew did not dignify him with an answer. He freed his hand from Duraunt, sorry to see the sadness on the old man's face. Duraunt was right: to continue a youthful argument for twenty years was foolish, but even setting eyes on Polmorva reminded Bartholomew of how much he had despised the fellow and his selfish schemes, and he discovered he was equally unforgiving. The strength of the emotion surprised him; he had not known he was the kind to bear grudges.

'Eudo?' muttered Michael, glancing around as if he imagined the tenant might still be lurking. He clutched Eu for support, making the man gasp and sway under the weight. Wormynghalle chuckled as Eu's legs began to buckle, and it was left to Abergavenny to try to relieve his beleaguered colleague. 'And that slippery Boltone? Where did they go?'

'Well away from *this* town, if they know what is good for them,' said Tulyet grimly. 'Your beadles will be after their blood for what they did to you, while my soldiers do not take kindly to men being left to drown in cisterns, either – not even scholars.'

'That is comforting,' said Michael. He reached out and seized the sniggering Wormynghalle when he found Eu unequal to the task of supporting him, snagging the ugly sheep's head pendant as he did so. The amusement disappeared from the tanner's face as he tried to prise it free.

'I kill him,' said Dickon, brandishing his bow in happy satisfaction.

'You took a long time to do what I asked,' said Bartholomew, somewhat ungraciously, since the boy had saved his life.

'That was not his fault,' said Tulyet defensively. 'He came long before dusk to tell me what he had seen, but I did not believe him. Only the fact that he refused to sleep until we had visited the cistern together brought me here.' He raised his hands. 'You must admit it sounds unlikely – you two playing a game with Eudo, which culminated in a leap down the well.'

'I kill him,' repeated Dickon with unseemly relish, leaving Bartholomew in no doubt as to what *he* considered the highlight of the whole affair.

'Did he?' asked Tulyet in a low voice. He had ordered lamps brought from the hall, and had been inspecting the ground while Michael recovered. 'Only there is a lot of blood here.'

'That is probably Chesterfelde's,' said Bartholomew. 'And perhaps some of it belongs to whoever else is in the pit.'

'The man you did not recognise,' mused Tulyet. 'How long has the body been down there, do you think? A day? A week? A year?'

'Not a day and not a year,' said Bartholomew. 'Somewhere in between.'

'Can you not be more specific?' asked Michael, releasing

the merchants and standing unaided at last. They backed away fast, to make sure they were not manhandled a second time. 'People often go missing, and I do not want to trawl through a year's reports to identify him. Neither will Dick.'

'Pull him out, and I will try to narrow it down,' offered Bartholomew. 'I only glimpsed him for a moment, but he may yield more information after a proper examination.'

'I suppose I can arrange for the well to be drained,' said Tulyet unenthusiastically. 'Not tomorrow – I am too busy with preparations for the Visitation – but perhaps the day after.'

'I kill him,' insisted Dickon, determined to have their attention and stamping his small foot to get it. 'He kill one man, so I kill him. Like my father.'

Bartholomew frowned, wondering whether from the vantage point of the wall the boy had witnessed other acts of violence. 'What exactly did you see, Dickon?'

'I saw him kill,' replied Dickon impatiently, as though Bartholomew had not been paying proper attention. 'And I kill him.'

'When?' pressed Bartholomew, aware that Tulyet was more anxious than ever. He imagined it would not be pleasant to have an infant son so eager to commit murder with his toys. 'Today? When you saw those two men fighting with Michael and me?'

'No,' said Dickon, as if it were obvious. 'When I played with my dog.'

'Before yesterday, then,' said Tulyet. 'That was when his dog died.'

'The dog *died*?' repeated Bartholomew uneasily. 'Did he shoot it?'

'He says not,' said Tulyet. He grasped another solution like a drowning man with a straw. 'Eudo must have done it, intending to aim at Dickon! Lord! What kind of man shoots at a child?'

'One whom that child is attacking,' suggested Bartholomew. He had seen for himself that Dickon was a fair shot, so it was entirely possible he had honed his skills on people.

Tulyet knelt next to his son. 'This is important, Dickon. What did you see?'

'The big one has blue eyes and a little knife. He was splashing in the water. Pow!'

'He means Eudo,' surmised Michael. 'Eudo is tall with blue eyes. And Eudo's victim must be the body in the cistern, not Chesterfelde, because Chesterfelde was never in the water. If he had been, he would have been left there, not fished out and dumped in the hall.'

'I kill *him*!' insisted Dickon, stamping his foot again when the adults insisted on ignoring him.

'Who?' asked Tulyet, becoming exasperated. 'The man with the blue eyes?'

Dickon nodded proudly, and Tulyet looked troubled.

'He did shoot Eudo,' acknowledged Bartholomew. 'He wounded him, but not seriously, although it was enough to make him think he was under attack by beadles.'

'God save us,' muttered Tulyet, rubbing his eyes. 'I have told him never to shoot at people, but the moment he disobeys me, he saves the life of two friends. And he knows it. He thinks he has done the right thing. What shall I do?'

Bartholomew had no answer, and was grateful the child was not his to mould into a sane and law-abiding adult. He considered Paxtone's contention that Tulyet was not Dickon's father – that the Devil had had something to do with it – and began to think his colleague might be right.

'You should go home,' said Abergavenny, indicating the slime adhering to the scholars' clothes. 'If you hang around smelling like that, you will have half the dogs in the county slathering after you.'

178

'That is good advice,' said Duraunt. 'It is chilly, so you can borrow my cloak and . . .' He looked around for a suitable candidate '. . . and Polmorva's to keep you warm until you reach your rooms.'

'Not mine,' objected Polmorva. 'I do not want it smelling like a latrine, thank you.'

'You can buy another,' said Spryngheuse. 'Give it to them.'

Polmorva's expression was disdainful. 'If I lent it to Bartholomew, it would come back ruined. I remember how he treated his clothes in Oxford, and he has not changed.'

Spryngheuse removed his own, with its hem of coarse grey fur. 'Take mine, then. We are not all uncharitable, and I am happy to be of service to the men who will catch Roger de Chesterfelde's killer.'

Reluctantly, Michael stripped off his filthy habit, revealing baggy silken underclothes that would have had most of the women in the town green with envy; he was a man who knew how to cater to his earthly comforts. They, too, were stained, but he declined to remove them, despite Bartholomew's assurances that no one was very interested in what lay beneath.

'He will make an exception for the occasional whore, I imagine,' Bartholomew heard Polmorva mutter to Eu. 'I do not see a fellow like *that* depriving himself when the mood so takes him.'

Bartholomew set a cracking pace through the darkening streets to Michaelhouse, and when he arrived, he led Michael straight to the lavatorium, a sturdy structure behind the stables. It comprised woven twig walls, a thatched roof, and a stone floor inlaid with drains. Thick beams supported suspended leather buckets that contained water, so that bathers could stand under a trickle of water while they washed. An oversized hearth in the

179

middle of the shed not only supplied warmth on winter days, but allowed water to be heated, too.

Bartholomew decided vigorous scrubbing was the only way to deal with the unpleasant aroma that clung to him, and for some time his Welsh book-bearer Cynric was occupied with stoking up the blaze and fetching pail after pail of water from the well. The night porter, amused by the notion of two Fellows trapped in a well, repeated the tale to anyone who would listen, and it was not long before Michael had an audience of scholars and servants, eager to hear the details of his latest daring encounter with dangerous criminals. Even Agatha was present, despite the fact that the lavatorium was strictly out of bounds to the College's only female employee. She stood with her powerful hands on her hips, shaking her head in disapproval of the attack, and even Master Langelee was not brave enough to point out that she should not be there.

'Please, Brother,' urged Suttone. He was fond of a good story, especially one that might be adapted to fit with his predictions about the return of the plague – and what better example of human depravity than the attempted murder of two University officials? 'Tell us again how you came to be hurled into the cistern, and how you spent hours whispering words of encouragement to Bartholomew, to keep him swimming.'

'Go away,' ordered Michael imperiously. The massive silken under-tunic concealed most of his bulk, leaving only a pair of sturdy white calves for the curious to view. 'All of you. A man's ablutions are his own affair, and not to be carried out in front of a crowd.'

'We are here to make sure you do them properly,' said Agatha. 'After all, *I* am the expert on washing things around here.' She raised her chin and gazed around challengingly, and no one had the courage to point out that her expertise was limited to their clothes, and that their

180

persons were entirely outside her jurisdiction. She took a step towards him.

'Stay back, madam,' shrieked Michael, clutching a piece of sacking to his chin like a reluctant maiden on her wedding night.

'You have nothing I have not seen a thousand times before,' said Agatha contemptuously. 'Besides, I like men with a bit of meat on them, not skin and bone like you.'

There were a number of awed glances, as scholars and servants alike contemplated the kind of suitor favoured by Agatha, if Michael was 'skin and bone' by comparison. Bartholomew's imagination reeled, and he found himself reviewing the medical problems that would be associated with such elephantine proportions.

'She must like them immobile,' he heard Deynman whisper to his friend Falmeresham. 'Brother Michael is so fat he can barely walk, so anyone bigger must be unable to move at all.'

'Probably so they cannot escape,' Falmeresham whispered back. 'Poor bastards!'

'I do not care how you like them, madam,' snapped Michael haughtily. He glared at Deynman. 'And I am *not* fat; I just have big bones. But I am not going to wash with you watching me like cats with a mouse. Go away, or I shall fine the lot of you for . . . for pestering.'

'Pestering,' mused Bartholomew. 'That sounds a useful charge for a Senior Proctor's armoury.'

Deeply disappointed that they were to be deprived of an evening's entertainment, the onlookers drifted away, speculating about what might have happened to culminate in Michael falling inside a cistern. Bartholomew heard Suttone suggesting to William that Oxford men might have orchestrated the attack, and closed his eyes wearily, suspecting that William would repeat this as fact, and it would not be long before gossips like Weasenham the stationer began to spread the rumour. He hoped it would not result in Cambridge scholars accusing their Oxford rivals of trying to spoil their attempts to impress the Archbishop, sure it would be the first step in a violent altercation if they did. Polmorva would not pass up an opportunity to exchange inflammatory remarks, and then the situation would spiral out of control, just as it had done on St Scholastica's Day. Soon everyone had gone except Langelee and Cynric, who were stoking up the fire. And Agatha.

'You, too, madam,' said Michael coolly. 'I cannot do anything with a woman gazing at me.'

'I am here to help,' Agatha declared, waving a bag of lavender. 'I do not want my scholars smelling like latrines – imagine what *that* would do for my reputation as laundress.'

'My cloak desperately needs your attention,' intervened Langelee diplomatically, removing the garment and handing it to her. It was a handsome thing, with rabbit fur around the neck. 'Would you be so kind? The sooner you wash it, the sooner I can have it back.'

'It is grimy,' agreed Agatha, inspecting it. She yawned, to make the point that Langelee was asking her to work rather late that evening. Then she left, making for the area behind the kitchens where she usually pummelled the life out of the scholars' clothes. Michael tiptoed to the door and peered around it, to make sure she had gone. Satisfied she was not lurking in the shadows, longing for a glimpse of his flabby nakedness, he returned to his hot water.

'Use this,' said Langelee, proffering a block of hard fat that was strongly scented with mint and rosemary. 'It can disguise the most rank of odours. Chancellor Tynkell gave it to me.'

'Then it does not work,' said Bartholomew, declining to

take it. 'Besides, I do not want to "disguise" the smell. I want it gone.'

Prudishly, Michael retreated behind a screen before divesting himself of his under-tunic, then began to smear the bar all over himself, flapping and splashing like a beached whale, so Langelee was obliged to retreat or risk being soaked.

'I had the pleasure of speaking Welsh today,' said Cynric as he brought more water for the monk to fling around. It was the first civil word he had spoken to Bartholomew for two weeks. He was hurt and indignant that his master should visit Matilde at night, and risk moving around the dark streets without an escort. Cynric prided himself on his skill with stealth, and resented the fact that he was ordered to remain at home when he felt his role was that of nocturnal protector.

'With whom?' asked Bartholomew, dunking his head and repelled by the slime that still rinsed from his hair. 'Warden Powys of King's Hall?'

'William of Abergavenny, a visiting merchant from Oxford,' replied Cynric, hurling a bucket of water at Bartholomew before he was ready and making him splutter. 'We met when I was your book-bearer in Oxford some twenty years ago, although I did not expect to see him here. We recognised each other in the King's Head this afternoon.'

'That villain,' said Michael disapprovingly. 'He is travelling with a spicer and a tanner, but *he* is the one I regard as the most dangerous.'

'You are probably right,' said Cynric. 'He has a cunning mind, make no mistake about it. It comes from living among the English for so long.'

'Did he tell you anything about the case he is here to investigate?' asked Bartholomew. He did not point out that Cynric also spent a lot of time in England.

Cynric grinned. 'He cannot keep secrets from an old countryman like me. He was glad to be speaking the tongue of princes, you see, and barely stopped talking the whole time we were together. He is here to look into the murder of a merchant called Gonerby, who died during the Oxford riots.'

'That is no secret,' said Michael. 'He and his friends have been quite open about what they came here to do.'

'The secret is this,' said Cynric, enjoying the fact that he had information Michael did not. 'This Gonerby died not from a sword wound, as the tanner told you, but from a bite. They lied about what caused his death.'

'A bite?' asked Bartholomew. 'From a dog?'

'No,' said Cynric. 'Because then Abergavenny would have had an easy task in solving the murder: just find a man with a vicious pet. But no dog killed Gonerby. The bite was inflicted by a devil in the guise of a man: Gonerby's throat was torn out.'

Bartholomew gazed at his book-bearer in horror, while Langelee started to laugh at such a ludicrous notion. Michael paused in his scrubbing to regard Cynric sceptically.

'Someone *bit* Gonerby to death? But that is not possible! Is it, Matt?'

'Apparently, it is,' said Cynric stiffly, not liking the way his information was being received by the scholars, and replying before Bartholomew could speak. 'He was bitten in the throat, which severed some important vessel. He bled to death.'

'Can this be true?' asked Michael, turning to Bartholomew. 'Can a human bite kill like that?'

'Possibly,' replied Bartholomew, his thoughts tumbling in chaos. Michael regarded him oddly before turning his attention back to the book-bearer.

'How does Abergavenny know this? Were there tooth marks on Gonerby's neck? Did someone actually see what happened?'

'Both, apparently,' said Cynric. He looked pleased, gratified that Michael was sufficiently intrigued to ask questions. 'Abergavenny saw the rips himself, and said they matched those of a person's teeth in all respects. He said the wound was a terrible thing to behold.'

'I can imagine,' said Michael dryly, but still unconvinced. 'Who is the witness? Not Abergavenny, or he would have told us, surely?'

'Would he?' queried Langelee. 'He lied to you about how Gonerby died, so why would he confess that he had witnessed the murder? If it is true, then he will not want to bray it about, lest he become this maniac's next victim.'

'Nonsense,' said Michael. He regarded Bartholomew's pale face and haunted expression with raised eyebrows. 'Do not tell me *you* believe this ridiculous tale? It is a fabrication invented by these merchants to lend credibility to the hunt for their colleague's murderer. And do not forget where Cynric heard this tale: the King's Head, a tavern noted for the strength of its ale.'

'Abergavenny *was* a tad drunk when he confided in me,' admitted Cynric. He glared at Michael. 'But he did not relate his story salaciously, as he would have done had his intention been to shock or frighten. On the contrary, boy, he seemed shocked and frightened himself.'

'Then his witness – the man who saw this attack – must be a talented story-teller,' said Michael. 'He has ensured his account is terrifyingly macabre, even when it is repeated by others. It did not originate with Gonerby's wife, did it? She might have invented a wild fable to ensure her husband's friends really do track down his killer.'

'The witness was Polmorva,' said Cynric with satisfaction,

delighted when he saw the scholars' surprise. 'That is why he is here.'

Bartholomew gazed at him, facts and theories ricocheting about inside his mind like acrobats. None of them made sense, and he could not have reasoned a pattern into them to save his life. Michael remained dismissive, however.

'But Polmorva told us he came to escape the dangers of Oxford. And I have no reason to disbelieve him – he seems a cowardly sort of man.'

'He is,' agreed Cynric. 'He has not changed during the two decades since we last met.'

'He is also a liar,' mused Langelee. 'I heard him dissembling myself, in the stationer's shop last week. He told Weasenham that a pen he had recently bought was defective, and demanded two in return, to compensate for the inconvenience it had caused him. But I saw him break the thing himself. Weasenham obliged, of course, because Polmorva started speaking loudly about the poor quality of the goods on sale in Cambridge, and Weasenham wanted to silence him before he lost customers.'

'He cannot help himself,' said Cynric. He addressed Bartholomew. 'Remember when he told Duraunt that you spent the night with a prostitute? He knew full well that the miller's daughter was no whore, yet he landed you in a good deal of trouble with that falsehood. Then there was the time—'

'Thank you, Cynric,' interrupted Bartholomew. 'Suffice to say that he lies as easily as he breathes, and it does not surprise me to learn he has another purpose in coming here. However, I suspect he has concealed his real intentions from Duraunt.'

'Duraunt,' said Michael, winking at the book-bearer to indicate he would have the story of the miller's daughter later. 'He is not the saint you imagine, Matt.

186

First, there is the business about him being drunk to the point of oblivion when Chesterfelde died – and then denying it; second, there is the business of the poppy juice; and third there is his friendship with Polmorva, a known deceiver.'

'Duraunt is a good man,' insisted Bartholomew. 'He was kind to me in Oxford, and—'

'That was years ago,' interrupted Langelee. 'Men change, and not always for the better. But Duraunt *does* drink heavily, as it happens. I saw him myself in the Cardinal's Cap on Sunday, putting away enough strong claret to render half of Michaelhouse insensible.'

'No!' cried Bartholomew, dismayed. 'He encourages abstinence and moderation.'

'Then he does not practise what he preaches,' replied Langelee. 'I know what I saw, Bartholomew, and I have no reason to mislead you. Your old Warden is not the man you remember.'

'How did Polmorva come to be a witness to Gonerby's death?' asked Michael, changing the subject when Bartholomew fell silent. The physician could hardly point out that the Master tended not to stint himself when it came to alcoholic beverages, either, and that large quantities of ale might have coloured his own perception of what he thought he had seen in the Cardinal's Cap. 'Cynric?'

'Abergavenny said Polmorva was out with his sword during the unrest, intending to add to the mischief. Polmorva always did like a riot – remember how he was always first on the streets when the bells sounded the alarm? Anyway, he found himself in an area controlled by townsmen, rather than scholars, so decided to hide until it was safe to come out. It was then, as he peered through the window to assess the situation, that he saw this devil approach Gonerby and bite out his throat.'

'And Gonerby let him do it?' asked Michael archly. 'Polmorva did not try to intervene?'

Cynric shrugged. 'I only repeat what Abergavenny said. I had to loosen his tongue with a fair amount of ale before he confided that much in me, but it was worth the expense. It will make an excellent tale for Christmas, when we sit by the fire and frighten each other with accounts of demons and their evil doings.'

'It was a demon who inflicted this fatal wound, was it?' asked Michael, rubbing his thin, brown hair with a piece of sacking to dry it. 'Not a person?'

'Of course,' said Cynric, who was always matter-of-fact where diabolical powers were concerned. Bartholomew was sure he believed far more strongly in the wicked potency of Satan than he did in the good teachings of the Church. 'No sane fellow eats the neck of another person, so it must have been a fiend – one who looks like a man. And he fled here, to Cambridge, to escape justice.'

'Does Abergavenny know where to find this creature?' asked Michael, more concerned that such a mission might result in civil disorder than by the prospect of confronting a supernatural foe. No townsman would stand idle on hearing the news that there was a demon at the University who liked to chew people's throats, while masters and students would fight to prove their school's innocence.

'He knows he must look among the scholars,' said Cynric. 'He and his friends were in the King's Head again today, asking after any students who have arrived here since February. They also enquired whether there have been any peculiar deaths or injuries recently.'

'The man in the cistern,' said Michael to Bartholomew. 'You said he had a wound in his throat. Could that have been caused by a bite?'

'I do not know,' replied Bartholomew unhappily. 'It might have been.'

'We shall know soon enough,' said Michael, donning clean clothes and stepping out from behind his screen a new man. 'Dick promised to dredge the well, and we shall see what emerges. This case has suddenly turned nasty, but there is nothing more we can do tonight, and I am tired. We shall interview the merchants tomorrow and demand to know why they misled us about Gonerby's death. And we shall have words with Polmorva, too. I detest a liar, and he has told more than his share.'

'And Duraunt,' suggested Langelee. 'Do not omit him from your enquiries just because Matt says he was pleasant, kind and abstemious twenty years ago.'

That night, Bartholomew lay on his bed and watched the stars through the open window, thinking about Chesterfelde, Gonerby and the body in the cistern. Were the three deaths connected, or were they independent examples of human violence? He considered the various questions that had arisen since he had inspected Chesterfelde.

First, and most disturbing, was Duraunt and his relationship to Polmorva. When Bartholomew had been a student, Duraunt had defended him many times against his rival, but now Duraunt and Polmorva were friends – or, if not friends, then allies – and Duraunt was happy to allow him to stay in Merton property. Why? Was Polmorva blackmailing Duraunt, perhaps about his drinking or weakness for soporifics? Or was there genuine affection between the two that had flourished after Bartholomew had left? And what was Polmorva's purpose in visiting Cambridge? To escape Oxford's unrest, as he claimed, or because he was witness to the very murder the merchants had come to solve? If the latter was true, then did it mean Duraunt was also involved in Gonerby's death, and his decision to confront Boltone about dishonest accounting was incidental?

Mention of the bailiff brought other questions surging into his mind. The fact that Boltone and Eudo had been working near a cistern that contained a corpse was an odd coincidence, and Bartholomew was fairly sure, from the amount of blood at the pit, that Chesterfelde had died there. The stains had not come from the unidentified body, because that had been dead for much longer, and recent rains would have washed away any remaining spillage. There was also the curious fact that Chesterfelde and Eudo both had wounds on their arms. Eudo attributed his to staggering home from a tavern, while Chesterfelde was alleged to have been drunk. Did *that* hold any significance, or did it just mean a lot of powerful drink had been imbibed that night?

Bartholomew considered Chesterfelde further. He and Spryngheuse were accredited with starting the St Scholastica's Day riot, although Spryngheuse denied the charge. Was it possible the unrest had been deliberately engineered, to create an opportunity for Gonerby to be bitten? But then why had the affair come to Cambridge? Were the merchants right, and the killer was a Cambridge scholar? Or was he an Oxford man who had fled to Cambridge to escape the hue and cry after Gonerby's murder? Or was he from neither university, and his intention was to strike at both institutions? Not everyone thought scholarship was a good thing, and some folk believed it had been academic probing of matters best left to God that had encouraged Him to send the plague.

Bites. Bartholomew closed his eyes and hoped with all his heart that what Abergavenny had told Cynric was wrong. He recalled the gaping wound in the throat of the corpse in the cistern and knew it could have been caused by something tearing at it – including teeth. He wished he could have confided in Michael, but he had sworn to keep his silence, and so was condemned to struggle with his fears alone; he dared not even discuss them with Matilde. He thought about her, and smiled despite his agitation, then eased quietly off the bed, hoping his colleagues were asleep so he could leave without awkward interrogations. Lights burned in the chamber where William lived, so he forced himself to wait until they were doused. Of all the Fellows, William would be the one to issue a direct challenge if he caught someone leaving in the middle of the night, and the physician was far too tired to prevaricate convincingly.

Eventually, all candles were extinguished, and he left with the liripipe wrapped inexpertly around his head in the hope that the ruse devised by his sister would work. It was drizzling and, since his own cloak was being laundered, he donned Spryngheuse's instead, hoping the Merton man would not mind. He crept through the sleeping College and slipped out through the orchard door, careful to leave it unlocked, although he predicted he would find it barred from the inside by the time he returned.

He trotted along the empty streets to the Jewry, ducking into doorways in a feeble attempt at stealth. He saw no one watching him, but was painfully aware that his wits were dulled from exhaustion. His best hope was that the hated liripipe would do its work. It was scratchy, restrictive and uncomfortable, and he determined that if anyone recognised him that night he would never wear the thing again.

At last he reached Matilde's house, where he knocked softly. The door opened almost immediately, indicating she had been waiting for him. He stepped inside, then saw who was sitting on the bench near the hearth.

'Good evening, Matt,' said Michael, sipping from a goblet of wine. His eyes were irresistibly drawn upwards. 'Nice hat.'

*　*　*

'You could have trusted me,' said Michael reproachfully, as he sat with Bartholomew and Matilde in her tiny house later that night. They had spent at least three hours talking softly, ironing out all the misunderstandings that had accrued over the last fortnight. Bartholomew was indescribably relieved, and felt as if a great burden was lifted from his shoulders. Some of his tiredness began to dissipate, too, and he realised his nocturnal duties had placed him under more strain than he had appreciated.

'It was not my decision to make,' he replied, sipping the wine Matilde had poured him. It was sweet and pale, and he felt it warming him through to the stomach.

'It was bad enough placing Matthew in such an awkward position,' explained Matilde. 'I could not justify doing it to you, as well. You are a monk, and it would do your reputation no good at all to be seen coming out of my house at questionable hours.'

'It has not done much for his, either,' Michael pointed out. 'I bullied the Weasenhams into silence, but it is like using a twig to dam a river. The rumours are rife, and his refusal to deny them has made tongues wag all the harder.'

'We shall have to concoct an explanation that will restore our good names when this is over,' said Matilde unhappily. 'Folk respect Matthew, and will not believe ill of him for long.'

'People are fickle,' countered Michael. 'They may well like him, but that will not stop them from turning on him like wild animals, if properly incited.' He saw his friends wince at his choice of similes, and spread his hands in apology.

'How is our patient?' asked Matilde, indicating the upper chamber of her house with a nod of her head. 'You said last night that you thought he might be on the mend, Matthew.'

'His fever has lessened, and the wound does not burn so fiercely. I think he will survive now.'

Matilde heaved a sigh of relief. 'Thank God! I do not know what we would have done if he had died. We would have gone to the gallows.'

'You took a great risk,' agreed Michael. 'Especially to help someone like Doctor Rougham. He would not have done the same for you, Matt. On the contrary: he would have used the situation as an excuse to cause you as much damage as possible.'

'I am not doing it for him,' said Bartholomew. He looked at Matilde and his bleak expression softened with affection. She smiled back, but sadly, and it did not touch her eyes. Michael watched the exchange with frank curiosity, but kept his thoughts to himself.

'How did you guess what was going on?' Matilde asked the monk, twisting her empty goblet through restless fingers. 'Why did you not believe Matthew was enjoying the company of a harlot every night, as everyone else seems to have done?' Her voice was bitter.

'You cannot blame them,' said Michael reasonably. 'You must see how it looks for a man to slink away in the dark and visit you – Mistress of the Guild of Frail Sisters – night after night.'

Matilde shook her head, and the monk was startled to see the sparkle of tears. She was exhausted, and the relief of sharing her burden was almost too much to bear. Her voice was angry as she embarked on a sudden and uncharacteristic outburst. 'It is not fair! I was awarded my dubious reputation the moment I set foot in this town, although I did little to deserve it. I admit, I accepted the occasional man into my chambers at first – if he could afford my fees – but they were infrequent. Do you know that no man has secured my favours for more than two years now? I am as chaste as you are, Brother.'

Bartholomew stared into the fire, thinking that she might have chosen a better example of chastity than the fat monk. However, he was certain she was telling the truth about her own situation; she had mentioned several times of late that her days of frolicking with wealthy patrons were over.

'They jump to those conclusions because of your association with whores,' said Michael gently. 'You cannot stand up for their rights and expect not to be connected with what they do.'

Matilde was distressed. 'When I first came here, I thought it was amusing to be the subject of such exotic tales. But those things are for younger women, and now I am older, I crave respectability – I want an end to all this merry chatter. But this business with Rougham has done damage I fear will prove irreparable.'

Bartholomew watched the flames devour a log, destroying it slowly but inexorably, just as the town's gossip was doing to Matilde's chances of earning respect. She would never have it, no matter how long she remained in Cambridge, playing the role of an upright and moral woman. It was simply more interesting for people to believe otherwise, and he knew they would do so for the rest of her life. Her only recourse was to move away, but he hoped she would not. However, if she did want to leave, he decided to go with her, prepared to give up his life as a scholar for the woman he loved so deeply. He felt an urge to ask her to marry him there and then, but an uncomfortable shyness suddenly assailed him, and he knew he could not broach the subject when Michael was present.

'How did you guess, Brother?' he asked instead, dragging his thoughts away from a future with Matilde, and grateful that at least he would not have to lie to Michael any more. The monk was astute, and it had been difficult trying to mislead him.

'Through a few clues here and there, and a good deal

of cleverness,' said Michael, pleased with himself. 'But I put the last pieces of the puzzle together when Cynric told that outrageous story about Gonerby being killed by a bite. You were appalled, but not surprised. While I argued with Cynric that it is impossible to die in such a manner, you remained suspiciously silent. And you are not usually mute about such matters.'

'You mean on methods of killing?' asked Matilde, regarding Bartholomew uneasily.

'On anything to do with physiology. I had to ask him direct questions about these bites, whereas normally he would have volunteered the information in tedious detail. Also, he had mentioned a throat wound in the body in the cistern, but it was left to me to make the connection between that and Gonerby. He is not often slow to see such associations, and his reaction sent me a clear message: he had encountered such an injury before.'

'But how did you go from that to me?' asked Matilde.

Michael shrugged. 'It was obvious once I thought about it. I have been nagging him about his visits here for days, and I sensed there was more to them than romping in your attic. Nor is he a man to put personal enjoyment before the reputation of a lady, especially one he adores. Therefore, I reasoned that it was not you he was here to see, but someone else. A patient.'

'How did you guess it was Rougham?' asked Bartholomew, acutely aware of Matilde's flush of pleasure that accompanied Michael's words.

Michael smiled ruefully. 'I did not. He was the *last* person I expected to discover! But tell me again what happened.' He raised a hand when Bartholomew started to object. 'I know you swore never to reveal his secret, but I already know the essence of this tale, so it cannot harm to fill in the details. And I may be able to help. You two have aroused so much suspicion that you will be hard-pressed to remove him from this house without being seen. You will need my assistance.'

'He will not like it,' warned Matilde. 'He almost died before I persuaded him to summon Matthew, and he made us both swear, on our lives, that we would keep his story secret.'

'I do not care,' said Michael harshly. 'The man has been responsible for harming – perhaps permanently – two of my friends. I do not care what he likes or dislikes. And, what is more important, he is lucky I do not storm up to his sickbed and fine him for dallying with loose women.'

A weak knock sounded through the ceiling. 'There he is again,' said Matilde wearily. 'I thought you said he was better.'

'He is – and that will be the problem from now on,' replied Bartholomew. 'He is well enough to make demands. The sooner we take him to Gonville the better. Then his colleagues can tend him.'

'I am exhausted,' said Matilde, leaning against the wall and closing her eyes. 'You see to him, Matthew. I shall need all my strength to deal with him again tomorrow.'

'Now I understand why you refused to let me visit her,' said Michael softly. 'You knew she would either be sleeping or wrestling with Rougham's care.'

'His illness has been severe, and he has needed someone with him almost every moment for the past two weeks. We agreed that Matilde would tend him from dawn until I was able to escape at night, and I would care for him during the hours of darkness – I could not come during the day, not without affecting my teaching and other patients. And there was you to consider: you would have been suspicious, had I started to visit her at the expense of my other duties.'

'True,' acknowledged Michael. 'But this affair has worn both of you to the bone.'

Bartholomew grinned wryly. 'Weasenham and other like-minded men have assumed our exhaustion is due to energy expended on each other, but the truth is that we have been so weary that we can barely exchange greetings. Frolicking in any form has been out of the question.'

'Damn Rougham,' snapped Michael angrily. 'He does not know what he has done.'

'Come with me,' said Bartholomew, when he saw Matilde was sleeping. Tenderly, he covered her with a blanket, and led the way upstairs. 'Rougham can tell you his tale himself.'

Michael followed him to the upper room in Matilde's attractive home. A bed filled most of the chamber, loaded with furs and cushions. A man lay among them, his eyes bright with ill health and his face flushed. His breathing was shallow and rapid, but he seemed alert enough. To Bartholomew, he was dramatically improved; there had been times when he had been certain that his fellow physician would die. Now the fever was receding, and all he needed was to regain his strength with rest and a carefully designed diet.

'There you are,' said Rougham peevishly. 'I have been knocking for hours. You promised there would be someone with me every minute of the day.'

'You no longer need that degree of attention,' said Bartholomew, sitting on the edge of the bed, and holding the man's wrist to assess the rate of his pulse. 'You are on the road to recovery and will be able to go home soon.'

'No!' breathed Rougham. For a moment, Bartholomew thought he was objecting to leaving Matilde, and was about to say that he had imposed himself on her for quite long enough, when he glanced up to see Rougham's eyes fixed on Michael. 'You promised to keep my secret! You have broken your word!'

'He did nothing of the kind,' said Michael sharply. 'And you owe him a good deal. Do you have any idea what

197

coming here every night has cost him? And Matilde, who has been obliged to look after you all day while he teaches, tends his patients, examines corpses for me, and tries to maintain the illusion that nothing is amiss?'

'I will pay them,' said Rougham angrily. 'I am a wealthy man, and reward people for good service and discretion.' He glared at Bartholomew in a way that indicated he felt he had not been given either.

'Gold is not everything,' said Michael sternly. 'And before you abuse the two people who saved your life, let me inform you that they *have* kept their promise. I guessed Matt was coming here to nurse a patient, although I confess I was surprised when I learned it was you – I thought it would be one of the Frail Sisters. How in God's name did you allow yourself to be seduced by a whore?'

There was a pause, during which Rougham regarded Michael in disbelief, scarcely crediting that one man should ask such a question of another. Eventually, he answered. 'Surely even a monk must understand that normal males need women to rebalance their humours? I rebalance mine with Yolande de Blaston every first Monday in the month. It helps to be regular. That is a medical fact.'

'Is it?' Michael asked Bartholomew. The physician shrugged that he did not know, so Michael went back to regarding Rougham with distaste. 'You visit Yolande in her house? Where she lives with her husband and children?'

'Well, I can hardly invite her to Gonville, can I?' snapped Rougham. 'Besides, her family are very accommodating, and I always take marchpanes for the brats. Her husband, meanwhile, is grateful for any money that can go towards feeding them all.'

'That is true,' said Bartholomew, who had known about the Blastons' peculiar marital arrangements for years. Personally, he believed the family would have been a good deal smaller if Yolande's nocturnal enterprises had been

198

curtailed, and was certain very few of her offspring were fathered by the carpenter. But every child was deeply loved, regardless of the fact that several bore uncanny resemblances to prominent townsmen and high-ranking members of the University.

'I always hire her late at night, and tell my colleagues that I am going to see a patient,' Rougham went on. 'It is not unusual for physicians to be called out at odd times, so they never question me.'

'So, did Yolande or one of her family hurt you?' asked Michael, indicating the bandages that swathed the man's shoulder.

'Of course not! I am trying to tell you what happened, but you keep interrupting.' Rougham snapped his fingers at Bartholomew to indicate he was thirsty, and only continued with his tale when watered wine had been brought. 'I was approaching her house for our usual liaison, when I sensed something amiss. Someone was watching me. I could not shake off the feeling, but I had paid Yolande in advance and I was loath to waste my money by going home again; and there was my medical need to consider. I decided to continue with my . . . physic. I knocked on her door, and it was then that the attack occurred. I recall very little about it, other than that it was quick and very vicious.'

'Yolande could not keep a seriously injured man in her house,' elaborated Bartholomew. 'There is no room. So, she and her husband carried him here. The next day Matilde sent for me.'

'It is not a crime to be attacked,' Michael pointed out, puzzled. 'Why did they not take him to Gonville, where he could be nursed by his students?'

Rougham grimaced. 'I am a physician. I know what happens to men in the grip of fevers – and I felt a terrible one coming upon me. I knew I would rant in my delirium, and did not want my colleagues to hear me praising the delights of Yolande de Blaston. Bartholomew and Matilde agreed to treat me here, taking turns to watch over me as the fever peaked.'

'Most charitable,' said Michael dryly. 'But why were they so obliging?'

'Look,' said Rougham, pulling away the bandage to reveal the wound underneath. It was inflamed and raw with marks that were unmistakably the imprints of human teeth. Rougham had been bitten on the shoulder, near his neck. He shuddered as he covered the injury again. 'I had the sense that the man wanted to rip my throat from my body! It was horrible, like being at the mercy of a wild animal.'

'A bite,' said Michael, glancing at Bartholomew. 'That certainly explains why you needed Matt, but not why he agreed to help you – at such cost to himself.'

Rougham closed his eyes. 'Because of *who* attacked me.'

'You cannot know that,' said Bartholomew, and from the tone of his voice, Michael sensed this was something they had argued about before. 'Not for certain. You said you did not see him clearly.'

'I am not a fool,' said Rougham tiredly. 'And there was more than enough evidence to tell me who launched himself from the shrubs, just as I was raising my hand to knock on Yolande's door. It was Clippesby, Michaelhouse's resident madman.'

Michael's jaw dropped open in astonishment. 'Clippesby?'

'It was not him,' argued Bartholomew unhappily. 'Rougham accused him, but Clippesby says someone else is responsible.'

'Clippesby is a lunatic, who thinks animals talk to him,' Rougham pointed out. '*He* claims I was attacked by a giant wolf! Have you ever heard anything more ridiculous? The truth is that he bit me, but he is so deranged that he has convinced himself that someone else is at fault.'

Michael regarded Bartholomew soberly. 'He is addled enough to imagine such a thing, Matt.'

'The man is downright dangerous,' continued Rougham. 'You were right to take him away and lock him up where he can do no more harm.'

After a while, Rougham began to doze, exhausted by the effort of talking. With deft, instinctive movements, Bartholomew bathed his head, and adjusted the covers, so he would not be exposed to draughts. When his breathing became regular with sleep, Michael spoke in a low voice.

'So that is why you have refused to let Clippesby return to Michaelhouse. We thought you were being overly protective of him, but you are afraid he really did harm Rougham.'

'Rougham is often nasty to him, and Clippesby is not so witless that he cannot see when he is being derided. I decided to err on the side of caution. Rougham agreed to say nothing about Clippesby, as long as Matilde and I keep quiet about Yolande.' He gave a soft laugh. 'We even have a written contract to that effect, would you believe? The man was lying in bed with a wound that looked set to prove fatal, and he dictated a legal document! He is incorrigible!'

'And you did all this to protect Clippesby? You know that if Rougham told anyone else what had happened, Clippesby would hang?'

'And to help Matilde. She was kind to Clippesby, and he repaid her by commissioning a silversmith to make her a tiny carving of a dog. Weasenham saw it being crafted, and drew some spiteful conclusions about who would receive it. Rougham had heard these speculations, and spotted the ornament on Matilde's shelf. He said he would not tell Weasenham *she* was the recipient of Clippesby's gift, if we returned the favour by keeping his secret. It was all rather sordid, actually. I would have kept his confidences anyway, and there was no need for him to resort to black-mail.'

Michael sighed. 'What a mess! It is hard to know where the work of evil men ends, and where the work of good men and fools begins.'

'And which am I?'

'A bit of each. That is why Matilde thinks so highly of you.'

Bartholomew smiled. 'Do you think I should marry her?' The question surprised him as much as it did Michael, and he realised exhaustion was making him voluble.

Michael was silent for a long time. 'If you do, you will have to resign your Fellowship and give up your teaching. The University will no longer be open to you, and I will probably not be permitted to keep you as my Corpse Examiner – although I will apply for special dispensation.' He nodded towards the sleeping Rougham. 'He has always envied you that post, and will doubtless try to secure it for himself once he hears you are wed.'

'I will not miss inspecting bodies, but I cannot imagine life with no teaching. However, Matilde is worth the sacri-fice.'

'Do not ask her yet,' advised Michael practically. 'Wait until you have both rested, and then neither of you will make a decision that is influenced by weariness. Marriage is a big step, and should not be taken lightly. But we should not be discussing this with Matilde downstairs; she may wake up and hear us. Tell me about Clippesby, instead. Do you really believe he is innocent?'

Bartholomew stared at the floor. 'You know what he is like about animals. It is not such a huge step from imag-ining they talk to you, to thinking you *are* one – and it is not wholly beyond the realm of possibility that, in a moment of madness, he saw himself as a wolf. I have read about such cases, and once met a man who thought he was a squirrel. He kept his cheeks stuffed with nuts.'

'But this is different,' said Michael. 'And there is more, too. I can see it in your eyes.'

Bartholomew rubbed a hand through his hair, relieved to share his worries at last. 'Clippesby has not remained at Stourbridge since I put him there. He has escaped to wander at least three times – more, if we count that time last February, when he said he had been to visit his father.'

'We did not believe him at the time,' mused Michael, remembering. 'But he returned safe and sound, and we forgot about it. But what is so odd about that? Scholars often disappear without proper permission – look at Hamecotes and Wolf. And Clippesby was not locked away in Stourbridge then, anyway.'

'February,' said Bartholomew significantly. 'You know what happened in February.'

'The St Scholastica's Day riots,' breathed Michael in understanding. 'When Gonerby was bitten to death by a man about to travel to Cambridge. Clippesby was gone for about ten days. Is that enough time to travel to Oxford and back?'

Bartholomew nodded. 'And, since arriving at Stourbridge, Brother Paul tells me he left the precinct once about a week ago and again on Saturday night.'

'Saturday night was when Chesterfelde died,' said Michael, alarmed.

'Yes,' agreed Bartholomew soberly. 'And the body in the cistern looked to have been dead for several days – perhaps a week. I may be able to be more accurate when I examine it properly.'

It occurred to him that there was something horribly untimely about the demise of Okehamptone – the Oxford man who had died from the fever – too. He had perished the night Rougham was attacked, when Clippesby had been out without a credible alibi. Clippesby had even recommended that Michael should review Okehamptone's death, claiming that the Merton Hall geese had been suspicious about it. Bartholomew's nagging unease about the scribe's end was compounded by the fact that Paxtone was supposed to have examined the body, but had actually done no more than pray. He was torn between a desire to know for certain that Okehamptone had died of natural causes, and the fear of discovering teeth marks that would implicate Clippesby in yet another assault.

'But why, Brother?' he asked, declining to load all his concerns on to the monk. '*Why* would Clippesby go all the way to Oxford, bite a man and then come home? It makes no sense.'

'The insane are not bound by the same rules as you and me,' preached Michael. 'You will not understand Clippesby's motives if you think about them until Judgement Day.'

Bartholomew closed his eyes, then opened them again when he felt sleep begin to creep up on him. 'He has never been violent before.'

'That does not mean he will never start. You have often said you know little about ailments that afflict the mind. Who knows what Clippesby might be capable of? And you are clearly worried, or you would not have taken the dramatic precaution of locking him away.'

'I do not know what to think. The fact that I may have incarcerated an innocent man is not a pleasant thought, but neither is the notion of a maniac on the loose. Human bites are dangerous, even when they do not rip vital blood vessels.'

'You did the right thing, Matt. It would be terrible for Michaelhouse – and the University – if the news were to spread that one of our scholars likes to eat other men's throats. The town would rise against us for certain, and it could be the end of us all.'

'And definitely the end of Clippesby. I like him, Brother; I cannot believe he is a killer.'

'I shall reserve judgement. But proving him innocent will not solve *our* problems. If we learn he is not the man who attacked Rougham, Gonerby and the fellow in the cistern, then we shall be obliged to hunt another lunatic with roving teeth – one who has a far more deadly purpose than gnawing on a man who was unkind to him.'

'Perhaps these deaths are unrelated,' suggested Bartholomew hopefully. 'It is a pity Chesterfelde is buried. I feel I should assess him again, to see whether I missed tooth marks on his body.'

'He is not buried,' said Michael. 'The Franciscans initiated some tiresome theological wrangle over whether a man from a city under interdict can be placed in holy ground elsewhere, and the visitors from Merton are still awaiting the outcome. You *can* examine him, if you think you should.'

'The wound was messy, and I was not looking for teeth marks at the time. It would be useful to know for certain whether they played a role in his demise.'

'We will find out tomorrow. Then we will visit Stourbridge and make sure Clippesby is well secured. If he is guilty, then it can do no harm. If he is innocent, then it will protect him, should this story seep out. How much longer can you keep Rougham here?'

'He is on the mend, thank God, and will be able to return to Gonville in a day or two. He signed that contract, so he will not say anything to damage Clippesby.'

Michael was not so sure. 'As long as he thinks he is the only one Clippesby attacked, he will abide by what he agreed. But what happens when he learns about Gonerby and the man in the cistern? He will be afraid the killer might try to harm him again – to finish what he started – and will speak out, just to make sure his colleagues afford him an appropriate level of protection. It will not be many days before Clippesby is exposed. You must keep Rougham here for as long as possible, so he cannot hear town gossip.'

'I cannot, Brother. He is a physician and knows how to read the state of his own health.'

'Then you will have to bring about a relapse,' said Michael seriously.

Bartholomew regarded him in disbelief. 'There are laws against that kind of thing, not to mention issues of professional misconduct. I will not make a patient ill.'

'Then you may find you have even more victims to tend,' warned Michael. 'I sense we are on the verge of civil unrest that may see the University and its scholars gone from this town for ever. Look at Oxford. Do you want us under interdict, too? You may pray for Rougham's recovery, but I shall put in a request for a lingering convalescence!'

CHAPTER 6

Despite Michael's prayers, Rougham slept well that night. Bartholomew knew his colleague would remain weak for a day or two, and Matilde agreed to tend him for a while longer, although it was clear the prospect did not appeal in the slightest. She was relieved that Bartholomew was no longer obliged to spend his nights nursing the man, but was still concerned for his reputation and her own. Bartholomew thought it was far too late to worry – the damage had been done – and only hoped Clippesby was innocent, because he did not like to think he had squandered his good name to protect a guilty man.

Bartholomew and Michael took turns to watch Rougham, so both could rest at least part of the night, and left her house two hours before dawn. Then the physician had the satisfaction of entering Michaelhouse respectably, through the front gate and in company with the Senior Proctor. As if to announce the occasion to the rest of the College, the porter's peacock released several piercing shrieks that had a number of scholars peering through their windows to see what was amiss. Before he retired to his chamber. Bartholomew made a brief detour to the orchard, Michael in tow, and was not surprised to discover the small gate securely barred.

'Who keeps doing this?' he demanded, as he stumbled back through the dark garden towards his room. 'Someone who knows what I am doing for Clippesby, and who wants me to fail?'

'William, perhaps?' pondered Michael. 'Clippesby is a hated Dominican, after all.'

'Or Langelee, because he thinks a student is leaving it open? Or Wynewyk, because he dislikes the notion of any man having dealings with women? Or Suttone, because he believes crimes like fornication will bring back the plague?'

Michael sighed. 'It could even be the porters, doing their duty properly for once, and walking around the College to ensure it is locked. We could wait here one night, I suppose, and catch him. There is no other way to find out, because asking will beg the question of how we know it was left open in the first place.'

'As soon as I have organised my students for the day, I will examine Chesterfelde's body,' said Bartholomew, opening the door to his chamber and rummaging for candle and tinderbox. 'Did you ask Matilde about Eudo and Boltone, by the way? William said they had stolen something from her.'

'We spoke when you were changing the dressing on Rougham's shoulder,' replied Michael, plumping himself down on a stool that creaked under the weight. 'Eudo visited her several days ago, claiming his wife had female pains, and could she spare medicine to ease them. After he had gone, she noticed Clippesby's silver dog was missing, but she says she cannot be sure he was the thief, and declines to make an official complaint.'

'He is not married, although there is no reason for her to know that,' said Bartholomew, speaking softly, so he did not disturb those sleeping in the nearby rooms. 'Do you think he knew Rougham was upstairs, and wanted to learn more about the nature of his injury?'

'You think he has something to do with the murders,' surmised Michael. 'He and Boltone must be involved in something nasty, or they would not have tried to kill us for asking questions. Of course, Eudo may well have a lover, and really did need Matilde's medicine. Men *do* ask her to help with that sort of thing, you know. Those two missing scholars at King's Hall – Hamecotes and Wolf – are just two of many who rely on her for cures for their secret women. She told me so herself.'

Bartholomew grabbed Spryngheuse's cloak, not pleased to hear that the lady he intended to marry was the focus of so much male attention, and made for the door. 'I am restless and need to walk.'

Michael gave a startled laugh. 'You cannot go out now; it is pitch black outside! I do not want it said that Michaelhouse has two insane Fellows – you and Clippesby, both wanderers in the dark.'

'It is too hard to talk here. I am afraid our voices will wake the students sleeping upstairs.'

'You could sleep yourself,' suggested Michael. 'God knows, you need some.'

'My mind is too full of questions. Will you come with me?'

'I will not! Sit down, Matt.'

'I cannot stay here,' insisted Bartholomew, pacing in agitation. An idea occurred to him. 'I will visit St Giles's Church and inspect Chesterfelde. I have a great deal to do today, and it will help if I do not have to find time to examine him, too.'

'In the dead of night?' asked Michael uneasily. 'People will wonder what you are up to.'

'I have done it before – at your instigation, I might add. Besides, I am less likely to be seen now than if I go during daylight. Churches are very public places.'

'Not this one,' said Michael soberly. 'Chesterfelde is not in St Giles's, because its vicar objected over this interdict business. He lies in All-Saints-next-the-Castle.'

'But that has no roof,' said Bartholomew, startled. 'And it has no priest and no parishioners, either – not since the plague took them. Worse, it is sometimes used by folk who think God and His saints abandoned them during the pestilence – witches and the Devil's disciples.'

'I know,' said Michael grimly. 'But St Giles's vicar claimed there would be a display of divine fury if the corpse touched hallowed ground before the issues regarding the interdict are resolved.'

Bartholomew was uncomfortable. 'But that might take months. We shall have to ask the Archbishop for a decision, or Chesterfelde may still be waiting for his grave this time next year.'

'The Archbishop,' said Michael gloomily, following him to the door. 'He is due to arrive in five days, and I am still no closer to catching this killer. My confidence was sadly misplaced, I fear.'

The town was silent in the hour before dawn, always a time of day the physician found unsettling. It was when he lost many dying patients, and when everything seemed unreal – either because he had been up all night, or because he had been forced awake earlier than his body was ready. That morning was no different, and he felt slightly light-headed as he walked.

Michael chattered next to him, trying to establish links between recent events. He said he understood why Clippesby might have attacked Rougham, but saw no reason for him to have killed Chesterfelde and the man in the cistern. He determined that when he next visited Clippesby, he would ask whether the Dominican knew Eudo and Boltone; he was sure they were involved in the mystery, but uncertain as to how.

'And we cannot forget Abergavenny and his associates,' he added. 'If Gonerby did indeed die from a bite, then there is a connection there, too.'

Bartholomew was too tired to fit the facts into a logical pattern, and almost at the point where he did not care. He crossed the deserted Great Bridge and began to stride up Castle Hill, Michael wheezing at his side. It was a steep incline for Cambridge, topped by the brooding mass of the Norman fortress. This was a formidable structure, with a stone tower standing atop a sizeable motte, and sturdy curtain walls that defended its bailey. All Saints stood near its main gate. The church had once been impressive, and had served as castle chapel before a purpose-built one had been raised inside. Then All Saints had been relegated to parish church for those who lived in the nearby hovels. Poverty and dismal living conditions had conspired against these people when the plague had struck, and most had died. With no congregation and no priest, the building had crumbled from neglect. Now, when people referred to All Saints, most folk thought of the grander All-Saints-in-the-Jewry.

In the dark, it looked even more unprepossessing than it did during the day. The roof timbers were cracked and broken, giving its top a jagged, uneven look. Ivy climbed up its walls and seemed the only thing keeping them standing, and the squat tower with its broken battlements was a sinister and forbidding crag against the night sky. Bartholomew inched along the weed-encrusted path that led to the west door, moving slowly so his feet did not catch in the matted undergrowth. Michael followed, swearing when he stumbled and stung himself on nettles.

The physician pushed open a door that hung from broken hinges, and wondered what the Oxford men thought of being provided with an abandoned chapel in which to lay their dead. It was disrespectful, and it occurred to him that one might be so affronted on Chesterfelde's behalf that he might attempt to avenge the insult. Duraunt would not, Bartholomew thought: he would believe prayers would do Chesterfelde more good than fine surroundings, while Polmorva would do nothing that did not benefit him directly. And the others? Bartholomew did not know them well enough to say. He took a deep breath as he stepped through the door and into the black interior.

*   *   *

211

Water dripped in echoing plops, and the entire place stank of mould and rotting wood. The ivy that coated the outer walls had made incursions inward, too, crawling through windows and those parts of the roof that were open to the elements. People had been in to see what they could salvage, and most of the floor had been prised up and spirited away. Paint peeled from the walls, although, when Michael lit a lamp, Bartholomew could still make out some of the images that had been lovingly executed by some long-dead artist. St Paul was recognisable amid a host of faceless cherubs, while the Virgin Mary gazed from the mural over the rood screen.

Bartholomew took the lamp and made his way to the chancel, where he supposed the body of Chesterfelde had been taken. Even in a derelict church, this was the most sacred part, and it had not suffered as badly from looters as had the nave. It still possessed some of its flagstones, and it was on these that the water dripped, sending mournful echoes along the aisles. The altar had been left, too. It was oddly clean, and Bartholomew recalled events from several years before, when he had witnessed acts of witchcraft around it. He supposed the place was still used for devilish purposes, because it was apparent that someone visited regularly – the chancel was relatively free of the debris that littered the nave and there was evidence that candles had been lit. But then, perhaps someone loved All Saints, and performed small acts of devotion to ensure it retained some of its dignity.

Chesterfelde lay on what looked to be a door resting atop a pair of trestles. He was covered by a grey woollen blanket, and a piece of sacking moulded into a cushion near his feet suggested someone had been kneeling there. Since Duraunt was the only priest in the party from Oxford, Bartholomew supposed the crude hassock was to protect his ancient knees.

The body was much as Bartholomew remembered from his examination three days before, although someone had wiped its face and brushed its hair. He had assessed it meticulously the first time, and knew he would learn nothing new by repeating the process. All he wanted to do that morning was study the wrist and see whether he could identify teeth marks.

He peeled back the cover and pushed up Chesterfelde's sleeves. The body's right arm was unmarked, although there were patches of hardened skin around the thumb that were familiar to a physician used to treating scholars. They were writing calluses, caused by the constant chafing of a pen. Then Bartholomew inspected the left wrist. The wound was still there, ragged and open, but it was now washed free of blood.

'If Chesterfelde died near the cistern – and the stains there suggest he did – then someone cleaned him up before taking him to the hall,' he said. 'The only reason for anyone to do such a thing is to mislead those examining the body. I cannot begin to imagine why: it does not matter whether Chesterfelde died from a slash to his arm or a stab in his back. It is murder, regardless.'

'Are you certain the wrist wound killed him? Is it possible he injured himself, but managed to stem the bleeding, and died from some other means? Poison, maybe? Or suffocation?'

'It is possible, but this wound unattended would certainly have brought about his death. Look. You can see the severed blood vessels.'

Michael made a disgusted sound at the back of his throat. 'A simple yes or no would have sufficed, Matt. But what made the injury? Can you tell whether it was teeth?'

'It is ragged,' said Bartholomew, inspecting the gash carefully. 'And longer than it is deep.'

'Meaning?' asked Michael impatiently, uninterested in

213

the mechanics of the damage and wanting only to know what it implied for his investigation.

'Meaning it is a slashing wound, not a stabbing one.'

Michael considered. 'Well, you do not *stab* with your teeth – unless you have long fangs like Warden Powys of King's Hall. You are more likely to slash with them.'

'But not in this case, Brother,' said Bartholomew, straightening up. 'I see no evidence that teeth were used, just some blunt old knife that was in sad need of sharpening.'

'Clippesby did not do it, then?' asked Michael, relieved. 'So, we are back to our original suspects – Eudo and Boltone, and the Oxford men: Polmorva, Spryngheuse, Duraunt and the merchants.'

'Not Duraunt,' pressed Bartholomew doggedly. 'But do not leave Dodenho of King's Hall off your list. He knew Chesterfelde, and he lied about it. And there is that curious business about his silver astrolabe, which was stolen, then found, then appeared at Merton Hall in the tanner's hands.'

'I have not forgotten Dodenho,' said Michael. 'Nor his conveniently missing colleagues, Hamecotes and Wolf. Nor Norton, either, who also admits to knowing Oxford.'

'It is a pity Okehamptone is buried,' said Bartholomew, replacing the sheet over Chesterfelde, and glad that particular task was over. He recalled what Clippesby had said about the scribe's death: that the geese knew more about it than Michael. Was the man spouting nonsense in his deranged state, or was he playing some complex game in which only he knew the rules? 'I would be happier if we knew for certain Clippesby had nothing to do with that, either.'

'Okehamptone died of natural causes,' said Michael, surprised by the comment. 'Paxtone confirmed it – said there was no doubt at all. He even signed a document to that effect, at Polmorva's request, because Polmorva was Okehamptone's designated heir.'

Bartholomew stared at him. 'But Paxtone did not examine the body: he accepted the explanations of the dead man's companions, and he said a few prayers, but that is all. And now you say Polmorva had a strong motive for murdering him? He will inherit all Okehamptone owned?'

Michael's eyes were huge in the gloom. 'Are you saying Okehamptone's death might be suspicious, too?'

'I have no idea, but I doubt you will ever get permission to find out. People do not like disturbing the dead once they have been buried. Damn Weasenham's toothache! If he had not summoned me, I would have been able to examine Okehamptone in the first place.'

Michael scratched his chin. 'Damn indeed. I should have known to look more carefully at a death in which a man like Polmorva was involved. Let us not forget that business about how much wine was swallowed on the night of Chesterfelde's death, either. Spryngheuse said Polmorva drank very little. Perhaps he waited until the others were suitably insensible, and then used the opportunity to rid himself of Chesterfelde, buoyed up by his success with Okehamptone.'

'But why?' asked Bartholomew. 'Even Polmorva would not kill without a motive.'

'Who knows what disagreements they might have had in the past? He has not seen you for twenty years, but his enmity towards you has grown no less intense. For all we know, Okehamptone and Chesterfelde were his rivals, too. We do not know his motive, but that does not mean he does not have one.'

Bartholomew was disgusted. 'So, if Polmorva did kill Okehamptone, then he has got away with it. We will never know whether he killed Chesterfelde, either, because no one will tell us the truth.'

'Not so. There are questions I have yet to ask about Chesterfelde – particularly of Eudo and Boltone. I have sent the reliable and determined Beadle Meadowman to hunt for them, so it is only a matter of time before they are caught. I have not given up on Chesterfelde, believe me. And if Polmorva killed Okehamptone, then he is out of luck, too.'

'What do you mean?'

Michael's eyes gleamed in the darkness. 'Okehamptone is not buried. I told you earlier that there is a theological query about whether men from a city under interdict can be buried in hallowed ground – that is why Chesterfelde lies here in the chancel. The same is true for Okehamptone. His body is temporarily consigned to the vault, right under our feet. All you have to do is open a coffin.'

'No,' said Bartholomew firmly. 'There is a big difference between looking at Chesterfelde here, and burrowing in crypts after corpses that have been interred for two weeks. I will not do it.'

'You must,' said Michael. 'You are my Corpse Examiner and that is what you are paid to do. I cannot do it myself – I would not know what to look for. Besides, do you *want* Polmorva to evade a charge of murder in your own town? Here is your chance to strike back at the man, and show him he cannot go a-killing wherever he pleases.'

He had a point: Bartholomew *was* reluctant to see Polmorva commit murder and enjoy what he inherited. There had been times in the past when he had suspected his sly adversary of ridding himself of men he considered a nuisance, although he had never managed to obtain proof. Okehamptone offered a chance to investigate one death properly, and Michael was right to urge him to seize it. He followed the monk to where a stout door marked the entrance to the undercroft, and watched him struggle with the bars and bolts that were designed to keep dogs and wild animals at bay.

When the monk eventually prised it open, Bartholomew saw it led to a flight of damp, slime-covered steps that descended into a sinister blackness. Taking the lamp, he climbed down them, bracing one hand on the wall when his feet skidded on the uneven surfaces. As he went deeper, an unpleasant smell assailed him. It was a combination of the recently dead, the mould that pervaded every stone and scrap of wood in the abandoned building, and the rankness of a place that had been derelict for too many years.

When he reached the last step, he raised the lamp and looked around. The vault was a simple affair: a single chamber that was about the length of the chancel. Its ceiling was low, and thickly ribbed to shore up the weight of the building above. A number of stone tombs were placed at intervals along the walls, some adorned with metal crosses that were green and crusted with age. Several had collapsed, leaving hefty slabs lying at odd angles and rubble littering the beaten earth floor. Niches cut into the wall held coffins, all crumbling and fragile, indicating that they had lain undisturbed for years. One was not, however, and was fashioned from bright new wood.

'I assume that is him,' he said, turning to look at Michael only to find he was alone. He sighed impatiently. 'I need you to hold the lamp,' he shouted up the steps.

'Set it on a shelf,' Michael called back. 'I shall stay here, and say prayers for Okehamptone's soul. But hurry. It will be light soon, and I do not want anyone to catch us here. It will look macabre, to say the least.'

Muttering resentfully under his breath that Michael should order him to do something so deeply unpleasant and then decline to help, Bartholomew grabbed the coffin lid and tugged, anticipating that he would need to find something to use as a lever, but it yielded easily. The wood was cheap and the barest minimum of nails had been used. He leapt in alarm when a rat shot out and ran across his hand, and he became aware that more of them were moving in the darkness to one side, rustling and scratching. Hurrying to be away before they decided that fresh meat might make an interesting change from old, he turned his attention to the contents of the coffin.

Okehamptone was not a pleasant sight, and Bartholomew was grateful the lamp was dim and masked some of the more grisly details. He had seen corpses aplenty, but not many after they had been buried or interred, and although there was little difference in the appearance of one that had been left above ground for two weeks and one that had been in a crypt, there was a subtle distinction between the two in his mind. He regarded one as part of the duty demanded by his office; the other made him uncomfortable.

Breathing as shallowly as he could, he began his examination. Okehamptone was swathed in a blanket, and the liripipe Paxtone had mentioned was still around his head and neck. Bartholomew observed that no one had done anything to the body except move it into its coffin – no one had washed it, brushed its hair or performed any of the usual acts of respect accorded to the dead.

Wanting to be thorough, Bartholomew ran his hands over the man's head to assess for bludgeoning, then pulled back some of his clothes to look for other injuries. If Polmorva had poisoned Okehamptone, then there was nothing Bartholomew could do now, but he could ascertain whether the cause of death was due to a wound. He completed his examination, careful not to rush and miss something vital, then shoved the lid back on the box with considerable relief. He used a lump of stone to hammer the nails home again and left, slipping and stumbling up the slick steps in his eagerness to be away.

When he reached the chancel, he did not wait for Michael to secure the door after him, but darted straight into the graveyard, where he stood taking deep breaths of cool, fresh air, savouring the clean, fragrant scent of wet earth and living vegetation. His legs were unsteady and he was aware that the miasma of old death clung to his clothes. He walked to a nearby ditch, and crouched down to rinse his hands, using fistfuls of grass to scrub them clean.

'Well?' asked Michael, coming to stand next to him. 'Did he die from a fever?'

'He may have had one,' replied Bartholomew, still breathing deeply. 'But it is not what killed him.'

'What then?' asked Michael, although Bartholomew could tell from the expression on his face that he already knew the answer.

'A wound to his throat,' said Bartholomew. 'It was completely concealed by the liripipe. Paxtone heard he had a fever, and thought nothing odd about the victim being wrapped up for warmth. However, Okehamptone bled to death, which explains why Paxtone said his face – what he could see of it without moving the hood – was pale and waxy.'

'But even I know a good deal of blood escapes from a throat wound. Surely Paxtone would have noticed that?'

'I imagine that is why the body was wrapped in the blanket – to hide the blood.'

'Damn Paxtone! I thought I could trust him. No wonder he refused to accept payment. I thought he was being noble, but it was because his conscience would not let him take money for something he did not do. So, Okehamptone was murdered after all?'

'I have seldom seen a more savage injury, and there is no earthly possibility that he could have inflicted it himself.'

219

Michael sighed. 'Then there is one more thing I need to know.'

'You want to know what caused it. It looks like a bite, Brother. Okehamptone died from a wound that shows clearly etched teeth marks.'

Neither Bartholomew nor Michael wanted to linger near All-Saints-next-the-Castle, so they left the churchyard and walked briskly down Castle Hill towards the town. Dawn was close, and here and there were signs that folk were stirring. Smoke wafted through the air as fires were kindled, and lights could be seen through the cracks of the window shutters of those wealthy enough to afford lamps. A cockerel crowed and a dog barked at the sound of Tulyet's soldiers marching back to their quarters after a night on duty.

It was Michael's turn to conduct the daily mass – although he was a monk, he had been granted dispensation by his bishop to perform priestly duties during the plague, and he had continued the practice since – and Bartholomew was scheduled to assist him, so they made their way directly to St Michael's. While Michael laid out the sacred vessels, Bartholomew busied himself by checking the level of holy water in the stoup, sweeping the porch and lighting the wax candles that stood on the altar. Neither spoke, and Bartholomew found himself unsettled by what he had discovered – not to mention the uncomfortable sensation that Okehamptone had not approved of his meddling. He felt as though something was watching him, and edged closer to the monk.

'The wick on this candle is defective,' announced Michael, breaking into his uneasy musings. His voice was loud in the silence, and Bartholomew jumped. 'I do not want it to extinguish itself just as the miracle of the sacraments is about to take place. There are those who would consider it a sign of divine disapproval.'

'Do you want me to trim it?'

'No, I want a new one. This is almost finished, and it looks miserly when Michaelhouse always burns its candles down to the very last scrap of wax.'

Bartholomew left the chancel and went to the large cupboard at the back of the nave where candles and incense were stored. He thought he saw a flicker of movement behind one of the pillars and his stomach clenched in alarm, but when he went to investigate, there was nothing to see. He chided himself for his overactive imagination, and supposed it had been a bat, flitting about in search of insects. He groped for the key that was 'hidden' on the windowsill, then removed the bar that kept the cupboard door from swinging open when it was not locked. He knelt on the floor and began to rummage for the candle, straining to see in the darkness.

When he felt a breath of movement on the back of his neck, he assumed it was Michael, treading softly on the stone floor. He was about to tell the monk that there were no candles left, but that he would remind Langelee to order more, when he became aware that the presence at his shoulder was closer than Michael would have stood. His mind full of Okehamptone's indignant spirit, Bartholomew leapt to his feet and backed away, heart thudding in panic. It was his rapid response that saved his life, for the heavy spade that had been aimed at his head missed, and smashed against the wall with a clang that echoed all around the building. He jerked away a second time as the implement swung again, and yelled for Michael. Even his tired mind had registered the fact that spirits did not wield agricultural tools and he knew it was no ghost that was trying to kill him.

The spade descended again, and Bartholomew found himself backed against the cupboard with nowhere to go. He tried to make out the features of the shadowy figure that lurched and ducked in front of him, and which seemed so determined to dash out his brains. Was it a thief, who had seen him enter the church, and thought he would be easy prey before the other scholars arrived? Was it someone connected to the peculiar case that involved Okehamptone and others being bitten? Foremost in his mind was Polmorva, who would not want the news spread that Okehamptone's death was suspicious – even if he had not killed the man himself, he would lose what he had inherited. Or was Polmorva innocent, and it was someone else who wanted Okehamptone consigned to the ground with no questions asked?

'Clippesby?' he whispered, voicing a terrible fear that his colleague might have escaped from the hospital again. 'Is that you?'

'Matt?' called Michael, much further away. 'What are you doing?'

The silhouette faltered, then the spade came at Bartholomew in a jabbing motion. The physician twisted out of the way, lost his balance and toppled into the cupboard. Sprawled among the incense, he was an easy target, so he was bemused when there was a loud crash and he was plunged into total darkness. For several moments he did not understand what had happened, then he heard footsteps and Michael's querulous voice. The cupboard door had been slammed closed and barred. He kicked and hammered furiously, but it was still some time before it was opened. He scrambled out and looked around him wildly. There was only Michael, standing with a pewter chalice clutched in one meaty hand, held like a weapon.

'What?' the monk demanded. 'I thought there was something wrong when you started yelling, and now I find you playing a practical joke. I was praying, man! Have you no respect?'

'Someone was here,' Bartholomew shouted, pushing

past him and aiming for the porch. 'The door is open. You let him escape!'

'Let who escape?' asked Michael irritably. 'There is no one here.'

'Someone attacked me with a spade,' yelled Bartholomew in agitation. He wrenched open the porch door and darted into the graveyard, looking around to see if he could spot someone running away or hiding. But the only movement was a cat tiptoeing through the dew-laden grass, trying to keep its feet dry.

'A spade?' echoed Michael, following him. 'Who?'

'I could not see his face,' said Bartholomew, exasperated.

'He was not a very efficient assassin, or you would not be here now, screeching like a demon and waking our neighbours. Keep your voice down, Matt, or we will be accused of conducting satanic rites that entail hurtling through dark graveyards and shrieking with gay abandon.'

'Someone *was* here,' Bartholomew insisted, although he spoke more softly. Michael was right: window shutters were beginning to ease ajar in the houses nearby. 'Surely you saw him?'

'I heard a good deal of yelling and crashing – all of it coming from you. And, as for the porch door being left open, it could have been the wind. You know what that latch is like. You are overwrought after examining Okehamptone, and—'

'I did not imagine anything,' said Bartholomew firmly. 'Someone tried to hit me, then locked me in that cupboard, so he could escape.'

'The bar *had* been placed across the cupboard door,' said Michael thoughtfully. 'I assumed you had rigged it somehow, so it would drop down on its own, to make me wonder how you had done it. But this attack on you makes no sense. From what you say, the fellow had you at his mercy but gave up at the last moment.'

'Probably because you were coming to my aid.'

'Look,' said Michael, crossing the grass to point at something. It was a sturdy spade of the kind owned by every man with a patch of ground to cultivate for vegetables. 'This was not here when we arrived, so I suppose it is the weapon your would-be murderer intended to use.'

Bartholomew nodded, feeling weak-kneed now the excitement was over. 'I saw nothing, other than the fact that he wore a hood to conceal his face. It could have been anyone: the Oxford merchants, Eudo or Boltone, Polmorva. Or someone from King's Hall – Wolf, Norton or Hamecotes.' He hesitated. 'Or Clippesby.'

'Damn!' muttered Michael. He scratched his chin, fingernails rasping on his bristles. 'Did he say anything to you? Did you recognise his voice?'

'He said nothing. I asked whether he was Clippesby.'

Michael was thoughtful. 'I wonder if that is what saved you.'

'What do you mean?'

'Your question may have told him you were not who he wanted. Think, man! Look at what you are wearing: a distinctive grey-hemmed cloak lent to you by Spryngheuse. And Spryngheuse's friend Chesterfelde has been murdered.'

Bartholomew considered. 'We have just walked from Castle Hill, which is the direction we would have taken had we been coming from Merton Hall. I suppose it is possible that someone mistook me for him in the dark.'

'So, he followed you, grabbing a spade in anticipation. His first blow missed, you began to yell and he realised he had the wrong man.'

'What does this tell us – other than that the attacker is not Spryngheuse?'

'It suggests it is not Clippesby, either.'

'No,' said Bartholomew sadly. 'It does not. If Clippesby

really is losing what little reason he has left, then it may just mean that my calling his name brought him to his senses. And it complicates matters. We have at least two deaths caused by bites, but this man did not use his teeth.'

'That does not imply we have more than one killer. It might just mean that our man is flexing his wings, learning to experiment and use whatever comes to hand.'

Bartholomew rubbed his eyes. 'Lord, Brother! The sooner we resolve this, the happier I will be. I do not feel safe, and I sense that other people will die if we do not have some answers soon.'

'I agree. My students will have to do without me for a while, because I should devote myself to this problem until it is solved. Only then can I be certain that the Archbishop's Visitation will take place without some madman racing around wielding spades and flexing his jaws. Will you help me?'

When Bartholomew returned to Michaelhouse, a messenger was waiting with notification that his postgraduates' disputations had been scheduled a week earlier than anticipated, and abandoning them to help Michael was out of the question. The monk went alone to his office at St Mary the Great, to look at the records that would tell him exactly when Clippesby had applied for leave of absence over the past year – and when he had been fined for going without permission. He had not been working long when he saw a familiar figure pass his window. He set off in pursuit, catching up with the fellow as he was lighting candles in the Lady Chapel.

'Warden Duraunt,' he said pleasantly. 'All alone this morning?'

The elderly master smiled. 'Polmorva is attending a lecture at the Dominican Friary. He is a dedicated scholar, and always seizes any opportunity to hear other academics speak.'

'He will not find much to stimulate his intellect among the Dominicans,' said Michael, voicing what every Cambridge man knew for a fact. 'What about the merchants?'

'Eu is in Grantchester, to see whether the lord of the manor might buy his spices; Wormynghalle went with him, because Eu is a good businessman and our tanner is hoping to learn the secret of his success; and Abergavenny followed them, to make sure they do not argue and kill each other along the way. I find their constant squabbles a sore trial, Brother.'

'You do seem tired,' said Michael. 'Did you sleep poorly?'

'I always sleep poorly – it is one of the burdens of old age. When it becomes too bad, I leave my bed and visit a church, just to sit in a quiet, peaceful place. Last night, for example, I went to St Giles's at two o'clock. Polmorva escorted me, then returned to collect me just after dawn. Spryngheuse usually obliges but he has grown jittery since Chesterfelde died, and is reluctant to go out. He says he sees his Black Monk everywhere, but of course no such person exists. He invented the fellow, to take the blame for the riots, and has become so unstable that he now believes the lie.'

While he spoke, Michael watched him lighting candles, trying to assess whether he was strong enough to brandish a spade. He did not think Duraunt would harm Bartholomew, but he might have wanted Spryngheuse out of the way for reasons the monk had yet to fathom. But his examination was inconclusive, and in the end he had no idea whether Duraunt's weariness came from attempting to kill someone with a hefty tool or from a genuinely restless night.

'We saw Sprynglheuse on the Great Bridge on Sunday,'

he said. 'I am sure he intended to throw himself over the edge.'

Duraunt did not seem surprised. 'I thought he would feel better, once away from the city where he is accused of bringing about a massacre, but first Okehamptone died, then Chesterfelde, and he is becoming increasingly distraught.'

'Where is he now?'

'I sent him to the stationer's shop, just to get him into the fresh air. Now Boltone has absconded, I am obliged to make sense of the accounts he left behind, and I need more ink.'

'Tell me about Polmorva. Why did he really agree to accompany you to Cambridge?'

'Because he dislikes being in a city under interdict, like any Christian soul. It is a pity Matthew will not accept his offer of a truce. I had hoped they would have forgotten their differences after all these years, but Polmorva tells me Matthew rejects all his friendly advances.'

'Polmorva is a liar,' said Michael bluntly. 'I am reliably informed that he witnessed the murder of Gonerby, and *that* is the real reason why he is here.'

'No!' exclaimed Duraunt. 'I do not believe you!'

'I am also told that he only pretended to be drunk the night Chesterfelde died,' Michael went on. '*He* might be the one who cut the man's wrist and allowed him to bleed to death.'

Duraunt considered, then shook his head. 'He would have been covered in blood, and he was not. Perhaps he did deceive us about the amount he drank, but I am sure there is an innocent explanation for that.'

'And you?' asked Michael. 'What is your explanation for the amount *you* drank? No, do not look indignant. You may be able to divert Matt with your reproach, but not me. You were seen at the Cardinal's Cap the night after

Chesterfelde died. You were also intoxicated on the night of his murder. And then there is the poppy juice.'

'My habits are none of your affair,' said Duraunt sharply. 'I admit I like a cup of wine, and we all enjoyed several the night Chesterfelde was killed. Perhaps I did imbibe too much, but who does not, on occasion? And the night after, I needed wine to restore my spirits – I was distressed about Chesterfelde, and about the fact that Matthew insists on quarrelling with Polmorva. Polmorva is destined for great things, and Matthew should acknowledge his talents.'

'You mean Matt should grovel to him? You do not know him very well if you think he would demean himself to such a man.'

'I do not know him at all,' countered Duraunt. 'He has changed – and not for the better.'

Sensing they would not agree, and not wanting an argument that would serve no purpose, Michael took his leave of Duraunt. He strode out of the University Church and headed for the Dominican Friary, where he was not surprised to learn that Polmorva was not there or that no lecture was scheduled for that morning. He was retracing his steps to the High Street, when he saw the object of his enquiries trying to slip past on the other side of the road, Spryngheuse in tow. Smiling grimly, he waddled towards them and managed to snag a corner of Polmorva's sleeve before he could escape. He was not so lucky with Spryngheuse, who declared he was terrified of all Benedictines, and fled without another word.

'Brother Michael,' said Polmorva, not pleased to be waylaid by physical force. 'Have you identified Chesterfelde's killer yet?'

'Where were you last night? You took Duraunt to St Giles's Church, and collected him before dawn. Where were you the rest of the time?'

'Asleep, of course. I am no ancient, who needs prayers

228

to make me drowse, and I went to bed after escorting him to the chapel. Everyone else was already dozing, so I doubt they will remember me coming in. You will have to take my word for it.'

Michael changed the subject. 'The day after Okehamptone died, you told me that you were the sole beneficiary of his will, but only if he died of natural causes. If his life ended by violent means, his property would revert to the Church, to fund masses for his soul.'

'He did not own much,' said Polmorva. 'And I am already wealthy, so I shall probably donate his paltry leavings to my College – some impoverished student might cherish his cloak, two battered saddlebags and a handful of *exemplar pecia*. Now, if he had owned land, I might have been interested, but he did not.'

'What about Gonerby?' asked Michael, unsure whether to believe him. He was finding Polmorva almost impossible to read. 'I have it on good authority that you saw what happened to him.'

'Is that so?' said Polmorva coldly. He tried to walk away, but Michael grabbed his arm.

'Tell me the truth, because if you lie to me I will send word to Oxford's Mayor that you watched a townsman murdered, and declined to step forward and do your civic duty.'

Polmorva sighed, to indicate he was bored with the discussion and that Michael's threats were more tiresome than worrying. 'I took refuge in a chapel when the riots began, and I happened to look out of a window to see Gonerby walking along. He was strutting confidently, arrogantly, as if he imagined no one would dare lay a finger on him. Someone did, and he died for his lack of humility.'

'How was he killed?'

'It was difficult to tell – I was some distance away and

the killer had his back to me – but the merchants say there were teeth marks in his throat.'

'Did you recognise the murderer?' asked Michael.

'Of course not. All I can tell you is that he was a scholar, and he wore a hooded cloak that hid his face. There was nothing distinctive about him. However, I can tell you that he moved towards Gonerby with a definite sense of purpose.'

'Really?' mused Michael. 'Then he knew his victim. This was not a random stalking during civil unrest, when everyone was free to do as he pleased, but a deliberate assassination.'

'I do not speculate on such matters, Brother. That sort of thing is for proctors.'

Despite his determination to remain calm, Michael found the man's manner intensely aggravating. 'I shall be watching you very carefully, Polmorva, and if I find you played even the smallest role in bringing about these deaths – Gonerby's, Okehamptone's or Chesterfelde's – I will see you hang.'

Polmorva laughed derisively. 'Do not threaten me, monk. I am no undergraduate to be cowed by hollow words. If you want to charge me with a crime, then you had better ensure you have a very strong case, because if you do not I shall bring my own against you for defaming my good name. And, by the time I have finished, you and your pathetic little College will be ruined.'

When teaching was over for the day, Bartholomew went to visit a patient on the High Street. He was on his way home again when he met Paxtone and John Wormynghalle, walking back to King's Hall together after attending an afternoon of lectures on logic at Peterhouse. Paxtone, always hospitable, invited Bartholomew to his chambers, and Bartholomew accepted, thinking it would be a pleasant way to pass the time before a statutory Fellows' meeting at Michaelhouse that evening. As they crossed the yard, they saw Dodenho, rubbing his chin as if deep in thought.

'Look at him!' said Norton, who was watching. 'He is waiting for Warden Powys to come home, and has been strutting around in that affected manner for the best part of an hour. He is not thinking up new theories; he just wants to impress Powys, in the hope that *he* will be one chosen to sit next to the Archbishop of Canterbury next Monday night.'

'Powys will not select him,' said Paxtone with considerable finality. 'He will spout some of his ideas on theology, and Islip might recognise them as his own. Dodenho will steal from anyone.'

'I need an astrolabe,' declared Dodenho, as he approached the gathering. 'I have several complex equations in my mind, but I cannot calculate them without an astrolabe. The world is suffering as long as I am deprived.'

'You claimed your own was stolen – and then it was not stolen,' said Norton. 'I heard it was last seen in the hands of one of those Oxford merchants. You should beware, Dodenho – you do not want people associating you with *their* crimes.'

'What crimes?' asked Dodenho in alarm.

'Murder,' replied Norton. 'They have been asking in the taverns about scholars who kill, and I understand *you* were in Oxford when the St Scholastica's Day riots took place.'

'Were you?' asked Bartholomew, startled.

Dodenho waved a dismissive hand, but his eyes could not conceal his unease. 'Only briefly, and I saw nothing of the fighting. Now, if you will excuse me.'

He scurried away, and he did not resume his scholastic pose, despite the fact that Warden Powys entered the College at that point. He merely shot across the yard like

231

a child caught misbehaving and entered his room, where he slammed the door behind him.

'Well,' said Norton, amused. 'There is an odd thing! But I cannot stand here all day. I must see a man about a dog in the King's Head – a hunting dog.'

Bartholomew and Wormynghalle followed Paxtone to his chamber, but they had done no more than pour wine when a servant arrived with a summons for Paxtone; there had been an accident with an oven at the Mortimer bakery, he said, making graphic gestures with his hands to indicate that flames were involved. Bartholomew offered to go with him, but Paxtone assured him no help was needed and that it would not be long before he had discharged his duties. A less charitable mind might have thought Paxtone did not want another physician to watch how he treated burns, but Bartholomew was tired and had no desire to assist with someone else's patients anyway. Wormynghalle was more than happy to keep him company, and was hauling a copy of Grosseteste's *De veritate* from the shelf almost before Paxtone was out of the door.

'Now,' said the young scholar, plunging without preamble into the debate he had proposed the day before. 'Grosseteste maintains that certain aspects of geometry are useful in representing "cause and effect whether in matter or the senses". Without representation by geometric angles, lines and figures, it would be impossible to know why natural effects are as they are.'

'*Per contra* abstraction is possible, of course,' expanded Bartholomew, 'giving us mathematical objects, and these may have accidents – that is, properties of a substance that are not part of its essential nature – of another sort, namely ones of mathematical character. Grosseteste abstracted magnitude from matter-in-motion, so accidents can be assigned to . . .'

He trailed off when Wormynghalle, eager to listen,

leaned forward in his chair and knocked over a goblet of wine, which splattered over Paxtone's best rug.

'Damn! Damn! Damn!' Wormynghalle cried irritably. 'This will stain unless it is soaked immediately, and he is fond of the thing.'

He hurried to fetch water, but the spilled claret made the floor slick and he skidded. Bartholomew jumped forward, managing to save him from a nasty tumble by a well-placed arm across his chest. The physician's jaw dropped in shock, while Wormynghalle struggled from his grip and took several steps away, breathing heavily. The scholars regarded each other uneasily for some time before Bartholomew spoke.

'It is all right,' he said. 'I will not tell anyone, although I imagine it is only a matter of time before someone else finds out. You cannot live in a communal place like this without someone prying into your affairs and discovering incriminating facts.'

Wormynghalle's eyes filled with tears. 'There is nothing incriminating to find. Believe me, I am only too aware of what will happen if my colleagues discover I am a woman, and have taken steps to guard against every eventuality – except slipping on wine and being caught by a physician. I confess, that is something I did not anticipate.'

'What you are doing is dangerous,' said Bartholomew. 'You may cut your hair and wear loose clothes, but there are other things that will give you away. The latrines, for a start.'

Wormynghalle waved her hand at one corner of the room. 'Like Paxtone, I paid extra for quarters with a private garderobe and I never visit the public ones. I have lived here for two months now, and no one but you has the slightest inkling that I am not all I seem.'

'They think you care for nothing but your studies,' said Bartholomew, recalling the discussion with his Michaelhouse colleagues. 'They attribute any odd behaviour to your fanatical desire to learn.'

'What odd behaviour?' demanded Wormynghalle, affronted. 'I have been careful to blend into this society, and do nothing to draw attention to myself.'

'You do not frequent taverns or hire prostitutes.' Bartholomew shrugged. 'In a friar or a monk that is not unusual, but total abstinence is rare in secular masters with money to spare. Also, you tend not to engage in the usual sort of manly chatter, and only indulge in discussions of a scholastic nature.'

'Of course,' declared Wormynghalle, surprised anyone should expect otherwise. 'I did not come here to debauch and exchange intimacies. I am here at considerable personal risk, and I want only one thing: to learn. There are no universities for women, and convents are too restrictive. I tried one once, but the nuns would only give me texts they thought were suitable and I felt myself dying inside.'

Bartholomew nodded sympathetically, trying to imagine what it would be like if he could not read what he wanted. He was under certain restrictions as a medical practitioner, some of which he found inordinately frustrating, and supposed it was far worse for Wormynghalle.

'I have so much to offer,' she said in a wistful voice. 'I am a clear and insightful thinker, and all I ask is that I be allowed to use my intellect – just as a man is allowed to use his.'

'The situation is not fair,' agreed Bartholomew. 'And you *are* an excellent scholar. But is this the best way to go about it? What if it had been Paxtone who had grabbed you? He is an old-fashioned man, who would have been appalled at the deception you have perpetrated on his College.'

'But this is the only way I can debate with like-minded

people,' said Wormynghalle, tears spurting again. 'I could go to some remote place and surround myself with books, but that is not what I need. I want to argue my points, and to have people dispute with me and tell me why I am wrong. I want my mind to be stretched and challenged to its limits. And I want to write a great treatise on natural philosophy that will equal those of men like Grosseteste. *You* know how I feel, because you are equally passionate about new and complex theories. I can see it in your face when we talk.'

'Yes,' acknowledged Bartholomew. 'There is little that is more exhilarating than a debate with clever men . . . I mean clever people.'

'You are writing a treatise yourself,' pressed Wormynghalle, wiping her eyes. 'Paxtone gave me some of it, and it is novel and unorthodox. When it is finished it will be read and debated by the best thinkers in the civilised world. But what do you think will happen to mine, if they discover it was penned by a woman?'

'Trotula's theories on medicine and health are widely read – and she was a woman.'

'But they are not accepted with the same open minds as are works by men,' Wormynghalle pointed out. 'Your fellow medics, Rougham and Lynton, will not entertain her writings at all – not because they are flawed or inferior, but because Trotula was female, and therefore has nothing worth saying.'

'True,' admitted Bartholomew.

'Then, you see I have no choice. I *need* the stimulation this University provides and I am discreet. I am obliged to share a room with Hamecotes, but he is too absorbed in his own work to take notice of my occasional idiosyncrasies – such as the fact that I like to close the garderobe door when I pee. If he has even considered the matter at all, it will be to think that I am foolishly modest.'

'Hamecotes is one of several men who ask Matilde for remedies to help female pains,' said Bartholomew. 'Are they for you?'

She nodded. 'He thinks they are for my secret lover, and that I am too embarrassed to ask for them myself. Like many men, he is taken with Matilde, and is delighted by any excuse to visit her.'

'Is that so?' said Bartholomew with displeasure.

'All I have ever wanted is to study at a University and to pit my wits against my intellectual equals and betters,' said Wormynghalle beseechingly. 'Please do not make me give it up.'

'I would never do that,' said Bartholomew. 'Every man – and woman – should be free to exploit the gifts he has been given, and I understand perfectly why scholarship is appealing. I only warn that if you are discovered there will be no mercy. You may not even escape with your life. Men can be harsh and unforgiving when their domains are invaded.'

'I know. I plan to remain here for another term, then return to Oxford, where I will join a different College to the one I was in before. Then I will come here again, or perhaps visit Paris. As long as I keep moving, and allow no one to know me well, I can continue this life for years yet.'

'You do not look like a woman,' acknowledged Bartholomew. He realised that might be construed as offensive and struggled to make amends. 'I mean, you have a beard and . . .' This sounded worse, and he saw he was digging himself a deeper pit. He stopped speaking and gave an apologetic shrug.

Wormynghalle smiled. 'All woman have a certain amount of facial hair, which they usually remove, but I strengthen mine with an ointment of white lilies. Many young men do the same to increase their beards, so no one thinks I am odd – they simply see me as a youth desperate to shave. I have a naturally bristly chin and dark hairs on my upper lip. They are a nuisance when I wear kirtles and wimples, but a great advantage when I don a tabard.'

'What is your real name?' asked Bartholomew. 'It is not John Wormynghalle.'

'I chose "Wormynghalle" because they are a clan of Oxford upstarts that I imagined would never come here. You can imagine my shock when that tanner appeared! I was obliged to visit him, and pretend to see whether we might be kin, all the while making myself unattractive, so he would not assume a connection we do not have. I did not want him thinking a scholar–relative might give him more credit with his mercantile rivals. It was all very awkward.'

'It was lucky you chose Wormynghalle – Eu would have been far more thorough in exploring your origins.'

'I knew that when I took the name – I deliberately avoided prominent, established families. But Wormynghalle's relatives never leave Oxford. It was terrible bad luck that he did – and that he happened to come here, of all places.' She smiled suddenly, so her face became softer and less intense. 'My name is Joan.'

Bartholomew raised his goblet in a salute. 'Well, Joan. I wish you the best of luck with what I anticipate will be a celebrated career.'

She grinned, and Bartholomew noticed she had artificially darkened her teeth in an attempt to make herself rougher. She had obviously worked hard on her disguise, concentrating on the smallest of details. He thought about the way she walked, and realised she had even perfected a boyish swagger.

'Thank you,' she replied. 'Although your knowing my secret puts me at risk, it is actually a relief to confide in someone. A shared burden is easier to carry.'

'I know,' said Bartholomew sincerely.

'What burden?' asked Paxtone, bustling into the room with an amiable smile. 'Can I help? After all, a burden shared by three will be lighter still than one carried by two.'

'You can,' replied Joan without a flicker of hesitation, moving quickly to stand on the stained rug. 'We are talking about the burden of metaphysics to define the mode of existence and the essence of the separable. It would be very good to hear your thoughts.'

Paxtone was pleased to be asked to expound on such an erudite matter. 'Where shall we begin?' he asked. 'With Aristotle or Grosseteste?'

CHAPTER 7

For the first time in more than two weeks, Bartholomew enjoyed a full night of uninterrupted sleep. He had visited Matilde on his way home from King's Hall, and had found Rougham sitting up in bed demanding chicken broth. His fever had gone completely, and Bartholomew knew he could not keep him there for more than a day or two. He was already planning how to reach Gonville Hall without being seen by the gossiping Weasenham, whose house he would have to pass, and then it would not be long before he heard rumours about other men with damaged throats – especially the one in the cistern. The dredging was likely to be a public affair, as it involved soldiers from the Castle, and the news would spread quickly. Okehamptone would not feature in the talk, of course, because only Bartholomew and Michael – and the killer – knew what had happened to him.

The following day, Michael took Bartholomew with him when he went to talk to the Sheriff about the search for Eudo and Boltone. Tulyet was frantically busy, organising bands of itinerant labourers to continue scraping the streets clean of ordure, renovate the Great Bridge so it at least did not look dangerous, and paint the livestock pens in the Market Square. It was not only scholars who wanted the Archbishop to be impressed: the townsfolk were determined that he should think well of them, too. As a result, Tulyet had scant resources to search for criminals in the vast wilderness of the Fens, nor had he found time to drain the well. He promised to do both as soon as he could, and

Bartholomew and Michael escaped from his house when they heard Dickon making his way towards them, the army of servants who had been detailed to entertain him powerless to prevent the invasion.

Since a heavy spring shower was in full flood, they ducked into St Clement's Church. They were not the only ones who had been obliged to take shelter, and Michael's eyes gleamed with predatory anticipation when he saw that the entire party from Oxford, on their way to terce at St Mary the Great, had been caught in the deluge, too. On spotting Michael and Bartholomew, Polmorva promptly aimed for the door, claiming he was going to the Dominican Friary for a theology lecture.

'I hope you find it as stimulating as the one you attended yesterday,' said Michael casually.

Polmorva shrugged, knowing he had been caught in a lie, but not really caring. 'It will be more rewarding than talking to you, Brother. But then, so is wallowing in pig dung.'

'That is an example of Oxford subtlety, I suppose,' said Michael, regarding him with disdain. 'Do not leave, Polmorva. I want to talk to you.'

'You have no right to order him around,' objected Wormynghalle indignantly. 'What do you want, anyway? More excuses for not finding Gonerby's killer?'

'You have not been successful with that, either,' snapped Michael in return. 'And do not pretend you do not know what I am talking about, Abergavenny. You have been in the King's Head, asking questions of the locals, when I explicitly told you not to.'

'What of it?' demanded Eu. 'We have businesses waiting at home, and we need to secure our culprit as soon as possible. Besides, you cannot stop free merchants from holding innocent conversations in taverns.'

'I can prevent you from causing trouble,' said Michael.

'Because that is what you do when you ask townsfolk to list those scholars they think are murderers. And how can I hope to find your culprit when you are not honest about his crime? I was obliged to learn for myself that Gonerby was bitten to death. Why did you not tell me the truth?'

'It was not necessary,' replied Eu, unrepentant. 'All you needed to know was that Gonerby was killed by a man who fled to Cambridge.'

'Then what about Polmorva's role? Why did you keep that from me, when speaking to an eyewitness might have increased my chances of success?'

'He saw nothing useful,' answered Eu. 'And he asked us not to involve him.'

'Is that true?' asked Bartholomew of Spryngheuse, who was peering into the shadows of the aisle with a haunted expression stamped on his sallow features. No one took any notice of the question: the merchants were defending their actions to Michael, while Polmorva listened disdainfully and Duraunt closed his eyes in despair as another argument unfolded.

Spryngheuse spoke in a low voice, so only Bartholomew could hear. 'Polmorva said Gonerby's killer might hunt *him* if he learns there is a living witness to the crime, and he only agreed to come here if the merchants promised to tell no one what he saw. I understand his fear; I am terrified myself.'

'Here is your cloak,' said Bartholomew, tugging it from his bag and hoping it was not too badly crumpled. 'Do you really think someone might harm you? You have been uneasy ever since you arrived.'

'You would be uneasy if *you* were accused of starting a riot that left hundreds dead. Some of the victims have powerful friends, and they want revenge. And there is that damned Benedictine! He will not leave me alone – he

241

seems to be everywhere I look. He may even be here, in this church, stalking me.'

Bartholomew strode into the shady aisle and looked around him carefully. 'There is no one here.'

Tears shone in Spryngheuse's eyes. 'I cannot tell you what it is like to be terrified every living moment of the day. I do not sleep; I cannot eat. My only solace is poppy juice, but Duraunt will not give me any more.'

'So that is why he had it,' said Bartholomew. 'But he is right: soporifics will not solve your problems. Do you think this Benedictine killed Gonerby? Or is he one of these avenging angels who lost influential friends in the fighting?'

'I do not know. But my days are numbered, just like poor Chesterfelde's, although *he* would never believe it. The Black Monk is playing with me, prolonging my agony. I wish he would just get it over with.' He stiffened suddenly, and his voice became full of panic. 'Is that him? Behind the altar?'

'No, those are John Wormynghalle and Thomas Paxtone, sheltering from the rain because they are carrying library books,' replied Bartholomew patiently, wondering whether Spryngheuse was becoming deranged; he looked unbalanced, with his frightened eyes and unkempt appearance. 'They will be fined if one is stained with even the smallest drop of water. You know this: it is the same at Merton.'

'True. But why are they skulking over there, rather than standing in the nave with the rest of us?'

'They are not skulking. I imagine they are keeping their distance because Wormynghalle does not want another awkward encounter with his unmannerly namesake.'

'Yes, of course,' said Spryngheuse, relieved. He rubbed his mouth with shaking fingers, while Bartholomew raised his hand in greeting and the King's Hall men returned his salute with friendly smiles. 'But what shall I do? How can I be rid of this spectre that is so determined to drive me from my wits?'

'Stay with Duraunt,' suggested Bartholomew, wondering whether Spryngheuse might benefit from a sojourn with Brother Paul and Clippesby at Stourbridge. 'He will not—'

'Why would Duraunt protect me? He lost loved friends in the riot, too. But you are a physician. Will you calculate my horoscope and tell me when the Black Monk plans to strike? I have my dates written out, and you can borrow the tanner's astrolabe . . . no, you cannot. It is missing.'

'Someone has stolen it?'

'For its metal, presumably. But it is no great loss, scientifically speaking. Astrolabes are better made of brass than silver, and this one is hopelessly inaccurate – made for display, rather than use.'

'Did Dodenho reclaim it?' wondered Bartholomew. 'It was his to start with.'

Spryngheuse did not understand the question, but nor did he care. 'Will you help me?' he asked desperately. 'I do not think I can stand the anticipation much longer.'

'I cannot predict when you will die,' said Bartholomew gently. 'No one can, not even with the best astrolabe in the world.'

'I visited a wise woman yesterday, and *she* said it would be soon, but refused to tell me the exact day. She said there is a black shadow following me – Death in the guise of a Benedictine.'

'She was guessing. You look like a man at the end of his tether, and she used it to make her so-called prediction. Fight this, Spryngheuse. Or leave Cambridge and go to some remote village where you can use a different name and no one will know who you are.'

'Yes,' said Spryngheuse wearily. 'That is what I should

do. The only problem is finding the courage to ride off alone, to somewhere the monk will never find me.'

'Enough!' roared Michael suddenly. The merchants' quarrel had reached screeching proportions. 'You have lied to me and misled me, and nothing can change that. But I do not want to talk about Gonerby today. I want to talk about Okehamptone, who was also foully murdered.'

There was a tense silence, as the party from Oxford digested this information. Bartholomew watched them carefully, but their faces told him nothing he could not have predicted: Spryngheuse, Duraunt and Abergavenny were shocked, Polmorva and Eu were unreadable, and Wormynghalle was incensed, seeing the statement as an accusation that somehow besmirched his personal integrity.

'Okehamptone died of a fever, Brother,' said Duraunt eventually. 'You said so yourself.'

'I have reconsidered in the light of new evidence,' replied Michael. 'So, what have you to say?'

'There is nothing *to* say,' said Polmorva. 'Okehamptone was hired as the merchants' scribe, and he died when we arrived in Cambridge. Fever deaths are not uncommon after long journeys.'

'England's roads *are* dangerous, Brother,' Abergavenny pointed out. 'It is not just outlaws who present a risk, but sicknesses caused by rotten food, cloudy ale, dangerous animals, filthy beds . . .'

'Strange whores,' added Eu. 'My father always taught me never to romp with harlots I do not know personally. Of course, getting acquainted with them first is not always—'

'Bad water killed Okehamptone,' declared Wormynghalle. 'He drank from streams and wells, when the rest of us took ale. I warned him it was foolish, but he would not listen.'

'Where did he drink this tainted water?' asked Bartholomew. 'How long before he died?'

'He was always doing it,' replied Wormynghalle. 'He disliked the flavour of ale, although he adored wine. He gulped a vast quantity of well-water in a village called Girton, and was feverish that same night. It is obvious what killed him.'

'Not Girton's well,' said Bartholomew immediately. 'It is good—'

'Did Okehamptone have enemies?' asked Michael, before his friend could hold forth on the topic of water.

'No,' said Eu, surprised by the question. 'We have already told you: we hired him because he was likeable. He had a habit of gabbling Latin with Chesterfelde, which was annoying . . .'

'And he sang,' added Polmorva. 'All the time. Now *that* was really irritating. He was always a tone below where he should have been, and it was hard on the ear.'

'Anything else? Was he quarrelsome? Aggressive?' Michael fixed Eu with a stare. 'Pompous?'

'He was a scholar-scribe,' said Abergavenny before Eu could respond. 'So, of course he was pompous. But, as Eu said, he was a pleasant fellow – not wealthy, but his clothes were of a decent quality and he was clean.'

'And that cannot always be said of scholars,' added Eu, determined to have his say. He did not look at anyone, but Bartholomew assumed he was thinking of Tynkell.

'You say he was murdered,' said Duraunt when Michael looked indignant. 'How do you know?'

'That is a good question,' said Polmorva. 'What have you done? Been to the church and dragged the poor man from his coffin?'

Duraunt turned appalled eyes on Bartholomew. 'Please tell me you did not disturb a man's mortal remains. I know there are universities in Italy that condone that sort of unchristian behaviour, but I thought English schools were above such barbarism – especially scholars I once taught.'

'Of course they have been in Okehamptone's grave,' said Eu. 'How else could they have "new evidence"? They cannot solve Chesterfelde's murder, so they have turned to Okehamptone instead, in an attempt to prevent us from finding Gonerby's killer – to muddy the waters.'

'Okehamptone died from an injury to his throat,' stated Michael baldly.

'His throat?' breathed Duraunt, shocked. 'I did not see anything amiss with his throat.'

'Did you look?' Michael pounced.

'Well, no, but—'

'Then someone must have invaded Merton Hall during the night and killed him,' said Polmorva with a shrug, to indicate he considered the matter of scant importance. 'He was alive when we went to bed, but dead by dawn.'

'Wormynghalle provided us with a casket of wine the night Okehamptone died,' recalled Duraunt. 'He drank some of that, but we all did. Besides, wine does not wound a throat.'

'It was our first night here, and I felt we should cele- brate our safe arrival,' said Wormynghalle, a little defen- sively. 'Duraunt will accept no coins for our board, so I decided to repay his hospitality in time-honoured fashion.'

'Just like the night Chesterfelde died,' said Michael pointedly. 'You provided wine, then, too.'

'That was claret,' said Duraunt, as if such a detail made all the difference. 'We had *white* wine when Okehamptone was . . . taken to God.'

'Did anyone see blood on his body?' asked Bartholomew. 'There would have been a lot of it.'

'He was wrapped in a blanket and he wore Worm- ynghalle's liripipe for warmth against his fever,' said Abergavenny thoughtfully. 'We did not notice blood,

246

because we did not unwrap him. All we did was cover his face and summon the appropriate authorities.'

'Wormynghalle's liripipe?' asked Michael, turning to the tanner with questioning eyes.

'He did not ask to borrow it,' said Wormynghalle, a little angrily. 'But once he had died in it, I did not want it back. I do not wear clothes that have been donned by corpses.' He gazed at Eu in a way that suggested he would not put such grotesque behaviour past him.

'And none of you touched the body?' Michael asked, cutting across Eu's angry retort. 'No one anointed it with holy water, dressed it in clean clothes?'

'We did what was required of us,' replied Polmorva coolly. 'No more, but no less, either.'

'You are a friar,' said Bartholomew to Duraunt. 'Surely you gave him last rites?'

'He was dead,' replied Duraunt. 'I know some clerics believe a soul lingers after death, but I am not among them. I feel it is wrong to place holy things near corpses, and Okehamptone had been dead for some time before we found him. He was stiff and cold.'

'Since the pestilence, we are all wary of cadavers,' added Wormynghalle. 'There are rumours that it originated when an earthquake burst open graves, and I, for one, refuse to touch them. We had Okehamptone removed as soon as your other Corpse Examiner had finished his business.'

'Wormynghalle is right,' agreed Abergavenny. 'You cannot be too careful these days, and we were only too happy to let others deal with Okehamptone's remains. None of us knew him well, but we attended his requiem mass and prayed for his soul. We did all that was expected of us.'

'Except notice that his throat had been cut,' said Bartholomew in disgust.

*   *   *

That afternoon, Bartholomew concentrated on his teaching, grateful to relegate the Oxford murders to the back of his mind for a while. Since the plague, physicians had been in desperately short supply, and there was a huge demand for qualified men to fill empty posts. Bartholomew felt it was his duty to train as many students as he could, and was hard-pressed to supervise them all, even when he was not helping Michael. He was more than happy to spend time in Michaelhouse, his apprentice medics perched on wooden benches in front of him, as he vied to make himself heard over the other lessons that were taking place. William was a particular nuisance, with his loud voice and bigoted opinions, and it was invariably a challenge to keep the students' attention once the Franciscan was in full swing. That morning, William had taken it upon himself to hold forth about the Dominicans again.

'Dominican,' he announced in a bellow, as soon as the bell had rung to announce the lectures' start. Michael and his quiet theologians jumped in alarm at the sudden yell, while Bartholomew's lively youngsters nudged each other and grinned, anticipating that they were going to be in for a treat. Langelee raised his eyes heavenward, while Wynewyk sighed in irritation.

'Yesterday, you were read Galen's theories relating to black bile,' said Bartholomew, to regain his class's attention. He spotted a number of guilty glances, and was not pleased to think that some had evidently been less attentive to their studies than they should have been. 'What are they?'

A pregnant silence greeted his question, and Bartholomew saw several lads bow their heads to write on scraps of parchment. Since he had not yet said anything worthy of being noted, he assumed it was a ruse to avoid catching his eye.

'Domini. Can,' bawled William. 'From the Latin *Domini*,

meaning our Lord, and *canna*, meaning dog.' The sinister emphasis he gave to the last noun indicated that he did not consider it a flattering term. Bartholomew regarded him uncertainly, not sure whether he had used the wrong Latin intentionally, to test whether his students were paying attention, or whether he had made a mistake. One eager Franciscan immediately raised a hand, and the fact that William ignored him suggested the error was a genuine one, and that he did not want to be side-tracked by linguistic niceties.

'Flies do not like it,' said Deynman brightly from the front of Bartholomew's class.

The physician dragged his attention away from William. 'What?'

'Flies do not like black bile,' repeated Deynman patiently. 'They think it tastes like the Dead Sea.'

'And we all know about dogs!' boomed William in a voice loud enough to make the windows shake. 'Disgusting creatures!'

'Lord!' muttered Langelee, looking up from where he was writing something on a wax tablet for some of the younger scholars.

Bartholomew glared at his best student, Falmeresham, who was laughing in a way that made others smile, too. He could not tell whether the lad was finding William or Deynman more amusing.

'Galen said most creatures avoid black bile, just as they do saturated brine,' Bartholomew explained, to correct Deynman's misinterpretation before the other students could write it down as fact. 'Excessive salt is poisonous to life, and—'

'I do not think the sea tastes of black bile,' said Falmeresham to Deynman, puzzled. 'I have tasted seawater myself, and it is nothing like it.'

'You should not drink bile!' exclaimed Deynman in horror. 'Did you not listen to the reading yesterday? It is a deadly poison and an excess of it causes all manner of ills. Besides, I referred to the *Dead* Sea, not any old ocean. You have not tasted the Dead Sea, so you cannot know whether it has the same flavour as black bile or not.'

'Dogs push their noses into the groins of passers-by and fornicate whenever the mood takes them,' ranted William, causing Michael's Benedictines to exchange shocked glances and Wynewyk to falter in his pedantic analysis of Roman law. Bartholomew saw he was losing the attention of his own students again: Deynman frowned as he absorbed the friar's statement with the same seriousness that he applied to all his lessons, while Falmeresham began to snigger a second time. So did Michael.

'Name one of the diseases caused by an excess of black bile,' Bartholomew said quickly.

'Melancholy,' said Deynman. Bartholomew gaped at him. 'What is the matter? Am I wrong?'

'You are right,' said Bartholomew, trying to regain his composure. He did not add that it was one of the few correct answers Deynman had ever given, and felt a sudden lifting of his spirits. His jubilation was not to last.

'And they eat the excrement of other animals,' raved William, pacing back and forth as he worked himself into a frenzy.

'They do not!' objected Falmeresham. He kept a hound himself, and was fond of it. 'Dogs just like the smell.'

'Pay attention to your own lesson,' snapped William. 'We are discussing theology here, not medicine, and it is too lofty a discipline for your feeble mind to comprehend. Besides, I am not talking about dogs, I am talking about Dominicans.'

'They do not eat excrement, either,' argued Falmeresham.

'People are always melancholic when they have an excess of black bile,' elaborated Deynman, pleased he had

250

his teacher's approval. Bartholomew struggled to ignore the burgeoning debate between Falmeresham and William, to concentrate on what his student was saying. 'And that is because they are distressed over the loss of their haemorrhoids.'

Bartholomew closed his eyes. Deynman's brief foray into accurate understanding had been too good to be true. Once again, certain points had stuck in his mind, but had then rearranged themselves in a way that allowed him to draw some very bizarre conclusions.

'Dominicans are afflicted with haemorrhoids,' declared William matter-of-factly, indicating that he was listening to other lectures, too, as he cut across Falmeresham's spirited defence of dogs and Dominicans alike. 'It comes from sitting in cold, dark places while they plot their satanic acts. And *that* is what makes them morose and melancholy.'

'Galen says that the removal of organs that contain blood – such as veins and haemorrhoids – might cause black bile to get the upper hand in the balance of the humours and bring about melancholy,' said Falmeresham, deciding that taking issue with William was a lost cause. 'He is referring to a loss of *vessels* causing the imbalance; he is not saying patients become depressed because they are sorry to see their haemorrhoids go.'

'Dominicans are proud of these marks,' William went on. 'It is the communal suffering they endure that makes their brotherhood so powerful. After all, what more shameful secret can you share than intimate knowledge of each other's haemorrhoids?'

'I cannot teach in here,' said Bartholomew abruptly, gathering his books and heading for the door, indicating that his students were to follow. 'I am going to the orchard. It may be cold and it may even rain, but at least I will not have to do battle with this kind of rubbish.'

'Dominicans such as Clippesby,' said William loudly,

'who lounges comfortably in his hospital, while his hapless colleagues are compelled to do his work.'

'Is that the reason for Clippesby's absence?' asked Deynman, wide eyed. 'Haemorrhoids? I thought it was insanity.'

'I will come with you, Matthew,' announced William, preparing to follow the physician outside. 'It is too hot in here. Besides, I will be able to speak properly in the orchard – I am tired of being forced to whisper all the time.'

Langelee gave a startled gulp of laughter, which encouraged his students to join in, and the hall was soon filled with hoots and guffaws, while William's face expressed his total bemusement.

'He really has no idea,' said Wynewyk to Bartholomew in wonderment. 'Is he quite normal, do you think? He accuses Clippesby of madness, but there are times when I think he is worse.'

'You go,' said Langelee to William, stepping forward to take control and wiping tears from his eyes. 'You are right, Father. It is stuffy in here, and it is a shame you are obliged to speak softly. Sit in the orchard and expound your theories so they can be properly heard.'

'They will be heard in Ely,' said Michael in alarm, as the friar left with his reluctant students in tow. 'And worse, at the Dominican convent! We will have enraged Black Friars at our gates within an hour, and you know how keen I am to keep the peace until the Visitation is over.'

'The Dominicans are perfectly aware that William's opinions do not represent our own,' said Langelee, relieved to have the Franciscan gone. 'Besides, would you really object if they silenced him by force? I would not. He is becoming a liability with his stupid ideas and braying voice. Perhaps we *should* summon a few Dominicans to shut him up – preferably before he has an opportunity to regale the Archbishop with his nasty theories.'

Michael sighed, unable to answer. It was a good deal quieter in the hall without William, and Bartholomew made rapid progress on Galen and black bile. Even Deynman seemed to have improved by the end of the lesson, and the physician was encouraged. He spent the second half of the afternoon teaching a combined class of his own students and Clippesby's how to calculate the speed of the planets through the sky using different geometrical techniques. Afterwards, leaving the students reeling from their mental exertions, he visited Rougham, and was pleased to find him sleeping peacefully.

Matilde was sleeping peacefully, too, so he crept out of the house so as not to disturb her, knowing that neither patient nor nurse would require his services that night. Rougham would soon be gone from her life and at that point, Bartholomew decided, they would discuss the future, and whether it would be one they might share. He returned to Michaelhouse, read until he started to feel drowsy, then went to bed, where he slept deeply and well.

Michael cornered Langelee the following morning, and confided that he was now seriously worried about the Oxford murders and the damaging effect they might have when the Archbishop arrived in three days' time. Unlike Bartholomew, he had slept fitfully, and Gonerby, Okehamptone and Chesterfelde had paraded through his mind like lost souls. His beadles informed him that the merchants had been at the Cardinal's Cap the previous evening, and had befriended a number of locals with their deep purses: the resulting discussion had included the notion that the University might be harbouring a killer. Rougham's medical students had overheard, and there had been an unpleasant exchange of words before the beadles were able to remove the scholars and fine them for drinking in a tavern.

Langelee was a practical man, ambitious for his University, and he desperately wanted Islip to found his new College in Cambridge. He understood perfectly that three tradesmen hunting a scholar for murder would not make for peaceful relations, and was willing to do whatever was necessary to help. He immediately agreed to release Michael and Bartholomew from their teaching until the Visitation was over. Bartholomew was not pleased to be informed that his classes were to be suspended while he chased killers, but appreciated the now urgent need to solve the case before the Visitation. Langelee ordered the fiscally talented Wynewyk to manipulate the College finances so that two postgraduates could be paid to stand in for the absent masters, and Bartholomew set his students an unreasonable amount of work, hoping they would become alarmed by the number of texts they would eventually need to master and would settle down to some serious study.

First, Bartholomew and Michael decided to see Clippesby at Stourbridge. The physician wanted to assess whether it was he who had attacked him in St Michael's Church, while Michael was keen to question him about the deaths of Okehamptone and Gonerby. When Langelee urged Bartholomew to bring Clippesby back, sane or otherwise, Michael confided that he was a suspect, although he prudently kept Rougham's name out of the explanation.

Langelee was appalled. 'But I was under the impression you had him locked away for his own sake, so he could enjoy a little peace, away from the strains of academic life.'

'I wish that were true,' said Bartholomew unhappily.

'Then I hope you are wrong,' said Langelee fervently. 'We all know he is insane, but it has always been a charming kind of madness, not the kind that makes him rip out men's throats like a wild beast. But it makes sense, I suppose. He has always claimed an affinity with animals, and it is not such a great leap from that to imagining he *is* one – the kind that likes to savage its prey.'

Michael complained bitterly that there were no horses available for hire – they had all been put to pasture until after the Visitation, so they would not make a mess on the newly cleaned streets – and that he was obliged to waddle the mile or so to the ramshackle collection of huts that comprised the hospital at Stourbridge. His temper did not improve when they were obliged to battle with a powerful headwind that drove rain straight into their faces. It snatched the wide-brimmed hat from his head and deposited it in a boggy meadow that was difficult to traverse. Bartholomew's boots were full of muddy water by the time they had retrieved it, and Michael's normally pristine habit was streaked with filth.

'Damn Clippesby,' the monk muttered venomously when the thatched roofs of Stourbridge finally came into sight. 'Why has he so suddenly taken it into his head to chew necks? He has never shown cannibalistic tendencies before.'

'He may be innocent,' said Bartholomew, although he could see the monk was unconvinced. 'But you should put your question to Brother Paul, who has much more experience of insanity than I. He may tell you that this kind of violence is not a factor in Clippesby's particular condition, and that we should be looking to another madman for our culprit.'

Michael knocked at the hospital's gate, then looked around with interest as they were ushered inside. He did not visit Stourbridge often, and always forgot how impressed he was by its orderly cleanliness. 'We shall see Paul first, and then . . . what in God's name is he doing?'

'That patient has acute lethargy, so Paul is attempting to cure her by setting her feet in salt water, ringing bells in her ears, and placing feathers under her nose to make her sneeze.'

Michael regarded him askance. 'Will it work?'

Bartholomew shrugged. 'Such a course of treatment has sound classical antecedents, although I am sure there must be gentler ways to treat her, as yet undiscovered. In a moment, he will put the feather in her throat to induce retching, then he will bleed her, to rid her of excessive humours.'

'We should talk to him before he starts, then,' said Michael hastily. 'I am already covered in mud, and I do not want to be sprayed with blood and vomit, too.'

'What do you think?' asked Brother Paul worriedly, when he saw Bartholomew approaching. 'Does she seem any better to you?'

Bartholomew considered. 'No. She seems more listless than ever. But intensive humoral therapy is exhausting, so perhaps you should allow her more rest between sessions.'

Paul regarded his charge with sad eyes. 'We can try, I suppose, since nothing else seems to be working. What about electuaries and embrocations? Can you recommend any that might help?'

Bartholomew shook his head slowly. 'Ailments of the mind are a complete mystery to me, and all my training and experience seem to count for nothing when I meet cases like these. You are far wiser about them than I, and you should trust what your own instincts tell you to do.'

'My instincts are failing me dismally at the moment.' Paul nodded at the drooping woman who sat disconsolately, with her legs in a bucket and a down scarf around her neck. 'I make no headway with her, while Clippesby is entirely beyond my skills. I misjudge him at every turn.'

Bartholomew regarded him in alarm. 'What is the matter? Has he harmed someone? Or himself?'

'No, no,' said Paul quickly. 'Nothing like that. But he seems recovered one moment, and mad the next. I cannot make him out. I trust him completely to help with the others – he is patient and gentle with even the most vicious and ungrateful of them – but he seems unable to follow orders about his own well-being. And he will insist on quitting the hospital, when he knows he must stay. He left us again on Tuesday evening – he was gone when I looked in his room after dusk, but was back for prime on Wednesday morning. I beg him not to wander off in the dark, but he cannot seem to help himself.'

Bartholomew and Michael exchanged a glance: so, it could have been Clippesby who had attacked Bartholomew with the spade. Nervously, Bartholomew wondered what else he might have done.

'Did you ask where he had been?' asked Michael.

'He does not know,' said Paul tiredly. 'He is not lying – he really does have no idea. There is not much more I can do for him, Matt, other than offer company, a little recreational work and a safe haven – which will not be very safe if he continues to escape.'

'How does he get out?' asked Bartholomew. 'I thought you locked his door at night, and his window has mullions that are impossible to squeeze through.'

'I forgot to bar the door,' said Paul apologetically. 'I was busy. Ned Tucker was dying and Clippesby slipped my mind. It was my fault, but I am sorry he took advantage of my lapse. Speak to him, and explain again that he is here for his own good.'

While Paul turned his attention to the unresponsive woman, Bartholomew and Michael looked for Clippesby. He was not in the peaceful little chapel, saying prayers for Ned Tucker like many other inmates, nor was he in the kitchen helping to prepare the next meal. Next to the church was a large dormitory that contained the beds of those who required constant care; the fitter residents slept in smaller buildings, some of which could be locked to ensure they did not escape to harm themselves or others. It was in the hall that they found Clippesby, reading to a patient who was in the last stages of a disease that had ravaged his face. He raised his finger to his lips when Bartholomew and Michael entered, and continued speaking. It was only when the man slept that Clippesby left him.

He looked healthy and cheerful, and his eyes had lost the wild expression that had so unnerved Bartholomew the day after Rougham had been attacked. He had combed his hair, so it lay flat and even across his tonsured pate, his face was shaved to a rosy pinkness, and his habit was scrupulously clean. It was difficult to see him as a deranged lunatic who bit the necks of his victims and wielded spades in dark churches. He smiled at Bartholomew, then clasped Michael's hand.

'It is good to see Michaelhouse men,' he said, leading them to his own room so that their voices would not disturb the sleeping leper. 'It is dull here, with no one of any intelligence to speak to. Paul is always too busy or too tired, and most of the others are beyond caring about decent conversation.'

'I am sorry you have to be here,' said Bartholomew sincerely. 'But Paul tells me you made a bid for freedom on Tuesday night and were gone until dawn the following day. Why?'

Clippesby shrugged. 'Why do you think? I have been here fifteen days now, and I am bored. I went for a walk, although I cannot tell you where. I just followed a mouse.'

'A mouse,' said Michael flatly.

'Well, a field mouse, naturally,' elaborated Clippesby. 'But you would know that, of course. One is hardly likely to find a dormouse with time on her hands at this time of year!' He laughed, to indicate he considered the notion preposterous.

'Did this mouse eventually lead you to Cambridge?' asked Michael. 'To St Michael's?'

'I do not recall,' replied Clippesby. 'I was too absorbed in what she had to tell me.'

'And what was that?' asked Michael suspiciously. 'It was nothing to do with the gnawing of throats, was it? Or the wielding of spades?'

'Hardly!' said Clippesby, startled. 'Her conversation was rather more genteel, and involved a discussion between St Benedict and his holy sister St Scholastica three days before her death.'

'Scholastica?' echoed Michael immediately. 'Did this mouse mention riots, by any chance? On Scholastica's feast day in Oxford?'

'She did, but those are of scant importance when compared to the dialogue between the two mystics. I am sure you are aware, Brother, that no one knows exactly what was discussed the night Scholastica summoned a great storm to keep her brother from returning to his monastery – so he would stay with her. But the mouse knew.'

'This mouse must be a considerable age,' said Bartholomew, amused. 'This alleged conversation is said to have taken place eight hundred years ago.'

'She did not hear it herself,' said Clippesby, irritated by the lack of understanding. 'It was witnessed by an ancestor, and the information has been passed through the family from century to century. The same sort of thing happens with humans. Generations of first-born Clippesbys have been called John, to name but one example.'

'Well?' asked Michael. 'What did St Benedict and his sister talk about that stormy night? What they were going to have for breakfast?'

'That would no doubt be *your* choice of subject,' replied Clippesby crisply. 'But pious folk are not obsessed with such earthly matters. Benedict and Scholastica talked about the power of creation, and how one life is so small and insignificant compared to the living universe.'

'Well, that very much depends on whose life we are talking about,' said Michael, smarting over the accusation that he was venally minded. 'For example, I would not consider Matt's unimportant, and someone tried to take it before dawn on Wednesday morning.'

'Really?' asked Clippesby, his eyes wide. 'How terrible! But you are unharmed, so whoever tried to rob you was unsuccessful.'

'How do you know it was a robber?'

'Why else would anyone attack him?'

'Have you encountered two men called Boltone and Eudo?' asked Bartholomew, seeing Clippesby was not going to admit to being in St Michael's at the time of the attack – if he even knew. But the mention of robbers had brought to mind the dishonest residents of Merton Hall.

'The Merton Hall chickens detest Boltone,' replied Clippesby. 'They say he has been cheating his masters for years. Meanwhile, Edwardus Rex, the dog with whom Yolande de Blaston lives, tells me that Eudo may have stolen the silver statue I gave to Matilde.'

Michael nodded. 'It seems he took it when he visited her to get a remedy for women's pains – for the wife he does not have.'

'Many men do that,' said Clippesby. 'Matilde is good and generous, and people trust her. You should marry her, Matt, before someone else steals her heart.'

'Yes,' agreed Bartholomew, aware that Clippesby was regarding him expectantly. He hesitated, on the verge of confiding his decision to make her his wife, but then Clippesby's attention was snatched by a flock of pigeons landing in the yard, and the moment was lost.

'Do your chickens know anything about an astrolabe owned by Geoffrey Dodenho?' asked Michael hopefully. 'It was sold to someone at Merton Hall.'

Clippesby shook his head. 'No, but the King's Hall rats

told me that Dodenho claimed it had been stolen by another Fellow – probably by his room-mate, who is called Wolf – but that he suddenly went quiet about it. They think he later found it again, but because he had made such a fuss about its "theft", he was obliged to sell it – so he would not have to apologise for making unfounded accusations. The rats say *that* is why Wolf ran away: he did not like being considered a felon.'

'When you say "King's Hall rats" are you referring to small furry rodents or to men in tabards?' asked Michael cautiously.

'Rodents, of course,' said Clippesby, annoyed. 'I do not insult rats by likening them to people.'

'Do they or the chickens know anything about Eudo or Boltone?' asked Michael. He sounded uncomfortable, unsure of how to deal with the strange realities of Clippesby's world.

Clippesby scratched his head. 'I do not think so, but I can ask. The problem with hens is that they are not always interested in the same things as us, and one needs to question them very carefully to determine whether or not they know anything of relevance. It is quite an art.'

'I can well imagine,' said Michael dryly. 'I have encountered similar problems myself. But I need to ask you more questions, if you have no objection. Matt and I have been investigating a very complex case, and you may be able to help us.'

Clippesby nodded sombrely. 'Of course. I am always willing to be of service to you, although you should be aware that a *desire* to help is not the same as being *able* to help. But ask your questions, and we shall see. As the hedgehogs of Peterhouse always say, if you do not ask, you will not receive.'

'Right.' Michael cleared his throat uneasily. 'Where did you go in February, when you abandoned your teaching for ten days without permission?'

261

'You have already fined me for that,' said Clippesby, immediately defensive. 'You cannot punish me twice for the same offence. Besides, I told you what happened: an owl came and told me my father was ill, so I went without delay to visit him in Norfolk.'

'Norfolk?' asked Michael. 'Not Oxford?'

Clippesby grimaced. 'Certainly not. I dislike Oxford, and would never go there willingly.'

'Was your father unwell?'

'No,' admitted Clippesby. 'The owl must have confused him with someone else.'

'Then what about your more recent absences? Where were you on the eve of Ascension Day?'

'That was the night Rougham was attacked and I saved his life,' replied Clippesby resentfully. 'I wish I had not bothered, because then I would not be incarcerated here. However, I do not recall exactly where else I was that evening. You had plied me with too much wine earlier, Brother, and my wits were addled.'

'That had nothing to do with the wine,' muttered Michael. 'Then what about last Saturday?'

'You think I had something to do with the murder at Merton Hall – the man with the cut wrist?' asked Clippesby. He saw Michael's surprise that he should know about Chesterfelde, and smiled enigmatically. 'The chickens mentioned what had happened – I told you I am friendly with them. But I did not kill anyone, Brother. I do not waste time with people when there are animals to talk to. What *they* say is worth hearing, unlike the vicious ramblings of men.' Abruptly he turned his attention to Bartholomew, who was simultaneously disconcerted and startled by the penetrating stare. 'I know what you are thinking.'

'You do?' asked Bartholomew, sincerely hoping he did not. He had lost interest in the discussion, and his thoughts had turned to Matilde. In the dusty gloom of Clippesby's chamber he had reached a decision, and he knew with absolute certainty that it was the right one. He would marry Matilde. He loved her more than he had ever loved anyone, and his Fellowship was a small price to pay for the honour of spending the rest of his life with such a woman. His mind now irrevocably made up, he felt strangely sanguine about the University and its various mysteries. It occurred to him that he should probably confide his plans to Matilde before resigning and making arrangements to secure them a house, and determined to do so at the first opportunity. He did not countenance the appalling possibility that she might decline his offer.

Clippesby frowned slightly, noting the distant look in his colleague's eyes. 'I know what you think about me,' he said, correcting himself.

'And what is that?' asked Bartholomew pleasantly, ready to embrace the whole world in his new-found happiness and serenity.

'You order me to stay here, because you say folk do not understand my kinship with animals and you are afraid someone may hurt me. But the reality is that *you* are one of those people. You may not wish me harm, but you no more understand my relationship with the natural world than they do. You are just like them, only you hide your opinions behind a veil of concern.'

'He is worried about you,' said Michael gently, while Bartholomew gazed at him in dismay, uncomfortably aware that he was right. His brief surge of bliss vanished, leaving him with the sense that he had let Clippesby down. He did not understand him, and was probably no better than others in that respect – worse, even, because his inability to physic him had led to his incarceration.

'And *you* want me here because you are afraid my idio-syncrasies might reflect badly on Michaelhouse when the

Archbishop comes,' said Clippesby, rounding on the monk. 'You are afraid I will say or do something that will make us a laughing stock. After all, what College wants a Fellow whose behaviour is so unlike anyone else's?'

'You are right,' agreed Michael bluntly. 'I *was* relieved when Matt suggested you come here for a few days. The Visitation is important, and I cannot risk anything or anyone damaging our prospects.'

Clippesby laughed harshly. 'Honesty! Well, at least that is refreshing. But you need to open your mind, Brother. Just because I do not distil my knowledge from books does not make me insane.'

'Talking to animals is not something normal men do,' said Michael with an unrepentant shrug.

'Saint Francis did it,' countered Clippesby. 'And no one accused him of madness.'

'He was *kind* to animals – he did not ask their advice and repeat their philosophical theories. There is a difference. But this debate is going nowhere, because we will never agree.'

'No,' said Clippesby softly. 'We will not. So, what will you do? Lock me here until I conform to your way of thinking and admit I am wrong? Send me to some remote parish, where I will never see an Archbishop's Visitation? Or slit my throat and be rid of the embarrassment permanently?'

'No!' cried Bartholomew, appalled he should think they would consider such dire options.

'No?' asked Clippesby sharply. 'No what? No to murder or exile, or no to letting me return to my duties at Michaelhouse?'

'No to the latter, and that is for certain,' said Michael firmly. 'Two men, possibly more, have died from peculiar wounds and Rougham was seriously injured. He says he *saw* you attack him, so you are currently at the top of my list of suspects. I want you to remain here until you are

264

either exonerated or we have positive proof of your guilt. Only then will we discuss what to do next.'

'I have not killed anyone,' reiterated Clippesby angrily. 'I cannot imagine why you insist on believing Rougham over me, when you know what the man is like. He lies. Have I ever lied to you?'

'Not exactly,' said Michael. 'But I never know when to believe you. Sometimes you speak gibberish, while other times you make perfect sense.'

'I will stay,' said Clippesby, gesturing to his bed. 'But you will find I have nothing to do with these crimes. When you do – and only then – we shall talk sensibly, and discuss how best to live with each other's oddities.'

Michael gaped at him. 'Some of us are more odd than others, so will have to make bigger concessions.'

Clippesby smiled. 'I am willing to be flexible, Brother. However, it is not *your* gross eccentricity I was referring to. It is Father William's.'

'Now there we do agree. I just have one more thing to ask. When you talked about us keeping you here or killing you, why did you select a slit throat as the means of execution?'

'Because that is what I saw the wolf trying to do to Rougham,' replied Clippesby. 'And then there was the man in Merton Hall's cistern.'

'What man?' asked Bartholomew, an uneasy feeling beginning to gnaw at the pit of his stomach.

'The one who died near the well,' elaborated Clippesby patiently. 'There was him a week or so ago, and there was Chesterfelde on Saturday night.'

'Chesterfelde?' asked Bartholomew, bemused by the sudden stream of information. 'You saw what happened to him? But you just said you did not.'

'No, I told you I did not *kill* him,' corrected Clippesby pedantically. 'However, I did not see what happened,

265

because I could not bring myself to watch. You know how I deplore violence. The hens were braver: they saw his wrist cut, resulting in his death. The first man was different, though, because it was his *throat* that was gashed, not his arm.'

'The first man,' said Bartholomew uneasily. 'You mean Okehamptone?'

'No, Okehamptone died when the wolf had him – the chickens told me about it. Chickens do not like wolves. I am talking about the man who was put in the cistern *after* Ascension Day.'

'He is talking about the body you found when you were rescuing me,' said Michael to Bartholomew, although the physician did not need him to state the obvious. 'We have four victims with throat injuries now: Gonerby, Okehamptone, the cistern man and Rougham.'

'But I cannot say for certain whether all four of those were claimed by the wolf,' said Clippesby. 'Just the two I was watching when the wolf found them – Rougham and the man in the cistern – and Okehamptone, because the chickens told me about him. I know nothing about your Gonerby, while Chesterfelde was most certainly *not* killed by the wolf.'

'This wolf,' said Bartholomew carefully. 'Have you spoken to him at all?'

'I would have nothing to say to a creature like that. I do not associate with rough beasts that kill for pleasure, only with those who can help me understand the natural universe.'

'Then what about the chickens?' pressed Michael. 'Did they talk to it?'

'Do not be ridiculous, Brother! I have already told you that hens dislike wolves.'

'Hopefully, Tulyet will retrieve this other body today,' said Michael. 'Then we might have some answers – some *rational* answers.' He shot Clippesby a reproachful glance.

'It happened more than a week ago now,' mused Clippesby, lost in reverie. 'I went to the towpath, where there are always birds ready to talk – moorhens, geese and ducks. I met the hens, and we were appalled when our philosophical debate was interrupted by murder.'

'Tell me what you saw,' said Michael with a sigh, valiantly striving to distil truth from the confused jumble of information that Clippesby was spouting. 'Exactly.'

'I saw nothing, as I told you already. But the chickens saw the man's throat bitten out.'

Bartholomew and Michael argued all the way back to Michaelhouse. Bartholomew thought Clippesby had picked up snippets of gossip when he had escaped to wander in the town, while Michael claimed he knew too much for his knowledge to have been innocently obtained. He believed Clippesby's inexplicable absences from Stourbridge were proof that he was deranged enough to kill and remember nothing later, except for the snatches of information he attributed to his animal friends.

'You know he is good at eavesdropping,' Bartholomew insisted. 'He always has been, ever since he arrived in Cambridge. He sits very still for long periods of time in odd places. He may well have witnessed these murders.'

'I cannot believe you trust him. He is demented! You are a physician – you do not need me to tell you this. He cannot distinguish between reality and fiction, and he genuinely believes animals talk to him. *He* is the chickens and the rats who saw these murders, and he is also the wolf that committed them.'

'He cannot be both.'

'Then how is he aware of the man in the cistern? The only folk who know about him are you, me and Tulyet. And the killer, of course.'

'Not true. All sorts of people will have heard about him by now: Dick's soldiers, the inhabitants of Merton Hall who came to haul us out. And what about Eudo and Boltone? They knew about the corpse, or they would not have attacked us when we approached the place where it was hidden.'

Michael declined to be diverted. 'Clippesby might not understand what he has done, but he is our man. I am becoming increasingly certain of it.'

'Well, I am not. He seems so rational at times.' Bartholomew rubbed a hand through his hair. 'I am completely out of my depth with him, Michael. Most of the time he is gentle and innocently fascinated by the natural world, no matter how bizarre his methods of gathering information about it.'

'I see we will not agree until we have more evidence.' Michael sighed. 'I am grateful Paul has agreed to keep him under lock and key until we tell him otherwise. It is better this way – for him as well as for us. I do not want him racing up the High Street and biting the Archbishop of Canterbury's throat, while the rest of us are all busily trying to impress the man.'

Bartholomew was deeply unhappy with the step Michael had insisted they take, which entailed securing Clippesby in his cell and not allowing him out to help with the other patients. Clippesby said nothing, but his eyes held an immense hurt that had cut Bartholomew to the quick. He only hoped the case would be resolved quickly, and the Dominican could be either freed or convicted. He was certain either would be preferable to the friar than an indefinite prison sentence. He promised to bring scrolls, to help him pass his long hours of solitude and, on a whim, offered to find a cat or a puppy to keep him company. Clippesby declined, claiming he would not wish imprisonment on any living thing, and that the hell visited on him for communing with nature was his to bear alone, and not to be inflicted on other innocent creatures.

Physician and monk were still quarrelling when they met Tulyet. The Sheriff was striding along the High Street with some of his men, all of whom were dirty, wet and scowling, and Bartholomew supposed they had just finished searching the cistern. Tulyet did not seem overly pleased to see his friends, and Bartholomew sensed something was wrong.

'Have you confiscated that bow from Dickon yet?' asked Michael, either not noticing Tulyet's cool manner or not caring. 'If not, I would like to borrow him for a while. There are a number of people in this town I would not mind him dispatching.'

'Do not jest about such things,' said Tulyet curtly. 'There are several folk he dislikes, and my wife is terrified he may try to shoot them, just as he did Eudo.'

'Dickon disliked Eudo?' asked Bartholomew. 'I was not aware they even knew each other.'

'Dickon likes to look over our boundary wall, but Eudo took exception, and words were exchanged. So were stones at one point. I did not know about this until today, because my wife was afraid I would be angry. She says Eudo came to complain about it.'

'Dickon lobbed rocks at him?' Michael was amused.

'They threw them at each other, apparently,' said Tulyet. 'But Dickon's were better aimed.'

'I am not surprised Eudo objected to a pair of curious eyes, given what has been happening around his cistern,' said Bartholomew. 'Clippesby claims to have witnessed a murder there a week ago, and says that was where Chesterfelde received his fatal injury, too. But Dickon saved us with his timely arrow, and I shall always be grateful to him.'

Tulyet gave a tight smile. 'That is the only spark of light in this nasty affair: Dickon rescued two dear friends.'

'Twice,' said Michael. 'Once when he shot Eudo and drove him away, and again when he fetched you to pull us out of the well. Has he told you about anything else he saw? I know Matt thinks Clippesby is a credible witness, who will impress any jury with his clarity and common sense, but I would sooner trust Dickon.'

'You could never believe anything Clippesby says,' said Tulyet, regarding Bartholomew as though he was insane himself. 'He told me he was a monkey last month.'

'Did he?' asked Bartholomew, troubled.

'He claims the similarity between men and apes means God used the same mould when He created them. Have you ever heard such nonsense? But I have questioned Dickon again and again about Eudo, and I still have no clear idea of what the boy saw. I suppose it is not surprising: he is very young and has no proper concept of time.'

'Then what did your dredging reveal?' asked Michael. 'Who is this man with the cut throat?'

'No one,' said Tulyet. 'We emptied the pit to the bottom, and nothing was in it except mud. Either you were mistaken, Matt, or someone was there before us and retrieved the body first. There is no corpse in the well, and no indication that there ever has been.'

CHAPTER 8

'I do not know whether to be relieved or alarmed,' said Michael, as he and Bartholomew took their leave of the disgruntled Sheriff. 'Without a body, we have no evidence of a crime, so I am not obliged to cram another investigation into my already busy schedule. However, assuming you did not imagine the entire incident and the corpse really does exist, then we have yet another mystery to look into: why did someone steal it?'

'I hoisted it up easily enough,' said Bartholomew. 'So, anyone else could have done the same once word was out that Dick planned to drain the cistern. Eudo and Boltone could have reclaimed it before making their escape a second time.'

'That assumes they put it there in the first place,' Michael pointed out.

'They must have done. Why fight us otherwise? It would not have been worth the trouble – or the risk. Boltone has a good job as Merton's bailiff, while Eudo is a local man with friends who say he likes living here. Neither would willingly turn outlaw without good reason.'

'Boltone is the subject of an enquiry. His life as a bailiff will never be the same, even if Duraunt deems him innocent, so perhaps he thought he had nothing to lose.'

'Perhaps,' acknowledged Bartholomew. 'It is a pity we do not know the dead man's identity. He was youngish, because his teeth were white, but that is all I could tell you about him.'

Michael was thoughtful. 'You should not be too

convinced that Eudo and Boltone are responsible for this mysterious corpse. As far as I am concerned, he is Clippesby's victim. I imagine *he* will be pleased to learn that the body could not be found.'

Bartholomew gave a triumphant smile. 'And that is something to consider, Brother! If Clippesby killed this man and threw him in the cistern, then who pulled him out? The only person to benefit would be Clippesby, and he could not have done it, because he has been locked up at Stourbridge.'

'Then what about all the times he escaped? He could easily have gone out, retrieved the body and been back before dawn, with no one any the wiser.'

'How could he have known that Tulyet planned to drain the well?'

Michael sighed. 'I imagine a robin or a weasel warned him. But I refuse to discuss this further until we have more information.'

'And how do we get that?'

Michael tapped his temple. 'By using our minds, as we have done on other occasions. We shall return to Michaelhouse, write down all we know, and analyse every eventuality until we see a pattern emerge. Are you prepared to spend a morning scribing for me? I do not trust anyone else.'

Bartholomew nodded. 'And we *will* prove Clippesby is innocent.'

'I see you intend to conduct the exercise with a suitably impartial mind.'

Since both had run out of parchment, they were obliged to visit the stationer's premises, to buy more. The shop, strategically sited on the High Street, was a grand affair with a tiled roof and several spacious rooms. Weasenham, Alyce and their servants lived on the upper floor, while the lower chambers were where they manufactured their writing materials, scribed their *exemplar pecia*, and made their sales. Bartholomew liked the shop with its sharp, metallic aroma of ink, and the warm, rich scent of new parchment, although he was less keen on its gossiping owner. When he followed Michael inside, he saw business was good: the place was crammed full of scholars and clerks, some trying to read the exemplars without actually buying them, some passing the time of day with acquaintances, and others waiting to be served.

Weasenham himself stood at a table, where he showed two customers an array of pens made from swan feathers, demonstrating how much easier they were to sharpen than those made from the more traditional goose. Alyce was near the back of the shop, engrossed in a deep discussion with Langelee. She was laughing, and their conversation was clearly about more than the glue Langelee was pretending to inspect. When he saw his Fellows approach, Langelee left abruptly and somewhat furtively. Moments later Alyce followed, and Bartholomew glimpsed them both darting down the small lane that led to the rear of the house.

'Weasenham will wonder where she has gone,' he said, thinking the Master overly bold in his courting. By contrast, his own meetings with Matilde were the picture of discretion – he had certainly not frolicked with a married woman in broad daylight, and in her husband's own back yard.

'He is run off his feet with customers,' said Michael, amused. 'He will not know whether she is here or not, so it is an excellent time for Langelee to seduce his wife. Do not look so disapproving, Matt, given what you have been doing of late.'

'You know what I have been doing,' said Bartholomew, offended. 'And it is not—'

Michael nodded towards the stationer. 'Weasenham's current customers are Dodenho and Wormynghalle.

Dodenho is fussy and pompous, and will keep him busy for hours with his exacting demands, while Wormynghalle probably takes his pens as seriously as he does the rest of his studies. Langelee is a genius to choose now to seduce Alyce.'

Bartholomew craned his neck to peer through the free-standing shelves, and saw the stationer was indeed serving the two scholars from King's Hall. He could hear Dodenho's braying voice as he demanded the best quality equipment, anxious that everyone should know him to be a man of means and good taste. Wormynghalle gave her full, quiet attention to the task in hand, and her face was intense as she considered the writing implements Weasenham displayed. Bartholomew saw that the incident in Paxtone's room had unnerved her, because she had been to even more trouble to render herself masculine. She had dirtied her clothes to emulate her more slovenly colleagues, and there was grime under fingernails that had previously been clean. She also had a brazenly feminine silk glove tucked into her belt, proclaiming to all who saw it that she kept a female lover. Michael saw it, too, and Bartholomew was certain it would result in a fine.

A group of Bartholomew's students were on the premises, too, under the loose supervision of Deynman and Falmeresham. They were assessing the cost of vellum, to use for the short treatises they were obliged to produce by the end of the term. Deynman had already purchased the most expensive kind, no doubt hoping that its superior quality would detract from the poor standard of what was written on it. The atmosphere was jovial, with light-hearted banter that resulted in a lot of laughter.

After a moment, the door rattled open and several Gonville Hall scholars bustled in. Bartholomew recognised their leader as William of Lee, Rougham's most senior student, who took his master's classes when he was away.

274

Lee looked more like a wrestler than a physician, and would have done better as a surgeon, where brute force was useful for setting bones and sawing off damaged limbs. When he saw the Michaelhouse lads, he swaggered towards them.

'Now there will be trouble,' muttered Michael uneasily.

'Stop it, then,' suggested Bartholomew, searching the shelves for the parchment he wanted. 'You *are* the Senior Proctor.'

'I will wait and see what happens. I do not want Lee to accuse me of heavy-handedness. He is quick to take offence, and if he insults me, your boys will rally to my defence with their fists.'

He edged closer, taking care to keep himself well concealed behind the labyrinth of storage furniture that displayed Weasenham's wares. Bartholomew followed, not to help, but because the type of parchment he was hunting for had been moved since the last time he had visited the shop.

'I am surprised to see you here,' said Lee tauntingly to Falmeresham. 'I did not think you could afford decent supplies.'

'You are right,' replied Falmeresham pleasantly. 'I do not come from a wealthy family, but Deynman is buying it for me, as payment for the help I have given him with his studies this year.'

'Then he is a fool,' said Lee contemptuously. 'Only an ass would waste money on such a stupid exercise.'

'Stupid exercise?' echoed Falmeresham innocently. He appealed to Lee's cronies, who were ranged in a pugilistic line behind him. 'Take heed, gentlemen. Lee thinks helping friends is a "stupid exercise". You should ask yourselves whether he is someone worthy of your companionship.'

'That is not what I meant,' snapped Lee, irked by the

way his words had been twisted. 'I meant he is squandering his gold by buying vellum for the likes of *you*. I heard you are a bastard.'

Michael stiffened, readying himself to intervene, while Wormynghalle tore herself away from the pens and listened to the burgeoning argument with an expression of alarm. She started to edge towards the door, unwilling to be implicated in an incident that might draw unwanted attention. Dodenho, however, was more interested in holding forth about quills, and Weasenham was too intent on securing a sale to notice the quarrel brewing under his roof.

'What *is* a waste of money,' said Falmeresham lightly, 'are lessons from Doctor Rougham.'

'True,' muttered Michael to himself. 'But this is not a good time to mention it.'

Lee's brows drew together. 'What do you mean?'

'I mean he is never here,' replied Falmeresham, who had meant nothing of the kind and was obviously enjoying playing with the slow-witted Lee. 'He has been gone for more than two weeks – in the middle of term and when his students need him most.'

'He is on leave,' replied Lee. 'We had a letter saying he has gone to visit his family.'

'Then I hope he returns as good a teacher as when he left,' said Falmeresham ambiguously.

Lee scratched his head as he considered the statement, and Falmeresham lost interest in baiting him. It was too easy; he preferred someone who provided more of a challenge. He doffed his hat in an insulting manner, then turned back to the vellum. His friends followed his lead, and were soon engaged in a good-natured debate that filled the room with ringing voices and boisterous laughter. Lee did nothing for a moment, but then moved to the back of the shop, where he and his cronies began to discuss whether Rougham would prefer his remedies book copied in brown or black ink.

Michael heaved a sigh of relief. 'That was close! Lee was determined to fight, but Falmeresham was too clever for him.'

'He *is* clever,' agreed Bartholomew. 'And I doubt he will forget what Lee said to him today – no man likes being called illegitimate. Those remarks will cost Gonville dearly in time.'

But Michael was not paying attention. He was leaning forward to eavesdrop on the discussion between Weasenham and the King's Hall men. Now the danger of a spat was over, Wormynghalle was back at the counter, fingering the glove in the hope that the stationer would notice it and begin a few rumours about her masculine lechery. Weasenham and Dodenho had agreed a price, and the stationer was regaling his customers with some post-sale gossip. The Michaelhouse students' cheerful banter was enough to mask any sound Michael might have made with his muttered asides, but was not sufficiently loud to drown out the words of the chattering scholars. The situation was perfect for the monk to listen unobserved, and he intended to make the most of it, keen to hear for himself whether the stationer was spreading lies about the Oxford murders.

'Gonville students are the worst,' Weasenham was saying. 'They are not too bad when Rougham is here, because he uses his sharp tongue to keep them in line, but now he is away, they are a menace.'

'When will he return?' asked Wormynghalle. She did not sound very interested in the answer and gave the impression she had asked only to be polite.

'No one knows.' Weasenham's voice dropped to a salacious whisper so that Michael had to strain to hear him. 'They say he has gone to enjoy himself with his lover.'

* * *

277

'His lover?' asked Dodenho, regarding Weasenham doubtfully. 'I doubt he has one. No woman would want him near her, when there are men like me to oblige.'

Michael scowled at Bartholomew when he started to laugh and almost gave away the fact that they were close by. 'I want to hear this,' he hissed irritably.

'Why?' asked Bartholomew, still amused. 'You know it is rubbish – Rougham's lover is a woman he pays every first Monday in the month, and he is definitely not enjoying himself with her now. Weasenham is a vicious-tongued snoop, and his stories are invariably lies.'

'Rougham's lover is no woman,' said Weasenham, snagging Michael's attention back again. Bartholomew peered through a gap in the shelving and saw the stationer's face was bright with malice, lips pressed firmly together in sanctimonious disapproval.

'It is not Chancellor Tynkell, is it?' asked Dodenho. 'I have heard he is a woman, and that is why he never washes – he does not want anyone to know what lies beneath his tabard.'

'Do not be absurd,' said Wormynghalle scornfully. 'That story came from Bartholomew's student – Deynman – and there are no grounds to it, other than his own ludicrously twisted logic. Of course the Chancellor is not a woman.' Her fierce words made Dodenho take a step back in alarm.

'You are getting away from my point,' said Weasenham crossly. He was not interested in ancient rumours when he had new ones to spread. 'Rougham's lover is someone you know: it is Hamecotes. Do not believe the tale that he is in Oxford collecting books. It is not true.'

'It *is* true!' cried Wormynghalle, outraged by the aspersions cast on her room-mate. 'I had a letter from him only this morning, telling me he has secured a copy of *Regulae solvendi sophismata*. It comes from Merton College, and he says it is annotated with notes in Heytesbury's *own hand*.'

She glared at Weasenham, waiting for him to be suitably impressed. Bartholomew certainly was, and wondered whether King's Hall would allow him to study it.

'Besides,' added Dodenho, equally affronted, 'Hamecotes is not inclined towards men. He prefers women – and so does Rougham, if Yolande de Blaston is to be believed.'

'Yolande is a whore,' said Weasenham nastily. 'She will say anything once she is shown the glitter of silver. Doubtless Rougham pays her to tell everyone he is a rampant and manly lover.'

Michael sniggered softly. 'Poor Rougham! After all he has been through to keep his dalliance with Yolande a secret, here is Weasenham telling people that it cannot be true because he is in love with Hamecotes!'

'Why pick on Hamecotes?' demanded Wormynghalle icily. 'Because he is away, and therefore cannot defend himself against these wicked fabrications?'

'Wolf is away, too,' said Weasenham, unperturbed by her ire. 'Perhaps *he* is Rougham's lover.'

'Wolf has a pox, caught from dalliances with unclean women,' confided Dodenho. 'That is why he cannot be seen around the town this term, and why he cannot be Rougham's lover. I should know, because I shared his room before he took himself off to the hospital at Stour . . .' He stopped speaking and bit his lip, aware that he had said something he should not have done.

'Now that is interesting,' breathed Michael. 'Here is something our friends at King's Hall did not deign to mention before.'

'You cannot blame them for that,' Bartholomew whispered back. 'Having Fellows with the pox is not something I would tell the Senior Proctor, either.'

'Well, it is a pack of lies anyway,' said Michael. 'Wolf is not at Stourbridge, or you would have told me so when

279

he first abandoned his duties. You have been there often enough recently, to visit Clippesby.' He glanced sideways. 'Right?'

'Wolf is not there now,' replied Bartholomew vaguely. He shook his head at Michael's exasperation. 'It is not my business to discuss the ailments of other scholars, Brother. That would make me as bad as Weasenham, and besides, who will hire a physician if he is the kind of man to spread embarrassing stories about his patients? It would not be ethical or proper.'

Weasenham's eyes gleamed with interest at Dodenho's slip, while Wormynghalle regarded her colleague in disbelief at his indiscretion. Weasenham was not so rash as to press Dodenho for details while she stood glowering, so he changed the subject back to Hamecotes.

'I asked those Oxford men about Hamecotes and his alleged visits to the Other Place,' he said snidely. 'And they said no self-respecting college would sell scripts to a rival university. Then Polmorva told me that Hamecotes must be using book-buying as an excuse to enjoy his lover with no questions asked. So I put two and two together and . . .' He raised his hands, palms upwards in a shrug, to indicate there was only one conclusion.

'And made five,' said Wormynghalle in disgust.

'Hamecotes and Rougham are *not* lovers,' said Dodenho, rallying too late to his colleague's defence. 'No self-respecting scholar would choose Rougham as a paramour.'

'Because he could have you instead?' asked Wormynghalle archly.

'Quite,' said Dodenho comfortably, thus telling anyone listening that he considered himself an excellent choice as a lover for people of either sex.

Wormynghalle grimaced in distaste at the conversation, and her expression echoed Bartholomew's own opinion. The physician started to move away, wanting to leave them to their nasty speculations. What he heard next stopped him dead in his tracks.

'Rougham is not the only scholar to have a secret lover,' said Dodenho, trying to make amends for his lack of loyalty by attacking someone else. 'Bartholomew of Michaelhouse is seeing Matilde, who lives in the Jewry. He is quite flagrant about it.'

Michael's expression hardened, and Bartholomew held his breath, wondering whether Weasenham would be able to resist the opportunity to tell what he knew. If he did, then he was certain Michael would act on his promise to ruin him.

'I know nothing of that,' said the stationer stiffly, after a transparent battle between desire and self-preservation. Michael grinned in satisfaction, while Bartholomew was simply relieved that he and Matilde were no longer a target for the man's spiteful tattle. 'They are honourable people, and I do not see him flouting University rules.'

'How dare you malign Bartholomew!' snarled Wormynghalle, so white-faced with rage that Dodenho jumped in alarm. 'He is a good man.'

Michael's eyebrows shot up and he began to cackle. 'You have an admirer – Wormynghalle has taken a fancy to you. You should take care you are never alone with the man, or Weasenham will be spreading rumours that half the Fellows in the University are in love with each other.'

Bartholomew said nothing, but was touched that Wormynghalle had come to his defence. After a few moments, she busied herself with selecting pens, while the stationer wrapped the ones Dodenho had already chosen. Dodenho looked around, then lowered his voice conspiratorially, although it was still loud enough to be audible to the eavesdroppers. 'Have you heard the news from the Castle?'

'Tulyet dredged Merton Hall's cistern,' said Wormynghalle

flatly, attempting to stall yet more idle chatter by showing she already knew the tale. 'Looking for a corpse. But he never found one, and there are rumours that it was never there in the first place.'

'I do not mean that,' said Dodenho, and Bartholomew saw him fixing the stationer with very beady eyes. Weasenham shifted uncomfortably. 'But I think *you* know what I am talking about, Master Stationer.'

'But *I* do not,' muttered Michael, peeved. 'I hope they do not go all obtuse on us.'

'I have no idea what you mean,' said Weasenham, slapping a wrapped pen on to the table to indicate that the sale – and the discussion – was over.

Dodenho had other ideas. He leaned forward and placed his hand over pen and the fingers that held it, making sure he had Weasenham's full attention. Wormynghalle looked from one to the other in confusion, while the stationer was visibly alarmed by the grip that pinned him to the bench.

'When Tulyet saw there was no body in the well, he abandoned his search,' whispered Dodenho. 'But a small crowd had gathered to watch the proceedings, and some folk lingered, disgruntled because they were deprived of the spectacle of a bloated corpse. One hovered longer than most, and eventually approached the cistern and had a poke around for himself.'

'You were watching me!' exclaimed Weasenham accusingly. 'Where were you?'

'Nearby,' replied Dodenho vaguely. 'I am not a man for obvious gawking, but I have no objection to witnessing such events from a discreet distance.'

'I do not think that is a very nice thing to—' began Wormynghalle uncomfortably.

Dodenho ignored her. 'I saw this onlooker fish about with a hook for some time before he snagged something

282

of interest. He took his find – a waterlogged sack – to some bushes, where he thought he could inspect it unseen.'

'What do you want?' asked Weasenham wearily. 'Half of what I found? You are welcome. Most of it comprised baubles that I shall toss into the river as soon as I have a free moment.'

'Blackmail!' cried Wormynghalle, looking at Dodenho in horror. He took no notice and fixed all his glittering attention on the unhappy merchant.

'There was a little silver dog. I saw it being made for mad Master Clippesby of Michaelhouse. That was no mere bauble.'

'It was a gift from Clippesby to Matilde,' said Weasenham. His expression became gleeful as he saw a way to change the subject. 'For services rendered.'

'For her kindness to an injured cat,' corrected Wormynghalle sharply. 'Clippesby is besotted with animals, and she helped one that was hurt. She is a good woman and he wanted to show her his appreciation, so do not make it sound sinister, Master Weasenham, when we know it was innocent.'

Bartholomew warmed to her even more, admiring her for speaking out in defence of two people whose reputations were currently compromised in the unforgiving little town.

'The dog was *stolen* from Matilde,' said Dodenho. 'There are rumours that Eudo took it, but the Sheriff found no trace of the thing when he searched Merton Hall. Now we know why. Eudo – aided by Boltone – kept his stolen goods submerged in the cistern, where no one would ever think to look. Tulyet's men missed them, because they were looking for a body, not a sack of treasure. But you did not.'

'I see,' murmured Bartholomew. 'Eudo and Boltone did not attack us because they were concealing a murdered corpse, but because they were protecting stolen goods.

283

They had been working on the pulley when we confronted them, either because they wanted it mended so they could retrieve the sack, or because they had acquired new treasures that needed to be hidden.'

'Interesting,' mused Michael. 'So, the bailiff and his tenant had nothing to do with the dead man. That particular corpse simply had the misfortune to be stored in the same place as Eudo's loot.'

Bartholomew reconsidered. 'Although we should not discount the possibility that they killed him *because* he discovered their hoard. Also, we should not forget that Chesterfelde probably died near the cistern – of a cut wrist. And Eudo also has a damaged arm.'

'Eudo would not have let you examine his injury if he thought it would lead you to connect him with Chesterfelde's death. The two gashed hands are coincidence, and the "connection" will mislead us if we pay it too much attention.'

'What else was in the sack?' demanded Wormynghalle of Weasenham, clearly disgusted by the stationer's dishonest activities. 'I assume you intend to return it all to its rightful owners?'

'Just trinkets,' reiterated Weasenham, with an anxious glance at Dodenho. 'It contained nothing any owners would want to see again, I assure you.'

'He is lying,' whispered Bartholomew. 'Eudo would not have tried to kill us for trinkets.'

'I do not believe you,' said Dodenho. 'Why would anyone hide a sack of rubbish?'

Weasenham sighed in resignation. 'I will show you, if you like. The dog was the only valuable piece, and you can have it – but only if you agree to say no more about the matter.'

'No, thank you,' said Dodenho with disdain. 'I have no wish to possess stolen silver. My belongings are regularly searched by students desperate for my learned writings, and I do not want them to discover contraband in place of my erudite scribbling.'

'What do you want, then?' asked Weasenham. 'My wife?'

'Lord, no! She does not have the time,' said Dodenho. Weasenham frowned, and Bartholomew was intrigued that the stationer should be observant in the affairs of others, but so blind in his own. 'I want nothing more than a decent arrangement over parchment. It is expensive.'

'I do not like this,' said Wormynghalle uneasily. 'I refuse to be involved in anything immoral, and—'

'Quite right,' agreed Weasenham. 'You are a sensible man, sir. The King will not be pleased to learn that scholars from the hall his father founded submit poor merchants to extortion . . .'

'I am not blackmailing anyone,' said Dodenho smoothly. 'I am asking for a mutually acceptable arrangement regarding the purchase of parchment. I go through a large amount of it when I pen my thoughts, and it would be of great benefit to the academic world if I did not have to worry about how much I consume.'

'Very well,' said Weasenham, defeated. He wrote a figure on a scrap of vellum.

Dodenho shook his head. 'If you want to keep the noose from your neck, I recommend you be a little more generous.'

Weasenham wrote another figure. 'And I will sell you this at a very reduced price,' he said desperately, placing something on the bench next to the pen. 'Every scholar should have one, and I hear you do not.'

It was Dodenho's missing astrolabe.

It was not long before Alyce Weasenham returned to her duties, flushed and with her hair in disarray. Bartholomew saw Langelee through the window, making no attempt to hide the fact that he was adjusting his undergarments. Michael paid Weasenham for a small quantity of parchment and ink, and the two scholars escaped from the shop in some relief.

'Lord, Matt,' breathed Michael. 'What a place! Did you see Dodenho's face when Weasenham offered to sell him the astrolabe that was once his anyway? He looked as if it might bite him.'

'Have you noticed how so many strands of this mystery lead back to Dodenho?' asked Bartholomew. 'He knew Chesterfelde – they laughed together in his chamber. He was in Oxford on St Scholastica's Day, and I am under the impression he is a fairly frequent visitor there.'

'He is – and he foists himself on Merton, to be precise. It is in our University's records; all applications to study away must be ratified by the Chancellor, as you know. However, the foray he made in February was unofficial, because there is no copy of a request, although we know he went: we heard him admit as much ourselves. And now there is the curious business of his astrolabe.'

'He accused his colleagues of stealing it,' recalled Bartholomew. 'Wormynghalle – and Clippesby – said Wolf may have disappeared as a result of the complaint, because he did not like being called a thief. Then Dodenho abruptly dropped the claim, and the astrolabe appeared in the hands of the tanner at Merton Hall. Then it was in Eudo's hoard at the cistern, and now it is offered to Dodenho again.'

'Can we be sure it *is* Eudo's cache?' asked Michael. 'Could it belong to someone else?'

'Such as who?'

Michael shrugged. 'Dodenho? But he is not the only member of King's Hall who has aroused my suspicions. Clippesby said Wolf fled because he was accused of theft, but Dodenho claims he was at Stourbridge with the pox,

286

while Norton maintains he disappeared because he could not pay his debts. Who is right?'

Bartholomew had no answer, and he and Michael were silent for a while, each engrossed in his own thoughts. Bartholomew considered the body in the cistern, pondering who might have salvaged it and why – and what might have happened to it later. The easiest way to dispose of an inconvenient corpse was to toss it in the river with a rock attached to its feet, and if that had already happened, then the chances of retrieving it were slim. He suspected Tulyet would not be prepared to dredge any more expanses of water in search of elusive cadavers, especially with the Visitation looming ever closer.

Michael was more concerned with the living, and was considering Wolf and Hamecotes. The gossiping stationer was not a man who allowed truth to interfere with his stories, and Michael was inclined to dismiss his tale about Hamecotes as groundless gossip. But Wolf was a different matter. How ill had his pox made him? Bartholomew had more or less confessed to spotting him at Stourbridge at the beginning of Clippesby's incarceration, but had not seen him since. Michael frowned. Poxes could be disfiguring, so it was possible the man had taken the scars of his shame to some remote manor until he was fit to be seen, but it was equally possible that he was still somewhere in the town – or even that he was the corpse in the cistern.

'I think we should revisit Merton Hall before we begin our written analysis,' said the monk, when no answers were forthcoming. 'I want to see whether I can catch any of that Oxford rabble in an inconsistency when I ask each one to repeat his story. Will you come and make notes on what they say? Or do you find the prospect of a morning with Polmorva too unappealing?'

* * *

At Merton Hall they were shown into the solar by an elderly servant. All the Oxford men were there, with the exception of Spryngheuse, who was in the garden. Bartholomew was surprised, having been under the impression that the soft-spoken Mertonian seldom went out alone, on the grounds that someone might try to kill him. The three merchants were eating nuts, while Duraunt and Polmorva were engaged in a debate. Duraunt was pleased to have visitors. Polmorva was not.

'What are you discussing?' asked Michael, sensing the debate had gone further than academic sparring and was moving to the point where feelings might be hurt.

'Yesterday we attended a lecture by a man named Dodenho,' said Polmorva. 'I thought it original and entertaining, while Duraunt maintains the central thesis was purloined from someone else's work. I believe he is mistaken, and we have been arguing about it ever since.'

'I attended that event, too,' said Michael. He explained to Bartholomew. 'It was about the dispute between Bonaventure and Aquinas on the notion of individuation: if matter is common to all bodies, and forms are objects of concepts, then what gives specific items their individuality?'

'Bonaventure argued – and I believe him to be correct – that it is the conjunction of matter and form that gives objects their individuality,' said Polmorva. He gave one of his patronising sneers. 'Let me give you an example, to help you understand, Bartholomew: imagine a ball of wax, which is then stamped with a seal. The conjunction of wax and seal thus makes an individual object – an imprinted disc – that is separate from either wax or seal, because of its form.'

'Bonaventure then went on to make an analogous statement,' said Michael, to show he was perfectly well acquainted with the debate and its issues. 'That human

288

individuality is assured only in the union of body and soul – and he considered the soul to comprise spiritual matter *and* spiritual forms.'

'But Aquinas disagreed,' said Bartholomew, placing parchment and ink on a table and preparing to take notes. 'He maintained that although the form of the spirit is shared by other members of the same species, a particular object is unique by virtue of its determinate quantitative extension in space and time. And, in knowing form, the mind knows matter only in general terms. *Ergo*, reason cannot know singulars directly.'

Duraunt clapped his hands in delight. 'I see you have not forgotten what I taught you all those years ago, Matthew. But you did not come here to debate the question of corporeal substances.' His expression was wistful. 'Or did you? Such a discourse would make an old man very happy.'

'That is not why we are here,' said Michael, although whether he referred to academic polemic or to pleasing Duraunt was unclear. 'We have come – yet again – to unravel the web of lies that has been spun at Merton Hall. First, there were untruths about Chesterfelde, then about Gonerby, then about Okehamptone, and now there is a fourth corpse to consider – one that has mysteriously disappeared.'

'That had nothing to do with us,' said Eu. 'We have been too busy trying to solve Gonerby's murder. Of course, that would not be an issue if your University was even remotely competent at deciding which of its members slaughters innocent merchants in alien cities.'

'Then what about you?' asked Michael, swinging around to Polmorva. 'You have had plenty of time to drop corpses in cisterns and fish them out again, because you have not had the burden of identifying a killer, like these poor burgesses. Or have you? Since you witnessed Gonerby's death, you are probably more than eager to see his murderer caught – so he does not try to silence you, too.'

Polmorva gave a tight smile. 'I saw nothing to identify the culprit, and I can defend myself anyway. Brawling with Bartholomew as a young man allowed me to hone my martial skills.'

'If you fight as poorly as Matt, then you should consider hiring a bodyguard,' advised Michael. 'But the body missing from the cistern is not my only concern today. I have recently learned that Eudo is a thief, and that he has been storing his ill-gotten gains on Merton property.'

'That is no surprise,' said Polmorva. 'The man lived here, for God's sake. Where else would you expect him to keep his loot? But this does not mean that you can charge *us* with his crimes.'

'We shall see,' replied Michael enigmatically. 'One of the objects recovered from his hoard was an astrolabe. A silver one.' He looked hard at Wormynghalle, who sat fiddling with his sheep-head pendant, although whether his restless twisting resulted from boredom, anxiety or a guilty conscience was impossible to tell.

'That was Polmorva's,' said Eu. 'But, not being brass, it did not work, so he sold it to our tanner.'

'Why did you sell it, Polmorva?' asked Bartholomew. 'Are you short of funds?'

Polmorva stared at him with glittering hatred. 'No, I am not,' he snarled. 'How dare you – with your patched tabard and frayed tunic – accuse me of poverty. Do I *look* poor, when my clothes are the best money can buy, and Queen Philippa herself uses me as her occasional confessor and rewards me accordingly? And how could I buy silver astrolabes, if I were impecunious? Your question is foolish as well as impertinent.'

'It is also unanswered,' said Michael. 'Why did you sell it?'

Polmorva turned his glower on the monk. 'Because it did not work – the alidade sticks. I should have given it to Bartholomew, who would not know the difference between a good instrument and a bad one, and who will never own such a fine thing unless someone makes him a gift of one.'

'Matthew was always better than you at astrological calculations,' said Duraunt softly. 'Do not accuse him of poor scholarship in an area where he excelled.'

'Why did you buy it in the first place?' asked Michael, while Polmorva reddened at the reprimand. 'Or do you make a point of purchasing inferior goods with your unlimited wealth?'

The look Polmorva shot him was supremely venomous. 'I have a liking for unusual objects – how many silver astrolabes have *you* ever seen? – and Dodenho asked a very reasonable price. Then Wormynghalle took a liking to it, and since it did not work well enough to be useful, I sold it to him. At a handsome profit.'

'How handsome?' demanded the tanner, not liking the notion he had been fleeced.

'And why did you buy a defective astrolabe?' demanded Michael, rounding on him.

'Because he thought owning one would make him appear erudite,' said Eu with a superior sneer. 'He buys anything he thinks will raise him in the opinion of his peers.'

Wormynghalle came to his feet, his thick features flushed with rage. 'What did you say?'

'You heard,' said Eu, leaning back in his chair and stretching his legs in front of him in an attitude that screamed disdain. 'No amount of good cloth and expensive jewels can change the fact that you hail from a ditch. You *should* have claimed a kinship with that grubby scholar from King's Hall, because even he would have improved your pedigree.'

'You vain cockerel—' began Wormynghalle, making towards Eu with a murderous expression on his face. Michael interposed his substantial bulk between them and Wormynghalle almost lost his footing when he cannoned into him and bounced off again.

'Now, now, gentlemen,' said the monk. 'I did not come to hear you quarrel. I want answers about this astrolabe. It belonged to Polmorva, who sold it to Wormynghalle. Then what?'

'It was stolen,' said Wormynghalle sullenly. He clutched his sheep-head pendant so hard that his fingers were white, and Bartholomew had the feeling he would dearly love to bludgeon Eu with it. It was heavy enough to do serious damage, and the physician made a mental note to check it for bloodstains, if Eu was ever murdered. 'And *I* know exactly who took it.'

'Who?' demanded Michael. 'Eudo? Boltone?'

'Bartholomew,' said Wormynghalle, pointing an accusing finger at the physician. 'I wanted to report him to the Chancellor, but Duraunt persuaded me to overlook the matter, on the grounds that I can buy a better one in Oxford anyway.'

'Of course it was him,' said Polmorva, so Bartholomew knew exactly who had planted the seed of that particular accusation. 'As I said, he will never earn enough to buy one for himself, so theft was his only recourse.'

'I do not want us associated with any more disagreeable matters,' explained Duraunt to Michael. 'And if Matthew needed an astrolabe, then I could not find it in my heart to take it from him.'

'I did not steal it,' objected Bartholomew, amazed Duraunt should think he had. A charge from Polmorva was one thing, but to have his old teacher convinced of his guilt was another altogether.

'You were the only one we saw looking at it,' said Duraunt. 'If it was not you, then who was it?'

'It was him,' snapped Wormynghalle. 'He is poor and of course will covet such a lovely thing – especially knowing it had once been the property of his rival.'

'But I do not want an astrolabe,' objected Bartholomew indignantly. 'I have no time for calculating pointless horoscopes that are of no use to man nor beast.'

'Matthew!' exclaimed Duraunt, shocked. 'You are a physician: you cannot manage without the calculations that tell you how and when to treat your patients. It would be grossly negligent.'

'He probably relies on the Devil to tell him what to do,' said Polmorva.

Bartholomew did not deign to reply, suspecting that anything he said would be twisted and given a sinister meaning. Suddenly he wished Polmorva and the whole Oxford contingent would just go home, taking their petty disputes and unfounded accusations with them. He was tired of them all, even Duraunt, and regretted agreeing to accompany Michael to Merton Hall.

'But if you did not swipe it, then who did?' demanded Wormynghalle.

'I imagine it was someone here,' replied Michael. 'Polmorva told us he purchased it because it was unusual, and he is an astute man, who would have tested the thing before parting with his gold. *Ergo*, he knew it was defective when he bought it, and so would not have sold it for that reason, as he has just claimed.'

'What are you saying?' demanded Polmorva, anger flashing in his eyes. Bartholomew saw something else, too. Alarm. Michael was coming close to the truth.

Michael shrugged. 'I was just thinking about one of the Sheriff's cases, where a man sold a horse, and then stole it back again to sell a second time. He was unable to resist the lure of a "handsome profit", you see. But suffice to say that the astrolabe was taken from Wormynghalle, and ended up in the cache recovered from the cistern, along with other stolen property.'

'The cistern?' asked Abergavenny. 'You mean the one that was emptied here? We have not been told about any cache. To whom did it belong? Eudo, I suppose. That must be why he fled with Boltone.'

'The astrolabe's travels are very confusing,' said Duraunt, while Polmorva scowled and Wormynghalle looked as though he was not sure what to think. 'It was originally Dodenho's, but it went missing from King's Hall before reappearing again. Dodenho sold it to Polmorva, Polmorva passed it to Wormynghalle, then . . .' he hesitated, not sure how to phrase the next part.

'. . . then it was removed from Wormynghalle,' said Michael smoothly, 'and found its way to the cistern hoard, and it is now in the care of Weasenham the stationer.'

'Then Weasenham will restore it to its rightful owner,' said Duraunt with a pleased smile. 'And we need say no more about the matter.'

'That is me,' said Wormynghalle, 'although I am not sure I want a defective instrument. I will offer to sell it to him – for a "handsome profit".' He glared at Polmorva.

Polmorva was outraged with Michael. 'You have accused me of the vilest of crimes. Me! A one-time Chancellor of Oxford University and a Fellow of Queen's College! I demand an apology.'

While Polmorva was ranting, Bartholomew had been gazing out of the window, thinking about the astrolabe and wondering whether its travels between various murder suspects were significant. He could see the cistern in the distance, surrounded by muck from its recent dredging. As he stared, he became aware of something else, too. He frowned, and looked harder.

'Spryngheuse,' he said, interrupting Polmorva's tirade. 'When did he go out?'

'Hours ago,' replied Abergavenny. 'He is probably praying for Chesterfelde. Why do you ask?'

Bartholomew pointed. 'He is not in any church. He is there: I recognise his cloak.'

Duraunt joined him at the window, and his jaw dropped in horror. 'But he is dangling from that tree – by the neck!'

'Yes,' agreed Bartholomew softly. 'And he is almost certainly dead.'

Spryngheuse was indeed dead. When Bartholomew and Michael arrived in the garden, with the Oxford men behind them, it was obvious that the Mertonian was beyond any earthly help. Duraunt insisted the body should be cut down and removed to a church as soon as possible, and Polmorva and the merchants concurred in a rare consensus. They were furious that another of their number had perished, and Bartholomew had very little time to examine the body *in situ* before the rope around its neck was untied and Spryngheuse was lowered to the ground.

'I suppose he will be taken to that horrible All-Saints-next-the-Castle,' said Duraunt, looking sadly at the body as it lay in the damp grass. Bartholomew noticed his hands were shaking. 'Like Okehamptone and Chesterfelde.'

'It is outrageous,' declared Polmorva. 'When I return to Oxford, I shall complain to the highest authorities about our treatment here. Your town does not even allow us a consecrated church from which to bury our dead.'

'You hail from a city under interdict,' said Michael insolently. 'What do you expect?'

Polmorva ignored him. 'It may be too late for Okehamptone, but I shall do better for Chesterfelde and Spryngheuse. I want them buried deep in the ground – preferably hallowed – where they will be safe from physicians with macabre pastimes, and not in some vault where they can be picked at.'

'I will arrange for them to be buried in St Clement's,' volunteered Michael. 'Merton Hall is not in its parish, but the priest has plenty of room in his churchyard.'

'That surprises me,' said Polmorva unpleasantly. 'I would have thought it would be stuffed full, given how many folk die in this sordid little settlement.'

'The only people who have died recently are from Oxford,' said Michael acidly, irritated that his offer should be treated with contempt. 'But I cannot stand here all day when Spryngheuse lies without a coffin. I shall fetch one, and Matt will stay with the body until I return.'

'Thank you,' said Duraunt gratefully. 'I will wait with him.'

'There is no need for that,' said Michael briskly. 'Go inside. It looks as though it might rain.'

'He wants you out of the way, so Bartholomew can examine Spryngheuse alone,' said Polmorva astutely. 'Do not let him. We do not want another of our colleagues defiled by his pawing hands.'

'There will be no defiling here,' vowed Duraunt, and Bartholomew was surprised by the glint of determination in his eyes. 'Not on Merton land.'

'Then do not leave Spryngheuse alone for an instant,' advised Polmorva. 'Besides, I have heard that the man who "discovers" a corpse is very often the man who has taken its life, and it was Bartholomew who first saw Spryngheuse. He probably killed him to strike at us.'

'I have no reason to kill Spryngheuse,' objected Bartholomew, becoming tired of the stream of accusations. 'I barely knew him.'

'He lent you his best cloak,' snapped Polmorva. 'Perhaps you thought that murdering him was the surest way to make sure you can keep it.'

'Do not be ridiculous,' retorted Bartholomew impatiently. 'I have already returned it to him. And what makes you think his death is murder, anyway? How do you know he did not kill himself?'

'Did he?' asked Duraunt, concerned. 'If that is the case, then he cannot be laid in hallowed soil, nor can he have the benefit of a requiem mass.'

'He did not kill himself,' declared Polmorva. 'On the contrary, he was so determined to live that he spent the last few days telling everyone how frightened he was that someone might try to dispatch him. A man intent on suicide would not have cared.'

'He was horrified when he learned Bartholomew was attacked while wearing his cloak,' said Abergavenny thoughtfully. 'He was certain it was his Black Monk, coming to snatch *his* soul.'

'And he insisted on staying indoors, where he thought he would be safe,' added Eu. 'I wonder what induced him to go out today.'

'I heard Duraunt telling him he would benefit from fresh air,' said Wormynghalle, a sly and spiteful expression on his coarse features. 'He must have taken the advice to heart.'

Duraunt was shocked. 'I did nothing of the kind! Do not try to blame me for this death.'

'I thought it was *you* who suggested he go,' said Polmorva to the tanner, stirring already troubled waters, so that it was not long before everyone was shouting. Polmorva stepped back and folded his arms, and Bartholomew tried to assess what he was thinking. Was it simple satisfaction, because he had provoked another quarrel? Or was there a more sinister reason for his games – such as using the others' anger to divert attention from himself?

Then Bartholomew studied Duraunt, who was suspiciously vocal in his denials that he had recommended a walk to Spryngheuse. Did that signify a guilty conscience, or was he merely appalled that anyone should think he was responsible for the scholar's death? Bartholomew was deeply troubled by the notion that his old master might be involved in something untoward, but found the man difficult to defend when he thought about the poppy juice and what his sister had overheard in the apothecary's shop. Were Michael and Langelee right when they pointed out that men changed over the years? Bartholomew had the sickening sense that Duraunt might have turned into something he no longer recognised, just as Duraunt had claimed Bartholomew himself had grown unfamiliar.

The merchants were equally impossible to read. Wormynghalle was red-faced with indignation that he should be associated with any wrongdoing, while Eu was loftily careless about what anyone thought, stating he had had nothing to do with the misfortunes that had befallen his travelling companions, and that was that. Abergavenny tried to placate them all, but it was some time before the voice of reason quelled those of dissent and anger.

'Strong wine is the cause of all this,' said Polmorva. 'If you had not caroused so wildly the night Chesterfelde died, then he would still be with us and Spryngheuse would not have hanged himself.'

'You were just as inebriated as the rest of us,' snapped Duraunt. He realised he had admitted something he had denied before and a flicker of annoyance crossed his face. He gritted his teeth and continued. 'You pretended to abstain, but you did not – not that night and not on other occasions. I heard you snoring later, in the way a drunken man sleeps.'

Polmorva assumed an expression of weary patience. 'You lie, old man. You—'

'Hanged himself?' interrupted Wormynghalle, regarding Polmorva with raised eyebrows. 'You just accused Bartholomew of murdering him, and I assumed you had good reason for doing so. Now you say suicide. Which is it?'

'I do not know,' said Polmorva icily. 'I was not standing by this tree when he died to see what happened, was I?'

'Really,' said Michael flatly, in a tone that indicated he was not so sure. Polmorva bristled, but Michael turned to Duraunt before he could respond. 'We will give Spryngheuse the benefit of the doubt, and will ensure he has all the due ceremony appropriate to a recently deceased scholar from a respected Oxford College. It is often difficult to tell the difference between murder and suicide in hangings, and we may never know what really happened.'

He shot Bartholomew a look that the physician interpreted as a suggestion that he should inspect the body later, without a hostile audience. It was a recommendation Bartholomew intended to follow, because he did not want to be accused of witchcraft or a morbid love of anatomy while he carried out his examination. Michael went to fetch the bier and Polmorva accompanied him, saying he wanted to ensure the monk left Merton Hall and did not go exploring by himself. The merchants declined to linger with a dead man – especially once it started to rain – and it was not long before Bartholomew was alone with Duraunt.

'Are Polmorva's accusations true?' the old man asked in a voice that cracked with sorrow. 'Do you defile corpses by prodding them after they have been laid to rest?'

'I did inspect Okehamptone,' admitted Bartholomew, not liking the way Duraunt considered his duties sacrilegious. 'But only to find out how he died. I imagine most men would want justice if their lives were snatched by killers, and I do not think Okehamptone would object to someone discovering he had been murdered.' He thought about the uneasy sensation he had experienced shortly after the examination, and sincerely hoped he was right.

Duraunt went to sit on the cistern wall. The pit was

already half full, recovering quickly from Tulyet's drainage. 'I find the notion of you caressing a two-week-dead corpse painfully disturbing. Did you "inspect" him with the help of a knife and rouse out his innards while you were there?'

'I did not,' said Bartholomew firmly. 'That would be illegal.'

Duraunt sighed, and was silent for a while, evidently too unsettled to discuss the matter further. Eventually, he changed the subject. 'The merchants are itching to be back to their businesses. I suspect they plan to blame Okehamptone or Chesterfelde for killing Gonerby, just to have something to tell this demanding widow. Both are dead, so not in a position to argue.'

'They may be maligning the names of innocent men.'

'Is that worse than seizing someone *en route* and dragging him to Oxford for hanging? Because that is what they will do if they fail to catch a culprit: they have vowed not to return empty-handed. I shall be glad to go home, though. Oxford is violent and unsettled, but I have friends there, and I know where I stand. Here I do not know who to trust.'

'Like Polmorva, you mean?'

'No, I do not mean Polmorva,' said Duraunt, although his eyes dipped away when he spoke. 'I know you dislike him, but it is the merchants I am worried about. Eu and Wormynghalle hate each other, and Abergavenny is hard-pressed to keep the peace. I would not be surprised to learn that one of them took the lives of Okehamptone, Chesterfelde and Spryngheuse. They hate my University with a passion, and may regard this as a good opportunity to rid themselves of a few of us.'

'Then why did you invite them to stay at Merton Hall?'

'Because I fear the St Scholastica's Day riots were started deliberately, and I do not want the same thing to happen here. I would rather have the merchants where I can see them.'

It sounded noble, but Duraunt no longer struck Bartholomew as a man who would put his own scholars in danger to protect a strange town. Once again he was not sure what to think.

Duraunt forced a smile. 'Let us talk of happier things, Matthew. Have you read any of the theories recently proposed by Heytesbury? We are proud to have him at our College.'

'A Fellow from King's Hall – Hamecotes – is visiting Oxford at the moment,' said Bartholomew, grateful to discuss a topic that would not be contentious. 'He has gone to buy books, and says he has already secured Heytesbury's *Regulae solvendi sophismata* from Merton.'

Duraunt shook his head. 'Not from Merton, Matthew. We never sell our books, because we barely have enough for ourselves, as I am sure you will remember. And Heytesbury's *Regulae* would be far too valuable to exchange for mere money. It would be priceless to us.'

'How odd,' mused Bartholomew. 'I wonder if Hamecotes made the story up, and has gone off on business of his own – or whether someone wants us to believe he is somewhere he is not.'

'You think he is dead? Perhaps he is the body you saw in the cistern.' Duraunt glanced behind him at the murky water, and stood quickly.

'There is no reason to think that. Perhaps he has escaped with a lover, as Weasenham says. Or perhaps he is with Wolf, nursing him through his pox.' Bartholomew went to where Spryngheuse lay, sorry he was dead and recalling the man's distress in the days before he died.

'Do not touch him, Matthew,' said Duraunt softly, watching the physician close the staring eyes. 'If you examine him and discover he committed suicide, then we shall have to inter him in unhallowed ground: my conscience will not allow anything else. But as long as there

301

is doubt, he can rest in a churchyard. Let there be doubt, so he can be given a Christian burial.'

Reluctantly, Bartholomew complied.

Suspecting his Corpse Examiner would never have an opportunity to examine Spryngheuse unless he took matters into his own hands, Michael abandoned the notion of taking the body to St Clement's, and arranged for it to go to St Michael's instead. This, he assured the suspicious Oxford contingent, was a great honour, and Spryngheuse would be guaranteed prayers from men who were members of a University, like himself. When they remained sceptical, he offered to bury Chesterfelde at the same time – two interments for the price of one. Father William had agreed to undertake vigils with his Franciscan students, and Michael said he would recite the requiem mass himself, which met with further suspicion from Polmorva, gratitude from Duraunt and indifference from the merchants. It was, after all, not they who would be footing the bill for the funeral expenses.

'And what about the interdict?' asked Polmorva archly. 'We have been told that prevents any Oxford citizen from being decently laid to rest.'

'We shall bury them first and worry about the relevant dispensations later,' replied Michael. He smiled at Duraunt. 'Then, even if permission is refused, no one will want to exhume them, especially once Matt has described the diseases that might be unleashed in so doing.'

'Thank you,' said Duraunt, taking Michael's hand in both of his own. 'When will you perform the rite? It is Friday now and Chesterfelde died on Saturday. The sooner he is laid to rest the better.'

'Today,' said Michael, wanting the bodies out of St Michael's well before the Visitation. He did not like the notion of the Archbishop stepping inside and declaring it reeked of the dead. 'Before vespers. I hope you will all attend.'

'We might,' said Eu cautiously. 'It depends on what else is happening.'

'I will come,' declared Duraunt. 'And so will Polmorva.' Polmorva looked none too pleased that he had been volunteered, but he inclined his head in reluctant assent.

Michael had arranged for Spryngheuse to be carried away by pall-bearers he had commandeered from Michaelhouse. Deynman and Falmeresham were more than happy to escape the monotonous tones of Master Langelee reading a text he did not understand, while Cynric was always willing to help the monk. The book-bearer nodded amiably at Abergavenny and exchanged a few words in Welsh, while Bartholomew and the students lifted Spryngheuse into the parish coffin. Then Cynric and Bartholomew took the front of the box, and the others grabbed the back.

'What did he say?' asked Bartholomew of the Welshman.

'He asked me to keep you from dissecting Spryngheuse once you have him in your domain – but that if I cannot, then I am to make sure Duraunt and Polmorva do not find out.'

Bartholomew frowned. 'What did he mean by issuing such a request? That he hopes no one will examine Spryngheuse, because there is evidence that he did not kill himself? And that Duraunt and Polmorva have a good reason for wanting such information kept hidden?'

'Or that they are more likely to make a fuss,' suggested Falmeresham practically. 'That pair seem opposed to anatomy in any form, but especially when practised by you.'

'Or that you may discover Spryngheuse *was* a suicide, which means he cannot be buried at St Michael's,' offered Cynric. 'A suicide *and* a man under interdict is banned from hallowed ground on two counts.'

Bartholomew recalled Michael's contention that Abergavenny was a man clever enough to kill and evade justice, and wondered whether the monk had been right. Tulyet was still convinced Eu was involved in more than he had revealed, while Bartholomew had not shaken his conviction that the blustering Wormynghalle was the villain. He grimaced when he recalled the way the tanner had levelled his accusation regarding the astrolabe, and supposed the dislike was mutual.

They reached the church, where Bartholomew ensured Spryngheuse was arranged neatly and covered with a clean blanket. Polmorva watched him with the eyes of a hawk, while Duraunt knelt nearby and prayed. Neither scholar made a move to leave the chapel, so Michael announced it was time for his mid-morning repast and begged them to excuse him. Bartholomew was bemused, because Michaelhouse did not run to additional meals during the day, and supposed the monk intended to inveigle an invitation to King's Hall again. He followed him along the High Street and into St Michael's Lane. After a few steps Michael doubled back, peering around the corner.

'There they go,' he said with satisfaction. 'I knew they would not linger once we had gone. Come on, before the Franciscans arrive for their vigil.'

He grabbed the physician's arm and hauled him back to St Michael's, where he barred the door to make sure the Oxford men did not return and catch them unawares.

'Hurry,' he ordered peremptorily. 'We do not have long, and I need answers.'

'I am not sure about this,' said Bartholomew unhappily. 'Duraunt asked me not to determine whether the death was suicide or murder, because he wants Spryngheuse buried in the churchyard.'

'We shall put him there regardless,' said Michael. 'The wretched man was terrified out of his senses these last few days, and we always bury lunatics in hallowed ground, no matter how they die.'

'He claimed a Black Monk was following him,' said Bartholomew, making no move to comply.

'Then that proves he was addled,' said Michael. 'I know every Benedictine in this town, and none is in the habit of stalking people. Spryngheuse imagined this spectre, which is why no one else ever saw him. Come on, Matt. I need to know what happened.'

Bartholomew examined the marks around the dead man's neck, trying to be fast and thorough at the same time, eager to be done before Polmorva or Duraunt returned. It was not long before he had learned all he could. He turned to Michael.

'When we stood by the tree, looking at Spryngheuse's body, I noticed fresh scratches on the bark, and here you can see corresponding marks on his shoes. They suggest he climbed the trunk of his own accord. His hands are not tied, and there are no signs of a struggle. Also, the noose's knot is just behind his ear. I have noticed it is nearly always there when death is self-inflicted, whereas it tends to be at the back when someone else lends a hand. Can you see the bruising caused by the rope is in an inverted V? With murder it tends to be more of a straight line, although there are exceptions, of course. However, in this case, I am almost certain it was suicide.'

'When did it happen?'

Bartholomew knew from experience that time of death was difficult to estimate with any degree of certainty. 'He was last seen at dawn – so some time between then and when we found him.'

'Thank you, Matt. However, I had worked that much out for myself. Can you not be more specific?'

'Not really. The body is cool to the touch, blood has pooled in its hands, and it is beginning to stiffen around the eyes and jaws, so I suppose he died closer to dawn than to now.'

'And he perished by hanging? You will not later claim there was a bite in his throat or that he was knocked on the head?'

'It is difficult to be sure about anything you do not actually witness, but you can see for yourself that his throat is intact.'

'Polmorva claimed that Spryngheuse did not want to die, and we saw for ourselves that he was terrified, which *does* indicate a desire to live. Why would he suddenly give up on life?'

'It was not sudden: remember what he was doing at the Great Bridge on Sunday? Perhaps he decided it was better to die than to live too frightened to eat, sleep, or even go for a walk.'

Michael sighed. 'There is only one thing that is clear in this case: all our victims are connected to Oxford. It started with Gonerby, bitten during that city's riots. Next was Okehamptone, an Oxford scribe, whose murder was disguised to appear as a fever. And now Balliol's Chesterfelde and Merton's Spryngheuse – two men accused of instigating the St Scholastica's Day disorder – are dead.'

'None of Okehamptone's companions examined the body, not even out of curiosity,' mused Bartholomew. 'Do you not think that is odd?'

'Most folk do not share your fascination with the dead, Matt. And anyway, the University's Senior Proctor and a Corpse Examiner came to do that for them. So, what does this tell us, other than that their trust in my abilities was sadly misplaced?'

'That the killer was relieved when his plan passed off without a hitch. Do you recall any odd reactions among the Oxford men that day?'

'They behaved then exactly as they have done since: Duraunt with wounded saintliness, Polmorva with smug superiority, Wormynghalle with aggression, Eu with indifference, and Abergavenny with tact. And Chesterfelde grinned and doffed his cap like a lunatic. Did *he* kill Okehamptone and Gonerby, do you think, and then someone dispatched him?'

'We have two distinct methods of execution: Okehamptone and Gonerby died from wounds to their throats; Chesterfelde bled to death from a cut to his arm. There could be more than one killer.'

'But they both involve incisions and bleeding,' mused Michael. 'Perhaps the murderer was aiming for Chesterfelde's throat but got his arm instead. I know you said a knife caused the wound, but perhaps he did not have time to use teeth, so resorted to his dagger instead.'

Bartholomew shook his head. 'That does not sound likely. However, with this latest death, our list of suspects is down to Polmorva, Wormynghalle, Eu and Abergavenny.'

'I note you do not include Duraunt, even though he has lied to us. But these are not the only ones with Oxford connections. We have Hamecotes, gone to Merton to buy books, and who sends messages about his purchases to his room-mate Wormynghalle, who has also studied in Oxford.'

'Duraunt said Merton would never sell a book, even though Hamecotes cited a specific volume by Heytesbury. Do you remember Heytesbury, Brother? He visited us himself not long ago.'

Michael nodded, but preferred to continue his analysis of the current case, rather than wallow in memories of past ones. 'We also have Dodenho, present in Merton during the riots, and who knew Chesterfelde well enough to invite him to his room. And there is Norton, who has stayed at Oxford Castle, and who knows so little Latin that you have to wonder why he is here.'

'Wolf, too,' said Bartholomew. 'He also spent time at Oxford.'

'And we do not know where *he* is now,' mused Michael. 'The three explanations we have been given are the pox, his debts and a lover. You saw him at Stourbridge – where another of our suspects currently resides, by the way – so you must have noticed whether he was covered in lesions.'

'Not really,' said Bartholomew, reluctant to disclose a man's personal medical details.

Michael regarded him irritably. 'Do not be coy with me, Matt, not when we are trying to solve murders. Tell me what was wrong with him and I promise the information will go no further.'

Bartholomew considered: Wolf had given no indication that he craved secrecy, and the truth was not especially awkward or embarrassing. 'He had a mild ague – the kind most of us ignore. To be frank, I thought he was malingering, and assumed he just wanted a respite from teaching. I am surprised he is still away, because medically, there is no reason why he should not have returned.'

'Perhaps he has been too busy killing old enemies from Oxford,' suggested Michael, going to unbar the door before someone demanded to know what they were doing. 'I do not like scholars disappearing without permission. Why do you think I tightened the rules about that sort of thing? It was so I would know where every clerk should be at any given time.'

'Was it?' asked Bartholomew, amused. 'You told everyone else it was so arrangements could be made to cover their classes before they left. I did not realise it was all part of the Senior Proctor's plan to create an empire in which he controls every man's movements.'

'Well, you do now,' said Michael, unrepentant. 'But here is William, come to pray for Spryngheuse. Do not tell him we have a suicide, Matt, or he will have the carcass tossed into the street.'

'Another murder!' boomed William as he entered. 'These Oxford men certainly know how to dispatch each other! How many is that now? Three? Four? All I can say is that I hope the Archbishop does not get wind of it and decide not to come. I have just paid to have my habit cleaned, and I would not like to think I have wasted my money.'

CHAPTER 9

Leaving William to his sacred duties with Spryngheuse's remains, Bartholomew and Michael returned to Michaelhouse and ate a meal of salted herrings and barley soup. Michael complained bitterly about the fact that it was a fish day, and sparked off a debate between Suttone and Wynewyk about whether it was right to abstain from meat at specific times during the week. Suttone maintained that the men who gorged on flesh on Fridays were the same folk who had provoked God to send the plague. Wynewyk declared that the definition of 'meat' was so vague – animal entrails, for example, were not considered as such, although muscle was – that He probably thought it was irrelevant. The argument was still in full swing when the hall was cleared of tables for the afternoon's lectures.

Bartholomew checked his students were on schedule with their reading, then left to visit his patient in St John's Hospital. Michael went with him, because the dying man was a Benedictine called Brother Thomas, who had been kind to him as a naïve and homesick novice many years before.

'You are fatter than ever,' said Thomas, when Michael followed the physician into the hall.

'Good afternoon to you, too,' said Michael irritably.

'If you continue to grow, you will be too big to fit through doors,' Thomas went on mercilessly.

'I am not fat,' replied Michael with a cross sigh. 'I just have big bones. Tell him, Matt.'

'You are fat,' said Bartholomew baldly. 'And it is not

good for your health. You puff and groan when you walk up Castle Hill, and you can no longer chase criminals.'

'I do not *want* to chase criminals,' objected Michael, while the old monk made a wheezing sound to indicate he was chortling his appreciation at the physician's blunt tongue. 'That is why I have beadles. Besides, it is inappropriate for a Senior Proctor to scamper through the streets of Cambridge like a March hare. I have a position of authority, and must move in a stately manner.'

'Like an overloaded cart pulled by a straining nag,' said Thomas brutally. 'Matthew is right: you do not look well with so much flesh on your heavy bones, and you are eating yourself into an early grave. And there is another thing: you often put your friend in dangerous situations. Imagine how you would feel if he needed your help and you could not move fast enough to save him.'

'Quite,' said Bartholomew. 'So, no dinner for you tonight, Brother.'

Thomas grimaced. 'I am serious, so listen to me! I am an old man and I know what I am talking about. Michael is obese, and such men often die before their time. I do not want that to happen to him, and I do not want you killed in some fracas, screaming for him while he waddles too slowly to your aid. Heed my words. I will meet God today, and you cannot refuse a dying man's last request.'

Bartholomew was silent, unnerved by the old man's gloomy warnings, while Michael busied himself by fussing with the bed-covers. They waited until he slept, and then left. Bartholomew knew he was unlikely to wake again, and that the frail muscles in his chest would soon simply fail to fill his lungs with air. Michael was pale when they emerged into the sunlight, and the physician saw Thomas's words had struck hard. They walked without speaking until they met Paxtone outside King's Hall, where Michael's expression went from troubled to angry. Bartholomew

311

sensed the monk was about to say something he might later regret, just because he wanted to vent his spleen.

'No, Brother,' he said quietly. 'Attacking Paxtone for being a poor Corpse Examiner will achieve nothing. He will not understand what he has done wrong, and you will offend a man who is a friend.'

'Perhaps I should include *him* on my list of suspects,' said Michael bitterly. 'He, too, visits Oxford with gay abandon, and may have his own reasons for disguising a murder.'

'If that were the case, then I doubt he would have confessed to performing an inadequate examination. He would have let us assume he was thorough.'

He greeted Paxtone amiably before Michael could reply, and told him about the mass arranged for Chesterfelde and Spryngheuse later that afternoon. Paxtone said he was saddened to hear about the deaths, and offered to attend the requiem with some of his colleagues.

'Why?' asked Michael, unnecessarily abrupt. 'Did you know them?'

'No,' replied Paxtone, startled by the monk's hostility. 'But they were fellow scholars, and it is the least we can do. Weasenham told me today that the St Scholastica's Day riots were started deliberately, and that someone intends to do the same here. We academics need to stick together, to show the town that we stand solidly with our Oxford colleagues.'

'Where did Weasenham hear this?' demanded Michael furiously.

Paxtone took a step back, unnerved by his temper. 'He did not say. Why? Do you think he made it up? It would not be the first time he invented tales when he found himself short of real stories.'

'Come with me to see him now,' ordered Michael. 'I want to know if there is a factual basis to his rumour-mongering, or whether he is speaking out of spite. In either case, he will desist immediately. I will *not* have him giving people ideas, and starting trouble when Islip is about to arrive.'

'You are right,' said Paxtone, starting to walk in the direction of the stationer's domain. Bartholomew followed, and could not help but notice that Michael was not the only large man who waddled. 'These tales that Oxford was ripped to pieces by townsfolk angered *me*, and I am a mild-tempered fellow. I cannot imagine what will happen if lads like Lee of Gonville or – I am sorry Matt, but it is true – Deynman and Falmeresham come to hear them.'

Michael stormed into Weasenham's shop. It was busy, with at least twenty students and Fellows inspecting the merchandise. Alyce was demonstrating a new kind of ink that dried more quickly than traditional ones, while Weasenham was deep in conversation with several scholars, all of whom were listening avidly to every whispered word. Bartholomew's heart sank when he caught the word 'Scholastica' among the muted diatribe, and it plunged even deeper when he saw that the eager ears belonged to Gonville's feisty students, including Lee. Michael surged up to them.

'Brother Michael,' said Weasenham, beaming falsely when he saw the monk's furious expression. 'Have you used all that parchment already? Do you want me to send you more?'

'What has he been telling you?' demanded Michael of Lee.

'Nothing about a certain physician's visits to a Frail Sister,' squeaked Weasenham in alarm, when he misunderstood what Michael was asking. 'I swear I have said nothing to anyone about that.'

'What physician?' snapped Lee. 'You had better not be gossiping about Doctor Rougham's meetings with Yolande de Blaston on the first Monday of the month, or you will have me to contend with.'

'Does he?' asked Weasenham encouragingly, eager for more details.

Bartholomew felt sorry for Rougham. It was the second time he had heard people refer to the dalliance, and, although *he* had been unaware of the man's penchant for Yolande, it was clearly no secret. Rougham could have gone to his College after the attack, and not imposed himself on Matilde, after all. He reconsidered: but then he would have told people about Clippesby, and the tale that a Michaelhouse Fellow had bitten a Gonville man would have resulted in trouble for certain.

'No,' Lee replied unconvincingly. 'It is a lie put about by his enemies. He goes to . . . to treat her bunions.'

'Bartholomew is her physician,' said Weasenham, not so easily misled. 'And Rougham would never physic her, because she would not be able to pay him. Bartholomew does not care about that kind of thing, but Rougham certainly does.'

'She has two physicians,' said Lee in a voice that was loaded with menace. 'One for her bunions, and one for everything else. So, we shall say no more about the matter. If I hear the faintest whisper against Doctor Rougham or Yolande, I will come to your shop and ram your parchments—'

'What was he saying to you just now?' interrupted Michael. He hoped the stationer would take Lee's threat seriously, because he was sure Rougham would assume Bartholomew was the source of any rumours that associated his name with that of Yolande de Blaston.

'He was telling us what happened in Oxford on St Scholastica's Day,' said Lee, still scowling at Weasenham. 'The men who started the riot were called Chesterfelde and Spryngheuse, both of whom have been murdered in Cambridge since.'

'Really,' said Michael flatly. 'And how do you come to be party to this information, Weasenham?'

Weasenham swallowed uneasily, and would not meet Michael's eyes. 'Spryngheuse told me himself. He and Chesterfelde are to be buried today, and everyone knows they are young men dead before their time. He said a Benedictine had followed him here, determined to exact revenge, and he was thinking of moving to another town. He planned to go today.'

'He left it a bit late, then,' muttered Lee.

'Tell him the rest,' said Paxtone to the nervous stationer. 'About the plot to spread unrest and bring down the universities.'

'I am only repeating what I have been told,' bleated Weasenham, unnerved by Michael's stern expression. 'The Oxford disorder was deliberately started, and it is believed that the same thing will happen here.'

'Who said this?' demanded Michael.

'Polmorva. He said he will abandon Cambridge soon, because it is on the verge of a serious crisis. He is thinking of setting up a new university in a different place – not Stamford or Northampton, because scholars have tried those places before, and their schools were suppressed – but somewhere really nice, like Haverhill in Suffolk, or perhaps Winchester.'

'Did he mention the names of the men who want to see us in flames?' asked Michael coolly.

'He did not know them, but obviously something is going on, because Chesterfelde was murdered, and now Spryngheuse is dead.'

Michael was sceptical. 'If Chesterfelde and Spryngheuse really did start the riots in Oxford, and someone wants to do the same here, then why waste two experienced rabble-rousers by killing them? Why not recruit them?'

'Perhaps there is more than one faction at work, Brother.

315

There may be those who want riots, and who may have brought Spryngheuse and Chesterfelde here. And there may be those who want peace, and who intend to punish that pair for what they have already done.'

'And it looks as if one group has been successful,' added Lee, in case Michael had not worked it out for himself. 'The two rabble-rousers are dead, so someone else will have to do their dirty work.'

'I have done nothing wrong,' said Weasenham with a sickly smile, as Michael regarded him with distaste. 'You cannot punish me for repeating facts.'

'They are not facts,' said Michael sharply. 'They are speculation, and if you spread any more tales that the town is about to be put to the torch, I shall arrest you. Do you want to see us under interdict, like Oxford? Do you want the Archbishop shocked by what he finds here?'

'No,' stammered Weasenham. 'But I—'

'If the University flounders, then Cambridge will have no need for a stationer. You will have to go to Haverhill or Winchester, and hope Polmorva manages to attract enough students to keep you in business. There are far too many secular clerks in Winchester for a university to be a success, while Haverhill is full of pigs. Rather like Oxford, I imagine.'

He turned on his heel and stalked out. Paxtone and Bartholomew followed, and the physician noticed that a number of Weasenham's customers had listened to the reprimand. As he closed the door behind him, a babble of excited conversation broke out, and he wondered if Michael had done more harm than good. In a few moments the door opened again, and Lee sidled out.

'Weasenham is not the only one who has been predicting unrest,' he volunteered helpfully. 'There was talk among the townsfolk in the Market Square this morning, because of Eudo.'

'Eudo?' asked Michael. 'The absconded tenant of Merton Hall, who robs the good citizens of Cambridge and hides his booty in a cistern?'

'Not according to him. He says he is innocent, and that the University fabricated the evidence against him because we are all corrupt and love to treat townsmen badly. He fled from the Square before the Sheriff could catch him, but he was very vocal in his denials.'

'Damn!' muttered Michael. 'This is not good news – not so close to the Visitation. I have a bad feeling Weasenham's predictions might be right, and someone really is trying to harm us.'

'Never mind the Archbishop,' said Bartholomew, worried. 'If rioting does occur, then people are going to be killed or maimed. I do not want that to happen, whether Islip is here to see it or not.'

'Polmorva,' said Paxtone uneasily. 'Is he trying to destroy us? Oxford has already been brought low, and if we are suppressed for violence, it means his new university will have a better chance of success. Winchester and Haverhill are lovely places, but I do not want them to flourish at our expense. Something must be done to stop him.'

'If it *is* him,' said Michael unhappily. 'We have no evidence, other than the suspicion that he would like to found a rival *studium generale*, which is hardly damning. What do you think, Matt? Is he the kind of man to destroy two towns for personal gain?'

'Yes,' answered Bartholomew without hesitation. 'But that does not mean to say he has actually done it.'

'I must go,' said Lee, edging away. 'Rougham sent word that he will arrive home from Norfolk soon, and I need to clean his clyster pipes. He will be angry if they are not spotless.'

'His imminent return is good news, Lee,' said Paxtone pleasantly. 'You must miss him.'

'Actually, I prefer it when he is not here,' said Lee baldly. 'But he is coming back, and there is not much I can do, except make sure his pipes are shiny. I do my best, but he is never satisfied.'

'I can imagine,' said Bartholomew wryly. 'I have the same experience with him myself.'

Lee strode away, while Paxtone invited Bartholomew and Michael to King's Hall for a cup of wine before the requiem mass, saying he had something he wanted to discuss. Michael accepted before Bartholomew could decline, and Paxtone took them to the refectory, where a pot of ale mulled over a brazier. He poured goblets for his guests, then led them to a table where some of the other Fellows sat. Dodenho was among them, holding forth on some aspect of philosophy that he claimed to have developed, while Wormynghalle was trying to look interested. She brightened when Paxtone, Bartholomew and Michael arrived.

Bartholomew grinned conspiratorially. 'You are looking especially manly this afternoon,' he said in an undertone.

She smiled. 'I rubbed oil into my hair to make it look greasy, and invested in a roll of material to bind my body. Now no one will feel what lies beneath when I slip on wine and a well-meaning physician dives forward to save me.'

'I am pleased to be here,' said Michael, settling on a bench and shaking his head when Paxtone offered him a plate of pastries. Bartholomew wondered whether he was unwell. 'I want to talk to you all about something.'

Dodenho looked pleased. 'You want me to give another University Lecture. My last one was very well received, and a number of people have asked when the next will be.'

'So they can avoid it,' whispered Wormynghalle to Bartholomew. 'But he is so convinced of his scholarly prowess that he does not realise they are insulting him.

318

Duraunt from Merton Hall said his lecture was enough to make the angels weep, and Dodenho interpreted it as meaning the heavenly hosts would shed tears of admiration at the power of his arguments!'

'Is he really so stupid?' asked Bartholomew, regarding the preening scholar wonderingly. 'Or is it all an act, and he is actually more clever than we think?'

Wormynghalle considered. 'No,' she said eventually. 'He really does believe he is Cambridge's answer to Roger Bacon. And speaking of Bacon, what do you think of his contention that—?'

'My question does concern King's Hall,' said Michael to the others, loud enough to distract her. 'But it is not about public lectures – it is about Hamecotes, who abandoned his duties without permission, and went to buy books. He claims to have purchased Heytesbury's *Regulae* from Merton. However, Duraunt informs me that Merton *never* sells its books, because they are too valuable a commodity. Hamecotes was lying.'

'We know,' said Paxtone, taking the wind out of Michael's sails. 'It is why I asked you to come here and share a cup of wine with us.' He swallowed uneasily, and glanced at his two companions. 'We had hoped to keep the matter quiet, given the disgrace it might bring to our College, but you are a sensible man and I am sure we can rely on your discretion.'

Michael narrowed his eyes. 'Why do I sense I am going to hear something I will not like?'

'Probably because you are,' said Wormynghalle softly. She grimaced, as if the subject was painful for her. 'You see, Hamecotes is not in Oxford. He is here.'

'Here?' asked Michael, startled. 'Well, I have written his absence in the University records now, and I cannot erase it. When did he return? Or are you going to tell me he never went?'

'We do not know whether he went,' said Wormynghalle. 'Although he sent us those letters, so I am inclined to believe that he stopped there briefly, even if it was not his intended destination. We discovered him an hour ago, which is why we have not yet had time to do anything official.'

'Send him to see me,' said Michael sternly. 'He owes two marks for being absent without leave, and we could do with the money before the Visitation.'

'It is not that simple,' said Wormynghalle. She looked at Paxtone and Dodenho. 'I do not know how to explain this.'

'I do,' said Paxtone. He stood and indicated that Michael and Bartholomew should follow him. 'The easiest way is to show—'

'No!' cried Dodenho, also coming to his feet. 'Do not make the situation worse than it is! Just tell them in a few words. They do not need *all* the grisly details.'

'I will not lie,' said Paxtone wearily, as if they had debated the matter too long already. 'We must do what is right, and Brother Michael is the Senior Proctor. I do not want King's Hall to become the centre of rumours and speculation when we have done nothing wrong.'

'King's Hall is not what *I* am worried about,' said Wormynghalle unhappily, indicating that Paxtone was to sit again. 'It is Hamecotes. I am obliged, as his room-mate, to protect him . . .'

'I am more concerned with the impact it might have on my scholarly musings,' said Dodenho. 'People might not want to read texts scribed by a man whose College . . . well, you know.'

'I do not,' said Michael loudly. 'What has Hamecotes done that is so dreadful?'

'It is better just to show him,' said Paxtone, raising his hand to quell the objections of his younger colleagues. 'Michael and Matt are friends, and will help us resolve this

320

unfortunate matter quietly and discreetly. Besides, they will not tell anyone else, because of the Visitation.'

Dodenho sighed. 'Very well, but you had better be right. If this misfires, I shall be cross.'

'Cross?' cried Wormynghalle in disbelief. 'Well, in that case we had better redouble our efforts. Hamecotes may be disgraced and the College shamed, but it would be worse if you were *cross*!'

Paxtone laid a sympathetic hand on her shoulder that made her flinch, while Dodenho merely looked bemused, as if he could not imagine what he had said wrong. Bartholomew and Michael followed Paxtone to the door, the physician doing so reluctantly, not sure he wanted to know what was about to be revealed.

'You are right to be uneasy,' whispered Wormynghalle. 'Do not allow yourself to become embroiled in this, Matt. Let Michael do it – this sort of thing is why he is paid such a princely salary.'

'I want him with me,' said Michael, overhearing. 'Where are we going, anyway?'

Paxtone did not reply, but walked into the yard, where he passed a number of buildings before reaching a disused stable block at the far end of the vegetable plots. It was near the river, and Bartholomew was aware of the water's dank fumes. Paxtone approached a ramshackle shed, and opened a door that creaked rustily. Everyone waited in silence while he took a lamp from a hook on the wall and set about lighting it.

'What are you doing?' came an appalled voice from behind them. It was Norton. 'Are you mad?'

'We have no choice,' said Paxtone, busy with the wick.

'You should have waited,' shouted Norton furiously. 'This should be for the Warden and *all* the Fellows to decide, not just you three. You have no right.'

'I do not care,' said Paxtone. 'I have seen what happens

321

when men try to deceive their way out of difficult situations. They always end up in deeper trouble. It is better this way.'

'I am not sure I want to remain here any longer,' said Norton coldly. Bartholomew saw unease and fear under the shell of anger. 'It is not how I imagined it would be. It is all gossiping in Latin and eating too much. I shall resign at the end of term.'

'Good,' said Wormynghalle, as Norton stalked away. 'At least something good has come out of this. That man has no right to present himself as a scholar. It is an insult to those of us with minds.'

Once the wick burned, Paxtone led the way inside the stable. Bartholomew could make out very little in the gloom, other than that it was dusty and dry.

'Here is Hamecotes,' said Paxtone, carrying the lamp to a table that stood in the centre of the room and tugging away a rug to reveal a body. It was swollen and black, and should have been in its grave days before. Michael gasped in shock, and backed away so fast that he collided with Dodenho. Bartholomew simply stared at the sorry sight in front of him.

'We found him here this morning,' explained Wormynghalle, putting her hand over her mouth and averting her eyes. Bartholomew saw she was struggling not to betray herself by fainting or being sick. Dodenho was not so iron-willed. He shoved his way past her to reach the fresh air outside, where he stood rubber-legged and breathing heavily.

'He has been dead a lot longer than that,' said Michael, stating the obvious. 'When did you say he left for Oxford?'

'The morning after Ascension,' replied Wormynghalle shakily. 'Fifteen days ago.'

'And how long has he been a corpse?' asked Michael, as Bartholomew studied the grisly spectacle.

'Less than fifteen days, but probably more than five. It is impossible to be precise.'

'I said farewell to him that morning, and he told me he was looking forward to his journey,' said Wormynghalle, fighting back tears. She turned away abruptly, and hurried to stand outside with Dodenho, staring up at the sky and blinking hard as she fought to regain control of herself.

Paxtone went to put a paternal arm around her shoulders, and Bartholomew saw her struggle not to recoil from his touch. 'I know this is hard,' Paxtone said kindly. 'You were friends as well as room-mates, and he thought very highly of your scholarship.'

Wormynghalle gulped and tears began to flow freely. 'He said that?'

Paxtone nodded. 'Many times. He said you were the cleverest man in the College, and boasted that he was the room-mate of the Fellow destined for widespread academic acclaim.'

Wormynghalle turned away in a flood of grief, while Dodenho straightened himself carefully. 'Surely you are mistaken,' he said. 'He must have meant *me*.'

'Never mind that,' said Michael. 'If Hamecotes died between the time he left for Oxford and five days ago, does it mean he fulfilled his book-buying duties and came back? Or did he not go at all – in which case who wrote the letters purporting to be from him?'

'They were in his writing,' said Wormynghalle in a muffled voice. She took a deep breath and entered the shed again, Paxtone and Dodenho following. 'You can see them, if you like. I retained them because I intended to scrape the parchment and reuse it later. Perhaps I will keep them now, to remind me of his friendship.'

'I wonder if he wrote them before he left, as a ruse,' mused Michael. 'That would have given him a few free days to go about his business – whatever that was. Was he with Wolf, do you think, looking after him at Stourbridge?'

'Possibly,' replied Paxtone. 'But Wolf was reasonably fit when I saw him a few days before he went missing himself – he had a summer chill, but we all suffer those from time to time. He stayed a day or two at the hospital, but he was malingering, medically speaking.'

'No sign of the pox, then?' asked Michael bluntly.

Paxtone did not like his supposedly celibate colleagues being accused of contracting sexually transmitted diseases. 'No,' he said shortly.

Michael turned back to the body, forcing himself to look at it. 'So, how did Hamecotes come to be in this building? Who found him?'

'I did,' said Dodenho hoarsely. 'I like to practise my lectures here, because it is more private than my room. I came on Tuesday evening – he was not here then – and I found his body today. Therefore, he must have brought himself here during the last two and a half days.'

'He did not come under his own power,' said Bartholomew. 'He has been dead too long.'

'I told you that,' said Paxtone to Dodenho, rather pompously for someone who knew so little about the dead. 'He was *put* here: he did not walk to this building on his own.'

'But who would do such a thing?' asked Wormynghalle in a small voice. 'And how did he die? Did he drown? I see from his clothes that he has been wet, and I know he cannot swim.'

'He may have been in the river,' said Bartholomew. 'But that is not what killed him. This is.' He eased away Hamecotes's liripipe to reveal a slashing gape across the throat, ragged and uneven, as if some blunt, crude implement had been used to inflict the damage.

Dodenho shot from the room, pushing past Wormynghalle and almost knocking her off her feet.

Paxtone reeled back with his hand to his mouth, while Michael inhaled sharply at the sight.

'And that is not all,' said Bartholomew softly. 'This is the man whose body was in the cistern in Merton Hall.'

Michael gazed at Bartholomew in the darkness of the dilapidated stables. The physician could hear Dodenho retching outside, while Wormynghalle and Paxtone stood well back, so they were not obliged to see the horror on the table. 'Are you sure?'

'Yes. I recognise the shape of his nose and the moss-coloured liripipe.'

'He often wore that,' said Wormynghalle in a cracked voice. 'He liked green clothes.'

'You told me that when I wrote Dodenho's prescription, and you gave me his emerald ink to use by mistake,' recalled Bartholomew. 'I should have put the facts together sooner, because I remember this garment quite clearly from the well.'

'But how did he come to be here?' demanded Michael.

No one could answer, and Bartholomew went back to his examination. He quickly established for certain that the throat wound was the cause of death, and ascertained from the state of the body that it had been immersed in water for some time. There was only one other thing that was pertinent: a rope around the corpse's feet, which had been cut. He supposed it had been attached to stones and used to weight Hamecotes down, to prevent him from floating. It explained why the body had been so heavy when he had pulled it to the surface in the belief that it was Michael. He realised it would have remained hidden indefinitely, had Michael not had the misfortune to fall in with it. He told the others his conclusions.

'But Sheriff Tulyet said there was no body in the cistern,' said Paxtone, bewildered.

'Obviously, it was moved before he conducted his search,' replied Michael impatiently. 'And now we know where it went, although I cannot imagine why. Did Hamecotes know Eudo or Boltone?'

'Not as far as I am aware,' replied Paxtone. 'But Boltone is sometimes obliged to travel to Oxford to present his accounts, and Hamecotes has . . . had friends there. Perhaps they had mutual acquaintances. It was because of his Oxford connections that we were not surprised when Hamecotes wrote to say he had gone there – we were annoyed and inconvenienced, but not worried.'

'He did know Boltone,' said Wormynghalle. She rubbed her mouth on her sleeve and Bartholomew saw that her hands were shaking. 'Boltone's brother was bailiff on a manor owned by Hamecotes's sister, or some such thing. They were not friends, but they passed the time of day when they met by chance on the street.'

'Boltone,' said Michael in satisfaction. 'This explains a good deal. It tells us why he tried to beat our brains out when we ventured too near the place where he had hidden Hamecotes's body. And Eudo must have helped him – either with the murder itself, or with disposing of the corpse.'

'Hamecotes died in exactly the same way as Oke-hamptone,' said Bartholomew. 'Do you see these inden-tations? They are tooth marks. I saw similar damage on Okehamptone's neck. Also, note the way the flesh is torn here, which is indicative of a puncture caused by a sharp canine . . .'

He trailed off. Was his analysis correct? Were the faint bruises caused by human fangs, or had he allowed Rougham's claims of being gnawed by Clippesby to influ-ence his conclusions? He found he was not sure. Then he became aware that Paxtone was regarding him with some shock.

'But Okehamptone died of a fever. I saw the body myself.'

'You did not,' said Michael tartly. 'You prayed over it, but you did not *examine* it. You missed the fact that there was a wound on Okehamptone's throat that was identical to this one.'

Paxtone was appalled. 'But Okehamptone was pale and waxen, not at all like Hamecotes, who is black and bloated.'

'That is because Hamecotes has been submerged in water for God knows how long,' said Michael impatiently. 'Of course they do not look the same now.'

'But how do you know Okehamptone had a wound in his throat?' asked Paxtone, regarding Bartholomew uneasily. 'You did not exhume him, did you? Like the medical men in Italy are said to do? I will not condone that sort of activity, Matthew. It is not right!'

'Okehamptone was not buried,' said Michael briskly. 'Which is just as well, given what we now know about him. No one wants his tortured soul roaming the streets of Cambridge, screaming for vengeance and haunting those who let him down, so you should be grateful for what Matt did.'

'We especially do not want him at large when the Archbishop is here,' agreed Dodenho. 'It would mean our suppression for certain. Perhaps I should offer my services to Polmorva, so he will take me with him to Winchester or Haverhill when he establishes his new school.'

'Yes, go and see him today,' encouraged Wormynghalle. She fixed Paxtone with accusing eyes. 'It sounds as though you almost allowed a killer to go free. How could you have missed a terrible injury like this on a man's body?'

'I am a physician, whose duty is to the living,' replied Paxtone angrily. 'I know there are men who learn anatomy from cadavers, but I am not one of them – I do not even touch them, if I can help it. That is why I did not see

327

Hamecotes's neck when Dodenho summoned me earlier, either.'

'No harm has been done,' said Dodenho, seeing Wormynghalle look angry at their colleague's negligence. 'Paxtone made a mistake, but Bartholomew has corrected it. Lesser mortals are prone to errors, and few of us are perfect.'

'True,' agreed Michael, evidently putting himself in the latter category. 'So, we shall say no more about it. What we will discuss, however, is what we can learn about Hamecotes's death now. Matt?'

'He and Okehampton have similar wounds, so they must have been killed by the same person or people.'

'Boltone is as good a suspect as any,' said Michael. 'He knew Hamecotes, and may have met Okehampton when he visited Oxford to present his accounts. Okehampton died in Merton Hall, and Hamecotes's body was concealed in Merton Hall – where Boltone lives. Eudo probably helped him.'

'But why?' wondered Bartholomew. 'Why would they kill these two men?'

'We will ask them when they are caught,' said Michael. 'I wonder why they moved Hamecotes from the cistern to here.'

'Because they did not want his body found?' suggested Paxtone. 'Tulyet made no secret of the fact that he intended to dredge the pit, so they were obliged to hide their victim a second time.'

'This does not make sense,' said Bartholomew. 'If they fished the body from the well, why did they not grab their sack of treasure at the same time?'

'Perhaps they intended to go back for it when they finished dealing with Hamecotes, but ran out of time,' said Michael with a dismissive wave of a fat white hand to indicate the point was unimportant. 'The question I want answered is why did they bring Hamecotes here, where he would be so easily discovered?'

'They probably did not know he would be "easily discovered",' said Paxtone. 'I had no idea Dodenho uses this abandoned shed to practise his lectures, and I am sure the killers did not, either. What do you think, Wormynghalle?'

'I saw Dodenho here once or twice,' recalled Wormynghalle thoughtfully. 'But I assumed he was meeting a woman, so of course I said nothing. We men must turn a blind eye to each other's dalliances from time to time.' She did not look at Bartholomew.

'I shall not come here again, though,' vowed Dodenho. 'I prefer my audiences alive. Perhaps I will leave Cambridge and go to Oxford instead. *They* do not have rotting cadavers in deserted huts.'

'Everything about this case points to Oxford,' mused Michael. 'We now have five men dead – Gonerby, Okehamptone, Chesterfelde, Spryngheuse and Hamecotes – all with links to the place.' He was silent for a moment, gathering his thoughts. 'Let us review what we know of these deaths chronologically. Gonerby died first, in February, during the riots. But who was next? Okehamptone died about two weeks ago, which is roughly the time you say Hamecotes left King's Hall.'

'Hamecotes did not kill Okehamptone,' said Wormynghalle, immediately defensive of her room-mate. 'Why would he do such a thing? They probably did not even know each other.'

'You cannot be sure of that,' argued Michael. 'You said yourself that Hamecotes had "friends" in Oxford. And Okehamptone may have killed Hamecotes, anyway, not the other way around. We have no idea who died first, because Matt refuses to be more precise about times of death.'

'I do not think either is guilty,' said Bartholomew. 'Their

throat wounds are virtually identical, and I doubt one killed the other, and then was slain in the same way by a third person. That is unlikely, to say the least.'

'I am not sure I agree with your assessment of bites,' said Paxtone, reluctantly inspecting the wound and clearly finding it distasteful. 'I acknowledge this rough gash was not made with a knife – even a blunt one – but teeth . . .' He shuddered at the notion.

Bartholomew pointed again to the marks still visible in the darkening skin. 'You can see their impression. It looks as if someone grabbed the throat with his teeth and pulled at it. Like this.'

Paxtone turned away with a gasp of revulsion, while Wormynghalle and Michael studiously refused to look until they were sure he had finished. Dodenho witnessed the demonstration, but only because he was too shocked to close his eyes.

'That was singularly nasty,' Dodenho said eventually, wiping his mouth on the back of his hand. His fingers shook violently. 'What are you trying to do? Unnerve us into having nightmares, with visions of human wolves tearing at the necks of their innocent victims?'

'Speaking of wolves, what do you think happened to Wolf?' asked Michael. 'We have ascertained that Hamecotes was not where you thought he should be, so what about your other absent colleague?'

'We do not know,' said Wormynghalle weakly. 'Paxtone says he does not have the pox, and I do not think he is Rougham's lover, because both men prefer ladies – as I do. Perhaps Norton is right, and he has absconded because he owes the College so much money. But I do not think he is the killer. Do you?' She addressed her question to Dodenho, his room-mate.

Dodenho considered carefully. 'No. He does not have the teeth, for a start. His are decayed, and biting some-

330

thing like a throat would probably make most of them snap off.'

'This is preposterous!' exclaimed Paxtone, suddenly angry. 'You must be mistaken, Matthew. People simply do not die in this way! I have been a physician for twenty-seven years, and I have never heard even the merest whisper of someone bitten to death by another person. I can see there are marks that *may* have been caused by fangs, but they must belong to a dog or a wild beast.'

'It is possible,' conceded Bartholomew, relieved that someone had suggested an alternative. 'Perhaps someone trained an animal to kill.'

Michael spoke in a low voice when the King's Hall men began a debate about which creatures might be trained for killing: Paxtone said only dogs were so inclined, while Wormynghalle opted for a bear and Dodenho elected a ferret. 'Or perhaps someone is so deranged that he *thinks* he is an animal. Do not forget Rougham, Matt – even I could tell a man had gnawed him. If I bit myself on the arm right now, I would see the same thing that I saw on *his* shoulder: a parabolic curve with oblong dents for choppers, and square ones for grinders.'

Bartholomew nodded, staring down at the body. 'The problem with Hamecotes – and Okehamptone, too – is that they have been dead too long. The skin has rotted and changed its texture, so the marks are distorted. There may be a parabolic curve here, and these marks may be molars and incisors. But it is impossible to be sure.'

Michael winced at what he considered unnecessary detail. 'I believe Hamecotes, Okehamptone and Rougham – and probably Gonerby too – were victims of the same person, because it is impossible that we should have two lunatic biters on the loose simultaneously. But this leads us to more questions: first, how is Rougham connected to the Merton Hall deaths, and second, who is this maniac?'

'It cannot be Clippesby,' said Bartholomew immediately. 'If it were, then we would have to assume that he also took Hamecotes from the cistern and brought him here. He has been at Stourbridge, and has had no opportunity to tote corpses around the town.'

'We have been through this before, Matt,' said Michael wearily. 'Clippesby *has* had the opportunity to retrieve and hide bodies. He regularly escapes from his cell, and he does not even bother to deny the fact. I know you are reluctant to believe he could do such a thing, but I think it is time we faced up to the truth, and took a long hard look at him.'

Bartholomew shook his head stubbornly. 'You can look all you like, but Clippesby is not our man. He has no reason to select these particular victims. I think you were right with your original theory: that there is something odd going on that involves Oxford – and Merton in particular – because all these deaths have some link to those places.'

'With the exception of Rougham.'

'He is in his fifties, and claims to have travelled. He may well have studied at Oxford in the past.'

'I do not like this,' said Wormynghalle, breaking into their discussion. 'Those Oxford men have no right to bring dangerous creatures to our city. It is only a matter of time before the thing attacks someone else, and I do not want it said that scholars harbour savage beasts for the express purpose of slaughter.'

'Nor do I,' said Dodenho. 'Eudo whipped the townsfolk into a frenzy this morning with his tales of scholars blaming him for crimes he did not commit. If word leaks out that we have killer ferrets in our halls, they will rise up against us for certain.'

'Then we must make sure they do not,' said Michael decisively. 'Keep this affair with Hamecotes quiet until I tell you otherwise. Bury him as soon as you can, but do

332

not tell the students what really happened. We have a great deal to lose, and we *must* be discreet.'

'You can trust us,' said Paxtone. 'We do not want our College attacked or the town in flames. Hamecotes will be buried tomorrow, but no one will know how he died.'

'Good,' said Michael. He glanced out of the window, gauging the hour by the angle of the sun. 'It is almost time for this requiem. Chesterfelde and Spryngheuse should go in the ground as soon as possible: I do not want dead scholars used as a rallying point as halls and Colleges rise up against the town.'

Bartholomew followed Michael to St Michael's Church, where the monk performed a moving and solemn mass. Bartholomew had expected Duraunt and Polmorva to attend, but he was surprised to see the three merchants, too. Eu and Abergavenny stood together near the front of the small gathering of mourners, but the tanner remained apart from them. Judging by the number of black looks he threw in their direction, they had had a serious falling-out over something.

Towards the end of the service, at its sacred climax, the largest of the altar candles began to gutter, and Bartholomew realised he had not changed it since Michael had complained about its defective wick. Before he could fetch a replacement, the flame had flickered and gone out.

'That is an omen,' he heard Eu whisper, while Wormynghalle began to cross himself. 'There is something amiss with this whole business, and God has sent us a sign.'

'Nonsense,' replied Polmorva. 'It tells us only that Michaelhouse did not have the decency to provide new candles for our dead.'

'It does not mean that either,' said Duraunt, sounding tired. 'It simply means one candle is finished and a new one is needed.'

'It means there are restless spirits here,' said Wormynghalle, looking around fearfully, as if he expected one to come and accost him. 'And they do not like what we are doing.'

'We are watching a holy rite,' said Polmorva archly. 'Why should spirits object to that?'

'It depends on the spirit,' said Eu in his laconic manner. 'Demonic ones will not appreciate a sacred office, I am sure. But perhaps the candle expired because God knows what really happened to Spryngheuse, and He does not want his sinful body in consecrated ground.'

'I do not like this,' said Wormynghalle. His face was white and his eyes dilated with fear. 'I am not staying here to be blasted by divinely inspired lightning.'

He clattered out of the building as fast as his legs could carry him, leaving Bartholomew staring after him in astonishment, amazed that a rough, insensitive man like the tanner should be so seriously agitated by the end of a candle. Eu laughed, hard and derisively, distracting Michael from his duties.

'Stop that!' said the monk sharply. 'Snigger outside if you must, but do not befoul my church with undignified behaviour. If there are bolts of lightning on their way, it will be because you have cackled and chattered during the Transubstantiation.'

'The candle going out *is* significant,' insisted Eu, chagrined and sulky at the rebuke. 'A flame extinguishing itself during the mass means something terrible will happen. You mark my words.'

The following day was a Saturday, so teaching finished early, and Bartholomew and Michael went to visit Rougham. They found him out of bed and sitting at the lower-ground window. His face was pale and he was thinner than he had been, but he had washed and shaved, and had lost the hollow-eyed stare that had made Bartholomew fear for his life. He was laughing when Bartholomew tapped on the door and entered. The physician had never seen Rougham laugh, except on occasions when a student or a colleague had done something stupid, when he made a braying sound full of derision. But this was an open guffaw, full of genuine mirth.

'Matilde has been entertaining me,' he explained when he saw his colleague's bemusement. 'She has tales about life at Court you would not believe. She is wasted here. She should be with Queen Philippa, employing her many accomplishments and securing herself a decent husband.'

Matilde gave a wistful smile that made Bartholomew wonder whether she might concur, and it crossed his mind to ask her to marry him then and there. He opened his mouth to say something, but Rougham chattered on, and Bartholomew did not want to propose in front of an audience anyway. He decided to ask later, when Rougham was back at Gonville and they could be alone.

'She plays the lute with a skill I have seldom seen.' Rougham continued with his eulogy when Matilde went to fetch cushions for her guests. 'And she sings with the voice of an angel. She reads better than any Bible Scholar I have heard, and she sees through the political manoeu-vrings of the King's Court with a skill any clerk would envy. I repeat: she should not be squandering her talents here.'

'You have enjoyed her company, then?' asked Michael wryly.

'I most certainly have!' declared Rougham with great conviction. 'I was horrified when Yolande and her husband brought me here: to the home of the woman who organ-ises the town's whores into an efficient and well-run guild. But Matilde is not like them and, since I have regained my wits, she has impressed me with her modesty and gentle-ness. It is not every lady who would take an ailing man into her home and risk so much for him. But Matilde did so without complaint, and my reputation remains intact.'

'Hers is not, though,' said Bartholomew, a little sharply. 'And besides, she only did it because you threatened to expose Clippesby.'

'Ah, yes,' said Rougham. 'Clippesby. We must decide what to do about him. I overheard Yolande and Matilde talking last night, discussing rumours that a man called Gonerby died from a bitten throat. Clippesby cannot be allowed to continue his reign of terror.'

'I am not convinced of his guilt,' said Bartholomew, alarmed that Rougham had learned about one of the other attacks already. 'The evidence against him is circumstantial, and—'

'I saw him with my own eyes,' said Rougham firmly. 'As I lay bleeding and dazed, there he was, looming above me, covered in my blood. That is not circumstantial, Bartholomew: that is fact.'

'He is right, Matt,' said Michael sombrely. 'Clippesby is a danger to himself and to others, and we need to make a decision about his future.'

Rougham touched Bartholomew lightly on the arm. 'I am grateful to you for helping me. We are not friends, and you would have been perfectly within your rights to take me to Gonville and explain I was attacked while visiting Yolande. But you have acted with decency and understanding, and I intend to reciprocate. I have given the matter a good deal of thought over the last two days, and I have a plan.'

'A plan for what?' asked Bartholomew warily.

'A plan for Clippesby. He cannot be allowed to return to Michaelhouse as though nothing has happened – not only because none of us want him to kill again, but because it would not look good for Michaelhouse to harbour homicidal lunatics.'

'I thought we could send him home to his father,' said Michael. 'We cannot grant him a benefice in some remote village, because he might start eating his parishioners.'

'His family might be as mad as he is,' Rougham pointed out, not unreasonably. 'But my brother owns large estates in Norfolk, and I established a hospital there a few years ago. It is remote, secure and run by an Austin Canon who asks no questions. He is a good man, and will treat Clippesby kindly.' He gave a wry smile. 'The hospital has its own chickens, geese, sheep and cows, so Clippesby will have plenty of suitable company.'

Bartholomew rubbed a hand through his hair. 'For how long?'

'For the rest of his life,' replied Rougham. He sighed in exasperation when he saw his colleague's shock. 'There is no other solution, man, and I am offering a haven, where he will be safe and cared for and where no one else will suffer as I have. I am even volunteering to pay for his keep.'

'You are very generous,' said Michael, before Bartholomew could refuse. 'And you are also right: there is no other solution to this problem. Clippesby should, by rights, answer for his crimes and pay with his life, but the town and the University are too unsettled to have that sort of scandal circulating.'

'You mean you do not want the Archbishop to know that Michaelhouse Fellows attack innocent men with their teeth,' said Rougham. 'Well, I happen to concur: I do not want Islip to build his new foundation in Oxford, when it should come here. We must unite on this, because it would be a pity to let Clippesby's illness deprive our University of what is its right.'

'But to lock a man away for the rest of his life . . .' said Bartholomew, troubled. He recalled Clippesby's distress when informed that he was to be incarcerated for a few days, and could not imagine how he would react to being told he would never be free again.

'It is horrible, but necessary,' said Rougham. 'Besides, he should be grateful his life is to be spared. You saw what he did to me, and perhaps you inspected the corpse of the man he murdered – this Gonerby. You cannot allow him his liberty.'

'It is settled, then,' said Michael. 'We should make arrangements as soon as we can – before the Visitation, if possible. Clippesby wants to see Islip, and I do not want him to escape from Stourbridge and bite the throat of the highest-ranking churchman in the country.'

'I have already sent word to my Norfolk hospital,' said Rougham. 'Matilde hired a messenger, and he is riding as we speak. I recommend Clippesby leaves on Monday morning. I would say tomorrow, but it is Sunday, and I do not want to despoil the Sabbath. The Archbishop will not be here until Monday afternoon, so it should work out nicely.'

'Good,' said Michael. He smiled when Matilde entered the room and handed him a goblet of wine. 'And when will *you* be ready to leave, Rougham?'

Hope flared in Matilde's eyes, and Bartholomew saw that while Rougham might be enjoying his sojourn now he was well enough to appreciate her lively and erudite company, she was tired of him, and wanted him gone.

'Tomorrow or the day after, God willing,' replied Rougham. 'Once I am at Gonville, I can blame my poor health on the journey from Norfolk. No one will question me, because it is common knowledge that travelling is dangerous. Look what happened to poor Henry Okehamptone.'

Bartholomew regarded him warily. 'How do you know his name was Henry?'

'We were friends,' explained Rougham. 'He wrote to say

he was coming, and I invited him to stay at Gonville. I was surprised – and offended – when he elected to remain at Merton Hall instead.'

'You *knew* Okehamptone?' asked Bartholomew. He exchanged a glance with Michael.

Rougham nodded. 'I went to see him the night he arrived – on Ascension Day eve – but was told he was indisposed, and too ill to receive me. The next day, the poor fellow was dead of fever.'

'Who told you he was indisposed?' asked Michael. 'Duraunt?'

'Someone I did not recognise. He was rather rude, given that I had gone to meet an old friend – I was not even invited inside. If I had been admitted, I would have examined Henry, and might even have been able to save him.' Rougham grimaced. 'And I would have been occupied with his care, so would have cancelled my appointment with Yolande. A great many things would have turned out differently, had I been allowed to see Henry that night.'

'What did he look like?' persisted Michael. 'This man who refused to let you in?'

'Fine clothes. Haughty and officious. He made me feel as though I was a beggar after scraps.'

'Polmorva,' said Bartholomew immediately.

'Why do you ask?' Rougham looked from Bartholomew to Michael. 'You seem to think my friendship with Henry is significant in some way. Why? What do you know that makes you glance so meaningfully at each other?'

Michael rubbed his chin. Since Rougham already knew Gonerby had died from a throat wound, there was no longer a need for secrecy, and he decided to be truthful. When he explained what had happened to Okehamptone, Rougham's jaw dropped in shock. By the time the monk had finished, tears were rolling down Rougham's cheeks, and it was some moments before he had regained control of himself.

'How shocking,' he said eventually. 'Poor, poor Henry! The killer clearly assumed that no one would inspect the body properly, and that he would get away with his deception. He was lucky it was Paxtone who made the examination, and not Bartholomew, or he would have been exposed immediately. You are always very thorough.'

'Weasenham demanded my services that morning,' explained Bartholomew. 'You were already here – and, although you did not ask for me until the afternoon, you were still unavailable to patients.'

Rougham gazed at him in confusion. 'Weasenham? Are you sure?'

'Of course,' replied Bartholomew. 'Why do you ask?'

'Because yesterday I sent a note to Lee asking him to prepare a list of all the summons I have missed during the last two weeks. Matilde persuaded him to provide her with a copy.'

'How did she do that?' asked Michael, startled. 'Surely he wanted to know why?'

Matilde's eyes sparkled; she loved a challenge. 'He was drafting it out in St Mary the Great, and I pretended to admire his writing. He gave it to me as a keepsake.'

The lad was besotted with her, Bartholomew thought, like so many other men. It occurred to him that he might have competition when he asked for her hand in marriage, and that he should place his request as soon as possible. 'Matilde,' he began, abandoning his hopes for more intimate circumstances. 'I have been thinking that you and I . . . that is to say, have you . . . ?' His heart was hammering so furiously that it was making him feel light-headed.

'That was clever of you,' said Michael to Matilde, when Bartholomew's stuttering sentences seemed to be leading nowhere important. 'But what does this list have to do with Weasenham?'

'His name is not on it,' explained Rougham, pulling it from his tunic. 'Look. You can see for yourselves. He is my wealthiest patient, and I was relieved I had not missed a consultation with him. But now I learn he has changed his allegiance, and favours Bartholomew instead. That is a blow.'

'Not necessarily,' said Michael thoughtfully. 'However, it does suggest that Matt was deliberately lured away by someone who knew Paxtone would do a less than perfect job. But who? Weasenham himself?'

'It was a summons under false pretences, too,' added Bartholomew, dragging his thoughts away from conjugal bliss and supposing there would be another opportunity to propose to Matilde. 'He only had toothache, and could have gone to the apothecary. He did not need a physician.'

'Interesting,' mused Michael. 'We must have words with him about this.'

'It is more than interesting,' said Rougham angrily. 'It smacks of a carefully laid plot. Henry was an Austin Canon and, although he did not often wear the prescribed habit, he *always* favoured clothes that were sober and functional. I never saw him don anything as frivolous as the liripipe you described. If there was a gaudy hood on his body, then someone put it there after he died.'

'To hide the wound,' surmised Michael. 'And with my Corpse Examiner otherwise engaged, and a room full of men prepared to swear that Okehamptone had died of a fever, the killer – or killers – had high hopes that the crime would go undetected.'

'It did go undetected,' Bartholomew pointed out. 'But if Clippesby is the killer, it means *he* put the liripipe on Okehamptone and convinced everyone that the man died

341

of a fever. It also means he persuaded Weasenham to summon me. It sounds too highly organised to be his work.'

'But he knows you are a careful Corpse Examiner,' argued Rougham. 'No one from Oxford does. It makes sense that *he* was the one who sent you on this wild-goose chase with Weasenham.'

Michael scratched his chin. 'I wonder whether Polmorva's refusal to allow Rougham into Merton Hall means Okehamptone was already dead – that he did not die in the night.'

'No, it does not,' said Rougham softly. 'The shutters were open on the upper floor, and I could see inside as I left. Henry was sitting in a window. Perhaps he *was* feverish at that point, but it did not prevent him from chatting merrily to his Oxford cronies. There was no reason for me to have been turned away, and I was hurt.'

'You definitely saw him alive?' asked Michael.

'Yes. We have known each other ever since we were undergraduate-commoners at Merton, forty years ago. We were boys then, and it was long before you studied there, Bartholomew, but we wrote and met whenever we could. At one point, I was going to marry his sister, but then I embarked on an academic career, and that put paid to thoughts of women – well, to marrying them, at least.'

'And Okehamptone was talking to his Merton friends that night?' pressed Michael, to be certain.

Rougham nodded. 'In the light of his murder, I can only assume this wretch Polmorva declined to tell him I had come a-visiting.'

Bartholomew rubbed a hand through his hair. 'Which means Polmorva decided in advance that Okehamptone was not to see any friends that night – especially a physician. But why? So no one could later claim he was fit, and had not died of a sudden fever?'

'If so, then it means Polmorva played an active role in

the murder,' said Rougham. 'Do you think Clippesby put him under his spell, or perhaps threatened to kill him, if he did not do as he was told?'

'No,' said Bartholomew immediately. 'Clippesby is not that forceful.'

'I agree,' said Matilde, taking part in the discussion for the first time. 'He is gentle, and abhors violence. And he is far too scatter-brained to have executed such a devilish plot.'

Michael was unconvinced. 'But it explains very neatly why he attacked Rougham later the same night – he knew Rougham was Okehamptone's friend, and did not want him looking too closely into the death that was to occur before the following morning.'

'But why would Clippesby want a stranger – an Austin Canon – dead?' pressed Bartholomew. 'Even the insane have their motives, even if they are not ones we understand or accept.'

'Perhaps he wanted revenge on the Order he knew would later incarcerate him at Stourbridge,' suggested Rougham. 'He claims his animal friends tell him things that will happen in the future, so perhaps he had an inkling that he would soon be locked away.'

'That is weak,' said Bartholomew doubtfully.

'But not entirely impossible,' argued Rougham. He shuddered. 'The sooner I am back at Gonville the better. Will you help me walk there on Monday, after Clippesby leaves for Norfolk? I would like to meet the Archbishop, and I can hardly ask him to visit me here.'

'No,' agreed Bartholomew harshly, thinking of Matilde's reputation. 'You cannot.'

Bartholomew and Michael left Matilde's house and started to walk back to Michaelhouse, discussing the difficulties inherent in taking Rougham to Gonville Hall with no one seeing. They considered various options, including disguising him as a leper, hiding him in a cart, and dressing him in one of Michael's habits. Mention of men in monkish garb reminded Bartholomew of Spryngheuse's imaginary Benedictine, and he was sorry the Merton scholar had died in such an agony of terror.

Preparations for the impending Visitation were all around them as they walked along the High Street. The gutters were being scoured yet again, and dung collectors were out in force, gathering as much ordure as they could find, for they had been offered double pay for every cart-load they procured. Apprentices scaled unsteady ladders to clean the fronts of their masters' houses and shops, and the demand for washes to paint over old plaster was at a premium. New shades were springing up everywhere, as the preferred cream and ochre became unavailable. Haralda the Dane's home was an attractive pastel green, while Robin of Grantchester, the unsavoury surgeon who killed more customers than he saved, had opted to make his own, because it was cheaper. It was a vivid pink, and there were rumours that he had added blood from his patients to colour it.

Michael stopped walking and regarded the High Street with a critical eye. 'It is looking quite attractive,' he admitted eventually, watching the frenetic activities as people tried to finish as much as possible before the Sabbath put an end to their work.

'It is a pity about the river and the King's Ditch, though,' said Bartholomew. 'The dung collectors have amassed such vast quantities over the last two weeks that there is too much to sell for fertiliser. For want of anywhere else to put it, they are dumping it in the waterways, which are now foul.'

'Archbishop Islip will be fêted with sewage-free streets, newly decorated houses, clean churches, and roads devoid of anything with four legs. He cannot expect the river to smell nice, too.'

'I was more concerned with the fact that at some point he will want to wash, and it will be unfortunate if he catches a disease because he dabbles his hands in polluted water.'

'He will be with Chancellor Tynkell for much of the time. And you know what *he* thinks about cleanliness, so I shall make sure he tells Islip just how dangerous it can be. Besides, he is only staying a week – not long enough for his hands to get dirty.'

Bartholomew gaped, then saw the monk was laughing at him. He smiled, then turned his thoughts to what Wormynghalle the tanner had said about Okehamptone's death: that bad water had induced a fatal fever. 'Okehamptone must have made some complaint about his health that night, because I do not think Duraunt, Polmorva, Spryngheuse, Chesterfelde *and* the three merchants would lie about it, and they all said he had retired to bed unwell.'

'They did,' agreed Michael. He was thoughtful. 'Chesterfelde was snuffling and sneezing the morning I was summoned to deal with Okehamptone's death, so perhaps Okehamptone had caught something from him. To some men, a summer ague is a minor inconvenience, but to others it is akin to having the plague. Okehamptone may have been one of the latter, and unwittingly provided a way for his killer to conceal his murder.'

'Some people do exaggerate the severity of their afflictions. I helped Paxtone devise a remedy for Dodenho's constipation last week, and he demanded last rites before he would let us begin.'

'There is something distinctly odd about Dodenho. I find it hard to believe he is so dire a theorist, yet considers himself brilliant. I do not like this affair of the astrolabe, either – his "stolen" property ending up in Eudo's hoard.

Nor do I like the fact that he knew Chesterfelde, but initially denied it.'

'Norton worries me – he reacted peculiarly when we examined Hamecotes. Since he is not here for his education – he cannot attend lectures, because he knows no Latin – I cannot help but wonder what is his real purpose.'

'It may be ensuring that our University does not gain Islip's patronage,' said Michael worriedly. 'Then there is Polmorva, who witnessed Gonerby's murder but agreed to travel to Cambridge despite knowing that his own life might be in danger if the killer found out about him. I want to know why he refused to let Rougham see Okehamptone, too. And there is John Wormynghalle to consider.'

'There is nothing odd about her,' said Bartholomew, and immediately winced. Mercifully, Michael did not notice his slip.

'There *is*,' he declared. 'He sometimes misses meals because he is reading.'

'How singular.'

'It is curious that he studied in Oxford, yet only made the acquaintance of his namesake here. That tanner stands out, with his ill-fitting clothes and his garish jewellery, and I imagine he would be highly visible in a small place like Oxford. It makes me wonder whether the merchant is as rich and influential as he pretends. Perhaps you were right to be suspicious of him at our first meeting.'

'He is very recently wealthy, and he is not yet comfortable with it. Not like Eu.'

'Or Abergavenny. I am certain there is more to his smiling diplomacy than meets the eye. But here comes a contingent of King's Hall men, all sewn into their best clothes in readiness for the Visitation: boastful Dodenho, bookish Wormynghalle and that reprobate Norton.'

'I have just been reading Ockham's distinction between kinematic and dynamic problems in relation to inertia,'

346

said Wormynghalle excitedly when she met Bartholomew. 'But I think he is wrong: where there is resistance, then surely a purely kinematic treatment will suffice?'

Bartholomew considered. 'Ockham was saying that he saw a way – although he does not explain what – of reconciling the law of ratios with movement in a finite time under zero resistance, and—'

'I have already ascertained that in my latest thesis,' interrupted Dodenho. 'It is a work containing dynamical considerations.'

'I read it,' said Wormynghalle shortly. 'It bears an uncanny resemblance to Bradwardine's *Tractatus de proportionibus velocitatum in motibus.*'

'Boring!' sighed Norton. 'You scholars are so dull, discussing such nonsense in the street. Why can you not talk about horses, like normal men? Come to the butts with me, Wormynghalle. You have a free afternoon, and I wager you a shilling you will not beat me again.'

'Another time,' said Wormynghalle, barely glancing at him as she turned her attention back to Bartholomew, the only man present she considered a worthy adversary. 'But resistance—'

'I would have done better if someone had lent me an astrolabe,' interrupted Dodenho, resentful that his work should be so summarily dismissed.

'An astrolabe,' mused Michael. 'There is a curious thing. You claimed yours was stolen, but later found it and sold it. Then it appears at Merton Hall, where it is owned by Polmorva and then by the tanner. And *then* it appears among the stolen treasure accrued by Eudo.' He did not add that it had completed the circle by being offered back to Dodenho by Weasenham, as part of the arrangement for his silence on the whereabouts of the hoard.

'So?' asked Dodenho furtively. 'I cannot be held responsible for what happened when it was out of my possession.'

'I have a confession to make about that,' said Wormynghalle, rather guiltily. 'I am sorry, Dodenho: I am afraid it just slipped out.'

'What slipped out of where?' asked Dodenho uneasily.

'Sheriff Tulyet was bemoaning the fact that he had not found evidence to prove Eudo and Boltone were thieves, and before I knew what I was saying, I had mentioned the fact that Weasenham had found a cache in the cistern, and that your astrolabe was among its treasures. I apologise, but my mind was so full of Ockham that I was not concentrating on the conversation. I did not mean to expose Weasenham, and I should have known better than to hold a discussion with a clever man like Tulyet when half my wits were occupied with kinematic inertia.'

'Damn!' cried Dodenho, annoyed. 'Now I will have to pay full price for parchment!'

Wormynghalle continued. 'Once the secret was out, Tulyet plied me with all manner of questions. However, I did stress to him that you categorically declined to purchase the astrolabe at Weasenham's much-reduced price, and I think he believed me. He said he was going to interrogate Weasenham, and I have the feeling that our stationer may think *you* told him what happened.'

Dodenho grimaced. 'Curse you and your loose tongue! You are worse than a woman, for chattering like a magpie.'

'I shall pretend I have not heard this conversation,' said Michael. 'Blackmail and concealing stolen goods are criminal offences, but I am presently concerned with more serious matters. Dodenho, your astrolabe links you to a place where two men have been murdered – three, if we include Spryngheuse. You are also a Fellow of King's Hall, where Hamecotes was found with a fatal wound similar to that of Okehamptone and perhaps Gonerby, and you were friends with Chesterfelde.'

'What of it?' snapped Dodenho, unsettled by the direction the discussion was taking. 'It is coincidence, and you cannot use it to tie me to these deaths. What about Wormynghalle? It was *his* room-mate who was killed.'

'But Wormynghalle did not know Chesterfelde, did he?' asked Michael coolly.

'Dodenho has nothing to do with these deaths,' objected Wormynghalle, loyally speaking up for her colleague. 'He is right: all the links you have listed are no more than coincidence.'

'We should not forget that Dodenho studied in Oxford, either,' said Michael, unrelenting.

'So have I,' Wormynghalle pointed out. 'But it does not mean I was acquainted with Spryngheuse, Chesterfelde or Okehamptone. It is a large community, full of transients, who come and go with bewildering rapidity. You can conclude nothing from the fact that someone has been there.'

'Then what about this astrolabe?' demanded Michael, fixing Dodenho with a glare. 'Explain that.'

'Very well,' said Dodenho, seeing the monk would not leave him alone unless he had answers. 'I made a mistake. I thought it had been stolen, because I could not find it, but I was wrong.'

'No,' said Michael, raising his hand to prevent Wormynghalle from speaking in Dodenho's defence again. 'It is more complex than that. Tell me the truth, or I *shall* press charges of blackmail and dishonesty.'

'All right, all right!' snapped Dodenho. 'I sold the thing to Polmorva and *pretended* someone had taken it. Hamecotes had a spare, you see – a better one than mine – and I hoped he might give it to me if he thought I had been the victim of a crime. He did not, and then Wolf thought my accusations were levelled at *him*. I saw I was in a fix, so I dropped the subject and hoped everyone would forget about it. Unfortunately, they did not, and the stupid thing ended up in a place where men have died.'

Michael was unconvinced. 'Well, we shall see, because I always uncover the truth, no matter how long it takes. Lying about a murder is a serious matter. Men have been hanged for less.'

CHAPTER 10

Michael was silent as he and Bartholomew continued their walk towards Michaelhouse, lost in speculation about how and why Dodenho should be involved with the men from Merton Hall. Bartholomew thought about Joan Wormynghalle, and her dedication to learning. She was insightful and intelligent, and he hoped she would be able to fool men over her sex for the rest of her life, and devote herself to something she loved – and at which she excelled. He was certain the discipline of natural philosophy would be the richer for her contributions, and felt it would be a pity if it were to be deprived because of an accident of birth.

When they reached the corner where Weasenham's shop was located, Michael stopped. Like most of the High Street businesses, Weasenham was doing his bit to make the town attractive for the Archbishop, and his apprentices had been released from their duties of scribing exemplars, making pens and preparing parchment, and were enjoying themselves with brushes and poles. The timbers were freshly treated with resin, to make them shiny and black, and the plasterwork had been washed in a delicate shade of amber. The front door was so new that two carpenters were still adding the finishing touches, and Alyce had placed pots containing colourful plants outside it.

'She will have to get rid of those,' said Michael disapprovingly. 'The Archbishop will think we only buy pens and ink because we like looking at her flowers.'

'He will not,' said Bartholomew, laughing. 'Besides, their scent is helping to disguise the stench from the river, so perhaps you should encourage other merchants to do the same.'

'We need another word with Weasenham,' said Michael, making for the door. 'I want to know why he summoned you at the precise time when your services were needed as Corpse Examiner, thus almost bringing about a gross miscarriage of justice.'

The shop was busy as usual and, without the help of his apprentices, Weasenham was overwhelmed with demands for pens, inks, sand, sealing wax, texts, vellum, parchment, and all the other clerkly supplies required by scholars. Bartholomew looked for Alyce, and was not particularly surprised to see her attention focused on a single customer, despite the fact that her husband was rushed off his feet. Langelee leaned close to her as she spoke, oblivious to all else.

'And he accused me of indiscretion!' muttered Bartholomew as he weaved his way through the throng towards his Master.

Langelee jumped in guilty alarm. 'I was just negotiating a better price for Michaelhouse's ink,' he gabbled. 'Wynewyk uses such a lot when he writes the College accounts.'

'I am sure he does,' said Bartholomew. 'You are always in here these days, and tongues will start to wag soon, just as they did with my visits to Matilde. You are carrying on your dalliance right under the nose of the biggest gossip in the town.'

'My husband is hardly likely to begin rumours that he is a cuckold,' said Alyce scornfully. 'Besides, he is so busy talking about other people that he never notices anything I do. He says producing such tales encourages you scholars to patronise us.'

'Is that why he does it?' asked Bartholomew. 'To improve his trade?'

'Why else?' asked Alyce with a shrug. 'Surely you do not believe he is genuinely interested in who sleeps with whom, or who has the pox?'

Michael raised his eyebrows. 'Why not? It seems most of his customers are.'

'Father William told him that Ralph here has a fondness for Agatha the laundress,' said Alyce, amused. 'Expanding that tale should keep him busy for a while.'

'Have a care, man!' breathed Michael to Langelee. 'Do you know what will happen if Agatha learns she is the subject of such a story? Your life will not be worth living!'

'She has heard already,' said Langelee resentfully. 'And she is being awkward – she is taking an age to launder my cloak, whereas she washed yours the same day. But they are right, Alyce; we should not linger here together. Thank you for the astrolabe. I shall treasure it.'

'Astrolabe?' asked Michael, when Alyce had gone to assist her beleaguered husband.

Langelee produced a cloth from under his arm, and unwrapped what was inside. Sure enough, it was the instrument that Dodenho had sold to Polmorva, who had in turn sold it to Wormynghalle, who had then lost it to Polmorva's sticky fingers, before Weasenham had retrieved it from the cistern.

'Well,' said Michael, raising his eyebrows in surprise. 'Now the thing comes to Michaelhouse.'

'Not for long,' said Langelee, lowering his voice. 'It is useless, because the alidade is broken, but it is silver, and so worth a tidy sum. We need new guttering for the hall, and this will pay for it – and more besides. This little liaison of mine is not entirely detrimental to Michaelhouse.'

'You just told Alyce that you would treasure it,' said Bartholomew accusingly.

'But I did not say for how long,' replied Langelee.

'I would not keep it for more than a few days, if I were you,' advised Michael. 'It is stolen property, although its list of owners is so convoluted that I have no idea who has the right to claim it.'

'Not Dodenho,' said Bartholomew. 'He sold it to Polmorva. And not Polmorva, either, because he sold it to Wormynghalle – before stealing it back.'

Langelee was not very interested. He cocked his head to one side. 'There go the bells to announce the midday meal. I will walk back to Michaelhouse with you.'

'I want words with Weasenham first,' said Michael. 'The Visitation looms ever closer, and my solution to these crimes does not. Food will have to wait.'

Langelee and Bartholomew gaped at him. 'You are willing to miss a meal?' asked Bartholomew in disbelief. He became concerned. 'Are you ill?'

'I am perfectly healthy,' snapped Michael haughtily. 'At least, *I* think so, although it appears others do not. Thomas unnerved me yesterday with his predictions of my early death, and I have resolved to eat a little less from now on.'

Langelee looked pleased. 'That should help the College finances. Will you be applying these new resolutions to wine, too?'

'No,' said Michael shortly. 'Wine is good for a man, because it increases the amount of blood in his veins. It is only green vegetables that make him fat, especially peas, because they adhere to his liver. I shall forgo those completely, and in a couple of weeks I shall be as lean as Matt here.'

'I think it might take a little longer than that,' warned Bartholomew. 'And peas do not . . .'

But Michael was already walking away, unwilling to hear that his dietary plans might be flawed. Bartholomew followed him to where the stationer was enjoying a brief respite from his labours. Most scholars preferred to be served by Alyce, particularly when they were in a hurry, because she fetched the goods they wanted, accepted their money and let them leave, whereas Weasenham waylaid them with chatter. With the Visitation only two days away, people were too busy to gossip, so while Alyce had a queue, Weasenham was temporarily at ease.

'I have a question,' said Michael, marching up to him. 'Who told you to summon Matt for your toothache on Ascension Day? He came at the expense of fulfilling certain obligations to me.'

'Then I am sorry, although it was hardly my fault. I sent for Rougham, but he was unavailable, so I asked Bartholomew instead. That is how these things work: if one man cannot help you, then you send for his rival. I was very satisfied with Bartholomew, in fact, although I will not hire him again because he is too friendly with you – and with that lecherous Langelee.' Weasenham glowered at the Master, who was wrestling with the door but failing to open it because he was exchanging smouldering simpers with Alyce.

'Why should his association with me be considered a negative?' asked Michael archly.

'You blackmail people, Brother,' said Weasenham coldly. 'I do not want Bartholomew giving you details of my ailments, which you can then use to expose me to ridicule.'

'I would never do such a thing,' objected Bartholomew, affronted by the insult to his professional integrity.

'I do not know what you might do,' snapped Weasenham. 'How can I trust the word of a man who visits a prostitute night after night? And now you have led Doctor Rougham astray, too! I saw *him* sitting in Matilde's window this morning, while his colleagues are under the impression that he is with his family in Norfolk. I suppose he will pretend to arrive home today, claiming he has been working for Gonville's good, and all the while he has been enjoying himself here.'

'You will say nothing about Rougham, unless you want me to tell folk that Langelee has made a cuckold of you,' said Michael coldly. 'Then you will learn first-hand how hurtful such chatter can be.'

Weasenham regarded the monk with such glittering hatred that Bartholomew was alarmed. He wondered to what lengths the stationer might go to avenge himself on the College that was home to his wife's lover and the man who so brazenly subjected him to extortion.

'You have not answered my question,' said Michael. 'Who told you to summon Matt? He says your case was not urgent, and that you could have waited until your regular physician was free – or even visited an apothecary for a remedy.'

'It *was* urgent,' insisted Weasenham. 'I was in pain. And, as I have told you, I summoned him when my first choice of physicians was unavailable.'

'Who told you Rougham was unavailable?' asked Michael. 'The Gonville porters? The messenger you used? Who?'

'A customer,' replied Weasenham. 'He offered to fetch Rougham, because he said he had nothing else that was pressing. I rewarded him with a pot of my best green ink for his kindness, and thought no more about it.'

'Who?' insisted Michael.

'Green ink,' said Bartholomew, turning to Michael. 'Who do you know who uses green ink?'

'No one,' said Michael. 'It would be an odd thing to do when brown and black are available.'

'Hamecotes,' said Bartholomew. 'Hamecotes had a penchant for green ink.'

* * *

'Hamecotes,' said Michael as they left the shop. 'We know he left Cambridge – perhaps heading for Oxford – on or just after Ascension Day. All his King's Hall colleagues agree on that point.'

'And it was on Ascension Day that he offered to fetch Rougham to tend Weasenham's toothache,' said Bartholomew. 'Rougham was with Matilde by then, so could not have obliged, but Hamecotes did not summon him anyway. We know this for a fact, because Rougham's students recorded all the consultations he missed, and Weasenham's name is not on their list.'

'He fetched you instead, so you would not be available to inspect Okehamptone. When I arrived – with the inept Paxtone in tow – the Oxford *scholars* harried me to be brief. They wanted to be done with Okehamptone's body, so they could go about the far more important business of praying for his soul. Meanwhile, the Oxford *merchants* had some guild meeting they were desperate to attend. They were not the only ones rushing me: Tynkell did, too. He told me to be quick, because he did not want trouble between us and Oxford so close to the Visitation. I should have resisted them all.'

'You probably thought Tynkell was right at the time,' said Bartholomew soothingly. 'You had no reason to think otherwise.'

'That will teach me to bend to the will of others in an attempt to be placatory. I should have waited for you to become available. But let us go back to this tale. Hamecotes ensured you were out of the way, probably hoping I would dispense with the services of a Corpse Examiner altogether. I did the next best thing, which was to secure Paxtone's help, not realising that he has an aversion to cadavers, and Okehamptone went to his grave unexamined.'

'You have left something out. The evening before

Okehamptone died, Rougham went to Merton Hall to visit him. He saw his friend through an open window, and said that although Okehamptone might have become ill later, he was healthy at that point. In other words, Rougham did not think he was on the brink of contracting a fatal fever.'

'And Polmorva, who answered the door to Rougham, declined to let him in. So, is Hamecotes our killer? Did he murder Gonerby in Oxford, then do away with Okehamptone here? We know he had Oxford connections.'

'And then bit out his own throat, before tying a rope around his legs and hurling himself in the cistern?' asked Bartholomew. 'I do not think so!'

'Was it suicide, then? Because he was overcome with remorse?'

'Can you reach your throat with your own teeth, Brother? Of course not: it is impossible. But the fact that Okehamptone, Gonerby and Hamecotes were killed in a similar – if not identical – manner means there is certainly a connection between them. Still, at least this exonerates Clippesby.'

'It does not. All it does is demonstrate that Hamecotes did not want Okehamptone's death investigated. Clippesby might still be our man – or perhaps he was in league with Hamecotes.'

'We cannot prove they even knew each other, let alone conspired to kill together,' objected Bartholomew. 'And all along you have been saying there is an Oxford dimension to these deaths. Clippesby has no links to Oxford. He loathes the place, and never goes there.'

'So he says, but we only have his word that he visited his father in Norfolk when he went missing in February. He may have gone to Oxford and lied about it.'

'So, after Hamecotes kindly helped Clippesby to conceal

Okehamptone's murder, Clippesby killed him, too?' asked Bartholomew. 'That does not make sense.'

Michael sighed. 'Clippesby is mad, so of course he will not act in a way we can understand. But perhaps I was wrong about this Oxford association. Hamecotes must have been taking orders from a *Cambridge* accomplice when he summoned you to Weasenham, because no Oxford stranger would know you are a diligent Corpse Examiner.'

Bartholomew scratched his head, uncertain. 'Yes and no. Rougham knows I am careful, and may have mentioned the fact to Okehamptone, probably as an example of the kind of colleague he is obliged to endure. Then his friend Okehamptone may have told others – Polmorva and the merchants.'

'Rougham,' mused Michael. 'That would explain why he was attacked, too. Rougham is fat, with plenty of flesh to be gnawed through before a throat can be reached, whereas Okehamptone was thin. It is possible that Clippesby's fangs were thwarted by Rougham's lard.'

Bartholomew glanced at the monk askance, thinking he would present no mean challenge to a set of teeth himself. 'I do not understand why Clippesby should want to attack these people.'

'We will not agree about Clippesby, so let us leave him for now and look at the other links between our town and Oxford.'

'Polmorva,' said Bartholomew immediately. 'He declined to let Rougham see Okehamptone, so it is clear he is involved in some sinister way.'

'Perhaps,' agreed Michael. 'But there is also you. You attended Merton College, and you have a previous acquaintance with Duraunt and Polmorva. Indeed, you know Polmorva well enough to have made an enemy of him. He hates you, and you would like to see him indicted for murder.'

'Only if he is guilty. I would not conspire to convict an innocent man.'

Michael shook his head despairingly. 'I have failed miserably in my training of you, if you decline to use the opportunities that come your way to strike blows at ancient adversaries.'

'Shall we confront Polmorva with our conclusions?' asked Bartholomew, ignoring the monk's levity – if levity it was. 'We may be able to gauge whether we are close to a solution.'

'We have not been able to gauge anything so far, and I think we should wait until we have more than a bag of unfounded speculations. Besides, we may just frighten our culprit – be he Polmorva or someone else – and cause him to flee, or even to kill again.' Michael sighed, and turned his mind to other matters. 'You should visit Stourbridge today and tell Clippesby he is going on a journey. He will certainly object, and I do not want a scene when my beadles arrive to escort him away on Monday.'

'Me?' asked Bartholomew in distaste. 'It was not my idea. You do it.'

'You are his physician. You must make him understand that this is the only way we can resolve the matter without harming him or compromising the College. The alternative is for him to throw himself on the mercy of the judicial system, and I do not think he should do that.'

'No, he should not,' agreed Bartholomew bitterly. 'He will be found guilty just because he is different. Our society is intolerant of those who do not conform, no matter how inane the rules.' He was thinking not only of Clippesby, but of Joan Wormynghalle.

'We are talking about murder here, Matt,' said Michael sternly. 'And they are not just simple murders, either, but ones that show a violent hatred towards the victims. You saw those corpses, and witnessed the savagery with which they had been defiled. I am sorry for Clippesby, but if he did these terrible things, then I do not want him in my town. Supposing he was to take against Matilde for losing that silver dog? How would you feel if she was his next victim?'

Bartholomew could think of nothing to say.

Bartholomew was deeply unhappy with the whole affair regarding Clippesby, and postponed his visit for as long as possible. It was with a heavy heart that he set out for Stourbridge the following day, immediately after the Trinity Sunday mass. It was a glorious morning, with birds singing shrill and sweet, the sun warm on his face, and a pleasant breeze wafting the scent of flowers and clean earth towards him. He returned the greetings of people he knew, many of whom were out enjoying the new glories of their freshly cleaned town. Folk were delighted by the changes, superficial though they were, and talk of the impending Visitation was on everyone's lips.

Bartholomew heard little of their excited babble, and felt burdened by the knowledge of what he was about to do. He walked slowly, although he knew it would only prolong the agony. He tried to tell himself that the Dominican would be well cared for in Rougham's remote retreat, and that they were lucky the Gonville man was prepared to spend his own money looking after an ailing colleague. But this did not blunt the knowledge that imprisonment was a very cruel thing to do to a free spirit like Clippesby.

Eventually he arrived at the hospital, where he spent longer than necessary talking to Brother Paul and examining two other inmates. When he could defer his unpleasant duty no longer, he walked to the house where Clippesby was installed, and climbed the stairs to the upper floor. The friar's cell was at the end of a corridor, and comprised a small room with a single window. The window had stone mullions that were less than the length of a man's hand apart, so it was impossible to squeeze between them and escape; the door was secured by a hefty bar placed between two iron wall loops, and a substantial lock. The key to the lock was on a hook outside the door, unreachable by the inmate, but conveniently accessible to anyone bringing food.

Bartholomew was shocked by the change two days had wrought on Michaelhouse's Master of Music and Astronomy. Clippesby's face was grey, and his hair was greasy and unkempt. He did not turn when Bartholomew opened the door, and did not react at all when told the news that he was soon to be moved to a distant place, where he would never see friends or family again. Bartholomew shook his arm, to try to gain his attention, but Clippesby simply continued to gaze through the window at the green fields beyond, and would not speak. Finally, Bartholomew secured the door behind him, and walked back to Cambridge feeling even more miserable than he had on the way out.

He spent the afternoon trying to concentrate on his treatise on fevers, a text that had already reached prodigious dimensions. Writing it usually relaxed him and, although College rules forbade any kind of work other than religious on the Sabbath, he felt the treatise was more pleasure than labour; he often spent his leisure hours scribbling down his ideas, ranging from fevers' symptoms and manifestations, to their treatment and how to avoid them. But even agues could not exorcise Clippesby from his mind, and he was grateful for even the smallest interruption that day.

He spent an hour helping Deynman with 'difficult' spellings, giving the student his entire attention on a matter he normally would have delegated to one of his teaching assistants. Then he joined in a lively debate among William's Franciscans, which focused on the work of the great Dominican known simply as Perscrutator. William was predictably frenzied in his claims that the Dominican Order never produced good scholars, although he was unable to refute any of Perscrutator's arguments pertaining to the definition of the elements. A large number of Fellows, students and commoners turned out to listen to the debate, although most were far more interested in William's rabid antics than in understanding Perscrutator's complex expositions.

At the evening meal, Bartholomew was pleased to note that Michael was as good as his word and ate only a modest portion of meat and a mere three pieces of bread. All vegetables, green or otherwise, were politely declined. That evening, when the sun was setting, sending rays of gold and red to play over the honey-coloured stone of Michaelhouse, Bartholomew wandered into the orchard, where there was a fallen apple tree that provided a comfortable seat for those wanting peace and silence.

He sat and stretched his legs in front of him, hoping Edith had reached London safely, and that her son was as delighted to see her as she expected. He thought about Matilde, and recalled her laughing at something he had said; he wondered whether she was smiling now, finding Rougham equally amusing. He considered visiting her, to ask the question that had been on his lips so many times that week, but was still not in the mood to propose in front of an audience. However, even the prospect of married life with Matilde could not take his mind off Clippesby, and his thoughts soon returned to dwell on the dull hopelessness he had seen in the Dominican's eyes.

He decided solitude was not what he needed, so went to the kitchens instead. These were off limits to scholars, because they were the domain of the formidable Agatha; but Agatha liked Bartholomew, and seldom ordered him to leave if he wanted company, or if he simply wanted to sit in the College's warmest room. He was surprised when he entered the steamy, fat- and yeast-scented chamber to find not only Michael, but Langelee, too. Agatha was in her great wicker throne by the hearth, sewing in the fading light that filtered through the windows. The Master reclined on a bench, playing with his new astrolabe, while Michael perched on a stool by the fire. Bartholomew was not impressed to see him devouring oatcakes thickly smeared with salted lard.

'I was hungry,' said the monk defensively when he saw the physician's disapproving gaze. 'And anyway, these are only oatcakes. They will not make me fat.'

'The white grease will, though,' said Bartholomew. 'Especially in that kind of quantity.'

'We were talking about Clippesby,' said Michael, changing the subject as he rammed one of the oatcakes defiantly into his mouth. 'I confided all our suspicions to Langelee and Agatha – along with what your medical colleague in Norfolk has agreed to do for us.' He looked hard at his friend, to tell him that Rougham's role in the affair had not been revealed.

'I cannot believe Clippesby would do such terrible things,' said Agatha unhappily. 'He is a gentle man, not a killer. Tell them, Matthew.'

'I have,' said Bartholomew, flopping on a stool next to Michael and taking one of the oatcakes. The fat was so generously applied that he thought he might be sick, and put it back half eaten. 'But no one will listen to me.'

'The evidence is there, plain for all to see,' said Michael patiently. 'I know this is an unpleasant – and even a painful – business, but we must be realistic. Occasionally, people change – they turn into something nasty, and Clippesby is a case in point. He has always been strange, and we have always been wary of him. We believed he was involved in something sinister during his first term at Michaelhouse – remember, Matt? – so we should not be surprised to learn now that his madness has transmuted itself into something dangerous with the passing of time.'

'You will find you are wrong,' warned Agatha. Bartholomew was surprised to see tears glittering in her small, pig-like eyes. He knew she was protective of all Michaelhouse's scholars, but he had not appreciated how deeply she cared for the quiet Clippesby.

'I do not see how,' said Langelee. 'There are too many arrows of circumstance pointing in his direction. If it were a case of one or two, I would be loath to send him away, too, but it is not. Some of our students are little more than children, Agatha, and we cannot risk their lives just because we want to believe in Clippesby's innocence. It is our duty to protect them.'

'We are lucky Matt has the contacts to arrange this solution,' added Michael. 'It is not unknown for Colleges to rid themselves of unwanted Fellows by murdering them, you know. I have investigated more than one case where a man has been killed because his colleagues did not like his scholarship, his religious ideas or his personality.'

'It would be a lot less expensive,' mused Langelee, looking as if he might consider such an option himself, should the need arise. Bartholomew was grateful Rougham had ensured it would not.

'He will die if you lock him away from his animals,' said Agatha tearfully.

Langelee frowned, and then looked at Michael. 'She is right. Are you sure there is no other way?'

'None I can think of, but I am willing to entertain any ideas you have. You need to come up with something quickly, though, because he leaves first thing tomorrow morning. It is better that way.'

'Better for whom?' demanded Agatha. 'For the Archbishop of Canterbury, so a lunatic will not assail his priestly eyes? For the University, because we can allow nothing to interfere with our plans to impress Islip, and risk him founding his new College elsewhere? For Michaelhouse, because we do not want the embarrassment of a Fellow who is unlike the rest of us? It is certainly not better for poor Clippesby, banished to the barren wastes of a foul and dangerous county.'

'It is Norfolk, Agatha, not Armageddon,' said Michael. 'Norfolk.'

'That is what I was talking about,' snapped Agatha. 'I know what that place is like. It is full of lunatics, lepers and heretics.'

'Clippesby should feel at home, then,' said Langelee, ignoring Michael's indignant splutter. The monk, like many Cambridge scholars, hailed from Norfolk.

'We will never know, will we?' said Agatha in a voice that dripped with hostility. She stood, snatched the oatcakes from Michael, and took them to the pantry, her large hips swaying purposefully. The monk watched his repast disappear with dismay. Her voice echoed from the cool room that was used to store perishable foods. 'After you have exiled him, we will never hear whether he is happy or sad, alive or dead.'

'I will make enquiries,' promised Bartholomew.

'You had better,' she said coldly, coming to re-occupy her chair. 'Because I can make life very uncomfortable for scholars who do not please me.' She gazed significantly at a pile of laundry, on the top of which sat Langelee's cloak.

'At last!' the Master exclaimed. 'I thought you had lost it, you kept it so long.'

'Perhaps it is ready now, but perhaps it is not,' retorted Agatha belligerently. She turned on Michael. 'And do not come here expecting edible treats, either. There will be no more of those until you convince me that Clippesby is content and thriving. And I may decline to do the laundry for a while, too. That will bring you to your senses.'

'The whole College will stink if no one has clean clothes,' objected Langelee. 'Within a month we will all smell like the Chancellor.'

'You are lucky to have me,' said Agatha sullenly. 'I am the best laundress in Cambridge, and every Michaelhouse scholar clamours for my services. It is not like that at King's Hall, where half of them do their own, lest their precious garments are ruined.'

'They manage their own washing because of cost,' corrected Michael. 'The King's Hall laundress is outrageously expensive.'

'Dodenho pays Wolf to do his, while Norton prefers to hire me,' Agatha went on. 'I charge him princely fees, but he makes no complaint. Meanwhile, Wormynghalle does his own, down by the wharves. I have seen him. He should not use the river for cleaning his clothes, though. It will make him reek.'

'Wormynghalle does not reek,' said Michael, starting to edge casually towards the pantry.

'That is because you are used to Chancellor Tynkell,' said Agatha. '*He* makes a cesspool smell like spring flowers.'

'Wormynghalle probably does not want to hurt the laundress's feelings by employing another washer-woman,' Bartholomew said, in an attempt to explain the scholar's odd behaviour in a way the others would understand, and so prevent rumours circulating about her. 'He rinses his clothes somewhere that is not overlooked, so she will not see him and be offended.'

Agatha regarded him beadily. 'You had better not be getting ideas. *I* am the laundress around here, and *I* wash the clothes. I do a good job, and I will not have you demanding to do your own. It would not be proper, and I would not stand for it.'

'Quite right, too,' said Michael ingratiatingly, taking another step towards the pantry. 'I would never consider managing my own clothes – you always do it so splendidly.'

Agatha looked pleased. 'I do,' she agreed immodestly. 'I *am* the finest laundress in Cambridge.'

'In England,' gushed Michael. 'In the world, even. But my innards ache with hunger, so I shall retire to my bed and pass a miserable night. Unless, of course, there are oatcakes available . . . ?'

'There might be,' said Agatha imperiously. 'Are you saying I am better even than the laundresses in the King's household?'

'There is no comparison,' said Michael desperately.

Agatha smiled in smug satisfaction. 'Then perhaps one of you will write to the King on my behalf, and tell him I am willing to be of service – subject to him bringing his Court to Cambridge, of course. I would not like to move away.'

'The oatcakes?' whined Michael piteously.

'They are for someone else,' replied Agatha maliciously. 'Matthew will collect them tomorrow morning and take them to Clippesby, to sustain the poor man on his journey to Hell.'

When Bartholomew went to bed, he was restless and unsettled, and found sleep would not come. He tossed and turned for what felt like hours before he finally dropped into a doze, but his dreams teemed with uncomfortable images of Clippesby. Deciding he would rather be doing something better than exhausting himself with nightmares, he rose, donned the hated yellow liripipe and left. Matilde would be asleep, and Rougham no longer needed his ministrations, but a patient called

Isnard was happy for company at any hour. He had recently lost a leg, and enforced physical inactivity meant he slept little and was always grateful when visitors relieved his boredom. Intending to leave Michaelhouse through the back door and use the towpath, Bartholomew aimed for the orchard.

He had not gone far when he became aware that he was not the only person out in the darkness. He glanced up at the sky, and gauged it was probably long past midnight: not a time when law-abiding scholars should be wandering around. He wondered whether it was a student, off to meet his paramour, and hoped it was not one of his own class. He had more than enough to worry about, without being concerned for errant students.

The figure making his way through the fruit trees was large and burly. The only one of Bartholomew's students with such a build was Falmeresham, and Bartholomew strained his eyes, trying to assess whether it was him. But it was too dark, and the person had taken the precaution of wrapping himself in a cloak with a hood that hid everything except his size. Bartholomew reflected. William and Langelee were also big men who owned long cloaks, and so was Michael. But the figure in the orchard was not quite vast enough to be Michael, and nor did it waddle.

When the man reached the gate he removed the bar and laid it gently in the grass. He opened the door, and looked carefully in both directions before letting himself out. Bartholomew followed, and watched him reach the High Street, then turn left. The physician trotted after him, hoping it was late enough for Tulyet's guards and Michael's beadles to have eased their patrols, and that neither of them would be caught. The scholar ahead of him did not seem to be suffering from any such qualms, and his progress along the High Street towards the Jewry could best be described as brazen.

As the figure passed King's Hall, the moon came out from behind a cloud and illuminated him, and Bartholomew recognised the cloak with its rabbit-fur collar. It was Langelee, wearing the garment he had retrieved from Agatha earlier that evening. Now he could see the mantle, Bartholomew thought the figure was unmistakably the Master's, with its barrel-shaped body and confident swagger; it was also very like Langelee not to care who saw him as he flouted University rules by striding around after the curfew. Bartholomew had kept to the shadows as he stalked his prey, but Langelee had not once glanced behind him.

Bartholomew immediately assumed that Langelee was going to meet Alyce Weasenham, and was staggered to think the Master would risk cavorting with her while her husband slumbered in the same house. Langelee reached the stationer's shop and eased himself into a doorway opposite. From this vantage point, he proceeded to stare at the silent building for some time. Then, abruptly, he darted out and shot towards the Jewry. Before he disappeared down one of its narrow lanes he paused and looked back, as if to ensure no one was watching. Bartholomew could only suppose he was making sure Alyce did not spot him as he embarked on a tryst with another woman.

With nothing better to do, Bartholomew followed him again, and for one agonising moment thought Langelee was going to knock at Matilde's door. But the Master did not give it so much as a glance as he strode past. Emerging from the tangle of alleys between the Round Church and the Franciscan Friary, he began to move purposefully along the marshy road known as the Barnwell Causeway. He paused at the small bridge that spanned the filthy waters of the King's Ditch, and Bartholomew saw a guard emerge from his hut to challenge him. The murmur of soft voices drifted on the still night air, and Bartholomew supposed coins were changing hands. When the transaction was completed, Langelee began walking again, and the soldier ducked back inside his shelter.

Bartholomew hesitated. He had no money to bribe guards, and nor did he want them gossiping about how Michaelhouse Fellows shadowed their masters at odd hours of the night. If he wanted to learn what Langelee was doing, there was only one course open to him: to bypass the sentry and try to sneak across the bridge without being seen. He was not especially talented at stealth, and it occurred to him to mind his own business and go home, but Langelee's odd mission had piqued his interest, and he wanted to know where the philosopher was going.

He walked as close to the shelter as he dared, then scrambled off the causeway to the lower ground surrounding it. He tiptoed clumsily through rutted fields until he reached the stinking black ooze of the King's Ditch. The bridge was just above his head, so he climbed up the bank and listened hard. The soldier was singing to himself, and he concluded the man would not be doing that if he thought someone was trying to creep past him. As quickly as he could, Bartholomew darted across the bridge and dropped down the bank on the other side. He waited, breathing hard, and pondering what explanation he would give if he was caught. But the guard continued to warble, and Bartholomew felt fortunate that the fellow was so pleased with the money Langelee had given him that he had relaxed his vigilance.

After a moment, Bartholomew began to move forward again, creeping through the fields until he deemed it was safe to climb back on to the causeway. In the faint moonlight, he saw that Langelee had made good headway, and was obliged to run hard to catch up. Despite the noise he was sure he was making, Langelee still did not look around.

The causeway skirted St Radegund's Priory, where the

Benedictine nuns were known to entertain men on occasion, and Bartholomew supposed Langelee had secured himself an appointment. But the Master stalked past the convent with its untidy scattering of outbuildings and headed for the Fens. And for Stourbridge, Bartholomew thought grimly, at last understanding what was happening: Langelee was going to visit Clippesby.

Bartholomew hung back, not sure what to do. Was Langelee planning to warn Clippesby that he was about to be spirited away to a remote institution from which he would never escape? But Langelee had thought that an acceptable option the previous evening, and Bartholomew did not see why he should change his mind. Was he going to say his farewells? Langelee was an odd man, bluff and thoughtless one moment, considerate the next. Perhaps he had a soft spot for Clippesby, and wanted to wish him well before he began his exile. But what really concerned Bartholomew was a darker, more sinister option: murder. No Master wanted it said that his College had lunatic Fellows locked away in distant parts of the countryside, and Bartholomew had a sick feeling that Langelee intended to resolve the Clippesby problem once and for all.

He followed the Master to the outskirts of the hospital, and watched as he opened a gate and headed for the house that had become Clippesby's prison. Bartholomew followed, thinking no further ahead than his intention to protect Clippesby, but bitterly aware that he would need the element of surprise if he wanted to win the confrontation. Langelee was an experienced and able brawler, and Bartholomew doubted he could best him in a fair fight. He took one of the surgical knives from his medical bag, and hoped that would even the odds – at least for long enough to allow Clippesby to escape.

Langelee crept up the stairs, and Bartholomew heard

the key being taken from the wall. He winced when the wooden steps creaked under his own feet as he climbed in stealthy pursuit. He watched Langelee remove the heavy bar, then open the door to Clippesby's chamber. He realised he would have to make his move immediately, since he did not think the Master would engage in pleasant conversation before he executed his troublesome Fellow. As quickly and as softly as he could, he sped along the corridor and burst into the room, wrapping one arm around Langelee's throat and pressing his knife against it firmly enough to ensure Langelee would understand he meant business.

Clippesby was sitting inside his cell. He had been reading by candlelight, and gazed in astonishment at the sudden and violent intrusion.

'Matt! Did you bring those books you promised? You forgot to leave them yesterday – perhaps because I was not very welcoming when you came. I was grieving, because the wren who comes to take crumbs from my windowsill had died.' He swallowed hard, and a tear rolled down his cheek.

'Died?' asked Bartholomew warily, wondering whether Clippesby, deprived of human victims, had resorted to dispatching his beloved animals as a means to satisfy his bloodlust.

'The cat got her – it was my fault for encouraging her to be trusting.' Clippesby's voice wavered, but then he took a deep breath and pulled himself together. 'Put down the knife, will you? This is a small room and I do not want an accident, especially one resulting from horseplay.'

'I am not playing,' said Bartholomew, bemused.

'Let me go!' ordered a familiar voice that shook with indignant fury.

'Agatha?' he asked in astonishment.

'Of course it is me!' she snapped, throwing him off and

adjusting the clothes he had ruffled. 'Who did you think it was?'

'Agatha has been bringing me food and other supplies ever since I was brought here,' said Clippesby when all three were sitting comfortably, and Agatha had finally, if reluctantly, accepted Bartholomew's increasingly effusive apologies for daring to lay hands on her person.

'It rained when I came here last night,' explained Agatha. 'I was drenched by the time I returned to Michaelhouse, and my cloak is still wet. Langelee forgot to take his with him earlier, and we are about the same height, so I decided to borrow it. I do not think he will mind.'

'I am not so sure,' said Bartholomew, thinking the Master certainly would object if he thought the laundress was wearing his distinctive clothes to conduct dubious nocturnal errands, particularly when it had led to at least one person assuming he was up to no good.

'I suppose you saw the garment and thought I was him,' said Agatha, affronted. 'I do not know how you could confuse us, Matthew. Langelee is hefty, while I retain the slim figure of my youth.'

'I see,' said Bartholomew, not sure what else to say without incriminating himself. If the truth were known, Agatha was larger than Langelee, and there was little to choose between them from behind. 'You hesitated when you went past the stationer's shop, and I concluded you were Langelee looking for Alyce,' he added, when she looked peeved that he had not immediately agreed with her assessment.

'Of course I was careful when I passed *that* place,' stated Agatha belligerently. 'Weasenham would have invented all manner of lies, had he seen me. Did you know he has been telling people that I seduced the Master?'

'Has he?' asked Bartholomew, appalled how an idle quip by Michael had taken on a life of its own in the mouths of Deynman, William and the stationer.

'I suppose he must have spotted me coming here one night,' she went on. 'However, it is Langelee who usually lingers around that shop after dark, not me. He is conducting astrological observations that he cannot perform at Michaelhouse, because it is too near Saturn. He told me himself.'

'He has a lover,' supplied Clippesby helpfully. 'Edwardus Rex told me – he is the dog who lets Yolande de Blaston and her family share his house. It is none other than Alyce herself, and they often meet to frolic in Weasenham's back yard.'

'Do they?' asked Agatha distastefully. 'I should have known Langelee was not hanging around at that time of night for the benefit of his studies. Nor should I be surprised that *you* knew what he was up to, Clippesby. Very little happens that escapes your attention.'

Clippesby gestured around him. 'And look where it has brought me.'

'My nephew guards the bridge over the King's Ditch,' said Agatha, unable to think of anything to say to comfort him, so resorting to practical matters. 'He knows better than to ask *me* questions, but how did you get past him, Matthew?'

'I was quiet,' said Bartholomew, unwilling to admit to climbing down river banks and creeping through fields. 'Does no one else ever challenge you? You must have met soldiers or beadles at some point.'

'A couple of watchmen looked as though they fancied their chances,' she replied grimly, 'but they backed off when I drew my sword.'

'Your sword?' echoed Bartholomew weakly, grateful he had not confronted her on the causeway.

She hauled a substantial weapon from the belt around her waist. 'It belonged to my father, and is no longer sharp, but it does what I want: makes people mind their own business and leave me to go about mine.'

'I can imagine,' said Bartholomew. 'I had no idea you were so well prepared.'

'She has been good to me,' said Clippesby fondly. 'I would not have survived here without her friendly face coming to me every night.'

'Every night?' Bartholomew was astounded. 'How do you manage to leave the College without the porters seeing?'

'Through the orchard door,' explained Agatha. Her expression became disapproving. 'But I am not the only one who uses it – someone has been leaving it unbarred. Still, I thwart his nefarious plans by locking him out when I get back.'

'That is you?' asked Bartholomew, startled.

Agatha was equally astonished when she realised what had happened. 'But you do not need to sneak around like an errant undergraduate – Langelee has given you permission to see your patients at any time, so you can come and go as you please.'

'He has been visiting Matilde in the Jewry,' said Clippesby, keen to be helpful. 'That is why he could not use the front gate. The College cat told me all about it.'

'Did she, indeed?' asked Bartholomew, supposing Clippesby had heard the rumours during one of his bids for freedom.

'William told me you were courting Matilde,' said Agatha. 'But I did not believe him. I know you have a liking for her, but I did not think you would spend every night at her house for nigh on three weeks because of the damage it might do to her reputation.' She regarded the amber liripipe with rank disdain, and reached out to finger it. 'This is nasty.'

'Yes,' agreed Bartholomew tiredly. 'It is.'

'It will not make you more attractive to Matilde, either,' predicted Agatha authoritatively. 'It is not the kind of garment she would admire. Like me, she has elegant tastes. I recommend you dispense with it, and let me sew you something more suitable. But why have you chosen to woo the poor woman so flagrantly of late?'

'He is doing it for me,' said Clippesby. He started to explain with a clarity Bartholomew found disconcerting. 'Rougham was attacked one night by a wolf. I drove the beast away, but the poor doctor had been so badly mauled that his senses were disturbed. Unfortunately, he then claimed that *I* was the wolf rather than his saviour. He agreed to keep his accusations to himself, but only if Matilde allowed him to recuperate at her house, and Matthew provided the necessary medical care. I told them it was not I who did him the harm, but no one would believe me.'

'And that is why you are here,' said Agatha in understanding. 'We were told it was because your wits are awry due to the warm spring weather.'

'They *are* awry,' said Bartholomew, defensive of his medical diagnosis. 'More than usual.'

'They are going to send you to a hospital in Norfolk,' said Agatha to Clippesby. 'That is why I came here tonight: to set you free.'

'Do not run,' said Bartholomew to Clippesby. 'It will only confirm your guilt in the eyes of the others, and I am still working to exonerate you.'

'Yes,' said Clippesby thoughtfully. 'You have at least tried to believe in my innocence, although I know it has been difficult for you. But I think I will take Agatha up on her offer. I would rather be free and outlawed than living here like a criminal.'

'But where will you go?' asked Bartholomew, alarmed.

'I have friends. Sheep are accommodating creatures, and there is a siege of herons at the river—'

'Stop!' commanded Agatha angrily. 'It is when you talk like this that people doubt your sanity. You are more of an enemy to yourself than anyone else will ever be. At least *pretend* to be normal.'

'Very well,' said Clippesby with a sigh. 'I shall go nowhere very far. There are plenty of woods where I can sleep during the day, while at night I shall go to Cambridge and try to find the real killer, since Michael seems unable to do it. It is the only way I will ever clear my name.'

'You cannot,' said Bartholomew, appalled. 'It is only a matter of time before someone associates you with these murders and harms you. Let Michael do his work. He will find the culprit.'

'Perhaps he will, but by that time I will be in Norfolk,' argued Clippesby. 'Locked away with lunatics. And Langelee may find he prefers Michaelhouse without me, and will see my absence as an opportunity to secure himself a new Master of Music and Astronomy. I cannot take that chance.'

'Hide well,' advised Agatha. 'I will bring you several different sets of garments. Matthew believed I was Langelee, just because I was wearing his cloak, so you should take advantage of the fact that people *look* but they do not *see*.'

'No,' said Bartholomew, standing to block the door. 'This is madness.'

'A poor choice of words, Matt,' said Clippesby with a rueful grin. 'But you are wrong: what would be madness is to stay here. Who knows? Perhaps someone will shoot me as I am escorted into exile, just to bring this case to a satisfactory conclusion. You obviously believed that was what Langelee intended to do, or you would not have pressed a knife to the throat you thought was his in an attempt to save me.'

Bartholomew shook his head, and wished Clippesby was

not quite so astute. 'Escaping will solve nothing. Let me go to Rougham and say you cannot leave tomorrow. I will tell him you have an ague and need to rest. Then—'

'He will know you are buying time,' said Clippesby. He stood and walked towards the door. 'I am leaving now. Please do not stop me.'

'But someone may harm you if you are caught, or the merchants may drag you back to Oxford to answer for Gonerby's murder.' Bartholomew appealed to Agatha. 'Surely you can see the sense in what I say? Help me persuade him.'

'Once he is in this Norfolk hospital, he will never be allowed out. He will talk about his animals, and the physicians there will insist he stays, even when Michael proves he had nothing to do with biting people. Let him through, Matthew.' Agatha's sword was still drawn and she waved it at him.

'What will you do?' demanded Bartholomew. 'Stab me with it? Sit down, Clippesby, and . . .'

Clippesby turned, and Bartholomew assumed he was going to recline on his bed again, but at the last moment he swivelled around and barrelled towards the door. The physician braced himself, but Clippesby had gathered considerable momentum, and he was bowled from his feet. He recovered quickly, and grabbed one of the Dominican's legs. He was far stronger than Clippesby, and could easily have overpowered him, but he had reckoned without Agatha. She ripped his fingers away from the friar, and Clippesby wriggled free to race down the short passage. The Dominican's feet thundered on the stairs and then there was silence.

While Clippesby's footsteps faded into nothing, Bartholomew tried to struggle free of the suffocating grip Agatha had managed to secure on him, but she tightened her hold in a way that threatened to break his neck, and he found himself growing weak from lack of air. She eased off when she heard him choke, and, as soon as she did so, he shouted as loudly as he could, to raise the alarm. He still held his dagger, but he could hardly stab her with it, so he dropped it and used both hands to break free. She grunted in pain as he forced her away, and almost took a tumble. Bartholomew took a moment to ensure she was unharmed, then tore after Clippesby, almost falling down the stairs in his haste.

Clippesby had a good start, and was running towards the dense woods that lay beyond the hospital's fields. The Dominican was good at hiding, and Bartholomew knew he would never find him once he had reached the trees. He ran harder, aware that Agatha was behind him, threatening all manner of dire consequences if he did not let Clippesby go. Lights were being kindled in Brother Paul's house, and Bartholomew could hear the agitated, fretful voices of the inmates as they demanded to know what was causing the disturbance.

Clippesby had just reached the edge of the copse when, by forcing a massive burst of speed, Bartholomew managed to catch up with him. He grasped the hem of the Dominican's flying habit and pulled hard, jerking him from his feet. Clippesby stumbled and Bartholomew dropped on top of him, aiming to hold him down with the weight of his body until he had regained the strength to secure him properly. Then someone grabbed his hair and jerked his head upwards in a motion that made the bones in his neck crick in protest.

'Agatha!' he gasped. 'Let go!'

But he heard Agatha bellowing in the distance, and knew she was still labouring across the uneven ground towards him. He struggled. There was a flash of brightness in the moonlight, and something jabbed at his throat. He threw himself back, towards his attacker, aware of Clippesby wriggling away from under him. His assailant did not lessen his grip, and the metal glittered again as it descended towards his neck. There was a thick, rank smell, too, that made him want to gag.

Clippesby leapt at them with a wild screech, knocking them both off balance. Bartholomew's attacker grunted in pain as the full weight of two men landed on top of him. The physician twisted as hard as he could, aiming to break the grip around his throat, but the fellow held on with grim determination.

He saw a foot swing out and Clippesby reeled, stunned by a kick to the side of his head. Then the attacker turned his full attention to Bartholomew. Yet another flash, and Bartholomew felt something tearing at him. Again, he detected the stench. He wriggled and squirmed with all his might, determined to prevent the blade from landing on his neck. But he was running out of strength, and the vicelike grip was depriving him of air. He became dizzy, and weaker. Stars exploded before his eyes and he flailed around in increasing desperation as he sought to drag breath into his protesting lungs.

Just when he thought he would lose the battle, there was a thump and a grunt, followed by rapidly receding footsteps. Clippesby stood there with a stone in his hand, while Agatha still lumbered towards them. Bartholomew started to follow his attacker through the trees, but there was no power in his legs, and he knew there was no point in blundering through the undergrowth in the dark. The trees blotted out any light from the moon, and the copse was a tangled mat of vegetation that would make pursuit all but impossible. He dropped to his knees, the craven exhilaration of the chase replaced by a tide of exhaustion that left him shaking and sluggish.

'Who was that?' gasped Agatha, reaching them at last. 'What happened?'

Clippesby crouched next to Bartholomew and laid a reassuring hand on his shoulder. 'Do not worry, he has gone now. I hit him hard in the chest with a rock, and he realised he would have no luck here tonight.'

'Who?' demanded Agatha, her face flushed and sweat coursing down her red-veined cheeks. 'He tried to kill Matthew with something shiny. I saw it sparkling in the moonlight. I will have his guts out for this!' She wielded the sword in a way that indicated she meant what she said.

'It was him,' said Clippesby simply. 'The wolf.'

'That was no wolf,' said Agatha. A nightjar called, low and hoarse, and in the distance Bartholomew could hear Brother Paul trying to soothe Stourbridge's inmates, who were alarmed by the commotion Clippesby's flight had caused. 'It was a man. I saw him silhouetted against the moonlit sky. It was a man, with something brassy in his hand.'

'Metal teeth,' said Bartholomew. His skin crawled when he recalled them slashing at him, and he was unable to repress a shudder. 'That is how he kills his victims. I did not think human fangs could cause such damage, but these were made of steel, and were honed to a vicious sharpness.'

He put his hand against his neck, half expecting to find it gashed, but the liripipe and its voluminous folds had protected him. He pulled off the garment, and saw it was shredded to ribbons.

'I cannot mend this,' said Agatha, taking it from him. 'It is beyond my skills with a needle. Still, it did not suit you anyway; it made you look like a jester.'

'Are you sure he has gone?' Bartholomew asked, looking around uneasily and wishing he had not dropped his knife in Clippesby's room.

Agatha nodded. 'You were lucky to escape alive – he meant business. I could see it in the way he moved.'

'Who was he?' asked Bartholomew, climbing unsteadily to his feet.

'It was the wolf,' said Clippesby again. 'I have already told you.'

'I was too far away to see his face,' said Agatha, pursing her lips at Clippesby to warn him to curtail his animal fantasies. 'But he was as tall as you, Matthew, and he looked strong.' She wrinkled her nose in disgust, and turned her attention back to the liripipe. 'That is disgusting! He smeared dog turds on you. He must have done it to spite me.'

Bartholomew was bewildered. 'To spite you?'

'Because I will have to wash the thing,' explained Agatha impatiently. 'I am a laundress, am I not? He probably knows this sort of stain is not easy to remove.'

'Look on the bright side,' said Bartholomew, thinking that causing inconvenience in the College laundry was probably the last thing on the killer's mind. 'At least it is not stained with my blood.'

'Why did he do such a thing?' asked Clippesby, watching Agatha fling the garment away. 'What would be the point? To add insult to injury?'

'To make a wound fester,' explained Bartholomew. 'A cut with excrement driven into it may kill a victim later, if he survives the immediate injury. He is using it as a form of poison.'

'That must have been what happened to Rougham,' said Clippesby. 'His wound went bad, but I saw for myself that the actual injury was not a fatal one.'

Bartholomew took a few steps towards the woods, not sure what to do next, but unsettled by the knowledge that the murderer was not far away. 'We cannot let this man go, because he will kill again for certain. We must find him!'

Agatha grabbed his arm. 'We could search all night and

not succeed. Looking now is worse than hopeless, and he will be long gone, anyway. Tell Sheriff Tulyet to come tomorrow with some of his hunting hounds, and let him track this monster.'

'Do you think Michael will believe me now?' asked Clippesby. 'He *must* see I am innocent, given that you have just had a nasty encounter with the wretch while I was pinned helplessly underneath you.'

'Clippesby saved your life,' stated Agatha, lest the physician had not realised. 'I was too far away to help, and that lunatic – and I do not mean Clippesby – would have throttled you long before I arrived. This brave friar drove him off, armed only with a rock.'

'I understand now how the wolf kills,' said Clippesby, blushing at the compliment. 'It is not easy to slash a throat with something as unwieldy as teeth – metal ones or your own – so he partially strangles his victims, to subdue them first. That was what he was doing to Rougham when I intervened. Then he rips their necks with his tainted fangs when they are too weak to fight. Nothing is left to chance; he is a thorough executioner.'

'Not thorough enough,' Agatha pointed out. 'He did not kill Rougham, and now he has failed with Matthew – twice, if you include the time with the spade in the church.'

'That was not me, either,' said Clippesby firmly. 'However, I have been thinking about it – analysing the details you gave me, along with information supplied by Agatha and a crow who happened to be watching – and I have reached a logical conclusion, based on facts.'

'Go on,' said Bartholomew, not sure whether he could trust the 'facts' supplied by the crow.

'The wolf has a very specific way of killing. He claimed three victims – that we know about – before the assault on you. Therefore, we can assume that he is content with his method, and there is no reason for him to change it. By contrast, the man who attacked you on Wednesday morning gave up very easily when he thought he would not succeed, and I think the wolf is more determined than that. It was not easy to drive him off when he hurt Rougham, and it was not easy tonight. *Ergo*, the wolf and the man who attacked you with a spade are not one and the same.'

'Two killers on the loose?' asked Bartholomew uneasily.

'The spade-man did not *kill* you,' Clippesby pointed out. 'And, from what you say, he was clumsy and ill-prepared. He did not have a weapon with him, and was obliged to use a tool he found in the churchyard. He is not a killer, because, as far as we know, he has not yet taken a life.'

'Yes and no,' said Bartholomew. 'I think he believed I was Spryngheuse. He stayed his hand only when I said something that indicated he had the wrong man, but I am sure he had intended to kill. But Spryngheuse was dead within two days anyway, terrified into taking his own life.'

'You may be right about that,' acknowledged Clippesby. 'But I am right about there being two killers: the wolf and your attacker are not the same man. The wolf would have used his teeth, not a spade.'

'Metal teeth,' said Bartholomew, his thoughts whirling away in another direction. 'Polmorva once owned some of those, but Duraunt destroyed them years ago. Does this mean he did not, and that he kept them for future use? Or did Polmorva have another set made, after the originals disappeared?'

'What are you talking about?' asked Agatha, bemused. 'Are you saying the Oxford men have steel fangs instead of real ones?'

Bartholomew described Polmorva's invention. 'But they

disappeared after I accused him of complicity in the sub-prior's death. He thought I had stolen them while I assumed he had hidden them, ready to hire out again when the fuss had died down. Duraunt confessed to melting them down, although he did not see fit to mention this at the time, and exonerate me from Polmorva's accusations.'

'So, who is the wolf, then?' asked Clippesby. 'Duraunt or Polmorva?'

'Duraunt is too frail to fight me,' said Bartholomew. 'Polmorva is not, though.'

'And he hates you,' agreed Agatha. 'However, I am told you defeated him with ease when you fought at the cistern, so are you sure he is strong enough?'

'He must be, because otherwise it means the wolf is Duraunt. Duraunt does not want me dead.'

'How do you know?' asked Clippesby softly. 'The Merton Hall chickens heard him telling his friends that he offered you a Fellowship at Oxford, and was deeply hurt when you elected to come here instead. He also thinks you are different from the young student he knew and loved.'

'I grew up,' said Bartholomew tersely. 'I became more practical and less idealistic, but so do we all.'

'Not all,' said Clippesby pointedly. 'Some of us cling to our naïveté, hoping it will protect us from the horrors of the world. Sometimes it works, but most of the time we are exposed to it regardless. You should not dismiss Duraunt from your list of suspects too readily. The stoat who lives at the Cardinal's Cap tells me he is belligerent once full of ale. Drunks can be strong.'

'No,' insisted Bartholomew doggedly. 'Not Duraunt.'

'He lied about the teeth,' Agatha pointed out. 'He said they were destroyed, but they were not. They are here, in Cambridge, being used for a far more sinister purpose

386

than helping old monks gnaw their meat. The wolf *must* be him.'

'And it was definitely you he was after,' added Clippesby. 'He does not perceive me as a threat – he could have come to the hospital any time and dispatched me at his leisure. It was you he wanted, just as he wanted Rougham, not me, the first time I encountered him.'

'But why?' asked Bartholomew in despair. 'I do not understand!'

'He thinks you are close to revealing his identity and is determined to stop you,' said Clippesby. 'Whatever direction your investigation is taking is obviously the right one.'

'No,' said Bartholomew wearily. 'There must be some other explanation.'

'So you said, but speculating will get us nowhere,' said Agatha, looking up at the sky. 'Dawn is not far off, and we should be about our business before anyone finds out what we have been doing: Clippesby escaping, me visiting lunatics, and Matthew stalking College laundresses.'

'I still cannot let you go,' said Bartholomew to Clippesby, dragging his thoughts away from Duraunt. 'Especially not now. You have saved my life, and I want to do the same for you.'

'But we have established that the wolf does not have designs on me.' Clippesby smiled wryly. 'He probably believes I am too addled, which goes to show a little eccentricity has its advantages.'

'You are more than a little eccentric,' said Agatha bluntly. 'You are stark raving mad.'

'I am not worried about the wolf . . . about the killer harming you,' said Bartholomew. 'I am concerned about the Oxford merchants and others who may seize you as a scapegoat. You cannot stay at Stourbridge, though; you are not safe here, either. Not now.'

'Well, if he cannot stay here, and you will not let him

escape, then where is left?' demanded Agatha. 'He is not a bird, whatever he might think himself, and he cannot fly away.'

'I know somewhere,' said Bartholomew. 'No one will think to look there, and he will be safe until this is over.'

'Good,' said Agatha. 'Then lead us to it.'

CHAPTER 11

It was well past dawn by the time Bartholomew had secured Clippesby in his new hiding place, and he was late for the Monday morning mass. He noticed that the town was waiting in eager anticipation for the Archbishop, and even the beggars had made an attempt to spruce themselves up. He hurried to St Michael's Church and walked briskly to his place in the chancel. Michael was officiating, but took his mind off his sacred duties long enough to indicate he wanted to speak to the physician. Then he delighted the students and bemused the Fellows by speeding through the rest of the ceremony at a rate that was far from devout.

'I wish all our priests would do it like that,' remarked Langelee, as he led the procession out of the church and back to Michaelhouse. 'It would save us a good deal of wasted time.'

'Praying is not wasted time,' said William, shocked, despite the fact that his masses were usually even faster. He jerked his head at the listening students. 'And watch what you say when there are impressionable minds listening.'

'Our impressionable minds might be disturbed by witnessing the Master's hankering for Agatha,' said Deynman sanctimoniously. 'The news of *that* is all over the University.'

'The Master does not hanker after her any longer,' said William, who had heard the rumours that Langelee had shifted his affections to Alyce Weasenham. 'That honour now falls to Suttone.' He guffawed loudly, to indicate he was making a joke.

'Suttone,' mused Deynman, and Bartholomew saw he had just witnessed the birth of another falsehood that would soon be circulating around the town and paraded as truth.

Michael snatched Bartholomew's arm and pulled him out of the procession. 'Where have you been? You were needed last night, and there was no trace of you. Have you been with a patient?'

'Yes,' replied Bartholomew truthfully. 'Why? What has happened?'

'Matilde's house was invaded – by the killer, we think.'

Bartholomew gazed at him in horror, a stab of panic making his breath catch painfully in his throat. 'She is not . . . ? Is she . . . ?'

'She is unharmed,' replied Michael. 'Frightened and angry, but unharmed.'

Bartholomew closed his eyes in relief. 'I *am* going to marry her, Michael,' he said in a soft voice. 'I am going to ask her as soon as Rougham has gone and we can be alone.'

Michael smiled. 'Good. It is time you acted on this, and I am sure Matilde will think so, too.'

'Do you think she will have me?'

'Probably,' replied Michael carelessly. 'It will mean the end of your Fellowship, but I intend to order Tynkell to keep you as our Corpse Examiner. I doubt Rougham will be clamouring for your dismissal, given what you have done for him of late.' He smiled affectionately. 'I hope you will be very happy together – and that you will spare the occasional cup of wine for an old friend.'

'Always,' said Bartholomew. They were silent for a moment, as each considered the enormity of what Bartholomew was about to do. He would have to start hunting for patients who could pay him, and would have no time for his treatise on fevers. Meanwhile, Michael thought about how different life would be for him, too, and realised how much he had come to rely on the physician's insights and help in all manner of ways.

'Did Matilde see who broke into her house?' asked Bartholomew, pulling his mind away from the future. 'And what about Rougham? Did the killer come to complete what he started two weeks ago?'

'I think that is exactly what he was doing,' said Michael soberly. 'It happened at midnight precisely, because Matilde heard handbells jangling inside All-Saints-in-the-Jewry. Rougham escaped unharmed, too, although the shock has not been good for him.'

'Lord!' muttered Bartholomew. 'The wolf was busy last night. He must have gone directly from Matilde's house to Stourbridge.'

'The wolf?' echoed Michael.

Bartholomew shook his head, impatient with himself. 'That is what Clippesby calls him. I am sorry, Brother. He used it so often last night that it rubbed off on me.'

'You went to see Clippesby?' asked Michael warily. 'In the middle of the night? With a killer on the loose, who may decide you are to be next?'

Bartholomew described what had happened, leaving out only the fact that he had hidden Clippesby in a place only he and Agatha knew. Michael immediately jumped to the conclusion that Clippesby had been afraid the Oxford merchants would hang him, and had fled the area completely. Bartholomew said nothing to disabuse him of the notion.

'Damn! The Archbishop is due this afternoon, and we shall have to welcome him knowing there is a killer stalking our streets with a metal dentition. I hope to God this wolf does not have designs on Islip, because, if he strikes, our University will be suppressed for certain. I know

Canterbury became famous after the murder of Thomas à Becket, but I do not want Cambridge to be known for killing archbishops, too. *We* do not have a cathedral.'

'I do not think the wolf wants Islip,' said Bartholomew.

Michael raised his eyebrows. 'Do you not? You think this murder and mayhem just before the Visitation is coincidence? Well, you are wrong. I believe he is following a very specific agenda, which includes making Cambridge appear every bit as unstable and riotous as Oxford. Thus, he may well strike at the Archbishop. But we should go to see Matilde. She is worried about you.'

'Before breakfast?' asked Bartholomew, aware that Michael's good intentions regarding his diet had already floundered once in the face of his appetite.

'Yes,' said Michael, taking his arm. 'I want Rougham back at Gonville before any more of the day passes – for all our sakes.'

'What happened last night?'

'Matilde was sleeping on a bench in her parlour, while Rougham had the bed in the upper chamber. She fled upstairs when the wolf burst into her house, and together she and Rougham barred the door and managed to keep him at bay. He tried to smoke them out by lighting a fire under the door, but you had insisted that bowls of water be left upstairs lest Rougham's fever returned, and they were able to douse the flames before they did any serious harm.'

Bartholomew set a cracking pace along the slowly lightening streets. He left Michael far behind, puffing, wheezing and complaining that such frenzied activities were not good for a man with an empty stomach. When Bartholomew reached Matilde's house, he hammered furiously on her door, not caring that Weasenham's window shutters immediately eased open. She opened it, a little angrily, to see who was waking her neighbours with his racket, and he shoved his way inside and took her by the shoulders, looking her up and down in concern.

'I am all right,' she said, smiling reassuringly.

'And so am I,' said Rougham wryly, aware that his colleague had not so much as glanced in his direction. 'Together, we managed to repel whoever burst in last night. We were fortunate Matilde is a light sleeper, or who knows what might have happened?'

'Doctor Rougham tore a sheet into pieces, and was going to lower me on to the roof of the house next door,' said Matilde to Bartholomew. Her face was pale; glancing up the stairs, Bartholomew saw black marks where the killer had set his blaze. There were deep grooves in the door, too, as if he had used an axe. 'We were becoming desperate.'

'And who would have lowered you to safety?' asked Bartholomew of Rougham.

'I was going to fetch the de Blaston family,' said Matilde weakly. 'That was the plan we agreed on as we struggled to quench the flames: I would run for help, and return to rescue Master Rougham.'

'Yes,' said Rougham softly, and Bartholomew saw he had not expected her to be in time. He had been ready to sacrifice himself to save the woman he had come so suddenly to respect and admire.

'Weasenham,' said Bartholomew heavily, thinking about what must have happened. 'He saw you in Matilde's window the other day, and he must have chatted about it to his customers – one of whom is the killer, and who decided to come and finish what he had started.'

'Probably,' said Rougham tiredly. 'I did not see the fellow's face last night, but I can tell you with absolute certainty that it was not Clippesby – he moved in a completely different way – slower and less graceful. Do you have any other ideas, now my main suspect is exonerated?'

'None at all,' lied Bartholomew, refusing to entertain the possibility that Duraunt could be the culprit. 'But I know more about the teeth that were used on you now. They are metal, devised by an Oxford scholar many years ago, to help edentulous people to eat.'

'That is a good idea,' said Rougham, rubbing his chin thoughtfully. 'False teeth. But metal will be hard on ancient gums, and what will fit one man will not match another. They would have to be individually tailored. How were they made? Were there two separate pieces for upper and lower fangs, or were they linked?'

'Linked,' said Bartholomew. He remembered them vividly. 'With a hinge on either side.'

'Did they work?'

'Not very well. But these have been adapted for use as a killing weapon, because I am sure the originals were not honed so sharp. Someone came after me with them last night – after he realised he would have no luck here.' He glanced at Matilde. 'The thick material of that liripipe saved me.'

'My recollection of the night I was bitten is hazy, as you know,' said Rougham thoughtfully. 'I remember falling over and I certainly remember the agony, but the attack itself is a blur until I saw Clippesby standing over me. But your words have sparked a dormant memory. I did see a metal object during the fracas, just before the searing pain in my shoulder. It may well have been these teeth, and that would explain why they did me so much damage.'

Bartholomew thought about his shredded hood. 'Excrement was smeared on them, too.'

'To be certain of causing an infection, should the injury not prove instantly fatal,' mused Rougham, understanding at once. 'What does this mean? That our killer is a physician, because he knows how to make a wound turn rotten? It is not you or me, so we are left with Paxtone or Lynton. Lynton is too old and lazy for such activities, which leaves . . .'

'No,' said Bartholomew firmly. 'Not Paxtone.'

'He *is* at King's Hall,' Rougham pointed out. 'So was Hamecotes.'

'No,' said Bartholomew again, appalled that another person he liked should be accused. 'It is probably someone from Oxford. Polmorva, who owned the teeth. Or . . .' He trailed off.

'Or who?' asked Matilde. 'Duraunt? Your kindly old teacher, who drinks heavily in taverns and who lies about his love affair with soporifics? The man who seems rather too friendly with that nasty Polmorva, and who has a will of iron under that oh-so-gentle exterior?'

'Poppy juice and wine is a powerful combination,' said Rougham to Bartholomew. 'They could change him from a kindly ancient into something savage.'

Bartholomew recalled the demonic strength of the hands around his throat, and the grim determination of the wolf to rip his skin with the filth-smeared teeth. 'He is not strong enough.'

'Not even when intoxicated?' pressed Rougham. 'Your experience as a physician will have taught you that even the meekest of men can turn into raging lions when they swallow dangerous remedies.'

'I know, but . . .' said Bartholomew, feeling exhaustion wash over him as his conviction in Duraunt's innocence began to waver, '. . . but I do not believe it of him.'

Rougham laid a sympathetic hand on his shoulder in the first gesture of friendship he had ever offered, while Matilde took his hand and raised it to her lips. He looked into her eyes and was suddenly overwhelmed with the utter conviction that it was the right time to ask her to marry him, whether Rougham was present or no.

'Matilde,' he began. 'Will you . . . ?'

'Lord!' puffed Michael, gasping for breath in the doorway. 'I am exhausted after that run!'

Michael waddled across the room and flopped on to a bench, where he sat fanning himself with his loose sleeve. Matilde released Bartholomew's hand and went to fetch ale to help him recover, while Rougham lowered himself on a bench, wincing at the pain in his injured shoulder.

'Well?' Michael rasped. 'What have you deduced? Have you solved the case? Who is the wolf? You had better hurry with your analysis, because Islip will arrive in a matter of hours and we do not have time to waste. Who might have a reason to kill you, Rougham? We know it was not Clippesby, so who else could it be?'

'I have no idea,' said Rougham. 'And believe me, I have thought about little else these last few days. I have not lost any patients recently, so it cannot be a grieving relative. I am on reasonable terms with my colleagues at Gonville – we have our disagreements, but none are serious. I confine my amorous adventures to Yolande de Blaston, and I always pay handsomely for the privilege. And I owe no one any money. I cannot imagine why anyone would want to harm me.'

'What about your student, William of Lee?' wheezed Michael. 'He thinks you are a hard taskmaster, and says you are never satisfied with him, no matter how hard he tries.'

Rougham sighed. 'Some students respond to encouragement, and others need criticism to produce their best work. Lee is one of the latter. If I do not monitor him constantly, he grows lax. But I do not ride him hard enough to make him want to kill me.'

Bartholomew was not so sure, aware that students were sometimes delicate creatures, whose feelings were easily hurt. Insults were often felt more deeply in the young than in older, wiser people, who had learned that they could not please everyone all of the time. But did Lee have the intelligence to kill and hide his tracks? And why would he have been in Oxford on St Scholastica's Day, when the whole business seemed to have started, not to mention managing to lay his hands on the metal teeth? Lee as the wolf did not make sense, so Bartholomew eliminated him from his list of suspects, resigned to the fact that, once again, it comprised Polmorva, Dodenho and some of his colleagues from King's Hall. And Duraunt.

'What about Boltone?' suggested Rougham, racking his brains. 'He knows Oxford, since he is employed by Merton College, and he makes journeys there to present his accounts. I know, because he is my patient, and he has told me. He may have found these teeth and killed Gonerby.'

'We asked if he had been there recently, and he said he had not,' said Michael.

Rougham pursed his lips. 'Well, he is hardly likely to admit to a February visit, if he had murdered someone. And besides, he is not an honest man. You know that for yourselves, because Duraunt is here to inspect his dubious accounting – and do not forget that he was caught virtually red-handed with that treasure hoard in the cistern.'

'But if Boltone is the wolf, why has he started his murderous spree now?' asked Bartholomew. 'Why not years ago? And what is his motive?'

'You can ask him that when he is caught,' said Rougham. 'And he *will* be caught, because he will not go far. Cambridge is his home and I do not see him leaving to start a new life elsewhere. He and Eudo will be in the Fens together, waiting until the hue and cry has died down. Then they will return, and set about proving their "innocence".'

'But why would they harm *you*?' asked Michael, puzzled.

'Are you saying Boltone hates his physician enough to make two attempts on his life?'

'I do not know,' said Rougham wearily. 'Perhaps it was because I once wrote, in a letter to my friend Henry Okehamptone, that Boltone was a dishonest sort of fellow and that Merton College would be wise to examine his accounting.'

Michael stared at him. 'You did that? Then he *does* have a motive to kill you: revenge.'

'It was more than a year ago,' objected Rougham, 'and I thought no more about it until today.'

'We must move you as soon as we can,' said Bartholomew, aware that time was passing. 'You are not safe here. We can discuss Boltone later, when you are home.'

Rougham nodded weakly. 'I have imposed myself on Matilde long enough. I cannot walk far, but I think I can reach Weasenham's shop.'

'Why there?' asked Michael, startled.

'I have a plan,' said Rougham.

'Will you tell us what it is?' asked Michael, when the Gonville man said no more. 'I would sooner know what you have in mind before we help.'

'I shall decline your assistance,' said Rougham softly. 'You have done more than enough for me already, and I refuse to have this wolf stalking you, when it is me he is after.'

'It is too late for that,' said Michael. 'He almost had Matt last night.'

Rougham sighed with genuine regret. 'Quite. And I do not want you taking more risks on my behalf. So, I will walk – alone – to Weasenham's shop, where I will ask him to send one of his lads for my College's cart. I will ensure he knows I am going to Gonville, because then he will tell everyone I am home, and the wolf will not bother Matilde again.'

Bartholomew shot her an agonised look, afraid that Rougham moving out of her house might not render her that much safer.

'He is right, Matt,' said Michael. 'The wolf is selective. From what Matilde told me last night, he could easily have hurt her before going after Rougham. Mercy was a mistake on his part, because it allowed her to dart up the stairs and warn him. Think about Clippesby, too. The killer could have had him with ease – he was a tethered goat at Stourbridge – but he was only interested in you.'

'You cannot walk alone,' said Bartholomew to Rougham. 'You are too weak – and just imagine how it will look if you are found lying in the gutter outside Matilde's house.'

'Not as bad as it would have done last week,' said Rougham. He smiled, in a rare display of humour. 'They have been cleaned since then.'

'We will escort you to Weasenham's premises,' said Bartholomew firmly. 'Now, before there are too many people around. But we should hurry – folk are already beginning to gather in the Market Square, hoping Islip and his entourage will arrive early.'

Michael heaved himself up from the bench. 'And afterwards, I shall have words with Duraunt and Polmorva. I intend to demand the truth about these teeth.'

Matilde fetched an old cloak of Bartholomew's, which she arranged so that it concealed Rougham's face, and helped the Gonville physician to the door. Michael offered to go ahead and create a diversion so that no one would notice when Rougham entered the shop, or the direction from which he had come. The monk grinned, and informed them that he intended to lean on a set of shelves, claiming to feel faint, and bring the whole lot tumbling down around him. He was certain the prospect of ink leaking over valuable parchment would be more than enough to capture the gossiping stationer's attention – and that of any customers who might be present.

'It is too early for trade,' said Rougham. 'Especially today, when everyone will be thinking about what to wear for the Visitation.'

Bartholomew waited until he saw the monk disappear inside the shop, then looked in both directions to ensure they were not being watched. There was no movement from Weasenham's house, so he assumed Michael's diversion was already working. He hesitated, loath to leave Matilde when he felt his place was at her side, in order to protect her from whoever had tried to smoke his way inside her bedchamber. It took considerable willpower to step outside.

'Answer the door only to Michael or me,' he instructed anxiously. 'And stay indoors until we come to tell you it is safe.'

'Do not even answer it to Yolande,' Rougham added, equally unhappy at abandoning her. 'She is innocent of this vile affair, but she may be used to gain access to you. Trust no one.'

It was good advice, and Bartholomew urged Matilde to heed it. She was a headstrong and determined lady, who would object to being a prisoner in her own home, and he suspected she would not skulk inside for long. He helped Rougham into the street. The Gonville Fellow stood unsteadily for a moment, face turned towards the pale blue sky and breathing deeply of the first fresh air he had taken in almost three weeks. Then he bowed to Matilde, thanked her for her kindness, and began to walk as fast as he could, aiming to put as much distance between him and her as possible before he was seen. But his scant reserves of energy were soon spent, and it was not long before he was obliged to lean heavily on Bartholomew. They were forced to stop altogether when the effort made him dizzy, but eventually they reached the shop, where he stumbled gratefully over the threshold.

'I have just returned from my home in Norfolk,' he announced in a husky voice, trying his best to speak loudly and ensure that all in the room would hear him. 'The journey was long and arduous, and I have an ague. I do not think I can walk any farther, so perhaps you would be kind enough to send for Gonville's cart, Master Weasenham.'

'I do not think there is any need for wagons,' came a soft voice from the shadows. 'You are not going anywhere today, Doctor Rougham.'

'I am sorry, Matt,' said Michael. He was sitting on the floor holding a hand to his bloody nose, and Bartholomew saw he had been put there by a punch. 'I was going to warn you, but they anticipated me before I could call out.'

'They have loaded weapons,' came a small, frightened voice from a stool behind the table. It was Weasenham, looking terrified as he was held in place by a powerful hand on his shoulder.

'Eudo!' exclaimed Bartholomew. He saw someone else, too, moving behind him. He whirled around just in time to see Boltone push the door shut with his foot, and drop the bar across it, securing it from within. Both he and Eudo carried crossbows.

'I do not know why you are surprised to see us,' said Eudo in his penetrating voice. 'You must have known we would not stand by and let the University defame our good names. We have been obliged to skulk in the Fens these last few days, not knowing how to help ourselves. But now we have a plan.'

'You did the damage yourselves,' said Michael, probing his swollen nose with tentative fingers. 'You are the ones who have been stealing from people and falsifying manor records.'

'We have not *stolen* anything,' said Eudo indignantly. 'And eccentricities of accounting hardly count as theft, either! Every clerk from here to Jerusalem does that. Is that not so, Boltone?'

Boltone nodded. 'We have been doing well for twenty years, so why should Merton choose now to move against us? Someone must have told them – lied to them – about what we do.'

'Well, it was not us,' said Michael, climbing to his feet and not looking at Rougham. 'And if you do not mind, we are busy today. The Archbishop is due soon, and I must be there to greet him.'

'He will have to manage without you,' said Eudo coldly. 'What are you doing here, anyway? Weasenham said no one ever comes to his shop this early – especially not today, when everyone is preoccupied with Islip.'

'They were helping me,' said Rougham, collapsing white-faced on to a bench. 'They met me near the Barnwell Gate, and offered to assist me on the final leg of my journey *from Norfolk.*'

'But I saw you in Matilde's house yesterday . . .' began Weasenham immediately.

'No, you did not,' said Rougham with a conviction that Bartholomew could only admire. 'That must have been someone else, because I have only just arrived. I was afraid I would miss the Visitation, but I am just in time.'

'You will not be making the Archbishop's acquaintance, either,' said Eudo. 'I have reason to believe it was *you* who wrote to Okehamptone, telling tales about us, so *you* are the reason we are in this vile predicament.'

'Did you kill Okehamptone, Eudo?' asked Michael, before Rougham could admit to anything. 'Did you cut his throat because he believed you were dishonest?'

'We have not killed anyone,' said Eudo firmly. He indicated Bartholomew with a nod of his head. 'Not even him, unfortunately.'

'It was you who attacked me with the spade?' asked Bartholomew. The weaving, cloaked figure in St Michael's Church had been about the right size and shape for the tenant.

'I should have gone through with it,' said Eudo resentfully. 'But you made me panic with all that yelling, and then the monk came. I shoved you in the cupboard, when I should have finished the job.'

'But why?' asked Bartholomew. 'What have I done to you? We barely know each other.'

'Enough chatter,' said Boltone impatiently, seeing Eudo ready to oblige with an explanation. He stepped towards the stationer and brandished his bow. 'We are short of time, so do not sit there listening to talk that does not concern you. Write.'

Weasenham flinched at the anger in his voice, and turned his attention to the parchment that lay in front of him. It was covered in the stationer's small, neat script.

'I want to go home,' said Rougham feebly. He looked dreadful, with a sheen of sweat coating his pallid face. 'And I need my colleagues to help me. I do not care what you are doing here.' He attempted to stand, but Eudo strode towards him with a furious glower and he sank down again.

'He is ill,' said Bartholomew, moving instinctively to stand between his patient and the felons. He had a sudden inspiration. 'It is a contagion, contracted on his journey from Norfolk. Possibly a fatal one. You do not want him in here with you.'

'A contagion is the least of our worries,' said Boltone bitterly, although Eudo looked alarmed. 'But we will not catch it if he keeps well away from us. You two can sit next to him, and prevent him from coughing in our direction.'

'I will stay here, thank you,' said Michael, leaning against the shelves with his hand still clapped to his bruised face. He had no intention of going where they could all be conveniently covered with one weapon. 'A man with a broken nose is vulnerable to contagions.'

Boltone should have insisted on obedience, but instead he turned on Eudo, and Bartholomew saw they were incompetent criminals. 'I told you this was a bad idea, but you insisted it would work. Now what are we going to do?'

'We will kill them before we leave. It is not our fault: they brought it on themselves.'

'No,' said Boltone, alarmed. 'Not murder – especially of a monk! It will not matter that we are innocent of theft, if we then commit an even more serious crime.'

'Listen to him, Eudo,' recommended Michael. 'You say you have not killed anyone so far, so it would be foolish to begin now. Let Rougham go, and we can devise a solution—'

'We cannot be merciful. We have too much to lose.' Eudo took a step towards Weasenham and his handsome features creased into a scowl. 'Write! Or I will chop off your hands.'

'I am going as fast as I can,' bleated Weasenham. 'I have been scribing all night, and my fingers are so cramped I can barely move them.'

'You are preparing proclamations,' said Bartholomew, craning his neck to see what Weasenham was doing. There was already a substantial pile of sheets on the table, at least half in a different hand, and he supposed Boltone too had been writing before he had been obliged to abandon clerkly activities to point a crossbow at Michael.

'I *told* you to keep the door locked,' grumbled Boltone, rounding on Eudo a second time. 'But you would insist on looking outside every few moments to see whether Islip had arrived, even though it is still far too early. It is *your* fault we are in this mess. I would have devised a way to explain away Chesterfelde's blood when the Senior Proctor came prying, but oh, no! *You* have to start a fight and we end up accused of killing Hamecotes.'

'Write!' shouted Eudo at Weasenham, refusing to acknowledge his friend's accusations.

Bartholomew thought fast, rearranging facts and conclusions in the light of what he had just heard. Rougham had been wrong to think either Eudo or Boltone was the wolf. They were exactly what they appeared: cornered petty felons. They knew something about Chesterfelde's death, but nothing about the others, because the wolf was clever and this pair were not. They had mishandled the situation at the cistern, and now they had allowed themselves to become trapped in a position where they had four hostages to manage.

'You can still escape,' he said in a reasonable voice. 'Abandon what you are doing and leave. You will find another property to run, given the number left vacant by the plague, and you can begin your lives again somewhere else.'

'Why should we?' demanded Eudo. 'I will not be driven away by lies. This is my *home*.'

'They are not lies,' said Michael. 'You have stolen – from people like Matilde, and from Merton – and you have been found out. Personally, I would rather see you hang, but my colleague is offering you a chance. Take it, before you end up with a rope around your necks.'

'No!' shouted Eudo. 'None of it is true – except for the accounting, and that was Boltone. *I* have stolen nothing! I am the victim of a University plot, which blames me for its own crimes. But I have a plan. I will exonerate myself, and everything will return to normal.'

'These will not exonerate you,' said Michael, picking up one of the proclamations. 'Lies can be written just as easily

405

as they can be spoken, and putting pen to parchment does not produce a truth.'

'You see?' said Boltone. 'I told you it would not work.'

'People *will* believe what is written,' insisted Eudo stubbornly. 'Especially clerks. They will read what I dictated, and see that the real villains are scholars – Polmorva, Dodenho and men like them.'

'Chesterfelde visited Cambridge regularly,' said Bartholomew, turning over what he had deduced. 'I think it was he who helped keep your deception from Merton for so long – for a price, I imagine. What was it? A third of the profits?'

'How do you know that?' demanded Boltone, aghast. 'He said he never told anyone.'

Bartholomew did not want to admit that it had been a guess. 'You two and Chesterfelde met last Saturday night, to discuss what to do about Duraunt's inspection. You formulated a plan to evade exposure, and to demonstrate the depth of your commitment, you decided to sign it with blood.'

'To *mingle* blood,' corrected Boltone, glowering at Eudo. 'As a sign of undying brotherhood. It was a stupid idea.'

'A stupid idea devised by men in their cups,' agreed Bartholomew. 'Eudo had been drinking at the King's Head, while Chesterfelde was drunk on wine provided by the merchants.'

'The mixing of blood was symbolic of our loyalty,' protested Eudo. 'Knights do it all the time.'

'But Chesterfelde cut himself too deeply – or you did it for him.' Bartholomew considered. 'No, he did it himself. The wound was on his left wrist, and I know he was right-handed because I saw writing calluses on his fingers: he used his right hand to slice his left arm. Blood pumped from him as he stood by the cistern, and none of you could stop it.'

'We did not know how,' said Eudo resentfully. 'We tried holding the limb in the air, we hunted for leeches in the cistern, but nothing worked. Meanwhile, Tulyet's brat was watching everything.'

'Dickon,' mused Michael. 'So, it was Chesterfelde's death he saw – the splashing he mentioned was you searching for leeches, not the sound of Hamecotes's corpse being dropped down the well. He identified you as the killer, but was vague about the victim.'

'He shot me later,' said Eudo resentfully. 'Evil little tyke. I will put an end to his violent antics when I am reinstated as tenant of Merton Hall. He will not spy on me again.'

'*I* was not drunk,' said Boltone. 'Well, not very, and the brat cannot have me blamed for what happened to Chesterfelde.'

'And what was that?' asked Michael. 'Exactly.'

'Eudo frightened Chesterfelde with his fury over Duraunt's inspection. It made him cut himself over-vigorously – to demonstrate the extent of his kinship with us.'

'He should not have used such a large dagger,' said Eudo, sounding more indignant than sorry. 'It was unwieldy and he was clumsy from wine. He should have used my little knife instead.'

'And then you tried to make the accident look like murder, by dumping his body in the hall with the dagger in his back,' surmised Michael. 'His Oxford companions were all drunk, too, so they slept through the racket you must have made.'

'Except Polmorva,' said Eudo. 'The others were all snoring but he saw what we were doing. He promised to say nothing, in return for certain favours.'

'It was Eudo's idea,' said Boltone bitterly, before Michael could ask what favours the sly scholar had demanded. 'He said if we left Chesterfelde's body in their midst, the Oxford men would be blamed for his death, and we would not.'

'Your only crimes are dishonesty and stupidity,' said the monk, disgusted with them both. 'You are innocent of murder, and it was just unfortunate coincidence that someone used your cistern as a grave for Hamecotes, not knowing it was where you kept your hoard.'

'We *have* no hoard,' insisted Eudo. 'I keep telling you: we had nothing to do with that.'

'You stole Matilde's silver dog.'

'I visited her for a remedy – my woman will not lie with me as long as she has female pains; I gave Alyce the cure, but she still only has eyes for Ralph de Langelee – but I stole nothing from Matilde.'

Michael glanced at Weasenham, who sat scratching out his proclamations and weeping softly. 'Go,' the monk said to Eudo and Boltone, pointing to the door. 'Leave Cambridge while you can.'

'I will not, and I will kill anyone who tries to make me,' Eudo shouted, brandishing the crossbow in a way that made his prisoners flinch in alarm. 'No one saw you coming here – I watched you sneaking down the lane myself – and no one saw us, either. Therefore, no one will know it was us who killed you.' He looked pleased with his logic.

'Weasenham will know,' Michael pointed out. He rested a heavy forearm on one of the shelves and gave it a nudge to test its stability. Bartholomew saw what he intended to do, and started to edge slowly along the bench towards him.

'He will die, too,' said Eudo coldly. 'He has almost finished what he is writing, and we have no further need of his services.'

'No!' shrieked Weasenham. 'You said I would live if I did what you asked. You promised!'

'That was before *they* arrived,' snapped Eudo. 'I cannot release a witness to their deaths.'

'I can keep secrets!' howled Weasenham. 'I have kept

the one about Bartholomew visiting Matilde. Ask Brother Michael. I have not breathed a word about that to anyone.'

'Finish that document, and let us bring an end to this,' said Eudo, unbarring the door to glance outside. Bartholomew saw the streets were becoming busy, as people flocked towards the Market Square, and there was an atmosphere of excitement in the rattle of many foot-steps. He eased closer towards the shelves, gradually slip-ping down the slick surface of the bench, and trying not to let Eudo see what he was doing. 'We have one of those proclamations for every scholar, priest and clerk in the town, and a copy is sure to reach the Archbishop. He will recognise the truth and will take our case before the King.'

'He will not,' said Michael scornfully. 'And it will be obvious who killed Weasenham, since this parchment – covered in *his* writing – is to be distributed throughout the town. It is a ludicrous plan.'

'You see?' demanded Boltone of Eudo. 'I told you it would not work.'

'It *would* have done, if these scholars had not spoiled it,' snarled Eudo. A thought occurred to him, and a wicked smile crossed his face. 'We will shoot them first, then set the shop alight. All anyone will find is charred corpses, and no one will ever know what really happened.'

'But murder, Eudo!' whispered Boltone. 'And the Proctor is a monk, a man of God.'

'We have no choice. If you let them live, you will hang. Do you want to die just because you are too frightened to loose a judicious arrow against men who put us in this situ-ation in the first place?'

Boltone was obviously unhappy, but the increasing clamour in the street and its sense of urgency was begin-ning to rob him of his common sense. He nodded reluc-tant agreement.

'Good,' said Eudo, flexing his fingers around his bow. 'Then we must hurry, because we are running out of time. You shoot Bartholomew and I will kill the monk. Then we will reload and dispatch Weasenham and Rougham, who are weaker and less likely to stop us. Ready?'

As one, he and Boltone raised their weapons and pointed them at the scholars.

'Now!' shouted Michael, flinging himself backwards as hard as he could. Bartholomew did likewise, at the same instant that Boltone released his quarrel. The physician heard a snap and something hit his chest before he fell. For a moment, he felt nothing, then there was a dull throb. When he glanced down, his clothes were stained red, and he realised he had been hit.

Meanwhile, his and Michael's combined weight had been more than the shelves could support. With a tearing groan, they came away from their moorings and toppled, sending their contents skittering across the room. Bottles smashed, pens tapped on the wooden floor, and parchments soared from their neat piles like birds, covering the shop with a carpet of cream. Eudo began to reload, regarding first Michael and then Bartholomew with an expression of hatred, while Boltone was momentarily stunned by a box that had struck his head.

'Michael!' Bartholomew gasped, knowing the monk could disarm Eudo if he moved fast enough. It took a moment or two to wind a crossbow.

But Michael wallowed with agonising helplessness among the inkwells and scrolls, and seemed unable to climb to his feet. Bartholomew was sharply reminded of Brother Thomas's prediction that the monk's obesity would bring about his friend's death, and was appalled it should come true quite so soon. He saw Boltone shake his head to clear it, then scramble towards the weapon he had dropped. The physician managed to reach it first, struggling to keep hold of it while the bailiff tried to snatch it back.

'Michael!' he yelled again, watching Eudo load his weapon with all the time in the world. But Michael only rolled this way and that, like a landed fish among the sea of parchment.

Weasenham dived under a table with a petrified squeak, and it was left to Rougham to pick up a stone inkwell and lob it with his failing strength. It hit Eudo square in the face, and felled him as cleanly as any arrow. Boltone gazed at his fallen colleague in horrified disbelief, then abandoned his skirmish with Bartholomew to dart across the room, wrench open the door and flee as fast as his legs could carry him. Weasenham emerged from under the table to grab Eudo's weapon, but the man was deeply insensible, and posed no further threat. Rougham appealed to Bartholomew.

'I am feeling most unwell. Will you mix me a physic?'

'Never mind you!' shouted Michael furiously, finally upright. 'What about Matt? He has been shot and is drenched in blood.'

'Ink,' said Rougham dismissively. 'Weasenham threw it. He was actually aiming at Eudo and, since he missed his intended target, I was obliged to hurl a pot myself. I always say that if you want a job done properly, you should do it yourself, and this is just a case in point.'

'But I saw the bolt fly loose,' said Michael, while Bartholomew regarded the mess on his best tabard in dismay. He doubted it could be washed out.

'It is lodged in the ceiling,' said Weasenham, pointing with an unsteady finger. 'Eudo is no better a marksman than I am, it seems.'

'Tend me, please, Bartholomew,' begged Rougham. 'Before Weasenham really does have a corpse in his shop.'

The stationer, relieved and grateful that he had escaped with his life, offered his own bed to the invalid, which was accepted with poor grace – Rougham claimed he did not want to return to Gonville a few houses at a time. But he slept readily enough, and Bartholomew thought he should be able to complete his journey the following day. Meanwhile, Michael went to summon beadles to collect Eudo before the tenant regained his senses. He found Tulyet first, and they returned within moments. The Sheriff, clad in his finest clothes, stepped carefully through the rainbow spillages that adorned Weasenham's once-pristine floor.

'So,' he said, watching his men haul Eudo away. 'You deliver me a pair of thieves, but no killer.'

'A *pair* of thieves?' asked Michael. 'You caught Boltone?'

'He ran right into my arms. He was covered in blood – just like you, Matt. Are you hurt?'

'My best red ink,' said Weasenham sadly, gazing at Bartholomew's tabard as though he was contemplating wringing it out to see what he could salvage. 'What a waste! You will not get it off, either, and Agatha will be furious. Do not tell her it happened in my shop. I do not want her storming in and waving her sword at *my* throat.'

'How do you know she has a sword?' asked Bartholomew.

'I have seen it. She thinks she can slip past my house unseen when she goes to her lover, but she cannot. I know the way she walks, even when she wears Langelee's cloak.'

'My cloak?' came a familiar voice from the doorway. It was Michaelhouse's Master, and Alyce Weasenham was behind him. 'Why would Agatha wear my cloak?'

'Where have you been?' Weasenham demanded of Alyce. 'You said you would only be gone an hour, and you have been away all night.'

Langelee had the grace to blush, but Alyce began a

412

convoluted tale about being caught in a spring shower, taking shelter in a church, and then waking to find herself locked in.

'I have only just been released,' she concluded defiantly, while Tulyet raised laconic eyebrows and Michael sniggered.

'It is true,' said Langelee, gallantly stepping in to defend her virtue. 'We did indeed pass the . . .' He trailed off as Alyce shot him a withering glance.

'*We?*' asked Weasenham immediately. 'You mean you were with her?'

'Fortunately, yes,' said Langelee, brazening it out. 'I was able to reassure her that she would be reunited with you at first light, or she may have become hysterical.'

Alyce did not look like the kind of person who would lose her wits about being shut in a church, but no one said anything, and there was a short, uncomfortable silence. Then Langelee muttered something about being wanted at Michaelhouse, and escaped while he was still able.

'I needed you last night, Alyce,' said Weasenham reproachfully. 'I have been held hostage for hours, and I kept expecting you to come and rescue me. In the end Michael, Bartholomew and Rougham obliged, although they made a dreadful mess as they did so.'

Alyce gazed around her. 'This will not impress the Archbishop, and the word is that he is less than a mile outside the town. He will be here at any moment.'

'That is true,' said Tulyet, moving towards the door. 'And we still have a great deal to do. The Visitation will have to take place with this killer on the loose, because I do not think Eudo and Boltone are our culprits. They are not clever enough.'

'No,' agreed Michael. 'They were with Chesterfelde when he died, and tried to have the Oxford men blamed for it, but they did not kill Hamecotes, Gonerby or Okehamptone, and nor did they frighten Spryngheuse into taking his own life. Our list of suspects is growing shorter.'

'Who is still on it?' asked Tulyet.

'Polmorva, Duraunt and the merchants,' said Michael. 'And some of the Fellows from King's Hall – Norton, Wolf and Dodenho, whose silver astrolabe ended up in Eudo's hoard.'

'I have no idea what happened to that,' mused Weasenham. 'It was a pretty thing, so I put it in my chest upstairs, but . . .' He realised what he had just admitted in front of the Sheriff and the Senior Proctor, and the colour drained from his face yet again. Bartholomew felt sorry for him: he was not having a good morning.

'You swore you had handed *all* your findings to me,' said Tulyet sternly. 'Now you confess that you kept certain articles?'

'Only the astrolabe,' protested Weasenham, horrified at himself. 'And only briefly – I do not have it now. Alyce thinks one of our customers must have made off with it.'

Tulyet grimaced in disgust, then turned to Michael. 'Who else have you eliminated from your enquiries, other than Eudo and Boltone?'

'Clippesby. He was with Matt when one attack took place, so he is in the clear.'

'Where is he?' asked Tulyet. 'Brother Paul sent me a message saying he escaped last night.'

'I have no idea,' said Michael.

'Well, you should find him as soon as possible,' advised Tulyet. 'Personally, I believe we are not looking for a single killer, but a man who uses others to help him. It is the only way he could have perpetrated all these evil deeds, and you may find Clippesby is his accomplice.'

'I do not think so,' said Bartholomew, although he was aware of an uneasy sensation in the pit of his stomach.

Surely, Clippesby could not be guilty after all they had been through?

'You had better be sure,' warned Tulyet. 'This killer is ruthless and cold blooded, and he knows exactly what he wants. I suspect he manipulates people and, if you have hidden Clippesby somewhere, thinking to protect him, you may find yourselves in grave danger.'

'God's teeth!' muttered Michael, emerging from the stationer's shop and looking to where folk lined the High Street, as if anticipating that the King himself might ride down it. He watched Tulyet's men trying to move them back, but it was difficult when people were so determined to secure themselves a good view; they jostled and shoved, and in places they blocked the road completely. Tulyet's expression was anxious, and Bartholomew sensed something in the air that had not been there earlier: an aura of menace. 'I wish we had the wolf locked up in the Castle, not Eudo and Boltone. They are nothing.'

'I am not so sure,' said Tulyet, scanning one of the proclamations. 'If they had succeeded in distributing these, the Archbishop might have experienced at first hand how uneasy this town can be. They have accused the University of the most despicable of acts, and scholars would have fought to protect their honour. These would have caused a riot for certain.'

Michael disagreed. 'No one would fight over this rubbish: it is too ridiculous. For example, it claims Chancellor Tynkell is a demon, because he has an aversion to water.'

'I have always wondered why he never washes,' said Tulyet dryly. 'Now all is clear.'

'And it says King's Hall is full of men who cannot read,' said Michael. 'They would not fight over that, because it is true.'

'It also says the Senior Proctor eats seven meals a day at six different Colleges,' said Bartholomew, taking the parchment from Tulyet and reading it properly for the first time. He started to laugh.

'Scurrilous lies,' snapped Michael, trying to snatch it from him.

'But here is something that is neither amusing nor untrue,' said Bartholomew, pulling it back, so it tore. He glanced at Michael with a troubled expression, his jocundity evaporating. 'It says that the University is harbouring a killer, and it is only a matter of time before more Cambridge men fall victim to his lust for blood.'

'*More* Cambridge men?' echoed Tulyet. 'I thought the only people to have died so far were from Oxford: Gonerby, Okehamptone, Chesterfelde and Spryngheuse.'

'And Hamecotes,' said Michael. 'From King's Hall.'

'But no one should know about him,' said Bartholomew. 'Certainly not Eudo and Boltone, who have been hiding in the Fens these last few days. So, either someone from King's Hall told them about Hamecotes's fate, or the murderer did.'

'No scholar from King's Hall would spread this tale,' said Michael. 'Which leaves the killer.'

'Are you sure they are different?' asked Bartholomew uneasily.

Tulyet was angry at the notion. 'Damn these scholars! They had better not do anything untoward when Islip is here, not after all the trouble the town has taken to impress the man.'

'No one will produce a set of teeth and attack an Archbishop in broad daylight,' said Michael soothingly. 'So far, the killer has only claimed his victims during the hours of darkness. We will need to be on our guard tonight, but not now.'

'Not true,' argued Tulyet, unappeased. 'Gonerby was

murdered in the day, when the streets were awash with rioting people, and there was a witness who saw everything.'

'Possibly,' said Bartholomew. 'But the witness is Polmorva, who may have lied about the timing of the murder – and who may even be the wolf himself.'

Michael nodded. 'It would explain why the wolf tried to kill you, too. Polmorva would slit your throat in an instant, if he thought he could get away with it. He hates you with a passion.'

'I want this clear in my mind,' said Tulyet. 'Chesterfelde's death was an accident, and has nothing to do with "the wolf", as you so prosaically call him. We can forget Eudo and Boltone, because all they did was steal from Merton and try to kill you with a spade. But we still have Gonerby, killed in Oxford, and Hamecotes and Okehamptone, killed here. The wolf made an attempt to disguise both deaths – Okehamptone's by making sure Matt went nowhere near the corpse; Hamecotes's by hiding his body and sending false messages to friends claiming he was buying books.'

'Hamecotes may have sent at least one of those himself,' said Michael. 'His room-mate Wormynghalle seems certain they were penned by his own hand.'

'Oxford and King's Hall,' said Tulyet. 'The wolf retrieved Hamecotes from an Oxford-owned cistern and took the corpse to King's Hall. It is not easy to wander in and out of Colleges, with porters on guard and territorial students all over the place, so I suspect that Matt is right: whoever put him there was a King's Hall man.'

'You are right,' agreed Bartholomew, thinking hard. 'And only a King's Hall scholar would know which of the outbuildings was abandoned, too.'

'But he did not,' said Michael. 'He selected one used by Dodenho, and his secret was out.'

'Does this exonerate Dodenho, then?' asked Bartholomew. 'He found the body and told his colleagues about
it. If he were the wolf, then he would have kept quiet about
it.'

'Not necessarily,' said Michael. 'He could not expect to
keep a corpse hidden there for ever, especially with
summer on the way. He would know it was only a matter
of time before someone noticed an odd smell and went
to investigate.'

'And several people knew the shed was used exclusively
by him, so it would not have been long before fingers were
pointed,' acknowledged Bartholomew. 'You are right.
Dodenho could be covering his tracks by "finding" the
body.'

'There is something odd about him,' said Tulyet. 'It
would not surprise me to learn that he is the wolf. His
crude attempts at scholarship are all anyone ever remembers about him, but perhaps he is more clever than we
suspect, and he feigns stupidity because he thinks it will
hide his true character. But other members of King's Hall
are equally suspect: Paxtone, because he is a physician –
they travel a lot and bloody throats do not bother them;
Warden Powys because he is Welsh and the Welsh are
often abused in Oxford – he may have wanted to avenge
the honour of his countrymen; Norton because he is no
more a scholar than I am, and has no business being
here.'

'And Wormynghalle because he is *too* scholarly,'
suggested Michael. 'Wolf, because he is missing and no
one knows where he is.'

They glanced up as distant trumpets sounded, and all
along the High Street people began to speak a little louder.
The Archbishop was drawing closer.

'Wolf,' mused Bartholomew. 'It was Clippesby who
started referring to the killer as "the wolf". I assumed he

was talking about an animal, but I wonder if he was actually referring to the name.'

Michael sighed. 'Damn Clippesby and his obtuse way of seeing things! Of course it is Wolf. It makes sense now: Wolf is a King's Hall man, who travelled to Oxford, and who has been missing since the first of the Cambridge murders.'

'We have no time to discuss this now,' said Tulyet, beginning to move away. 'The Archbishop is almost here, and I must be there to greet him. You, too, Brother. And Matt should change his tabard before someone sees it and thinks either he has stabbed someone or has indulged in particularly gruesome surgery. Either may result in a skirmish, and that is something we must avoid at all costs.'

They hurried along the High Street, Michael walking in front of Bartholomew in an attempt to disguise the mess of red on his chest. However, even easing politely through the crowd drew hostile glances. Bartholomew was shoved in the back as he passed a tinker, and was only saved from falling because Michael was in the way. The physician heard bitter comments about Oxford men bringing murderous and dishonest ways to Cambridge, and supposed the rumour-mongers had made it known that *he* had once studied in Oxford.

When they parted at the High Street's junction with St Michael's Lane, Tulyet stopped and called back to them. 'I have just remembered something – I should have mentioned it before, but all this noise distracted me. When he was arrested, Boltone blamed Eudo for the dishonest accounting *and* for Chesterfelde. He also claimed someone else told Eudo what to write in the proclamations.'

'Who?' asked Michael. 'Wolf?'

Tulyet shrugged. 'He just said it was someone from King's Hall.'

*   *   *

419

Bartholomew ran down the lane towards his College, Michael puffing at his side. The porter opened the door, and Bartholomew saw that he, Michael and Tulyet were not the only ones to detect the atmosphere of unease among the townsfolk: Langelee also knew that large gatherings of people might result in trouble, and had taken the appropriate precautions. The gates were secured with heavy bars, and barrels had been filled with water and stood in rows near the hall, in case of fire. All the porters and servants were armed – and silently resentful that they were obliged to remain inside, when they could have been on the High Street admiring the pageantry.

'We will change into our finery and look for Wolf among the crowds,' panted Michael. 'I will not let him harm the Archbishop and damage my University.'

'I do not like the aura of unrest that pervades the town this morning,' said Langelee, coming to speak to them. 'Do you think this killer will attack Islip in order to thwart our chances of gaining his favour? Is he an Oxford man?'

'He probably has connections to the place,' said Michael, hurrying to don his best habit. 'I do not understand why he has committed these crimes, but I intend to stop him from harming anyone else. We can discuss his motives tomorrow, when he is safely inside the Castle prison.'

Bartholomew hauled off his ink-stained tabard and called for Agatha to give him his spare. It was in the process of being laundered, and he hoped she had not been as tardy with it as she had with Langelee's cloak. She hurried from the kitchens to hand it to him. He pulled it over his head and straightened it impatiently, while Langelee regarded him in dismay.

'You are not going to meet Islip in that, are you? He will think we are paupers!'

'Surely that is a good thing?' said Bartholomew,

unwilling to admit he did not own another. 'If he sees we have no money, he might give us some.'

'Interesting point,' said Langelee, looking down at his own ceremonial robes, then glancing at Michael, who was resplendent in a cloak of soft black wool. 'I shall have to change. It is a pity, because Alyce said I cut rather a fine figure in this, but it cannot be helped, and it is all in a good cause.'

'He knows,' warned Michael, before the Master could leave. 'Weasenham knows about you and Alyce.'

'Not much escapes his attention,' agreed Agatha, not entirely pleasantly.

'True,' conceded Langelee with a sigh. 'I knew our happiness could not last for ever. But now is not the time to discuss it. I hear Clippesby has escaped.'

'Yes,' said Michael. 'But we do not need to concern ourselves about him, and especially not today. We are fairly certain our killer is Wolf of King's Hall. Clippesby may only be his accomplice.'

There was another blast of trumpets, much closer this time, and Bartholomew could hear the rhythmic rattle of drums. The Archbishop was obviously intent on putting on a spectacle for the people of Cambridge, with music and a procession of handsomely attired churchmen and their scribes. He was sure it would be remembered for years to come, and only hoped the memories would be pleasant ones, and not of a murder that had taken place during it.

'Really?' asked Langelee. 'Wolf did go missing at about the right time, but I understood it was because he had a pox.'

'Only according to Weasenham,' said Agatha. 'But Clippesby has been talking about wolves these last three weeks, and he is no fool. I thought he meant animals, but he must have referred to Wolf the man.'

'How do you know?' pounced Michael. 'You have not seen him since he was sent to Stourbridge.'

Agatha regarded him coolly. 'I visited him. I know he *sounds* deranged, but to my mind he is far more sane than the rest of you most of the time. I need a word, Matthew, in private.' She gave him a monstrous wink that immediately secured Michael's keen attention.

'Why?' asked Bartholomew warily. 'Do you need a consultation?'

'Yes,' she replied, giving another indiscreet leer. 'But not the kind you are thinking about. I want to tell you something about a mutual friend.'

'Clippesby?' he asked in alarm. 'What has he done?'

'He has gone out. He—'

'Gone out from where?' demanded Michael. He gazed accusingly at Bartholomew. 'You have not been telling me the truth, my friend! You said he ran away after he saved you from the wolf, but that is not true, is it? You helped him to hide. And where safer than Michaelhouse, where there are strong walls and a sturdy gate to protect him?'

'I did not lie,' said Bartholomew defensively. 'You jumped to conclusions.'

'But you did not correct me. Are you insane? What if the rumour spreads that Clippesby is the killer, and people discover he is here? We will be in flames in an instant, and not even the Archbishop of Canterbury will be able to save us.'

'Do not exaggerate,' said Bartholomew uneasily. 'No one but Tulyet knows Clippesby was a suspect, and Rougham will say nothing. Clippesby is in more danger *from* others than he is *to* them.'

'He is right,' declared Agatha. 'And he promised to stay in Matthew's room, with the College cat for company.'

'I do not like the use of the past tense here,' said Bartholomew worriedly. 'Where has he gone?'

'He said he had been thinking about your mystery all morning, and he had reached a conclusion. He was wildly excited when I took him larded oatcakes a short while ago, and was talking about the wolf.'

'Then Tulyet was right after all,' said Michael. 'Clippesby has always known more about these killings than he should have done, and now it is clear why: he *is* the wolf's accomplice. Tulyet said the wolf could not have managed alone and needed help, and now I see who provided it: Clippesby, who is too addled to know the difference between good men and bad.'

'He knows the difference,' said Agatha angrily. 'He knows it better than you.'

'You have done him a grave disservice by helping him escape, madam,' said Michael, rounding on her. 'Your actions may lead him to commit another crime – or one he will be blamed for, whether he is responsible or not. And Michaelhouse may be forced to bear that responsibility with him.'

'Damn!' muttered Langelee. 'There goes our benefaction from Islip.'

'He said he left something in your chamber, Matthew,' said Agatha, treating Michael to a glower for his accusations. 'He said that you would understand what it was, and that you should go to Merton Hall as soon as possible.'

'Damn the man!' exclaimed Michael furiously. 'And today, of all days!'

Bartholomew darted towards his room, heart pounding as he wondered what the Master of Music and Astronomy could have left for him that would induce him to go to Merton Hall. It did not bode well for Clippesby's innocence. He wrenched open his door, then stopped in mute horror, so abruptly that Michael piled into the back of him and made him stagger. In the middle of the bed was a single object: a set of metal teeth.

CHAPTER 12

'I told you so!' gasped Michael as he hurried along the High Street with Bartholomew and Langelee in tow. 'Clippesby is our man. All this rubbish about the wolf was a ruse. There is no wolf. If Wolf is involved, then it is as a victim, and he is floating in a well somewhere with his throat bitten out.'

Bartholomew was finding it difficult to move as quickly as he wanted. People had poured into the town from the surrounding villages, and they blocked his way. Everyone was wearing his or her best clothes, so dull homespun browns and creams were virtually absent, and the streets were alive with tunics and kirtles of red, yellow, green, blue, orange and purple. There was a heady scent of perspiration and perfumes, and the more usual aroma of sewage was almost entirely absent. People's faces were intense, determined to see, touch or even speak to England's leading churchman, and Bartholomew was painfully aware that many of them would go to considerable lengths to ensure they did so. He heard townsfolk muttering about scholars monopolising the Archbishop, and scholars mumbling back that Islip's time was too valuable to waste on layfolk. It did not bode well for the Visitation passing off peacefully.

'It was not Clippesby who attacked me at Stourbridge,' said Bartholomew, trying to move through the crowd without jostling anyone and concentrate on refuting Michael's conclusions at the same time. 'I was sitting on top of him when that happened.'

'Dick was right: there are two of them,' said Michael breathlessly. 'Clippesby and someone else. I allowed myself to be influenced by your arguments, which were based on sentimentality: you are fond of the man and wanted him to be innocent. But he is not.'

'All I can say is thank God you did not treat him at Michaelhouse,' said Langelee. 'Perhaps *that* is why he ordered his accomplice to kill you: you are the reason he was exiled to Stourbridge.'

'Then why did he hit the wolf with a stone and drive him away?' asked Bartholomew, aware of the increase in noise as Islip's procession drew nearer. 'He saved my life.'

'That is probably how he wanted it to look,' argued Langelee. 'You have said all along that the killer is cunning, and Clippesby is a very clever man, for all his madness. Only a devilish mind would have thought to fish Hamecotes from the cistern and dump him in King's Hall before Tulyet's men reached it. And we know from Brother Paul that he has escaped several times.'

'This is a damned nuisance,' grumbled Michael, aware that his finery was becoming drenched in sweat. 'I should be greeting the Archbishop, not chasing lunatics.'

'Why does Clippesby want us to go to Merton Hall?' asked Langelee of Bartholomew. 'He told Agatha you would understand. Do you?'

'No – unless he has guessed the identity of the killer, and knows it is someone staying there.' A sense of unease gripped Bartholomew. 'I hope he does not attempt to confront the wolf alone.'

'Clippesby is the killer, Matt,' repeated Michael doggedly. 'And he has summoned us to engage in some kind of confrontation, after which he imagines he will emerge triumphant. We shall have to be careful he does not draw us into a trap.'

The bell of St Mary the Less began to toll, indicating

that the Archbishop and his entourage had reached the Trumpington Gate. The massive cheer that went up from the crowd was audible, even at the Great Bridge.

'He is here,' said Langelee grimly, as more trumpets blasted. 'A grand gate-opening ceremony has been arranged before Islip enters the town officially, which means we have about an hour before he reaches St Mary the Great.'

'We *must* have Clippesby under lock and key before then,' said Michael. 'All of us – Masters, Fellows and certainly the Senior Proctor – are supposed to attend a service of thanksgiving before Islip processes to the Hall of Valence Marie for a feast. I do not want Clippesby seeing him as his own personal meal, and using his teeth on the man.'

'We have the teeth,' Bartholomew pointed out, feeling them bang up and down in his medical bag as he moved. 'The killer cannot bite anyone without them.'

'He may apply his own,' said Michael, struggling to keep up with his more agile colleagues.

Bartholomew saw the monk's flushed face and heaving chest, and slowed further still, not wanting him to have a seizure. He pulled the steel fangs from his bag as he walked, and inspected them properly for the first time. They were more or less how he remembered them, although they were tarnished with age. The only difference was that the incisors had been honed to a vicious sharpness – keen enough to draw blood even from the lightest touch. They were expertly made, and the hinges on either side were well oiled and in good working order. Uncomfortably, he wondered how they had come to be in Cambridge, and kept returning to the same conclusion: Duraunt had brought them. He had not destroyed them, as he had claimed, but had kept them for some reason he had declined to share.

They arrived at Merton Hall to find it strangely deserted. No servants were in the grounds; Bartholomew supposed they had all gone to watch the Archbishop. The silence was unsettling, and he thought Michael was right to be worried about a trap. The monk hammered on the door, then opened it when there was no answer. He leaned against a wall to catch his breath, and indicated with a wave of his hand that Bartholomew and Langelee should look upstairs. While they obliged, he used the time to inspect a pile of saddlebags that were packed and waiting by the door.

Bartholomew and Langelee crept up the stairs and entered the hall. Bartholomew held one of his surgical knives, while the Master produced a massive ornamental dagger with a jewel-studded hilt. The hall was empty, so they aimed for the solar. When Bartholomew hauled open the door, Langelee shot inside with his weapon raised, but no one was there. The grubby possessions of Eudo and Boltone were still scattered around, but there was no sign of the three merchants or the two surviving scholars. By the time they had finished searching the house, Michael had been through the saddlebags.

'These belong to Duraunt and Polmorva,' he said, pointing at the smallest two. 'There is poppy juice in one and an academic tabard in the other. I think they intend to slip away during the Visitation.'

'What about the others?' asked Bartholomew, hoping the monk was wrong, although flight at such a time looked suspicious, to say the least.

'They belong to the merchants, judging by their contents,' replied Michael. 'Do you think this means they have a culprit to take back to Gonerby's vengeful widow?'

'You mean Clippesby?' asked Bartholomew in alarm. 'I hope they have not harmed him, on the grounds that it will be safer to take a corpse than a live victim.'

'He told us to come here,' said Langelee, annoyed. 'But the place is empty. Was he trying to draw us away, do you think, sending us chasing shadows so he can kill the Archbishop more easily?'

'No,' said Bartholomew shortly. 'He does not want to kill Islip. Why would he do such a thing in sight of the entire town? It would ensure he is incarcerated permanently – assuming, of course, that he is captured alive and Tulyet's men do not shoot him.'

'He is mad,' explained Langelee. 'He does not see things in the same light as you and I.'

Bartholomew shook his head. 'He wanted us here for a reason, and I will not leave until I know what it is. I am going to search the grounds. Will you come with me?'

'No, I will go to tell Tulyet what has happened,' said Langelee, beginning to move away. He called back over his shoulder. 'If you do find Clippesby, do not let him escape again. We will send him to this hospital in Norfolk first thing tomorrow.'

When he had gone, Bartholomew led Michael through Merton Hall's vegetable plots. They were still and silent, contrasting starkly with the colour and movement along the High Street. A blackbird suddenly flapped away from a patch of peas, squawking its agitation and making them jump in alarm. And then it was gone, leaving them grinning in rueful amusement at the way it had startled them so badly.

They were almost at the end of the garden, near the Bin Brook and the cistern, when they heard the first sound. It was a voice and a splash. Raising his hand to warn Michael to take care, Bartholomew inched forward, watching where he put his feet, so he did not step on a dead twig and warn Clippesby – or whoever was there – that he was coming. Michael was less cautious, and there was a loud crunch as he trod on a snail. It sounded like

428

thunder in the otherwise silent garden, and Bartholomew turned to give the monk an agonised scowl.

'That is far enough,' said a soft voice. 'Do not move, or it will be the last thing you do.'

Bartholomew looked around slowly, and was startled to see a woman standing there. She wore a white wimple, while a light veil covered her nose and mouth in a fashion that had been popular among ladies some ten years before. Bartholomew looked hard at her, and saw a fair curl that was redolent of Alyce Weasenham. Her long blue kirtle accentuated the attractive curves of her sensual figure, and he was not surprised Langelee had been lured by her charms. But, at that moment, he was more concerned by the fact that she held a bow, and that she handled it in a way that suggested she knew how to use it. Around her shoulders was a quiver containing more arrows, and from its position Bartholomew sensed she could whip out a second one even as the first sped towards its target.

'Where is Clippesby?' demanded Michael. He took a step forward, then stopped when a quarrel thudded into the ground at his feet. As Bartholomew had anticipated, she had nocked another missile into her bow before the astonished monk had looked up from the spent one. 'There is no need for that,' he objected.

'Do as you are told,' she snapped. 'Or the next one will be through your heart.'

Her determined eyes, and the way her hands were absolutely steady on her weapon, convinced both scholars that she was in earnest.

'Help!' came a weak voice from the cistern. Bartholomew saw that the heavy lid preventing leaves and other debris from falling inside the well had been replaced since Tulyet's dredging. All that was open was the square hatch, which allowed a bucket to be raised and lowered. And someone had evidently gone through it.

'Who is it?' he asked, taking a tentative step forward. The woman did not object, so he took another, and another, until he was able to see. What he saw shocked him.

Four white faces gazed at him. They belonged to Polmorva, Duraunt, Eu and Abergavenny. The water was not far from the top of the well, but the walls were still slick, preventing anyone from climbing out. The lid made matters worse: it was so heavy that no one would be able to raise it from within. He heard Michael's horrified gasp as he recalled his own recent experiences.

'That witch has blocked the outflow,' called Polmorva desperately. 'It is only a matter of time before enough water floods in to drown us. There is no escape and we are too far away for our cries to be heard.'

'There is always that nosy child,' said 'the witch'. 'Perhaps his mother will bring him home from the Archbishop's parade early, but perhaps she will not. At least you have a chance of life down there. You will die for certain if I shoot you.' She waved her bow to indicate that Bartholomew and Michael were to join the Oxford men.

'No,' said Michael. His voice was unsteady and there was a sheen of sweat on his face. 'I am not going in there again. Loose an arrow at me if you will, but I will not jump in the pit.'

'I will not shoot you,' she said softly, swinging her bow round to point at Bartholomew. 'I will kill your friend. You do not want him to die because you decline to obey a simple instruction, do you?'

'Why are you doing this, Alyce?' asked Michael, desperately trying to buy time in the distant hope that Langelee might bring Tulyet to scour Merton Hall's grounds for the missing Clippesby. But Bartholomew knew Tulyet and

Langelee thought the killer intended to strike at the Archbishop, and would never abandon their duties protecting him to engage in a search a mile away from the Visitation. 'Are you this wolf, who kills with metal teeth?'

'How is it that you think you know my name?' she demanded in her turn.

'Your veil does not hide your eyes,' replied Michael. 'What are you hoping to achieve by condemning us to such a dreadful death? To run off with Langelee? I can tell you now that he will not go. He likes being Master of Michaelhouse, and has already annulled one marriage to ensure he can continue. You will never be more than something pleasant to occupy his spare time.'

'Shut up and get in the well,' she ordered, beginning to draw on her bow. Her aim was unwavering, and Bartholomew was under no illusions of survival once she had loosed the thing.

He glanced inside the cistern, and saw water lapping not far from the top. Abergavenny was struggling to hold Duraunt high enough for him to breathe, while Eu and Polmorva were gasping and retching. It was an ugly way to go, and he knew Polmorva was right: they could shout and scream all they liked, but no one would hear them, particularly on the day of the Visitation, where every soul was watching the ecclesiastical pageant and cheering at the top of his voice.

Michael edged towards the hatch, and threw Bartholomew an agonised glance. The monk swallowed hard, and Bartholomew saw he was shaking as he sat slowly on the well's low wall.

'Where is Wormynghalle?' the monk asked, lifting one leg so it trailed in the water. He could not prevent a shudder as wetness lapped across his foot. 'Has he escaped? If so, then he will raise the alarm. Give yourself up, before any more damage is done.'

'Wormynghalle is fetching horses,' said Polmorva, shivering partly from the cold, but mostly from fear. He also saw the advantage of talking, to keep the hatch open for as long as possible. 'For their escape. They are in this together.'

'Wormynghalle and *her*?' asked Michael in surprise.

Eu spat water from his mouth. 'The tanner is too recently rich to be trustworthy. I should never have agreed to travel with such a man – such a *killer*.'

'I do not understand,' said Michael, making no move to jump. 'Are you saying *Wormynghalle* murdered Gonerby, Okehamptone and Hamecotes?'

'I witnessed Gonerby's death,' said Polmorva, coughing as Abergavenny tried to find a better way to hold Duraunt, and the water was churned into waves that slopped into his face. 'The killer was not Wormynghalle, because I would have recognised his shape. But it could have been that witch. The villain wore a cloak with a hood, but he was the right size and height to have been her.'

'Then it is good you will not live to tell anyone about it,' she said coldly. 'But you knew little to put us at risk. My brother and I never had anything to fear from you.'

'Your brother?' asked Michael, startled. 'You are Wormynghalle's sister? But he is too fat and pig-like to be related to you.'

'Insult me again and I shall shoot you myself,' came another voice from the path. The woman did not look around, but moved to one side as Wormynghalle came to stand by her side. They exchanged a brief glance, and Bartholomew saw with a sinking heart that the tanner also held a bow.

'I might have known your motives were sinister,' said Eu in disgust. 'An upstart family like yours can know no honour. You are two of a kind – ambitious, greedy and cowardly.'

Wormynghalle raised his bow, his face flushed with fury, but his sister poked him with her elbow, and indicated he was to lower his weapon. Bartholomew was astonished that an aggressive, confident man like Wormynghalle should take orders from a woman, but she was most definitely the one in charge. The tanner hesitated for a moment, then trained the bow on Michael. His sister's, meanwhile, had never wavered from Bartholomew.

'We leave today,' she said. 'I can do no more in Cambridge, and it is time to go home. Now, for the last time, get in the cistern.'

Michael lifted his other leg over the wall. 'I cannot swim.'

'Then you will die quickly,' she replied.

The water was now very near the top of the well, and Eu, appalled by the grim death that awaited him, decided to take matters into his own hands. Claiming that only Wormynghalles should die like rats, he grabbed the edge of the hatch and started to heave himself out, legs flailing as he fought to gain purchase. Michael scrambled out of the way as both Wormynghalle and his sister brought their bows to bear on the escaping merchant.

'Cover Bartholomew,' she snapped, when the physician, taking advantage of the diversion, ran several steps forward, intending to disarm at least one of them. Wormynghalle obeyed and Bartholomew stopped dead in his tracks when he saw the determined expression on the tanner's face.

'You will not kill me,' said Eu, continuing to climb. 'And I am weary of this charade. When I return to Oxford and report this matter to the burgesses, none of your ignoble clan will ever—'

There was a hiss and a thud. Eu gasped as the arrow struck him in the chest. He gazed down at it in disbelief, then looked up at Wormynghalle before toppling back-wards. There was a splash as he hit the water and sank out of sight. Neither Abergavenny nor Polmorva made any attempt to retrieve the body, while Duraunt began to pray in a frail, weak voice. Meanwhile, Eu's executioner snatched another missile from her quiver and set it in the bow before anyone could do more than stare in horror.

'Who will be next?' she asked, backing away, so she would have plenty of time to notch another arrow, if necessary. 'Abergavenny?'

The Welshman said nothing, but clutched harder at Duraunt. Bartholomew had assumed it was to keep the old man's head above the water, but now he realised Duraunt was being used as a shield. Duraunt, already resigned to his fate, looked as if he did not care.

'Now move,' said Wormynghalle to Michael. 'Hurry, or I shall shoot you where you stand, and you will have no chance of life at all.'

'We have none anyway,' said Polmorva piteously, as Michael sat, very slowly, on the cistern wall and lifted the first of his large legs over it again. 'The Archbishop's parade will go on for hours, and every man, woman and child will be watching it. Even if someone does walk along the towpath, he will not hear us, because of the trumpets and shouting.'

Wormynghalle shrugged. 'A small chance is better than none.'

'You said you could do no more in Cambridge,' said Bartholomew, looking at the cold eyes glittering over the veil. He felt sick when the last piece of the puzzle fell into place: he had finally recognised them. 'But you are not talking about murder. You are talking about your scholarly work.'

'Shut up,' she snapped.

'Joan,' said Bartholomew softly. 'You are not Alyce Weasenham. You are Joan Wormynghalle.'

'You know her?' asked Michael, astounded, moving his leg across the wall as slowly as he could.

434

'It does not matter,' she said, scowling at Bartholomew.

'She is King's Hall's best scholar,' said Bartholomew, hoping to draw her into conversation and give them more time, although he was not sure what he could do with it. 'She will make a name for herself at the greatest universities in the world.'

'She is a scholar?' asked Michael, startled. 'But she is a woman!'

'Exactly!' snapped Joan, rounding on the monk and leaving her brother to cover Bartholomew. 'You think that because I am a woman I am incapable of rational thought? Well, I am not, and some of my mathematical theories have been very well received by my peers.'

'Then why do this?' asked Bartholomew reasonably. 'You are as good as a man – better than most – and your prospects are endless. Why jeopardise them?'

'I am jeopardising nothing. You are the only one who knows my secret, and you will not live to tell it. I shall return to Oxford today, and secure myself a Fellowship at a new College – Balliol this time, I think – and later I shall move to Salerno. As I told you before, as long as I am transient, and do not allow anyone to know me too well, I can continue this life indefinitely.'

'It is all she has ever wanted,' said her brother. 'And I like to see her happy. She tried a term at Oxford last year, to see if she could carry it off, and was so successful that she decided to come here. As you saw for yourself, she is very convincing.'

'I am confused,' said Michael. 'Is this John Wormynghalle of King's Hall, wearing a kirtle to disguise himself as a woman? Or does Joan Wormynghalle dress like a man?' He frowned. 'And perhaps more importantly, have we just deduced that he . . . she is our killer?'

'I should have guessed you two were related,' said Bartholomew, angry with himself for not seeing something so transparently obvious. 'I should not have fallen for your tale of choosing the name of a wealthy Oxford merchant who you thought would never visit Cambridge. You simply changed your Christian name – John for Joan.'

'Congratulations,' said Joan coldly. She raised her eyebrows at him. 'But how did you recognise me? I thought my disguises were good.'

'Your eyelashes,' replied Bartholomew. 'And I am a physician, well able to tell the difference.'

Joan sneered at him. 'Hardly! It took a grab before you were able to work it out.'

'It could only happen in King's Hall,' muttered Michael, poised over the water but not making the final jump. 'They accept anyone with money, and now it transpires that they even take females.'

'Norton admired your skill as an archer,' recalled Bartholomew, thinking of another reason why he should have guessed her identity – there were not many bow-wielding females in Cambridge.

'I am an excellent shot.' She turned to Bartholomew, and seemed to soften slightly. 'I am sorry, Matt. You were kind to me, not revealing my secret to men who would have seen me burned as a witch. But I have no choice but to dispatch you – if I want to continue my career, that is.'

'I do not understand,' said Bartholomew. 'Polmorva says you killed Gonerby, which means you also killed Hamecotes and Okehamptone, since they died in an identical manner. I see why you killed Hamecotes: he was your room-mate and, although you said he was not observant, he would have had to be singularly dense not to have noticed he was sharing his chamber with a woman.'

'He was not as nice about it as you were,' said Joan. 'He threatened to tell the Warden.'

'Why did you take his body to King's Hall after it had been in the cistern?' asked Michael.

'Because Hamecotes was killed with metal teeth,' replied Bartholomew, when it looked as if Joan would bring an end to the discussion by forcing the monk into the water. It was conjecture, but he hoped that even if he were wrong, she would correct him and delay their deaths until he could think of an argument that might reprieve them. 'She did not want us to associate Hamecotes's murder with Gonerby's, because that would reveal an Oxford connection – and a possible link to her and her brother.'

'I did not anticipate Dodenho stumbling on him quite so soon,' she admitted. 'I thought I had plenty of time to bury him, and planned to let folk assume he had been killed by robbers on the Oxford road. I wash my clothes regularly at the end of the garden, and I have never seen Dodenho using that shed before, despite what I said to you later. It was a shock when he came screeching about his discovery.'

'You forged letters from Hamecotes, claiming he had gone to Oxford,' said Bartholomew. 'He had been there for books before, so no one was surprised when he did it again. But I should have seen something sinister in that explanation long ago – especially after Duraunt told me that Merton never parts with its books.'

'There was no need for you to hide Hamecotes from Tulyet,' said Michael, trying to help Bartholomew occupy her with questions and observations. 'We had already established a link between Gonerby and a Cambridge murder: Okehamptone's. But you did not know that when you dragged a rotting corpse from here to King's Hall; if you had, you could have saved yourself a lot of trouble. So, why did you pick our poor town? Do you intend to set it alight with riots, and ensure our University's suppression?'

'Of course not,' cried Joan, appalled. 'It is not in my interests to see a school flounder, and I do not care whether

437

the Archbishop builds his new College here or in Oxford. I know you think there is a plot to deprive both universities of his beneficence, but you are mistaken. The disturbances on St Scholastica's Day had nothing to do with Islip and his money.'

Michael nodded. 'I imagine you started those because you wanted to kill Gonerby, and a riot provided the perfect diversion.'

'His business was located near the Swindlestock Tavern, and a little civil disorder was a good way to disguise his murder,' acknowledged Joan. Her brother made an impatient sound; he was becoming restless and wanted to be away.

'How did you do it?' asked Bartholomew. 'Pay Spryngheuse and Chesterfelde to start a fight?' A thought occurred to him. 'No, it was the Benedictine! Spryngheuse did not imagine him after all. He was you – another of your disguises. It makes sense now. You needed a screen to conceal Gonerby's murder, and you knew Spryngheuse and Chesterfelde could be goaded into violence.'

'I did not anticipate it would flare up quite so hotly,' said Joan. 'The town was like a tinderbox, and the affray was quickly out of control. I did not intend sixty scholars to die, but it is done and there is no going back. Chesterfelde was no problem, because he was a sanguine sort of man who pushed the whole matter from his mind, but Spryngheuse became obsessed by his Black Monk.'

'So, you decided to hound him to suicide,' said Bartholomew in distaste. 'Your brother helped you appear at times when the others would not see you, and you literally haunted him to death.' He turned to Wormynghalle. 'And the day he died, it was *you* who suggested Spryngheuse went for a walk in these gardens, knowing Joan would be waiting for him.'

'He took little convincing to hang himself,' said Joan,

438

as if it did not matter. 'I am good with logic and I told him he had no choice.'

Wormynghalle looked uneasy, and Bartholomew recalled his curious behaviour during the requiem mass, when Eu had declared the spluttering candle to be a portent of doom. Wormynghalle, like many men, was superstitious. Bartholomew wondered whether he could use the tanner's fears to his advantage.

'Spryngheuse was an insignificant worm,' called Polmorva, doing his part to prolong the discussion when Bartholomew and Michael fell silent. 'Even Duraunt tired of him when he became too big a drain on his poppy juice. It is easy to procure enough for one man's needs, but not two. Eh, Duraunt?'

The elderly scholar's eyes remained closed, but his prayers became more fervent. Bartholomew was disappointed in his old teacher – for his lies as much as his dependence on soporifics.

'Eudo helped, albeit unintentionally, by killing Chesterfelde,' said Joan. 'And then, when Spryngheuse learned that a man was attacked while wearing his cloak, it was the last straw. Justice was served with his death – his and Chesterfelde's – because it was their fault that the chaos escalated. I only wanted Gonerby dead.'

'Why?' asked Bartholomew. 'Did he discover you were a woman when you were at Merton?'

'You are missing a vital piece of information,' called Polmorva. His eyes showed fear, although his voice was steady. 'The Wormynghalles marry well when they can – as Eu said, they are ambitious.'

Bartholomew gazed at Joan, recalling the name of the murdered merchant's wife. 'You are Joan *Gonerby*? But it was she who insisted the burgesses came to catch her husband's killer. Why would you do that, if you were the one who dispatched him in the first place?'

'To rid *me* of a man who blocked my election as Mayor, and who damaged my business,' replied the tanner. 'And because he interfered with *her* ambition to study, by threatening to expose her.'

'I see,' muttered Abergavenny, still keeping Duraunt between him and the bows. 'Gonerby refused to buy your skins to make his parchment, did he?'

'I understand why you accused Matt of Gonerby's murder,' said Michael to Wormynghalle. 'You were trying to confuse me with wild charges and irrational statements of dislike. It was you who said Gonerby was killed with a sword, rather than teeth, too. And you, alone of the merchants, did not want me to look for Gonerby's killer – you were afraid I might find her.'

'As he lay wounded, Gonerby heard Joan advising someone – probably her brother – that she was going to Cambridge,' said Bartholomew. 'And he passed the information to the men who found him dying. Wormynghalle's presence was no coincidence, of course: he was there to prevent Gonerby from saying anything incriminating. But why involve Eu and Abergavenny in this hunt?'

'To lure them to a distant town where they, too, would die,' said Wormynghalle, pleased with himself. 'Like Gonerby, they were going to vote against my election as Mayor, and their removal will see me win.' He raised his bow, and Bartholomew saw he was impatient to use it.

'So, you killed Gonerby to rid yourself of a tiresome husband and an annoying business rival,' gabbled Michael. 'Hamecotes was murdered because he discovered you were a woman, and Spryngheuse because he was unstable. But what about Okehamptone?'

Bartholomew scratched around for the few facts he knew about the scribe's death. Duraunt's prayers had petered out, and Polmorva seemed to have abandoned his delaying tactics. Abergavenny was exhausted from keeping himself and Duraunt above water, while Michael was trying not to reveal the depth of his own terror. Bartholomew saw he was on his own in keeping Joan and her brother occupied until he could conceive of a way to best them. He hoped something would occur to him soon, because he sensed he would not keep them gloating over their successes for much longer.

'It was you who claimed Okehamptone's fever came from bad water on the journey from Oxford,' he said to Wormynghalle. 'It was also your liripipe that hid the fatal wound. You said he had borrowed it, and that you did not want it back – not because it had adorned a corpse, but because it continued to conceal the gash in his throat.'

Wormynghalle addressed his sister. 'I told you strangling was a better way to kill. They would never have deduced all this if you had used a more conventional method of execution.'

Joan shrugged.

'It was you who refused to let Rougham see his friend, too,' Bartholomew continued. 'He said the door was answered by someone with fine clothes and a haughty manner, and we assumed it was Polmorva. But that description applies equally to you.'

'I turned no one away,' said Polmorva, sounding surprised.

'Everyone drank heavily the night Okehamptone died,' continued Bartholomew, wishing Michael would help, because he could not talk and devise an escape at the same time. 'Of wine *you* bought.'

'I should have noticed that,' said Polmorva feebly. 'Every time the tanner provided wine, someone died. But why kill Okehamptone?'

'He overheard us talking the night he arrived in Cambridge,' replied Joan. 'He promised to say nothing, but we killed him anyway, just to be sure. While I disguised the wound on his body, my brother gave the meddlesome Rougham a good fright. He fled to Norfolk, I hear.'

'Is that why you attacked me at Stourbridge?' asked Bartholomew. 'To make sure I did not reveal your secret, even though I gave you my word that I would not?'

'Men break oaths all the time,' said Joan. 'Eu and Abergavenny swore to avenge my husband's death, but were happy to forget their pledge once he was dead. None of you can be trusted.'

'These teeth,' said Bartholomew, removing them from his bag. 'How did you come by them?'

'I gave them to my predecessor at Merton,' said Duraunt, barely audible. 'He used them for years, but he died recently. Then I kept them in my room, but one of my students stole them.'

'You,' said Bartholomew to Joan. 'You studied in Merton – *you* took them.'

'They fascinate me,' admitted Joan. 'And I knew no one would guess *I* had killed my husband if I used the fangs to dispatch him. But they disappeared from my chamber this morning, and I wondered where they had gone. It was you, was it?'

'No,' said Bartholomew, wondering how Clippesby had managed to do it without being seen.

'Well, give them back,' ordered Joan. 'Be careful when you toss them over. I keep them very sharp.'

Bartholomew pulled back his arm and hurled them into the trees as hard as he could. Joan pursed her lips in annoyance.

'It does not matter,' said Wormynghalle. 'We have completed our business here, and it is time to return to a more civilised city. Now, jump in the water, monk.'

Michael began to slide with infinite slowness into the cistern. His face was as white as snow, but he refused to submit to the indignity of begging for his life. When he had gone, Bartholomew looked from Joan to her brother in despair. He suspected he could overpower the tanner, who was overly confident, but Joan was a different proposition. She had approached the problem of loose ends with the same precision she applied to her studies, and would never risk her safety by exercising mercy.

'Eudo,' he blurted, desperately trying to think of some way to delay the inevitable. 'You told him what to write in his proclamation. You chose carefully, so something in it would be certain to incite unrest.'

Joan gave a tight smile. 'I only want the beadles and the Sheriff distracted until we have left. We probably do not need a diversion with the Visitation, but there is no point in being careless.'

'Joan,' Bartholomew began. 'I—'

'No more talk,' said Wormynghalle, pulling back his arm as he aimed his arrow.

Bartholomew willed himself to keep his eyes open and fixed on the man who would kill him. Neither Wormynghalle nor Joan showed remorse or distaste for what they were about to do, and he supposed it was such cold-blooded ruthlessness that had allowed their family to prosper so abruptly.

'Spryngheuse's soul will never let you rest,' he shouted, resorting to desperate tactics. 'He is there, in the trees, watching you sell your soul to the Devil.'

Joan's eyebrows shot up in surprise, but Wormynghalle paled, and his bow wavered. Then there was a loud crack, and he toppled backwards. Without waiting to see how or why, Bartholomew launched himself at Joan, wrenching the weapon from her hands while she watched her brother stagger. She saw instantly that Bartholomew would overpower her with his superior strength, so she abandoned her attempts to retrieve the bow, and grabbed a knife from her belt. She stabbed wildly, and the physician leapt away. With a gasp of horror, he lost his balance and toppled into the cistern, bowling over Michael, who was halfway out.

For a moment, Bartholomew's eyes and ears were full of water. Then he surfaced, gagging and choking. He looked around, anticipating that the lid would be slammed down and he and the others would drown. The level of water was now so high that the heads of anyone inside would be forced under as soon as it dropped, and he braced himself for a final ducking as Joan completed her work. But the hatch remained open, and he was aware of someone thrusting him roughly out of the way to reach the rectangle of light that represented air and life. It was Polmorva, kicking and punching others in his determination to escape.

As Polmorva hauled himself out, Bartholomew expected him to be shot, but nothing happened, so he grabbed Michael, who was floundering nearby, and shoved him to where he could reach the hatch. The monk was strong, despite his lard, and his powerful arms propelled him upward as though he were on fire. Bartholomew saw him glance around quickly before leaning into the cistern to help the others. Duraunt went first, followed by Abergavenny, and Bartholomew last.

Of Joan, there was no sign, and Polmorva had also gone. While Michael hunted for them among the trees, Bartholomew knelt next to Duraunt, who was shivering in a crumpled heap on the ground.

'I recognised her,' the old man said in a whisper. 'As soon as she started talking about her crimes, I recognised her as my brilliant young student who disappeared after a term. She looked different here – her hair is longer and darker. But it was she who stole the teeth from me.'

'Damn those things!' said Bartholomew. 'They have caused problems from the moment they were made.'

'My predecessor had twenty years of pleasure from them,' objected Duraunt. 'Do not be so quick to condemn new ideas, Matthew. One day, many ancients may own devices like those, to make their final years more enjoyable.'

'Never,' vowed Bartholomew. 'No one will want foreign objects in his mouth while he eats.'

'It is a case of what you are used to,' said Duraunt. 'Your fat friend will not decline a set when he wears out his own and he wants to continue to devour good red meat.'

'What happened to the tanner?' asked Bartholomew, suspecting they could argue all day and not agree. He was angry with Duraunt for keeping something that should have been destroyed, and for lying to him about the poppy juice. He felt betrayed, but told himself that Duraunt was just a man, not a saint, and that men had human failings.

'There,' said Abergavenny, pointing.

Bartholomew scrambled towards him, but could see Wormynghalle was dead. There was a graze on the side of his head, where something had struck his temple. It was not a fatal wound, though: the tanner had died because the chain of his sheep's-head pendant had caught on the cistern's pulley and was tight around his neck. He had been stunned, then had hung unconscious while his jewellery deprived him of air. Bartholomew recalled the sharp crack before he had fallen, and glanced around uneasily, wondering whether his words about Spryngheuse's soul had been prophetic. He was not normally given to superstition, but whatever had happened to Wormynghalle had been uncannily timed. He looked up as someone knelt next to him. It was Clippesby, with Michael looming behind him.

'You threw me the teeth as I watched what was happening from the trees,' Clippesby explained. 'I knew exactly what you wanted me to do. Unfortunately, I missed

445

Joan and hit her brother instead. You probably did not intend me to throw them quite so hard, and I am sorry I killed him.'

'Well, I am not,' said Michael fervently. He clapped Clippesby on the shoulder. 'You and Matt saved us with your quick thinking.'

'Not me,' said Bartholomew, realising he should have guessed Clippesby was somewhere close by, doing what he did best as he listened to a conversation undetected.

'Do not be modest,' said Clippesby. 'I would not have known what to do without your prompt. I was beginning to think I might have to watch you die, because I have no idea how to confront people with loaded weapons. Such folk are beyond my understanding.'

'Well, they are not beyond mine,' said Michael grimly. 'And I have a feeling Joan is not finished with us yet. She will not be pleased that you killed her brother, and she knows her life as a scholar is over now. I think she will do something dreadful, to ensure she leaves academia with a flourish.'

'What can she do?' asked Abergavenny reasonably. 'If she has any sense, she will jump on one of her brother's horses and leave while she can.'

'Polmorva took them all,' said Clippesby. 'I saw him tearing along Merton Lane as if the hounds of Hell were after him. He is not a brave man, and his only thoughts were for his own safety once he was free. But it means Joan cannot go anywhere, because she has no transport.'

'Why did Polmorva run?' asked Bartholomew. 'He is not in league with Wormynghalle, is he?'

'Probably because he saw at first hand the trouble murders can bring,' replied Duraunt enigmatically.

Michael frowned. 'What are you saying? That he has it in mind to commit one of his own?'

'I suspect he has been put off by the chaos they cause,'

446

replied Duraunt, still annoyingly obtuse. He relented when he saw Michael's stern expression, realising the time for prevarication was over. 'You are not the only one with whom he has a feud, Matthew. I am fairly sure he had planned to put an end to the Master of Queen's, so he could be elected in his place.'

'Is that why you brought him here?' asked Michael. 'Not because you had developed a friendship with the man, but because you were hoping to prevent a crime?'

'It worked,' said Duraunt with a tired smile. 'I think he will be so grateful to reach home unscathed after this escapade that he will count his blessings, and think of less permanent ways to rid himself of rivals.'

'I do not think Joan will run away, though,' said Bartholomew, more concerned with her than about a man he felt was beneath his contempt. 'Scholarship was her life, and she will never be accepted into a College now. She has nothing left to live for.'

'What do you think she will do?' asked Michael anxiously.

'She will want revenge, and she knows how to get it. She said she did not want the universities suppressed, because she wanted to enrol in them. But she probably thinks that if she cannot study, then others should not have that privilege, either.'

'Yes,' agreed Duraunt sadly. 'That is exactly what my ambitious student would think. She will attack Cambridge – and she will succeed. Look what she did in Oxford.'

'The Visitation!' Michael cried in horror. 'I was right all along. She plans to spoil the Visitation!'

'She has the teeth, too,' said Clippesby unhappily. 'She grabbed them as she fled, and I was too far away to do anything about it.'

'We must stop her,' said Michael, seizing Bartholomew's sleeve. The physician hesitated, worried about Duraunt's pale face and sodden clothes.

'Go, Matthew,' said Duraunt weakly. 'You can visit me later, when you have her safely under lock and key.'

'I will stay with you,' said Clippesby, slipping a hand under Duraunt's arm to help him to his feet. 'I deplore violence, and want no more of it. It serves me right for spending so much time with people today – visiting King's Hall to look for the teeth, then coming here. Animals are not so vicious.'

'Wolf,' said Bartholomew, before following Michael. 'What did you mean when you insisted the killer was a wolf? It was Joan, and she is not wolf-like in the slightest.'

'Joan is not heavy enough to have flattened us both last night: that was her brother,' replied Clippesby. He grimaced. 'She would have been far more efficient, so we are lucky she asked him to do it, and did not come herself. I heard them discussing it this morning, after I left your room and went to meet the Merton Hall geese. She was furious when he told her he had failed.'

'So why did you say the killer was "the wolf"?' pressed Bartholomew.

'Because the man wears a locket around his neck in the shape of a wolf's head. I saw it when he attacked Rougham, and again last night. It fell out of his clothes as he struggled.'

'That is not a wolf,' said Bartholomew, exasperated. 'It is a ram. He is a tanner, and a ram's head is supposed to represent his trade of steeping sheepskins, to make leather.'

'Oh, well,' said Clippesby carelessly. 'It looked like a wolf to me.'

Michael raced towards the High Street as fast as his fat legs could carry him, while Bartholomew strode at his side. They crossed the Great Bridge, where a solitary guard was on duty; his colleagues had been dispatched to deal with the crowds massing for the Visitation.

'Where will she go, Matt?' gasped Michael. His wet

clothes did not make running easy, because his woollen habit was heavy when waterlogged. He stopped to catch his breath, clinging to the physician like a drowning man. 'I do not understand her, so I cannot predict what she might do. Do you think she might attack Islip tonight, thinking we will lower our guard?'

'There are crowds to hide among today. If she is going to act, then it will be now.'

The folk who had gathered to catch a glimpse of the Archbishop stretched as far back along the High Street as St Michael's Church. Bartholomew could tell from the sound of trumpets that the ecclesiastical procession had reached St Mary the Great, where Islip was expected to stop for a few moments, and allow people to view him.

Michael began to shove his way through the crowd, earning hostile glowers as he went. His Benedictine habit protected him from retaliation, although Bartholomew was repaid with one or two hard shoves. The physician did not dare look around, afraid that even a glance might initiate the kind of skirmish that had so damaged Oxford. Every man, woman and child carried a knife for general use, and any fight that broke out would almost certainly end in deaths and ugly injuries.

'Slow down, Brother,' he hissed, as he followed the monk's flailing elbows. 'You will start a riot without Joan's help, if you are not careful.'

'We are almost there,' muttered Michael. 'I beg your pardon, madam. *Pax vobiscum.*' He sketched a blessing at the furious woman he had jostled and gave her one of his best smiles. She relented, although her husband did not, and Bartholomew saw a dagger start to emerge from its sheath. He took a coin from his scrip, hoping it would appease him. It fell to the ground, and the fellow's attention was immediately taken with trying to retrieve it from among the churning feet.

'Here we are,' said Michael in relief. 'St Mary the Great. And there is the Archbishop being greeted formally by Tynkell.'

Bartholomew stood on tiptoe and saw the glorious white robes of the Archbishop, who stood next to the equally splendid Chancellor in his ceremonial red. He saw Islip duck to Tynkell's left, presumably to stand upwind of him. They were flanked by town dignitaries on one side, and the University's most senior Fellows on the other. Surrounding them was a heaving throng of dark-robed students and brightly clad townsmen. It was an uneasy combination, and Bartholomew's only consolation was that they were so tightly crammed together, there was not much room for swinging punches.

'There is Lee,' he said urgently, pointing to one side. 'Rougham's student. And he is far more interested in the silversmith's apprentices than in Islip.'

'Stop him, Matt,' said Michael. 'A fracas is just what Joan is waiting for. She will kill the Archbishop while everyone's attention is on the brawl, just as she has done before. I will warn Islip.'

'There she is!' cried Bartholomew. 'She is talking to Lee!' He watched helplessly as Lee started in surprise, then regarded the silversmith's lads appraisingly. 'She is encouraging him to argue, just as she induced Spryngheuse and Chesterfelde to quarrel in Oxford.'

'Go and grab Lee,' ordered Michael. 'I will get her. Damn it! I cannot see the woman! Where did she go?'

'Next to Father William,' said Bartholomew, trying to move towards his quarry but finding his path blocked by the sheer crush of people. 'Now she is pointing at the Dominicans. She knows what she is doing, Brother: she is aware of how much he hates them.'

'He is heading towards them,' said Michael in alarm.

'And his face is like thunder. She has made up some tale to get him aroused. Do something, Matt!'

'I cannot stop him *and* Lee,' cried Bartholomew, appalled. 'She is making sure there are too many skirmishes for us to control.'

Michael used every ounce of his strength to forge a way through the hordes, smiling benignly and informing people that he was the Senior Proctor and that he needed to reach the front. He sketched benedictions in all directions in the hope of mollifying those he shoved and trod on, but he was leaving a trail of anger behind him nonetheless. Bartholomew heard a merchant telling Paxtone that the monk was a godless oaf, at the same time that William reached the Dominicans and began to hold forth. Meanwhile, Lee and the silversmith's apprentices were already embroiled in a push-and-shove that looked set to spill over into something violent. Bartholomew saw a flash of steel in Lee's hand.

'It is too late!' he shouted. 'She has set her fires and we can do nothing to stop her.'

Michael reached Joan, and one of his meaty hands closed around her shoulder. Bartholomew looked behind him, and saw the Dominicans starting to yell back at William, while Lee's dagger was in his hand and he was waving it at a loutish looking lad who carried a cudgel.

'Help!' screamed Joan. 'I am a Cambridge wife, and I am being ravaged by a scholar! Help me!'

Several townsfolk immediately went to her assistance, and Bartholomew saw the monk quickly surrounded by men who looked ready to show impudent scholars what happened to those who assaulted their women, monastic habits notwithstanding. Meanwhile, one of the Dominicans pushed William hard in the chest, and the friar responded by lashing out with his fist. Michaelhouse's students surged forward to support the Franciscan, while Lee and the others were suddenly engaged in a furious battle. Small fights were beginning to break out elsewhere, too, and Bartholomew watched the unfolding chaos with a sense of helpless despair, knowing there was nothing he could do to prevent a massacre.

'LET US PRAY.'

The voice that cut across the sounds of fighting was so loud and compelling that it stopped a good many brawlers in their tracks. Lee jumped in alarm and the knife dropped from his hand, while the Dominicans and William were stunned into immobility by the words that were such a large part of their lives. Several friars grinned sheepishly at the Michaelhouse students as they placed their hands together in front of them.

'I said, *LET US PRAY*!' boomed Islip again, even more thunderously.

The apprentices looked at each other in bemusement, but obediently lowered their weapons. One or two even knelt, while the students, conditioned by the routine of their daily offices, formed tidy lines and stood with bowed heads. Bartholomew was astounded to see that everywhere people were assuming attitudes of prayer, either standing devoutly or dropping to their knees. The silence was absolute, and all signs of hostility gone, like blossom in a spring gale.

'Help me!' cried Joan in desperation, when she saw her plan about to be thwarted.

The townsmen who had come to her rescue edged away uncomfortably as she shattered the reverent stillness. Michael released his grip and folded his arms, smiling in satisfaction.

'Rape!' shrieked Joan in final desperation, appealing to her rescuers. 'He tried to—'

'Hush!' hissed Lee angrily. 'The Archbishop is praying.'

A communal growl of agreement accompanied his

words, as the crowd indicated that they wanted her to shut up until the great man had finished.

Tulyet approached, and spoke softly in her ear. 'It is over, Joan Gonerby. My men and Michael's beadles are all around you. You cannot escape.'

'Help!' yelled Joan, not one to give up easily, although her face was frightened. Her furious howl drowned Islip's next words, and those around her began to complain, outraged that she should dare to screech over the most venerable churchman in the land.

'Be still, woman!' snapped William. 'I cannot hear what he is saying.'

Joan, seeing she had lost, ducked away from Michael, and people hastily moved out of her way, not wanting to be associated with someone who made a racket during an Archbishop's devotions. Sheriff and Senior Proctor followed. Bartholomew winced when Tulyet tripped her from behind and Michael, to make sure she did not escape again, sat on her. He hurried forward, genuinely afraid she would be crushed to death. Two of Tulyet's sergeants took her arms, and he saw she was limp and unresisting, squashed in spirit, as well as in body, as they hauled her away.

'I said "Peace be with you",' said the Archbishop, in response to William's demand that he repeat himself. Bartholomew glanced at Islip, and saw the faintest of smiles touching his lips as he regarded the confused crowd. 'The usual response is for you all to say that it is also with me.'

'Forgive me, my Lord,' said William, bowing absurdly deeply. 'You spoke English, and I only ever make such responses in Latin. But I shall make an exception for you.'

'Thank you, Father,' said Islip, now unable to suppress the grin. He raised his hands and appealed to the crowd. 'Well come on, then.'

There was a disorganised rumble of voices.

'No,' said Islip patiently. 'You all speak *together*. Loudly and clearly, so I can hear you.'

'And also with you,' bawled William, all on his own.

'Well, that is a start, I suppose,' said Islip. 'Now how about the rest of you?'

Scholars, clerics and townsmen alike exchanged bewildered glances, but did as they were told. Then they did it a second and a third time, until Islip was satisfied. By this time, the beadles had interposed themselves between Lee and his adversaries, and the antagonism between Dominicans and Michaelhouse had been forgotten in the unprecedented phenomenon of making priestly responses to an Archbishop in English. The townsfolk were delighted, and began to shout their appreciation. The scholars joined in, and it was not long before the atmosphere had changed from unease to jubilation.

'That was clever,' said Michael admiringly. 'I heard Islip is a genius, and now I see why he has that reputation. But let us see to Joan. I want her locked up before she tries any more mischief.'

They edged through the cheering crowd until they reached the soldiers who had arrested her. Bartholomew immediately sensed something was wrong. He started to run towards them, but stopped abruptly when he saw Tulyet. The Sheriff's hands were sticky with blood.

'Help her, Matt,' he said.

'I cannot,' said Bartholomew, kneeling to confirm what he already knew just by looking. 'She is already dead.'

'What happened?' asked Michael.

'Those damned teeth,' said Tulyet unsteadily. 'She used them to cut her own throat.'

EPILOGUE

'It was all very simple in the end,' said Michael, as he and Bartholomew sat together on the old apple tree in Michaelhouse's orchard. Clippesby was with them, and Bartholomew was teaching him to juggle with stones. Michael was chewing on a stick in an attempt to assuage the pangs of hunger that racked his portly frame. The Visitation had lasted a week – Islip had left that morning – and Bartholomew was impressed by the way the monk had kept to a rigid dietary regime of his own devising. Michael had been deeply alarmed by his inability to come to his friend's rescue in the stationer's shop, and had taken Brother Thomas's warning to heart. He was determined to be slender.

'Yes,' agreed Clippesby, attempting to juggle and talk at the same time. 'Joan Gonerby wanted to be a scholar, and completed a term at Merton College in Oxford, but her husband disapproved. So, with the blessing of a cunning brother, she instigated a riot that would serve as a way to murder him without anyone knowing what had really happened.'

'Unfortunately, she did not kill him instantly, and he heard her talking about going to Cambridge,' continued Michael. 'He charged Eu and Abergavenny – and Wormynghalle, without knowing his role in the affair – to bring his killer to justice. Then Joan and her brother decided to turn what could have been an awkward situation to their own advantage. We might have had the answer to this sooner, Matt, if you had mentioned that King's Hall was recruiting women. I could have told you no good would come of it.'

'She was an excellent scholar,' objected Bartholomew. 'Besides, I see no reason why women should not be allowed to study.'

'Neither do I,' said Clippesby, throwing his stones in the air. 'Pigs do it, and the world has not tumbled around our ears. There is very little more erudite than a sow, you know.'

'I shall take your word for it,' said Michael shortly. He resumed his analysis before Clippesby could lead them off into some strange world of his own. 'Joan exhorted the merchants to investigate her husband's death, then came to enjoy herself at King's Hall.'

'Polmorva had witnessed Gonerby's murder and was encouraged to accompany the merchants,' said Bartholomew. 'Joan did not care – she knew he had seen nothing of import or she would have killed him – but Duraunt extended the invitation because he thought Polmorva planned to dispatch the Master of Queen's College for personal gain.'

'Wormynghalle wanted Eu and Abergavenny to come, because it was a chance to rid himself of two burgesses who would vote against him as Mayor,' continued Clippesby. 'Duraunt suggested they should all travel together, and offered them accommodation at Merton Hall when he realised they were likely to cause trouble. But why was he so magnanimous? The Merton Hall cat told me he is not an especially good man, just an average one.'

'Because Oxford is under interdict, and he does not want Cambridge to fall into the same pit,' replied Michael. 'Cambridge is Merton's bolt-hole, should Oxford be suppressed or collapse. It is in his interests to preserve Cambridge.'

'So, you were wrong to assume that the Oxford men came to cause trouble,' said Clippesby, jigging and dodging to keep his stones in the air. 'None of them cared anything for Islip and his rumoured foundation. It was something *you* might have done, Brother, but nothing they considered.'

Michael ignored the accusation that he was a schemer. 'As soon as her brother arrived, Joan went to visit him, but she was heard discussing her success by Okehamptone. Joan killed him with her teeth, and they hid the wound, so I would think a fever had claimed him.'

'But Joan knew – probably through Paxtone – that the Senior Proctor has a Corpse Examiner who is thorough,' said Clippesby, putting his hands over his head as his stones plummeted around him. 'So, she arranged for Weasenham to summon Matt for his toothache and prevent him from looking at the body.'

'How did she do that?' asked Bartholomew. 'Weasenham did have toothache, but how did she persuade him to choose me over Rougham, his regular physician?'

'The bat, who lives in Weasenham's roof, told me that Joan promised him all manner of gossip if he did as she asked,' replied Clippesby. 'Then, while her room-mate Hamecotes – who likes green ink and who was always in Weasenham's shop buying it – obligingly fetched you, she regaled him with wild lies to keep her end of the bargain. This all happened a matter of hours before Hamecotes made his devastating discovery about her sex and threatened to expose her.'

'A bat,' said Michael flatly. 'I do not suppose *you* happened to be lurking in the shop at the time, and also heard this chatter?'

'Well, yes,' admitted Clippesby, gathering his stones. 'I was there, too. Joan also made sure that Paxtone was available when you needed a Corpse Examiner, knowing he dislikes touching the dead and would never properly investigate a body. So, that was Okehamptone dealt with. It transpired that Polmorva was the sole beneficiary of his will,

457

which made you suspect him of murder, but he was innocent.'

'The same night, they decided to get rid of Rougham,'
said Bartholomew. 'They were right to try: Rougham would
have made a fuss about his friend Okehamptone's sudden
death. The tanner was supposed to kill Rougham with the
teeth, but he was not as proficient as Joan, and he failed.'

'There was also me,' said Clippesby. 'I disturbed him
before he could finish.'

'Joan probably smeared the teeth with excrement,' said
Bartholomew. 'She knew her brother was not as efficient
as her, and added the filth as insurance against his failure.
Clippesby saw Wormynghalle's medallion during the
attack, which he thought was wolf-shaped.'

'Rougham was lucky you helped him, Matt,' said
Clippesby, hurling the stones in the air again, far too high.
'He is not a good *medicus*, and if he had tried to physic
himself he would be dead for certain. Your kindness came
at high cost, though – for you and Matilde, as well as for
me. It occurred to me to do nothing to ward off the attack,
because he is an unpleasant man who I once saw kicking
a cat, but I found I could not stand by and watch someone
slaughtered.'

'And that was Rougham finished,' said Michael. 'When
he disappeared, they assumed he had run away. The
following day, while he lay gripped by fever in Matilde's
house, Clippesby was sent to Stourbridge. But speaking of
Matilde, it has been a week since you told me of your intention to marry her, Matt. What did she say?'

Bartholomew glared at him. 'You know I have not been
able to see her, because of all the extra duties imposed by
the Visitation.'

'She wants you to ask,' said Clippesby. He smiled shyly
when Bartholomew raised his eyebrows in surprise.
'Edwardus Rex, Yolande de Blaston's dog, often hears

Matilde talking about you. He says she will take you tomorrow, if only you would speak to her about it.'

'I will, then,' said Bartholomew softly. 'I will ask her tomorrow.'

'Good,' said Clippesby. 'Do it straight after prime. I will watch your class until you come back. Do not delay, because Edwardus says she will not wait for ever.' He resumed his juggling, leaving Bartholomew determined to erect some strong gates when he was married, to prevent Clippesby from eavesdropping on Matilde's confidences with her friends again.

'Then Hamecotes died,' said Michael, going back to their analysis. 'Murdered by Joan because he stumbled across her true identity, but was not sympathetic. When Matt unveiled her on Wednesday, she set her brother to kill him, too. She trusted no one.'

'Do not take any notice of what Duraunt said, Matt,' said Clippesby, blanching as one of his rocks landed in Michael's lap. 'He claimed you were insular, because you disapproved of the false teeth. You have your foibles, but who does not?'

'You do, and that is for sure,' muttered Michael, snatching up the stone and threatening to lob it back. Clippesby sat down quickly. 'So, Hamecotes was hidden in the Merton Hall cistern, where she imagined his body would remain for ever. But then Chesterfelde died, killed by a friendship pact, and Matt saw the blood. We asked Tulyet to drain the well, so Joan moved the body to King's Hall, where she anticipated she would have time to work out what to do with it.'

'But Dodenho practised his lectures there, and her secret was out,' said Bartholomew. 'Joan did an excellent job of brazening out the situation. She told us Hamecotes had sent letters, and seemed heartbroken by his death. She had me fooled.'

'Me too,' admitted Michael. 'Meanwhile, she was afraid that Spryngheuse, who was frightened and unstable, would also cause problems. When Chesterfelde died, he became even more distressed, and it was an easy matter for her to don a Benedictine habit and urge him to kill himself.'

'Wormynghalle knew that would work, because he was afraid of spirits himself,' said Bartholomew. 'He ran screaming from the church when your candle went out at Spryngheuse's requiem. But none of these deaths had anything to do with the Visitation. And they had nothing to do with Oxford, either, except for the fact that some of the victims happened to hail from there. Joan tried to bring about a riot by telling Eudo what to put in his proclamation, but that was to create a diversion and allow her to escape, simultaneously leaving her last remaining adversaries to drown.'

'Duraunt really did come to assess how far Boltone had been cheating his College,' said Michael. 'Okehamptone mentioned the deception to him a year ago, but he only acted now, because Oxford is under interdict and it is a good time to inspect distant manors. Chesterfelde also knew about the irregularities, because he was Boltone's accomplice.'

'I was wrong about Duraunt,' said Bartholomew unhappily. 'He drinks, swallows soporifics that he cannot bring himself to share with others, and lies to cover his weaknesses. But he had nothing to do with the murders. He told the truth about that, at least.'

'Norton, Paxtone and Dodenho are innocent, too,' said Michael. 'And the travels of the silver astrolabe are irrelevant – all it did was pass through the hands of some very dishonest men.'

'Nasty,' said Clippesby with a shudder. 'My advice to you is stay away from people, and look to animals. They never lie, nor do they murder. And speaking of animals, Wolf is back.'

'He no longer matters,' said Michael. 'We have all our answers now.'

'Not quite all,' said Clippesby. 'It was *his* hoard Weasenham found – the one with my silver dog and the astrolabe. He is your thief, not Eudo. You know Polmorva sold the astrolabe to Wormynghalle the tanner, then stole it back, and passed it to someone else before it arrived in the cistern?'

'Yes,' said Michael. 'Are you saying Polmorva sold it to Eudo? Why? Eudo is not the kind of man to buy a scientific implement.'

'Polmorva did not *sell* it to Eudo,' said Clippesby. 'He *gave* it, in return for a favour. I watched the transaction myself, and so did the Merton Hall chickens. *And* I, in company with the King's Hall rats, saw Wolf steal it from Eudo one night in the King's Head.'

'Lord!' muttered Michael. 'That thing certainly travels! It is almost as though it is cursed, and can only stay with one owner for a few days. I wonder where it is now.'

'Nowhere,' replied Bartholomew. 'It no longer exists, because Langelee had it melted down to pay for our new gutters.'

'Eudo *was* innocent of the thefts, just as he claimed,' said Clippesby. 'He did not steal the astrolabe. He did not take the silver dog, either – Edwardus saw Wolf do that, when he visited Matilde to beg a remedy for his lover's female pains.'

'Why did Eudo try to kill us at the cistern, then?' demanded Michael. 'It was nothing to do with the fact that Hamecotes was there, either, because he knew nothing about that.'

'Because Matt found Chesterfelde's blood. It was wretched bad luck for Eudo and Boltone that Wolf used the well for his hoard, and that the Wormynghalles used it for Hamecotes.'

461

'And *that* is an odd coincidence, too,' remarked Michael.

'Not really,' replied Clippesby. 'The Merton Hall hens told me that Wolf gave Joan the idea: she saw him use the pit for his treasure when she was visiting her brother, so she did likewise with an inconvenient corpse. Wolf had fled Cambridge because of Dodenho's accusations, and it was doubtful whether he would return. Eudo just chose a remarkably bad week to mend the pulley – the pulley that was broken by Wolf's excessive use of it.'

'I still do not understand why Eudo tried to kill me with a spade, though,' said Bartholomew. 'Was it because I was the one who found Chesterfelde's blood?'

'The answer is there,' said Clippesby. 'You just need to review the evidence. First, as I have told you, Polmorva gave Eudo the astrolabe in return *for a favour*. Second, Eudo mentioned that Polmorva witnessed him dumping Chesterfelde's body in the hall, but agreed to remain quiet in return *for a favour*. And third, Polmorva ran away very quickly when we all escaped from Joan and her brother.'

'He did not even stop to see if anyone needed his help,' said Michael.

'He had good reason. Duraunt thwarted him over the murder he wanted to commit in Oxford, so he intended to try his hand at another instead. I heard the entire trans-action, as I told you. Polmorva hired Eudo to murder you, Matt – for old times' sake.'

'Lord!' breathed Michael, appalled. 'He may come back and try again.'

'Yes,' agreed Clippesby soberly. 'He might.'

The following morning, when dawn heralded the start of another glorious sun-filled day, a small cart clattered along the tangled lanes of the Jewry and headed for the High Street. It was still early, and the wispy clouds were not yet tinged with the sun's golden touch, although the birds were awake and sang loud and shrill along the empty streets. Folk were beginning to stir, and the air was full of smoke as people lit fires to heat ale and breakfast pottage. Bells announced the office of prime, and here and there neat lines of scholars and friars made their way to the churches for their devotions.

Matilde urged her horse to trot a little faster, not wanting to meet the men of Michaelhouse, but the cart was heavy – it was loaded with all her possessions and the beast was not able to move as briskly as she would have liked. She passed King's Hall with its magnificent gatehouse, and ducked inside her hood when she saw Paxtone, Norton and Dodenho emerge, and walk to St Mary the Great together. They did not so much as glance at the cart and its single occupant, but she kept her face averted anyway. Then she passed sturdy St Michael's, and her eyes misted with tears. She glanced down St Michael's Lane and saw Langelee striding along it, his scholars streaming at his heels as he led his daily procession. Matilde could not see whether Bartholomew was among them because her tears were blinding her.

She reached the Trumpington Gate and passed a coin to the man on duty, knowing he would barely acknowledge her. Guards were trained to watch who came into the town, but they did not care who left it. He waved his hand to indicate she could go, and she flicked the reins to urge her horse into a trot, wanting to put as much distance between her and Cambridge as she could before any of her friends realised she had gone.

Matilde was going to Norwich, where she had a distant cousin. The Guild of Frail Sisters would survive without her, and she longed for the respectability that she knew she would never have in Cambridge. Folk had too readily believed she was the kind of woman to entertain men in her house all night, and she wanted something better. In

Norwich she could begin another existence, where she would be staid and decent, and honoured by all. She would be courted by upright men, one of whom she would eventually choose as a husband. After all, she could not wait for ever for the man she really loved, and it was clear he was never going to ask her to be his wife.

She did not look back as her cart rattled along the road that led to the future. She would not have seen anything if she had, with hot tears scalding her eyes. She did not hear the birdsong of an early summer morning, and she did not notice the clusters of white and pink blossom that adorned the green hedgerows. She wondered whether she would ever take pleasure in such things again.

When the service at St Michael's had finished, Clippesby nodded encouragingly to Bartholomew, who grinned back and slipped out of the procession to head for the Jewry. He heard the birds singing, and saw the delicate clouds in the sky, and his heart felt ready to burst with happiness. He was going to see Matilde, and it was the first day of his new life.

HISTORICAL NOTE

On 10 February 1355, all hell broke loose in Oxford. It was St Scholastica's Day, and several students had gone to an inn called the Swindlestock Tavern at the south-west corner of Carfax. There are conflicting accounts of what happened, but basically the scholars complained to the taverner, John Croidon, about the poor quality of the wine they had been served. A row ensued, and scholars named Walter Spryngheuse and Roger de Chesterfelde smashed the jug over Croidon's head.

Then accounts begin to diverge. The citizens claimed that their bailiffs had tried to reason with the scholars, but that the students had rushed out and armed themselves with bows and arrows. The bailiffs had then asked the University Chancellor to call for calm, but Chancellor Brouweon refused, and a throng of two hundred academics began looting, killing and setting the city alight. Meanwhile, the scholars maintained that the taverner had summoned a mob to attack them, and that Brouweon was almost murdered when he appealed for peace. It was only when the University men feared they were all about to be slaughtered that the bells were rung to summon them to arms.

Whatever the truth of the tale, it was clearly a terrifying incident. The homes of clerks and townsfolk alike were plundered and burned, and one account says sixty scholars lost their lives. The battle continued until virtually all members of the University had either been killed or driven from the city, and only then was peace restored.

Retribution came quickly. The town was immediately put under an interdict, which meant no religious ceremonies of any description could be carried out – no burials, baptisms or masses. This was considered dire punishment, given that religion was far more a part of daily life than it is today, and the threat of Hell and eternal damnation were genuine concerns.

The interdict remained in place for more than a year, and it was removed only on condition that the city authorities agreed to attend a special mass each year – financed by themselves – for the souls of the scholars who had perished. They were also to disburse an annual fine. Amazingly, this continued until 1865, when the University finally conceded that the town had paid its dues and agreed to forget about the matter. This was not the only punishment inflicted on the townsmen. They also lost vital privileges in a new charter. These included meeting standards imposed by the University for ale, bread and wine – which meant a loss of revenue for merchants – and breaches of the peace committed by laymen were to be resolved by the Chancellor. This gave the University a good deal of power, which was bitterly resented. The charter remained in force until 1543.

One of the earliest Colleges to be founded in Oxford was Merton, which began life in the 1260s. It was established by Walter de Merton, an influential clerk and later Chancellor to the King. When Merton drafted the statutes to govern his new institution, the universities at both Oxford and Cambridge were in a very precarious state, and migrations of scholars after periods of unrest were fairly frequent. One group had gone to Northampton, and the fledgling *studium generale* was still extant there (it was suppressed in 1265) when Merton built his Oxford College. Being a cautious man, he decided to provide his scholars with a bolt-hole, in case the town rose up and forced them

466

to leave. He decided Cambridge was as good a place as any, and bought several tracts of land in the nearby villages of Gamlingay, Chesterton, Over and Grantchester, along with a manor house in Cambridge itself.

The manor belonged to the Dunning family, and Richard Dunning sold it to Merton in 1271, probably because he was desperate for money. The College leased the property, and its tenant in 1314 was Eudo of Helpryngham, who did not pay what he owed, and eventually absconded with the colossal sum of £40 outstanding. The house was a sturdy building, L-shaped and with a hall and solar on the upper floor. It remained in Merton College's hands until the 1960s, when it was sold to St John's College, Cambridge. Visitors today will see remnants of the Norman building in the narrow windows and stalwart buttresses, but it has been altered and rebuilt over the centuries, and is much changed. Still, even surrounded by the twentieth-century dormitories, it is impressive. It acquired the name 'School of Pythagoras' long after Walter of Merton's day, probably in the Elizabethan era.

Many of the people in this story were real. The Warden of Merton in 1355 was William Duraunt or Durant, who was a Fellow in the 1330s and who held various benefices before his death in 1372. His name appears in writs with one John de Boltone, and he is buried in Merton's chapel. William de Polmorva held fellowships in Exeter, University and Queen's Colleges between 1333 and 1341, and he was Chancellor of Oxford from 1350 to 1352. He was a favourite of Queen Philippa, and was her confessor for a year or two before his death in 1362. Chesterfelde and Spryngheuse, the instigators of the riots, did not die in Cambridge: Chesterfelde eventually become rector of Ashley, Cambridgeshire in the 1380s, while Spryngheuse was involved in a dispute over his Somerset appointment, which resulted in him appealing to the Roman Curia. He was still alive in 1362.

Meanwhile, records tell us about several wealthy Oxford clans whose members were mayors and burgesses in the thirteenth and fourteenth centuries. The Eu family (various Philips, Johns and Peters) were mentioned between 1290 and 1329, and were still around in 1408. Their name suggests a French origin, and it is likely they had been wealthy Normans. By contrast, the Wormynghalles were thirteenth-century upstarts, a sort of medieval *nouveau riche*. They were mayors in 1298, 1310 and 1340, and were still prominent in the city in 1368, although they seem to have died out twenty years later. John Gonerby flourished in Oxford in 1346; he was the son of a burgess. William Abergavenny, whose name suggests Oxford enjoyed a cosmopolitan government, was a bailiff in 1352.

At Gonville Hall, early fellows included William Rougham and William of Lee. King's Hall's Warden was Thomas Powys (until 1361, when he died during the next wave of plague), while John de Norton, Richard de Hamecotes and Geoffrey de Dodenho were admitted in 1350, and Robert de Wolf in 1356. There was a John de 'Wormenhale' at King's Hall in 1350. He was given a benefice in 1362, although it is not known whether he was kin to the Oxford dynasty. Scholars tended to remain local, and there was no reason for a Wormynghalle to travel to Cambridge to study. The University stationer in 1361 was John Weasenham, who was married to Alyce.

Simon Islip, Archbishop of Canterbury, never did found a College in Cambridge. He waited until 1361, when he purchased a handful of houses in Oxford, and took the bold step of making his new institution a place of learning for both monks and secular clergy. His foundation struggled on for a while, although the experiment never really worked, and quarrels broke out between the two factions almost immediately. Four years after Islip's death in 1366, the Pope made the College a secular appendage of Christ Church. It became part of Cardinal's College in the reign of Henry VIII, which, later still, became Christ Church again.

Go back to the beginning

Discover the first three chronicles of Matthew Bartholomew

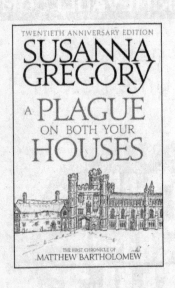

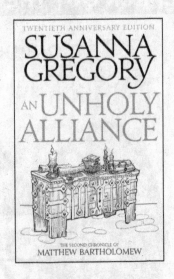

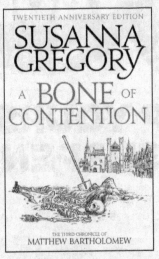